Praise for
THE WAVE TRILOGY

'If there were stars for world-building *Irenicon* would be a five plus, no question'

SFX

'Exciting and original amid the current fantasy landscape'

FANTASY BOOK CRITIC

'If you want something a bit different to traditional fantasy, *Irenicon* might just be the book for you'

I WILL READ BOOKS

'A fountain of gorgeous detail . . . well written and conceived, we look forward to Harte's future works with relish'

SCIFINOW

'A completely unique world, a plot that will prove you wrong time after time, and a whole cast of characters that you will learn to love and hate (as Harte sees fit), told through flawless prose'

FANTASY-FACTION

'A brilliant new voice in historical fantasy'

TTA PRESS

'An excellent piece of world building by someone with a real feel for renaissance Italy'

INTERZONE

'One of the best alternate history series in recent times'

UPCOMING4.ME

'I have to give Aidan Harte full praise to his world building

Also by Aidan Harte

THE WAVE TRILOGY

Irenicon
The Warring States

AIDAN HARTE

Spira Mirabilis

BOOK III OF THE WAVE TRILOGY

Jo Fletcher
BOOKS

First published in Great Britain in 2014 by Jo Fletcher Books
This edition published in Great Britain in 2015 by

Jo Fletcher Books
an imprint of Quercus
55 Baker Street
7th Floor, South Block
London
W1U 8EW

A CIP catalogue record for this book is available
from the British Library

ISBN 978 1 78087 155 4 (PB)
ISBN 978 1 78087 154 7 (EBOOK)

10 9 8 7 6 5 4 3 2 1

Typeset by Ellipsis Digital Limited, Glasgow

Printed and bound in Great Britain by
Clays Ltd, St Ives plc

To my hero, Bronagh

DRAMATIS PERSONAE

CONCORDIANS

Torbidda	The Last Apprentice
Girolamo Bernoulli	Long dead tyrant of Concord
Leto Spinther	Concordian General
Lord Geta	Disgruntled swordsman
Fra Norcino	Blind preacher; leader of the fanciulli
Madame Filangeiri	Brothel keeper
Scaevola	Leto's quartermaster
Collegio dei Consoli	Council of previous candidates for apprenticeship
Consul Numitor Fuscus	Influential consul
Consul Malapert Omodeo	Noble-born but self-made plutocrat
Horatius	Malapert Omodeo's nephew

RASENNEISI

Sofia Scaligeri	Former Contessa of Rasenna
Iscanno Scaligeri	Her son
Pedro Vanzetti	Chief Engineer
Salvatore Bombelli	Eldest son of Fabbro, the murdered ruler of Rasenna
Guido and Gasparo Bombelli	Middle twins
Costanzo Bombelli	Youngest of Fabbro's sons
Maddalena Bombelli	Fabbro's only daughter; Lord Geta's wife

Sister Isabella Vaccarelli	Young Reverend Mother of the Sisterhood
Sister Carmella	Novice
Uggeri Galati	Bandieratoro; young capo of Bardini Workshop
Polo Sorrento, the farmer	Wool Merchant and father of Rosa & Pablo
Pablo Sorrento	Rosa's brother; a bandieratoro
Rosa Sorrento	Young mother; daughter of Polo; Pablo's brother
Bocca, a.k.a the Brewer	Owner of Lion's Fountain; Prior of Vintners' Guild
Jacques Bonhomme	Frankish Blacksmith
Donna Soderini	Wife of a poor wool carder

OTHER ETRURIANS

Levi Azzarà	Podesta of Rasenna; General of Hawk's Company
Duke Grimani	Dictator of Veii
Poggio Marsuppini	Town elder of Veii; succeeds Duke Grimani
Doctor Ferruccio	Ambassador from Salerno; old Scaligeri ally
Sergio	A Salernitan buttero
Matron Trotula	A Salernitan doctor
No Man	Sybaritic youth
Hellebore	Top Man of Sybaris
Femus	Hellebore's son
Whisperer	Councillor of Sybaris
Befana	Prophetess

OLTREMARINES

Queen Catrina Guiscard	Queen of Oltremare
Fulk Guiscard	Queen's son; Grandmaster of the Lazar Knights
Basilius	Seneschal of Lazars
Gustav	Elderly Lazar
Patriarch Chryrsoberges	Queen's councillor
Baron Masoir	Rich Akkan noble
Melisende Ibelin	Baroness; wife of Baron Masoir
Prince Jorge	New ruler of Byzant
Captain Khoril	Captain of Oltremarine flagship, the *Tancred*
Abdel	Moorish slave

EBIONITES

Ezra	Old Ebionite sailor
Azizi, a.k.a The Moor	Usurping ruler of Ariminum; former pirate
Mik la Nan	Infamous chief of Napthtali tribe
Arik ben Uriah	Ebionite of Issachar tribe; Scout for Oltremarines
Yūsuf ben Uriah	Leader of Sicarii; brother of Arik
Bakhbukh	Yūsuf's unhappy advisor
Zayid	Heavy; Ally of Yūsuf
Jabari	Sicarii boy
Roe de Nail	Chief of Benjaminite tribe

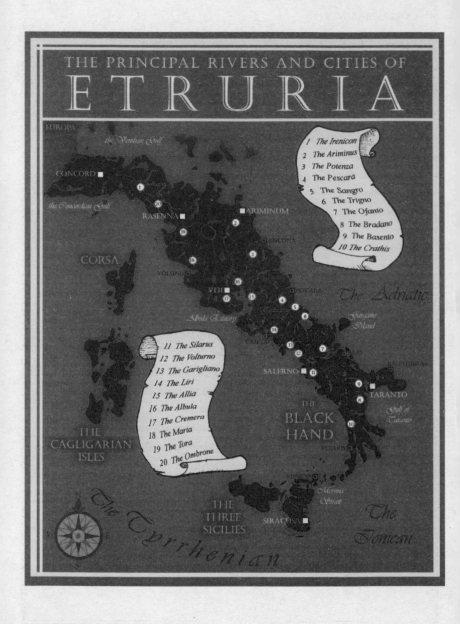

THE PRINCIPAL RIVERS AND CITIES OF
ETRURIA

1 The Irenicon
2 The Ariminus
3 The Potenza
4 The Pescara
5 The Sangro
6 The Trigno
7 The Ofanto
8 The Bradano
9 The Basento
10 The Crathis

11 The Silarus
12 The Volturno
13 The Garigliano
14 The Liri
15 The Allia
16 The Albula
17 The Cremera
18 The Maria
19 The Tora
20 The Ombrone

EUROPA

the Venitian Gulf

CONCORD

the Concordian Gulf

RASENNA

CORSA

VOLSINII

VEII

Albula Estuary

CORSA

THE CAGLIGARIAN ISLES

ARIMINUM

ANCONA

PESCARA

The Adriatic

Caieta

CAIETA

SALERNO

THE BLACK HAND

TARANTO

Gulf of Taranto

BRUNDISIUM

SYBARIS

MESSINA

Messina Strait

THE THREE SICILIES

SIRACUSA

The Tyrrhenian

The Ionican

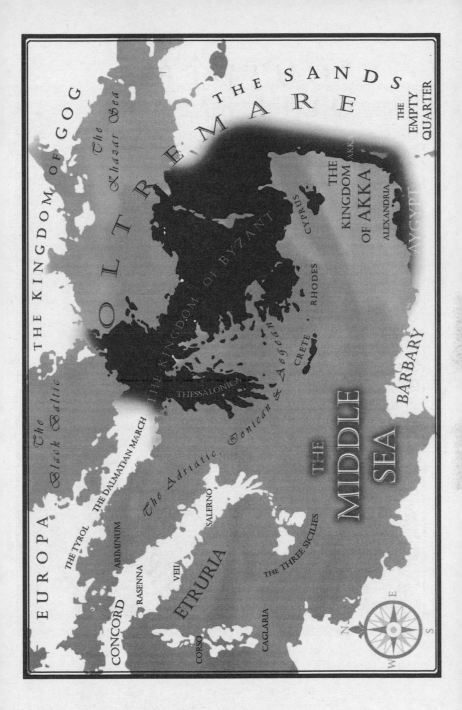

SOUTHERN
OLTREMAR

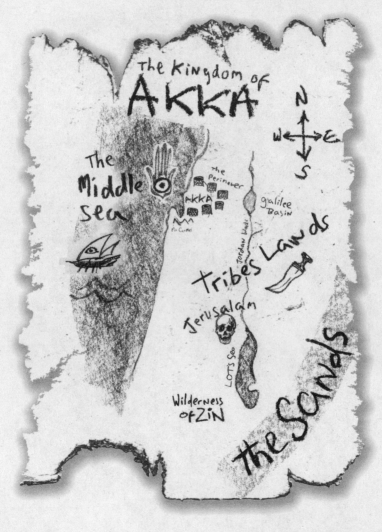

The Kingdom of
AKKA

N
W — E
S

The Middle Sea

the Perineur

AKKA

Mt Carmel

galilee Basin

Jordan Wadi

Tribes Lands

Jerusalem

LOT'S Sea

Wilderness of ZIN

the Sands

PART I:

EXILES

Verily thou art a God that hidest thyself
Isaiah 45:15

CHAPTER 1

Some doubted their eyes. The mutilated corpse, they argued, could have belonged to anyone. These doubters were swiftly silenced because believing that Fra Norcino – their shepherd, their teacher – had abandoned them was even more terrible than believing he was dead. The engineers had scourged Consul Corvis, the devil who ordered his execution; now, leaderless and denied even the solace of revenge, the fanciulli retreated to the Depths. Unity had been their great strength but they broke willingly into gloomy covens, to argue amongst themselves about what had broken them, and why. A deficiency of faith was the explanation that held sway for a few dismal days, before a sweeter notion suggested itself.

This was a test.

What was Consul Corvis? An engineer.

Who had shown them the body? The engineers.

And what was the First Apprentice but an engineer – the king of that benighted race.

Monte Nero might tower over the New City, but its foothills were in the Depths and those twice-orphaned wretches threw themselves, pushing and shouting, like a wave at the crags. When the folly of that became clear, they retreated to the *Umbilicus Urbi*, the cartographic navel of the Concordian Empire, whence the mapmaker's needle began its tireless revolutions, to meditate on the injustices done to them. The ancient stone pillar was not merely the point from where all imperial measurements began, it was the pulpit from which Norcino had preached. Here the truth had originated, and against it was measured the falsehood of all other positions.

They alternated chanting, *Abasso Torbidda!* – down with Torbidda! – with *Abasso Spinther!*

The objects of their hatred were the two boys who controlled respectively Concord's civic and military wings: First Apprentice Torbidda and General Leto Spinther. Though the mob did not know it, this singular pair were looking down upon them from one of the New City aqueducts. Both had devoted their lives to Reason, and both knew this sea of passion was capable of drowning them.

Beyond that, their reactions were very different.

'Look at it, Leto,' the First Apprentice marvelled. 'The great beast that is man in aggregate. What an army they would make!'

The young general was unimpressed. 'A man can be worth something, but men are generally worthless. I shall gather the praetorians. A charge will soon break up this rabble.'

'No, they'd just come back. I must speak to them.'

'You can't reason with a mob.'

Torbidda smiled so rarely that his gleeful laugh took Leto entirely by surprise. 'Who said anything about Reason?'

No one assaulted the boy in red as he pressed through the crowd – the praetorians saw to that – but once the masses would have parted like cattle before the First Apprentice. Concord's year of anarchy had made them bold.

'Down with the Guild!' they shouted as he stood with bowed head before the pillar from where the blind preacher had hurled his sermons. Bloody handprints marked it still. He turned and looked contritely at the hostile faces surrounding him, and they saw a boy not much different than them: paler, perhaps, but with his ox-like brow and large callused hands he looked like one who knew what it was to work.

It was hard to hear at first, so choked with grief was his voice. 'We mourn together, Children. Hear me not for my rank but for that woe we share,' he started solemnly. 'My rank is but an ephemeral vanity. Our grief is eternal. The saint's pillar is empty, and so it must stay. No one can take the place of Fra Norcino – not you, not I' – he stepped away from the protection of the praetorians and gestured contemptuously – 'and certainly not them.'

The crown lowed aggressively, but no longer at Torbidda.

'Nor can the Collegio dei Consoli replace him,' he continued, 'for all their claimed wisdom. A surfeit of Reason has enfeebled their minds. That scoundrel Bernoulli said that only philosophers could uncover truth, but I say that only *you* have that power! Your roar is the voice of God – give thanks that Bernoulli and his dogma are dead. Give thanks that Fra Norcino and his promise will live for ever! We, his children – we shall be tyrants to the world: we shall be a new breed, the tyranny of ten thousand! Cast off your petty bonds, your family, your names, and in this union forget your mothers, your brothers, your neighbours, your lovers. Forget all bonds and become something greater. Our unchained strength and collective stature is unbounded. O joy! O terror! How our senses will be magnified: a hundred eyes and ears, a thousand mouths to bite our foes! A million fists to smash the world!'

He walked amongst them so that that they could see he was just a boy like them. 'We are young, that is why the Fra believed in us. He showed us the path and gave us courage to follow it. He threw away his life to free us from the snares of Reason. The Molè was a temple to that discredited idol, and we shall have nothing to do with it. Tear up the stones of the streets with your fingers; carry all you can on your backs. Load them till your knees buckle – and there on the grave of idolatry we shall build a new church dedicated to youth! Come, climb the mountain with me! Lay out the site with me! Cut the foundation stone with me!'

'Lead us!' they cried.

'If you will follow me, then I will follow you. I tell you there is no greater rapture than to forget yourself. *Become* the Temple! Make stone of your flesh – make mortar of your bones and blood. Give your lives for Concord – for those who build and those who kill for Concord are equally brave, equally blessed: we are soldiers of God together.'

Leto, looking on, could hardly believe his ears. Instead of pacifying them, Torbidda was driving them mad.

'I have no need of this gaudy robe, for I am no Apprentice.' And as he spoke, Torbidda began to remove his clothes.

'Then you are the master!' cried an ecstatic girl, and the cry was taken up.

The surrounded praetorians, out of self-preservation, bowed low, and Leto bowed too, lower than everyone, to cover his indignation.

Torbidda, standing naked before them, picked up his Apprentice's robe and threw it into the throng. 'Tear it!' he shouted. 'Everyone take a share!'

'Master!' they insisted, 'Master!'

'We are all masters! Dip your wool in the blood of the lamb and be reborn. Children, we are Crusaders.'

Leto had to struggle to get to the head of the procession as Torbidda led a trail of naked children up the mountain. Like his followers, Torbidda's feet were bleeding. In all the years Leto had known him, he'd never seen such an ecstatic smile. He threw his cloak over his naked shoulders and whispered, 'Have you gone mad?'

Torbidda turned, and Leto fancied that he saw in his friend's face – for the briefest moment – a look of terrible entreaty. Then it was gone, glazed over by joyless glee. He threw off the cloak impatiently. 'On the contrary: I know now the true price of things. Concord is certainly worth a mass.'

CHAPTER 2

Serves you bloody well right for doing the right thing! Captain Khoril raged at himself. The diminutive, hirsute Levantine was waiting to be summoned, and sweating like the last hog of winter. This was the first time he'd returned to Akka since helping Contessa Scaligeri escape Ariminum and the Moor. It didn't help matters that the Moor's ensign was standing calmly beside him. The tall, handsome youth with skin the colour of liquid walnut had a noble mien and a haughty diffidence; Khoril had ferried the perfectly composed youth from Ariminum to speak on his master's behalf.

A black-robed cleric pushed open the door to the throne room and stared at them for an awkward moment, then, apparently satisfied, he ordered them to approach.

'I summoned the Moor,' said the queen. 'He sends his cup-bearer?'

The ensign's eyes, deep sleepy pools, opened wide. This was mild reproach for Queen Catrina, but the beautiful youth responded defiantly, 'Admiral Azizi sends his dearest friend. Loyalty keeps him in Ariminum. You would commend his prudence if you knew the Serenissima's reputation for treachery.'

She said with resignation, 'All the world knows that. He did as instructed and offered allegiance to Concord?'

'Yes and as you predicted, they stood by and let us take over Ariminum.'

'What then has your master so worried?'

'I would not say *worried*. As canaries are to miners are rats to mariners. He smells one.'

'I'm told it's quite a distinctive musk. Is that so, Khoril?' Before the captain could stammer an answer, the queen continued, 'You mean this boy king – the one who styles himself the— What is it your Beatitude? The journeyman?'

'I believe he calls himself the Apprentice,' said the patriarch, striking the appropriate note of scepticism.

'The *First* Apprentice,' the ensign corrected him. 'Mock all you like, but Admiral Azizi believes he will feed us to the beast as soon as he gets what he wants.'

'Which is the Contessa?'

'Just so, your Majesty, which is why my master recommends you *don't* hand her over.'

'And what am I to do with her instead?

The ensign, oblivious to the queen's sarcasm, looked surprised. After a moment, he answered, 'Kill her, of course.'

While Captain Khoril glared at his companion, torn between fear and hate, the queen glanced at the patriarch.

'Tell the Moor,' she said at last, 'that I have already decided what to do with that one. Tell him too that next time his queen summons him, he had better come himself, not send some over-bold Ganymede. Dismissed.'

Fury flickered across the ensign's handsome face and he looked about to retort, but then he thought better. He gave a shallow bow and turned on his heels.

Khoril did likewise, happy to escape the royal reprimand he'd been dreading, but her silky voice stopped him dead.

'I expect you are eager to see your family, Captain?'

Her voice paralysed him. ' . . . very much, your Majesty—'

'Then I will not detain you for long.'

The ensign shot Khoril a look of suspicion and warning before the cleric showed him out.

Khoril's mouth went dry and he resolved to head off whatever accusations she might make with his own. 'I must remonstrate, your Majesty – why did you not tell me the Moor was your servant?'

'You of all people know that a captain must not share everything with his crew. You are too hot-blooded to lie convincingly. Your enmity with the Moor is famous; the Ariminumese had to believe I wanted him dead too.'

'I played my part so well that I helped the Contessa escape.'

'Yes, an embarrassing episode – But irrelevant now that I have custody of her.'

'A captain needn't share all but neither should he leave his servants wholly blind. The better I know your will, the better I can serve. What are you going to do with her?' Khoril hoped he was doing a good job of keeping his sympathies concealed.

'The Moor's prescription is extreme. I buy time by keeping her alive. Contrary to appearances, my power is circumscribed. I cannot summarily dispose of her – sending her away or otherwise – and preserve Akka's reputation as a safe haven, so I have engineered a situation, one where my subjects will clamour for me to cast her out.'

Khoril concentrated on looking stupid. He was appalled by her callousness, but he knew better than to show it.

'But tell me, what is really on the Moor's mind?'

'His pretty friend spoke true: he's worrying about the First Apprentice. The Moor is one of these sailors ever watching for the next storm. You've put him on a throne in a rich city across the sea upon which Concord's shadow falls. He preyed on your ships as a pirate – what is to stop him doing worse now that he is Doge of Ariminum?'

'Gratitude?' the queen ventured, then laughed at her own joke. 'Please, Khoril: I don't need your counsel to navigate these seas. I'm well aware of the risks involved in employing such a duplicitous dog. But necessity obliges me to use the tools at hand.' She rose from her throne and turned to the balcony, gesturing with a flick of her head for Khoril to follow. 'I asked you here because of *this*.'

Akka had a natural harbour, and though the queen's predecessors had spent little bettering it, the trading fleets of magnates like Baron Masoir made it a busy one. The quickest way from Akka to Byzant had always been by sea, and thanks to the Sands' incursions, it was now the safest way too. As the faintly rotten smell touched her skin, she said musingly, 'Who controls the Middle Sea controls the world: so said the Etruscans, and it's as true today as it was then.' She turned back to Khoril and said, 'Within a year, Concord will have subdued all Etruria, from the Irenicon down to the Black Hand's filthy fingernails. It's inevitable. And when the final city falls, Concord's unsleeping eye will look to me. I have a reprieve, a few months at best. Whether the Moor gives Ariminum to Concord or they take it by force, the sword that will strike us will be the Ariminumese fleet. Our navy is old: a few worm-ridden cogs, barely adequate for patrolling our coasts. I want you to build us one that compares to Ariminum's.'

She stared at him, awaiting his reaction as he struggled to find a way to respond politely, 'Majesty, the Golden Fleet—'

'—is large, and the work of generations. I know that. "Compares to", I said. We don't have to equal them – our fleet need never leave its moorings to accomplish its job. It'll stay the ambitions of these Etrurian dogs simply by existing.'

'With all due respect, your Majesty, I think you underestimate the scale of the task.'

'I own the forests of Lebanon.'

'Besides *dry* timber, we'd need pitch, hemp, tow, cordage – and sailcloth by the acre besides. Not to mention skilled shipwrights—'

She handed him a parchment bearing the Guiscard seal.

'Bring this to the Moor. You sail for Ariminum tomorrow. You will deliver this, along with your other cargo.'

Khoril looked at the document with undisguised alarm.

'It's an official request for those building materials we lack,' she said, 'and arsenalotti who know how to use them.'

'The Moor won't be happy.'

'No, but he'll provide them to keep me happy. That's if he hasn't decided to betray me yet – in which case, he'll hang you. Get what you can. If it comes to it, I see plenty of merchant vessels I could confiscate.' She flashed a smile. 'Baron Masoir's, for instance. Any other objections? Good. When you reach Ariminum you might decide to betray me yourself – be assured that no matter what happens, my dear captain, I'll take care of your family as if they were my own flesh and blood.'

Sofia took aim at the empty eye, imagined it was Queen Catrina's and fired. '*Merda.*'

Arik was teaching her to sling in a derelict piazza in the Ebionite Quarter. For targets, they'd gathered shards of broken masks from under the Madonna Murtha niches. 'You're throwing from your elbow. You must use all your strength' – he swivelled at the waist – 'like *this.*'

'Easy for you. You wouldn't dance so pretty with a baby due.'

The palace was the domain of Catrina's retinue, so Sofia took every opportunity to escape. She was free to roam the bazaars, to attend mass and pageants – but she had been imprisoned before and she wasn't fooled. Her unborn child was a prisoner within a prisoner, surely, the worst confinement. At least Akka was not a maze any more: she'd gradually become familiar with the backstreets and the people who lived there. She knew now that the Sown, Akka's Ebionite population, were captives too – but one thing remained a mystery to her. 'Why don't you throw them out and take over?'

Arik picked up a stone and studied it. 'We are not so many as we were, and besides, it's not so easy.' He discarded the stone. 'To what are you loyal?'

Sofia thought a moment. 'Tower Scaligeri. The workshop. Rasenna.'

'Your home, your workplace and your city. Anything else? *Eu-toroor-eea*?'

She smiled, because it sounded exotic in his accent. She made a grasping-at-nothing gesture, 'That's like—'

'A mirage. We have no time for abstractions either. In the Sands, a man's first loyalty is to his tent: his parents, his sons and their children.' Piling one pebble on another, Arik showed her how the bonds of kinship came next: a typical lineage embraced fifty tents; lineages laid claim to certain wells and oases and fought together to defend those rights. Beyond that was the tribe. 'And here things again become' – he made the same grasping gesture – 'abstract. A tribe is composed of lineages that have traditionally allied. They claim common ancestors and common enemies. The head of each tribe is the nasi.'

'The king,' Sofia said sourly.

'Not quite. Nesi'im are more in the order of judges. So that is how it should be: tent, kin, tribe' – he suddenly smashed his little tower with a wave of his hand – 'but in these corrupt times one cannot trust a brother, so how could the tribes unite? And how, disunited, could we oppose Akka? One day things perhaps shall be otherwise, *be'ezrat HaShem*.'

'*Be'ezrat HaShem*,' Sofia repeated. 'You say that a lot.' She'd learned a smattering of Ebionite from Ezra on her voyage from Etruria and had plenty of practice since. She had an ear for music, and it made her a quick study of languages too, though to confuse matters, the Ebionites and Akkans communicated in a mongrel blend – and always in argument. But word by word, she was finding her way in.

'Do I?' He grinned bashfully. 'It means "God willing". God's will is all that keeps Akka's walls intact. Akkan unity is another mirage.'

This surprised her; she'd found ordinary Akkans almost as unfriendly as Catrina's courtiers. 'They all support her—'

'They rally round the throne because they're terrified. Never underestimate the value of an enemy with unknown numbers and seemingly limitless reach. Anyone the queen considers a threat gets his throat cut in the night, and the Sicarii get the blame.'

'That's one way to end an argument,' she said, picking up a pebble and tossing it in her hand. 'Do you imagine Fulk will ever realise how unworthy she is of his devotion?'

'*Be'ezrat HaShem.*'

'Do you see the Grand Master much these days? He's avoiding me.'

'That is discretion. If Fulk is seen with you, the queen will hear of it.'

'I don't care what she – *uhh!* – thinks.' The pebble left her sling smoothly and shattered the chunk of mask into shards.

'Good shot, Contessa – but you really should care.'

When the day got hotter, they went to the bazaar to find refreshment and Levi, who'd spent the morning circling the harbour, doing what he did best – talking. There was much trade between Akka and the Three Sicilies, so he swallowed his dislike of the slave-owning captains and struck up conversations where he could, pretending to be homesick. In reality, he was trying to find a ship they could stow away on to get back to Etruria.

The impending Haute Cour was an event rare enough to draw a crowd, and the bazaar was full of people, like Levi, enquiring into things that didn't concern them. Traders brought many treasures into Akka, but none was more precious than gossip from the Sands. Town-dwelling Ebionites might disparage their desert kindred as lizard-eaters, but they still yearned to hear of the comings and goings, marriages and funerals, raids and ransoms of the world they had abandoned. And each tribe's dearest wish was to see the Lazars set upon their rivals.

All the Sown were collaborators in a sense, but there was a special cloud of suspicion about Arik, in part owing to his antecedents, in part because of his friendship with the Grand Master. As she tried to keep up with the chatter, Sofia occasionally intercepted covert scowls directed at Arik, which he either missed or ignored, too busy was he sifting and comparing information to piece together a picture of the shifting sand that was the relative strengths of the tribes. His continuing interest, naturally, was the Sicarii.

The assassin band had been in decline before the recent skirmish at Megiddo. By blundering into an obvious Lazar trap, their nasi had dishonoured himself and them. For all their notoriety, the Sicarii lacked the one thing that kept tribes together in tough times: blood links. Many cells had evaporated by desertion. Arik listened to these reports so calmly that no one would ever guess that their leader was his brother.

Sofia spotted Levi in the midst of a heated conversation with an orange-seller. She'd seen him before, a big man with a body like a collapsed wall and a face defeated by hardship.

Levi waved excitedly to Sofia and Arik. 'Listen to this,' he said.

The orange-seller was not his usual miserable self, laughing as he punctuated his story with bright, animated gestures. Sofia's Ebionite was not good enough to keep up, but when he'd finished, Arik thanked the man effusively and walked away with three fresh oranges.

'Well?' said Levi eagerly.

Arik distributed the fruit before starting, 'I heard that story at my father's knee, Levi. The Sands are full of fantasies that drift like the wind from tribe to tribe, growing ever larger in the telling. Dreams acquire substance and wishes harden to facts.'

Sofia was annoyed at being left out. 'What did he say?'

'That the Day has come, that the people's burden has grown too onerous, that the Old Man has returned to make all things right. Every summer some fool stays out in the sun too long.'

'This is different,' Levi insisted. 'He's not repeating a rumour, he *saw* the Old Man himself. He heard him preach.'

'Levi, I know your mother told you those same stories but, believe me, the credulous are always disappointed.'

'He *heard* him?' said Sofia. 'What did he say?'

'That if tribes cease feuding, the Radinate can be restored.'

'And when it is,' she said warily, 'this preacher will lead it?'

Arik looked at her sharply, then admitted, 'That's the only thing that gave me pause, Contessa. Many pretenders have called themselves the Old Man, hoping to acquire power. This preacher, whoever he is, he says he's merely a herald. The nesi'im aren't happy that he's stirring everyone up, but he's so popular that they dare not molest him. So they let him preach, then urge him to go spread his message to the next tribe.'

'He has no affiliation?'

'Apparently not – another token of authenticity. All the old tales say the Old Man came from the East.'

Sofia saw that Levi's attention was elsewhere. She followed his glance to a dwarfish Levantine who was looking over his shoulder. 'Is that—?'

'The good captain? I do believe it is.'

Khoril was a dour fellow at the best of times, but the reunion was a happy one. 'I can't believe you're both alive!'

'Same here,' said Levi. 'I thought for certain the Moor would string you up after we got away with Ezra.'

'If I was not the queen's admiral he would have. He's got his shadow making sure I don't get up to more mischief – I only managed to give him the slip because the queen doesn't trust him either. Where is Ezra, anyway? The old sea-dog owes me a drink . . .' His voice trailed off as he saw their smiles suddenly disappear.

Briefly, Sofia told Khoril how their voyage had ended.

'Lost at sea? *Madonna*, I wouldn't have thought it possible. The things that lizard-eater could make the wind do. I'll miss him.'

'So will we.' Sofia steeled herself for the worst. 'Do you know what happened to Pedro Vanzetti after we left Ariminum?'

'Your friend, the young engineer? I understand the Salernitan ambassador helped him to escape.'

The news made Sofia's heart glow, and not just because Pedro was safe. 'See, Levi? I knew Doctor Ferruccio would never side with the Concordians.'

'Well, war makes strange bedfellows.'

'Speaking of which, Captain, there's only so much I can learn from harbour scuttlebutt. Is it true that Veii and Salerno have formally committed to the League?'

'True enough. I'll tell you all about it if you buy me a drink,' said Khoril, lowering his voice and looked at the Contessa. 'And I need to warn you—'

'—to keep out of the midday sun.' The intruding voice made all three of them jump. The ensign stood there, blandly smiling. 'You run the risk of ruining your wonderful complexion, or worse. Sunstroke would be *most* dangerous in your condition.'

Sofia stared back at him. 'Thanks for your concern.'

'Why don't you go on with Arik to the Haute Cour, Sofia,' said Levi. 'I'll find a suitable tavern for these gentlemen.'

It took two strong men to open the doors of the Haute Cour; Fulk took one side, Basilius the other. Beneath the marble floor of the court was a well-equiped dungeon – but though the foundation of Akkan justice was decidedly dark, the courtyard itself was awash with light. At the end of the courtyard was a wooden chair, well carved and jointed, but simple, unostentatious: a poor seat for a queen, but the Haute Cour and its customs had come into being when Akka's kings were weak.

Basilius might not care much for his Grand Master, but Fulk was glad to have him there; whatever else Basilius was, he was certainly efficient. Time was precious in the Order of St Lazarus, and talented brothers were swiftly promoted. As seneschal, he was responsible not just for maintaining the patrols' supply-lines but for keeping Akka's citadel and the network of towers in the Sands manned and in good repair. Basilius still appeared to be in good repair himself; the leprous teeth gnawing his extremities had not yet bitten too deep, for he could still deftly wield the cere-monial axe the younger Lazars could barely lift. But though his arms might be thick as old oak branches, the oak had a canker, and the hundred whispers telling a man his prime is past had become a constant harangue.

Stoic acceptance was a virtue that new recruits were taught, and for example they had only to look to their elders, for they endured terrible pain, especially at the end. Though many bore their trials with grace, some even being sanctified, an unhappy few found their faith decaying with their flesh, tormented by impious doubts worse than pain – for what sort of God repays a lifetime's fidelity so poorly? Basilius was one of these inconsol-ables, and the young knights soon learned to avoid his wrath. Those paying attention had begun to notice a reek of rotten flesh lurking underneath the aniseed and camomile in which he daily soaked his surcoat and cloak, and his breath through the thin partition lips of his helm had become a sulphurous cloud. Even in private he never removed his helm, something which his fellow brothers mistook for devotion. In truth, the mask had long ago fused to the bloody scabs underneath.

The patriarch entered the Haute Cour first, swinging an incense tabernacle that filled the chamber with pungent smoke; he was followed closely by the drone of dolorous chanting. Behind him pressed the jostling crowd, all eager to get a good position, and Basilius began pushing back and cursing them like livestock.

Fulk stepped in before he hurt anyone, shouting, 'Ease up at the back there! One by one, now – take your time. There's plenty of room for all–'

Basilius shook his head wearily. He had never said outright that Fulk was Grand Master only because Akka's queen was his mother, nor did he say in public that Fulk's mildness nurtured enfeebling effeminacy in the ranks; he only remarked from time to time that the Sands have no use for softness. Fulk tolerated the innuendoes because the Order's strength was as illusionary as Akka's. Basilius was meticulous, dogged and unforgiving, and on days like today, he needed men who looked the part.

Clerics and clerks slunk about the edges of the court, assessing and pricing the various petitioners huddling in small groups, muttering behind soft hands. The members of the baronial party milling around Baron Masoir were conspicuous by the din they made; though they dressed as nobles in sumptuous clothes, their vulgar braying revealed them to be *sang nouveau*, little better than warlords. Only Masoir had anything remotely resembling an aristocratic bearing, though his big-fisted arms were the equal of any of the hauliers he employed.

'Masoir thinks he owns the place,' Basilius grumbled.

'If he expects numbers to intimidate my mother, he doesn't know her like he used to.' Fulk gave the patriarch the nod, and as he and Basilius placed themselves either side of the empty chair, Patriarch Chrysoberges announced the queen.

A hush descended and the queen's handmaids emerged from a side-entrance, followed by their mistress. She took her place and looked slowly around the court, her eyes coolly appraising the various groups, but not once did she glance up. The balcony was the only place where the Sown and Akka's Small People could get a glimpse of what passed for justice in Akka.

Sofia and Arik were in the middle of that throng, watching.

The patriarch mumbled through a prayer for the queen's health, but before he could even finish intoning *Amen*, she exclaimed, 'What an august audience! When I wish to recruit irregulars to help defend Akka, I must plead with my lords to present themselves. Yet here you are, Baron Masoir, with all your little friends, unsummoned and unlooked for.'

The baron ground his teeth, his pugnacious jaw moving as if he were chewing his reply. There was no point trying to charm her.

'The baron comes from impoverished noble stock,' Arik whispered to Sofia. 'He was one of the queen's childhood friends.'

'Hard to believe she had any.'

'They were more than friends, according to some, but in any case, she found a richer baron to marry and Masoir rebuilt his fortune by marrying into a *noblesse nouvelle* family with impressive Byzantine shipping links.' Arik pointed out a petite, serious-looking middle-aged woman standing towards the back but watching the proceedings avidly. She was dressed in black silk and surrounded by a retinue of formidable-looking slaves. 'That's his wife, Melisende Ibelin. Old Akkan family with blood as pure as the queen's. They've known each other since girlhood – which is not to say they were ever boon companions. She was a Lady of the Privy Chamber but the queen considered her marriage to Masoir a great betrayal. She has never forgiven them.'

'I felt bound to come,' said the baron, 'as your Majesty lacks disinterested advisors to tell you that the course you're intent upon is folly.'

'When I need advice, I'll ask,' Catrina said curtly. 'All that's required of you is silent obedience.'

'Silence when the ship's bearing down on the rocks? I call that negligence.'

'I may not be the mariner you are, but I believe there's only one navigator, and when others attempt to steer, I believe that's called mutiny. I see no rocks.'

'Then it is well I have come. Now that your servant the Moor has won Ariminum for us, the Middle Sea lies open. For God's sake, let's enjoy it! With no competition, direct access to Etrurian markets, and Europa beyond, our prospects are immense—'

'You might think to thank me.' The queen's temper, never good, was shorter than ever since her uncle's attempted coup.

Baron Masoir ignored the mockery. 'You've handled the foreigners admirably, no question, but the domestic situation has never been so precarious. The Lazars' aggression is pushing the tribes together—'

'Enough! A slur on my soldiers is a slur on me. You talk of Akka, but your concern is to protect your myrrh caravans.' She turned from the baron and looked around the rest of the court. 'Is it so hard to believe that I see further from this throne than a peddler grubbing in the bazaar?'

Her ladies answered with loyal titters, but the men responded only with hostile stares. Under this daunting scorn, the noble faction shrank – all but the baron.

'Business *must* be good that you've time to waste interfering with affairs of state that are none of your concern. Perhaps I should have you – and that rabble you've brought with you – audited again?'

The baron recognised it was time to withdraw. 'When it comes to tithes and tolls, your Majesty knows well that we are adequately burdened. Thank you for the audience.' He bowed perfunctorily and retreated with his supporters to the back of the courtyard.

The queen glared and hissed through clenched teeth, 'Who's next?'

While Chrysoberges laboriously consulted the agenda, a husky voice rasped, 'Me.'

All heads turned to the court's entrance where an exotic figure stood silhouetted. He was very tall, and though he did not look it, old. His nose protruded like that of a bloodhound. His long, sharp teeth smiled from the middle of a cascading beard that was braided and ornamented with green and blue beads. His eyes were steady and lively with humour, as if everything he saw amused him a little.

'Thank you for answering my summons, Mik la Nan. We are honoured.'

'The honour is mine. I'm told that my unlucky race is not ordinarily permitted to speak here.'

'That might be the case ordinarily, but I am told you are exceptional.'

'I have always considered myself so,' he said, and ignoring the scandalised wispers, marched into the courtyard. He gave the impression of great power held in check in a way that reminded Sofia of the Doc. The two ragged but fierce-looking warriors following quietly behind carried tall baskets.

His aplomb amused the queen. 'How do you like my city? Better surely than tents that the wind may sweep away?'

He stopped in front of her. 'A strong enough wind sweeps away everything. Your walls seem to offer security – the illusion may be comforting, but it comes at a cost.'

'Let me guess: liberty. When one considers how the Ebionites cherish their freedom and how often they've lost it, they begin to look almost careless.' The court erupted in sycophantic titters until the queen silenced them with a testy gesture.

'O Queen. I have lived long enough to know few are truly free,' the old nasi said solemnly. 'I have come to discuss a matter of urgency. The Empty Quarter has become truly barren. Even my Napthtali' – he gestured to his two shadows – 'who live on nothing, even they cannot live there. Therefore we have moved into lands upon which your shadow falls. The other tribes know my name, and with words or other tools, I'll find an accommodation with them. To you, O Queen, I lay down my sword.'

Fulk and Basilius watched warily as he drew his great sword and kneeled. The pommel was carved in the shape of a mountain lion and the blade was curved like a crescent moon. Etched Ebionite characters made its surface dance. On cue, his men placed a reed basket either side of the sword. 'Besides my fidelity, I offer—' He paused and tipped the first barrel over '—these.' A dozen short curved blades scattered nosily on the ground.

Arik leaned forward. 'Sicarii blades,' he said, with an intake of breath.

'I am grateful,' the queen murmured, 'but assassins can always find new weapons.'

By way of answer, the nasi reached into the second basket. 'I did not know which flavour you preferred, so I brought one of each. Gad—' He took a head from the basket, then another, and yet another, displaying each to the queen while reciting, 'Benjaminite, Zebulun, and more besides.' He tipped the basket and the rest of its grisly contents vomited forth and thudded onto the marble. One head rolled right to the queen's feet and the horrified patriarch rushed to remove it, but she shooed him away and picked it up herself. The neck was cleanly severed and the hair was lank with clotted blood. Dried rivulets painted the broken contours of the face. The eyes were swollen black from a haemorrhage within; the teeth were bared as if surprised in laughter.

No one spoke. Fulk and Basilius looked to the queen while the old nasi's eyes strayed to his sword.

She solemnly kissed the cracked lips and exclaimed, 'What a handsome gift!'

Mik la Nan's relief turned to confusion as the queen leaped from her throne, brandishing the head like a lantern. She held it up to Masoir and his cronies. 'Behold, Baron, the fate of traitors! Is it not handsome?'

Masoir paled a fraction and agreed.

Mik la Nan grinned. 'I am pleased it pleases your Majesty.'

She turned and stood before him. '*You* please me. By all means, bring your Napthtali north and welcome. If the other tribes fail to make room, respond accordingly, with the assurance that I will not interfere.'

'Praise God, it is true what they say: verily, a new Sheba is come amongst us, as generous as she is wise. Were you not an idolater, you would be perfect.'

The patriarch, indignant after the nasi's gruesome exhibition, pounced on this heresy. 'To what idolatry do you refer?'

The nasi gave the priest a scornful look. 'I came to pay homage to a queen, not debate with her fool.'

'Please, O Nasi,' the queen dramatically intoned, 'this is the Haute Cour, where the weak speak truth to power. Here, I am obliged to listen to contrary opinions – so pray answer Patriarch Crysoberges' question – tell us all, how am I an idolater?'

Mik la Nan, a practised politician, understood that this was a game, intended to make some point to the queen's courtiers. Even so, he had been called to testify. He drew himself up stiffly, all mirth draining away, and said clearly, 'God is God, one and indivisible, but you would make the Prophetess into God's consort.'

The patriarch smirked. 'Small wonder the savage misunderstands. I could show you the holy writ where it says, "Thou canst not see my face: for there shall no man see me, and live," but doubtless you're illiterate, so I'll explain in your own words. If God is one, as you say, it follows that He cannot diminish Himself. Therefore a mediator is necessary. The Madonna is that mediator. Like a favoured daughter, she stands between God and Man, shielding us from His wrath. Therefore,' he concluded triumphantly, 'it is not us but the Ebionites who diminish God!'

'God will blacken your face for these lies,' the nasi responded.

'Thank you, Patriarch Chrysoberges,' said the queen sweetly, 'for reminding us all that theology is so unbearably tedious. I'd almost forgotten. Now, Mik la Nan, to practicalities. My permission to enter my lands you have. If you want my friendship, keep sending the baskets.'

'Any particular flavour?'

'I consider any tribe which fails to make war on the Sicarii traitors.'

And with that, the queen clapped her hands and declared the Haute Cour concluded for the day.

Arik was pensive as they descended from the balcony.

'She wants war amongst the tribes,' Sofia said, 'that's clear. But surely the Napthtali are more dangerous to Akka than any Sicarii dagger?'

'They'll be by far the largest tribe in all the Sands, but Mik la Nan knows his foe,' Arik agreed. 'The sight of blood excited her till she couldn't think straight – she should have immediately added Mik la Nan's head to that pile.'

As disappointed petitioners filed out of the court into the piazza Arik walked towards Mik la Nan's entourage, men with faces crossed and recrossed with scars.

'My eyes are liars if this this is not an Issachar,' said Mik la Nan as he came upon them. 'Uriah ben Sinan was almost as skilful a warrior as me.'

Though Sofia was standing next to Arik, the nasi didn't acknowledge her. She did not protest; she was becoming used to this blindness from Ebionites in formal settings.

'He was my father,' Arik said.

Mik la Nan glanced around at his followers. 'It is true then, that the sons of great men often disappoint. This one is a slave to the infidel. The other slides daggers between the ribs of sleeping merchants and bowstrings around the fat necks of their wives.'

Arik bristled. 'The man who leads the so-called Sicarii is

24

no longer my brother. As for me, my name is Arik ben Uriah. After the hospitality the Napthtali showed those Issachar who fled the Empty Quarter, I have longed to see you. God be praised, my prayers are answered. I will be blessed indeed if we meet in another venue, that I might give full expression to my gratitude.'

'Pray that never happens, boy. I no longer wish to slaughter Issachar. That sport has lost its novelty for me.'

Sofia wasn't prepared to stand by and listen. 'Don't let this dog bark at you, Arik,' she started.

'Woman,' said Mik la Nan grandly, 'do you not know who I am?'

'I know *what* you are. That's enough.'

Mik la Nan did not share his men's amusement at this re-joinder. 'It is not my custom to allow women to disrespect me—'

'Surprising. You're ready enough to bow to one.'

'Queen Catrina is the greatest nasi in the land,' he proclaimed, 'and there is no shame in giving one's sword to such a potentate.'

'No shame crawling before the persecutor of your race?'

'Beside my Napthtali I have no race!' he said with sudden fury – fury that was gone as quickly as it had arisen. 'Like your friend, I am a man of practicalities.'

'Please, Contessa,' said Arik, 'don't get involved.'

Akkans were staring at them now, enjoying the scene.

'I know not what a *contessa* is,' said Mik la Nan, 'but if it is some species of princess, be advised that that queen is not one to brook rivals. If I knew where your husband was, I would tell him to take you from Akka without delay.'

'God alone is above me. I am unmarried.'

The eavesdroppers gasped with pleasure to hear the rumours surrounding the foreigner confirmed by the girl herself.

The nasi however took no satisfaction in it. 'You have my sympathy,' he said, turning away.

That was worse than laughter. Sofia stared after him, trying to ignore the stares directed at her, trying to look like she didn't give a damn. She left before her tears could betray her.

Fulk entered the chapel and made the sign of the Sword before sitting down in one of the front pews. 'This place is only supposed to be for Lazars,' he said mildly.

A voice from the pew behind him said, 'Everyone avoids me. No one talks to me. I think I qualify.'

He turned around. 'They're afraid of the queen, Sofia.'

She sat up. 'And you're not? You're also only supposed to tell the truth here. Hadn't you better run along before she finds you've been talking to the *enemy*?' When Fulk didn't respond, she went on, 'I was at the Haute Cour today. She wants to start a war between the tribes, doesn't she?'

Fulk didn't try to deny it. 'The waste is that we could have peace with the Ebionites. They don't covet our cities – they never have. Jerusalem was all they craved, and now it's occupied by a force hostile to all men. The empire's fractured and our half is crumbling. We're spent, and the queen knows it better than anyone. She's content now to let the hourglass drain until her mask takes its place amongst her ancestors.'

'So why fight for her?'

'Because that's what our fathers taught us to do. A poor excuse, I suppose.'

She knew better than most the compulsion of feuds, however old. 'You'd be a better king than she is queen.'

'Impossible. "Who represents the whole people must himself be whole",' he quoted, 'and I am walking corruption.'

'Your affliction *is* terrible, but she's rotten from the inside.'

'Stop!' he cried, standing. 'It's sinful for any vassal to whisper against his queen, and still worse for a son.'

'And what of the patriot who foresees his kingdom's ruin? Should he too remain silent?'

He grabbed the pew for support and bowed like a penitent. 'You cannot turn me against her.'

'The truth at last. Not so hard, is it?'

CHAPTER 3

There was the mount, but surely this was not Jerusalem? The Winds had no dominion here. The Waters had deluged this city. Instead of an ark, she sat in a narrow little boat on a sea carpeted with bodies. More floated gently down about her like the leaves of autumn. She did not wish to see them and stared instead at her ferryman's back. It was not Ezra, no – it was someone much younger, with the bearing of an engineer. Might it be—? She longed to ask the stranger to turn around, but she knew that was forbidden.

One of the drifting bodies stirred as it came close. With white bloated hands, it pulled itself up onto the prow. The bloated, long-dead face next to hers was a face she knew. The ferryman raised his oar to stave in Giovanni's head, but before the oar descended, he cried, 'Wake up!'

Sofia opened her eyes to darkness. Lately she was grateful if she managed a few hours of rest uninterrupted by the baby's kicking or strange dreams. She felt her eyes: wet again. God, why was she crying so much? Expecting mothers, she knew from midwifing, were crazy as cats in a bag, but this was more than that. If even Fulk, who Catrina had sacrificed as a babe new-born, remained so blindly loyal there was every reason to be upset.

The door opened. 'Mistress? I heard you cry out.'

'Just a bad dream, Abdel.'

The sight of the Moorish slave who guarded her chamber door made her smile. She wasn't completely friendless. The queen expected Abdel to spy on Sofia; instead he told her the court gossip and found whatever foods she craved from the kitchen.

He looked into the darkness behind her. 'No wonder, Mistress! You left the window open – how often have I told you? That's how the Jinn enter.' He closed the lattice, then, after scolding her some more, left her to her thoughts.

Reclining there, staring at the moonlight diamonds the lattice scattered over her chamber, it was easy to recall that early dawn nine months ago in Rasenna, when she had woken to find a buio standing by her bed. The buio had asked her to be God's Handmaid.

Why had she answered as she did? In a word: Giovanni – but it wasn't logical. The two things she knew about the man she loved flatly contradicted each other: Giovanni was dead, but water could not die, so Giovanni was . . . what? To speak of individual buio was as absurd as speaking of the drops of water that made a river. Her lover had betrayed his country, sacrificed his name and, finally, his body. Even if the Handmaid's lot was ultimately grief, she owed him. And so she had said yes, and only months later had she realised to what she had consented. She had not sacrificed her life but her child's. No wonder she couldn't sleep. She was as bad as Catrina.

Suddenly she tensed, guilty ruminations forgotten. Abdel had said she'd left the window open, but she distinctly remembered closing it. Something *had* woken her. Slowly she turned. The shadow standing by the window was no buio. She reached under her pillow.

'Looking for this?'

The knife was illuminated in the moonlight.

'Fulk?' Sofia whispered to the chill night, balling her fists in anticipation. The queen had finally condemned her to die. Of course she would send her son to do it.

'Relax. If I'd come for that you'd never have awakened. I'm here to get you out. Morning will find Levi and Baron Masoir with Sicarii daggers through the chest.'

Sofia leaped up. 'I have to warn Levi—'

'Relax. Levi's the one who told me. Khoril told him after they got the Moor's ensign drunk. Arik is helping him now.'

'You expect me to believe the queen didn't share her plans with her loyal Grand Master?'

'Believe what you like – you know your child's doomed if you give birth within these walls. Arik said you know the Ebionite Quarter well now. Pay who you must to escape Akka – find a ship, or a caravan bound for Byzant.' Fulk threw a veil towards her. 'Change now, quickly. Basilius will soon be here.'

'Who is to be blamed for the murders?'

'Arik, of course,' he said, as though the question was naïve. 'In Akka, Catrina decides who's Sicarii. Considering Arik's brother is their leader, it'll be easy enough to convince the people that he was a sleeper.'

'But why?'

'Because you were right. She wants war. Any rapprochement weakens her rule. The baron's murder will cow the nobles and inflame the devout, but Levi's is intended to prove that the Sicarii will drive Oltremare to war with Etruria. Akka flatters itself that exiles can always find succour here, so this is a good way to get rid of you without looking heartless. She doesn't trust Concord, but handing you over will buy her time to prepare a fleet large enough to persuade them not to invade.'

'The First Apprentice doesn't want Akka. He wants me.'

'She doesn't believe that.'

'You can turn around now.'

He studied her critically, then adjusted her headdress. 'It'll do. It'll have to.'

Levi crouched behind Arik as they made their way through the empty corridors of the floor below to the battlements. 'Fulk won't be able to get Sofia out,' said Arik, 'not unless we create a distraction.'

They reached a doorway and together poked their heads out into the chill night air. Akka slept and there were few sounds: the wind's whisper, the plaintive cry of a night-fox from the Sands, the rhythmic gush of the filthy waves breaking upon the walls, the sound of half a dozen sleepy sentries occasionally stamping their feet to keep warm. The courtyard gate was being raised for Basilius and his men returning from their murderous expedition to the Merchants' Quarter.

'Can you swim?'

'Before I answer that, tell me you're not thinking of—'

A gong was struck, and as its sonorous echo died out, the blush of torches smeared the courtyard below. The wings of the palace lit up and the night's hush was ripped aside by shouts and a sourceless locust-hum as the clackers of Akka's churches spread the alarm.

'The baron's body's been discovered,' said Levi.

'Then what are we waiting for?'

The sentries' attention was on the streets below; the last thing they expected was a sword-wielding marauder charging them from inside the palace. Levi didn't try to fight them – the longer he was exposed, the greater the danger – but instead he shouldered them aside and swept by in a mad dash.

'He means to jump!' Arik roared from the point Levi had set out, and the Lazars in the courtyard below started raising ladders, trying to head Levi off. He stopped to tip them over, but Basilius waited for him to pass before raising his own ladder. Getting close to the sea, Levi cast his sword and helmet aside.

'Quick, Seneschal, throw!' Arik cried.

Thanks to quick reactions and considerable luck, Levi managed to duck the hurled axe.

Basilius cursed the Grand Master's pet Ebionite for a loud-mouthed fool and took a second axe from one of the unconscious Lazars. He calmly watched Levi weaving left to right, working out where he would be in a second's time.

Levi took the final few steps, held his breath and prepared to launch himself into space – just as Basilius released the axe. There was no pain, but Levi felt his legs and arms go dead as he dropped towards the scum-skinned sea and a darkness deeper than any he had ever thought possible.

Word travelled fast in Akka. The vessels belonging to the late Baron Masoir were already flying black flags – though his wife ensured that they continued to go about their business. The xebecs, Oltremare's native ships, were strange mongrels: a crossing of Ariminumese galleys, Byzantine dromons and the dhows of the old Radinate. With their lateen rigs and jibs projecting like antennae they resembled a horde of locusts spawned from the oily water, vibrating hungrily, waiting to take wing.

Levi smelled of death – but not because of his wound, though it looked ugly enough. The stench was due entirely to his dip in the Lordemare. Arik had fished him out of the filth and now sat on the side of the dock wringing out his own shirt. He looked and smelled no better.

Seneschal Basilius and the patriarch stood behind the Grand Master and the queen, looking down upon their strange catch. Levi dearly wished to ask Fulk if the Contessa had got away, but it was crucial that he play his part to the end. He tried to sound unruffled. 'Killing me will be a grave insult to the League.'

'Merely grave? I shall try to be more imaginative.' The queen was plainly furious. 'Your League has nothing to offer me. Where has the Contessa gone? You obviously helped her plan her escape.'

'I assumed I'd be captured, so I made sure I didn't know.'

'How very clever. Perhaps I'll torture you just for fun.' The queen turned to Chrysoberges. 'What say you, your Beatitude? What sentence is fitting for a mercenary who comes to disrupt my kingdom's peace?'

After Baron Masoir's assassination, the patriarch was eager to demonstrate his loyalty. 'Schismatics should be themselves parted' – he ripped his vestments, in passion or perhaps merely to illustrate his words – 'for he who divides his own kind—'

'But he's not your kind,' Arik interrupted.

Levi stared, numbed by this betrayal of confidence, but Arik did not meet his eye. Instead he risked a warning glance to Fulk before continuing, 'He's Ebionite, Majesty, by blood at least.'

'You know this – how?'

'He confessed to me that his mother was a slave. He even boasted how he had passed himself off as a Marian for years. It was *my* people he first betrayed. I should have let him drown.'

'Jackal!' Levi cried. He attempted to rise, but Fulk silenced him with a mailed fist. Levi fell back, nose and lip weeping blood.

'Then we are both wronged,' said Catrina. 'For your years of service, I give you the honour of sentencing him.'

'Most gracious,' said Arik with a bow. 'The punishment ought to fit the crime. He was born a slave, so put him to the oar and let him die one.'

'A judgement worthy of Solomon,' the queen said.

When the prisoner began to struggle, Fulk said, 'Obviously the first one didn't take. Care to try, Seneschal?'

Levi's blood struck the ground, and his head a moment after.

'Basilius!' the queen chided. 'He'll never fetch a good price looking like tenderised beef.'

'Don't worry, Majesty,' said Fulk carelessly. 'I'll see that he looks presentable when the time comes.'

'Very good,' she said. 'And now, Arik ben Uriah, what punishment would fit your own crime?'

'—Majesty?'

'Don't take me for a fool. You've been mooning over the girl for the last few months. I know you're behind this.'

'I will not deny it,' Arik said before Fulk could intervene. 'The Contessa asked for my aid when I first met her – I, who brought her to Akka. I am responsible.'

'There's more than that.'

'You mean to start war amongst the tribes. While I was helping you to defend innocent merchants from bandits, I could convince myself I was not betraying my people. At last I must choose.' He held up his head proudly so that she could see the martyr sincerity in his gleaming eyes and be persuaded.

It worked. 'Until this day you've served us loyally. Though it's more than you deserve, I will give you a soldier's death, Be so good, Grand Master.'

Fulk began to protest, but Arik stopped him. 'I've done my duty. Do yours swifly, my brother, and we shall see each other again, *be'ezrat HaShem.*'

'Seneschal?' said Fulk, holding out his hand, and Arik bowed his neck as the shadow of the axe blocked out the morning sun.

Levi opened his swollen eyes to see an Ebionite boy holding a pair of wool clippers staring at him. 'All of it?' the boy said again.

'The lot,' said Fulk. 'He won't sell with hair.'

As the boy drew close, Levi flinched, but the chain around his neck pulled him up short. His hands were manacled, so he raised a foot to try to defend himself.

Fulk caught it mid-air. 'Relax. You need to be gone from Akka before the queen changes her mind.'

'If Arik thought he was doing me a favour, he was wrong. I swore to protect Sofia—'

'And she has few friends left. Arik's dead, Levi. You getting killed too won't help the Contessa.'

'Then why are you selling me as a slave? I know these dogs

– they'll just chain me to a rowing station and work me to death–'

'—and feed your body to Leviathan. Yes, most likely, but there were few other options. The captain I'm selling you to is a Syracusan dog. Arik said you were raised in the Scillies.'

'So?'

'So I expect that you can speak the dialect. I know you can pick a lock. You have a gift for persuasion, though it availed you little here – my mother's court is not, alas, a reasonable place.' Fulk unpinned something from his mantel: a needle with a kink at one end and a small hook at the other. 'Hide this on your person – not under your tongue; they will examine your teeth and make you talk.'

'I'll think of somewhere.' He bowed his head, and told the boy to cut. 'See her to safety, Fulk, or Arik will have died for naught.'

'I know it, Brother.'

CHAPTER 4

The foothills of the ancient city of Veii shimmered in the silver light reflected from the Albula. The Rasenneisi engineers – Pedro Vanzetti and seven of his best – fixed their gaze on the majestically swollen flags snapping at the summit and began the arduous climb. The spectacle was spoiled when they came close enough to see the slain she-wolf depicted upon those yellow flags. It might have been a thousand years ago, but Veii's pride in conquering Rome remained undiminished. It was, according to most Etrurians, their last pride-worthy achievement.

The Rasenneisi were dressed sombrely in coarse grey cloaks worn over sleeveless multi-pocketed work jackets. Long hoods draped round neck and over chins, emulating their maestro. Pedro's resemblance to his father was strong now. The runt of yesteryear was completely gone, replaced by a youth with broadening shoulders and a tested strength behind his dark brown eyes.

As the gate was hauled open, Pedro rehearsed under his breath, 'I'm *so* sorry.' He tried again: 'My *deepest* condolences.' He considered afresh the wisdom of accepting Duke Grimani's invitation. When last year's summit broke down in Ariminum, the Veian ambassador – a cur who also happened to be the duke's son – had attempted to kidnap him – and he'd only escaped with the help of Doctor Ferruccio, the Salernitan ambassador. Yet here he was, putting his head into the noose again. But it was a necessary risk, for war, though long delayed, was upon them at last.

It was not Duke Grimani waiting to welcome him but the last man Pedro had expected to see in Veii.

'Doctor?'

When a Salernitan attains the age of two score and ten years, he is obliged to become an adult, leaving behind the rootless lifestyle of the butteri to pursue the life of the mind. Ferruccio, Count of Salerno, had been a doctor for decades now, but he had never quite abandoned the habits of his youth. Beneath his star-fretted blue cape he wore a faded mantle, and he carried his mazza still, though these days he used it to help him walk instead of herding buffalo. His hoary white moustache was styled in the buttero manner too, kept thick enough to protect from the dust of the trail, and swooping like the horns of their herds. All that was missing was the wolf-skin cap.

The old warrior pulled him into an embrace. 'Good to see you again, lad. I worried you had perished with the rest of the bandieratori.' He looked over Pedro's team of engineers, none much older than their maestro. 'Are these all who survived?'

'No, there are more back in Rasenna – but it was bad. We ought to have been more careful in our choice of podesta. Geta would never have been elected if the Contessa had been around.'

Ferruccio anticipated his next question. 'You'll be interested to know that shortly after the *Tancred* got off, it was escorted back to Ariminum by the *San Barabaso—*' Seeing Pedro's reaction, Ferruccio rested his hand on his shoulder. '*Tranquillo*, lad. Your friends weren't on it. Whether they made it to Oltremare, I don't know yet, but I'm making enquiries. I have some friends in Taranto who trade with the Akkans.'

It turned out Ferruccio was here for the same reason as Pedro: to lend his expertise to the defence of Veii.

'Droll, isn't it? The Concordians have made for us the alliance we failed to create ourselves a year ago. Let's go and see the duke, shall we?' He winked. 'Don't forget to give him your condolences.'

Castello Grimani topped the hill that overlooked the other five;

it was in every sense the peak of Veii. The duke's personal crest flew from its turrets and balconies: the Argus eyes of the peacock tail reminded the duke's subjects that his spies were everywhere. Deep within those walls, hidden away from the sun, was the ducal court. An army of fat candles tried in vain to hold back the gloom, barely illuminating the sullen, hollow-eyed busts in the niches that lined the windowless hall.

At the top of a small set of steps sat the current head of the Grimani family. The duke had once been delicately handsome; now, fat-padded and wrinkle-scarred as he was, he looked like a petulant dowager. He gestured to the long table at the bottom of the steps. 'You've come a long way, Maestro. Would you eat?'

'Thank you, Duke. I would prefer to survey the walls first.'

'My dear son was like you, full of vigour. The young are ever in a hurry.'

When Pedro attempted to offer his sympathies, the duke hushed him. 'Do not speak of my suffering, dear boy. I know Rasenna too has suffered at the hands of this usurper.'

'We'll win back control eventually,' said Pedro, 'but the loss of our city means the Concordians have no reason to delay. They'll soon be here.'

Ferruccio helped himself to some rabbit stew and a glass of wine while the duke led Pedro around the throne room, a limp, liver-spotted hand resting upon his shoulder like a dead fish.

'Don't worry,' Grimani said airily, 'when the time comes, Concordians always negotiate.'

'If you are so sanguine,' Ferruccio interrupted, 'why did you send an ambassador to the summit at Ariminum?'

Pedro felt his face redden and he stared at his feet, hardly believing that Ferruccio was bringing up *that* subject.

The duke's snarling reaction showed that however calm his outward appearance, he was nonetheless capable of passion. 'I sent him to ensure there was at least one voice of Reason present!

And my reward for being a good neighbour? To have my innocent son murdered in a sordid bridge brawl, and to win the enmity of the Concordians!' He looked disdainfully at Ferruccio, who was holding a haunch of meat in his fingers as he tore at it with his teeth. 'I can understand why Rasenna and Ariminum are intent on dragging the rest of us into this *northern* war – they need allies. But why you Salernitans wish to be involved is beyond me. Barbarians love fighting, I suppose.' He composed himself and gestured around at the tapestries that lined the room.Weaves with colours fresh as frescoes depicted horse herds running free over Arcadian pastures, stuffed horns of plenty, and coy goddesses, voluptuous and nude. 'Well, my people love peace. We have our city, our islands and our horses. The God of War is unwelcome here.'

'Come, Maestro Vanzetti,' said Ferruccio with barely concealed contempt. 'My appetite fails me. Let's see about defending these lambs.'

Pedro's quick survey gave reason to hope that Veii might be adequately fortified, and Doctor Ferruccio agreed; he might not be cognisant of the latest in siege-craft – although he was curious about the latest advances – but anyone who had been a buttero had sound instincts for territory. The Albula snaked around the southern half of the city like a moat, then broadened until she merged easefully into the Tyrrhenian Sea. They followed its course to the coast where fat, quarrelsome seagulls floated on the cool breeze and great waves smashed pointlessly against the cliffs. The doctor said the heavy rains that had swollen the Albula augured a tough winter – butteri knew such things, but the doctor had a solid grounding in Euclidian geometry too. They talked about the Contessa as they walked, and the doctor described the headstrong girl she had been growing up, and how like her grandfather.

'That's a handsome bay. I don't understand why they neglect

it so.' The memory of Ariminum's arsenal was fresh in Pedro's mind.

The doctor spat over the cliff. 'They wouldn't know what to do with a navy if they had it. They don't have the guile to trade or the guts to raid.' He grinned. 'I know what you're thinking, lad: "Of course a Salernitan would say that!" – but I don't say the Veians started out worthless; they've spent a lot of time and effort degrading themselves. Before the Grimani took charge, Veii aspired to be a maritime power like Ariminum and she chased business in every port of the Middle Sea from Byzant to Akka. The monarchy had been slumbering on the throne for centuries and was too indolent to interfere in its citizens' enterprises – which is the best that can be said for any government.'

Pedro smiled tolerantly. The doctor, like all Salernitans, was jealous of his liberty to a ridiculous degree 'So what changed?'

'One of the duke's ancestors convinced the king to grant him a monopoly on the Cagligarian Isles trade, but he quickly got bored with haggling with the Cagligarians and decided it would be easier to conquer the island, enslave the natives and mine its iron and alum intensively. Nobody objected – Concord's hunger for iron is boundless, and every town with any sort of textile industry requires alum.'

Pedro wasn't smiling any more. Rasenna was one of the latter.

'The Grimani were rich enough by then to overthrow the monarchy and "liberate" Veii. Every few decades the republic elects the latest Grimani as dictator-for-life. Sustained by the sweat of other men's brows, without reason to risk and without risk to vitiate, Veii's merchant class have become lazy living off rent.'

'And the Small People?'

'Keep them fed and they'll reserve their passion for games. Life is simple here. Why not turn your back on Etruria and its ceaseless wars.'

'So why are we here?' Pedro said despondently.

'Etruria's trade routes don't matter to Veii. While Duke Grimani thought Concord just wanted to control those routes, he wasn't bothered; that's why he wanted nothing to do with the League. I think the fate of Ariminum's Consilium made him realise his fate is bound up with the rest of Etruria, whether he likes it or not. Now he understands that Concord seeks a more lasting empire, one in which every Etrurian is a bondsman.'

'Just like the Cagligarians.'

'Aye, like the Cagligarians. Well, life's no fairy-tale. We can't choose our allies for their virtues.'

They completed their circuit and made their way back to the summit. The horseshoe-shaped piazza was Veii's exposed heart. It was dominated by Castello Grimani on one side and an old Etruscan temple on the other. The temple had been converted into a Marian cathedral centuries ago, but the leering gorgon on the pediment suggested that the Veians like to hedge their bets.

Ferruccio looked sideways at his companion. 'You're jumpy as a colt, Maestro. What's picking at you?'

'A riddle,' said Pedro. 'Why couldn't the southern states come to agreement in Ariminum? It was clearly in the interests of every party.'

Ferruccio chuckled. 'Seeking Reason in men's actions is a quick way to drive yourself *pazzo*.' He pointed to the cathedral's pediment. 'Look at the perpetually warring pantheon sculpted in yonder stone. Of course we are all Marian now, but I often think the gods of the pagans suit this fractious land a whole lot better. Domineering Concordians, turbulent Rasenneisi, perfidious Ariminumese – such varied terrain contains all the hues of humanity, lacking nothing but common ground. The League's hour was not yet ripe, Maestro, simple as that.'

'But why does it always have to come to crises? If we had presented a strong front in Ariminum – but General Spinther threw an apple of discord amongst us and that was all it took. If any ambassador had made a deal, it would have given his city a privileged position in the new order, so it became a race to betray each other.'

'You losing hope?'

'No, I think Etruria is. We need Veii to prove resistance is possible.'

'You're looking for a miracle, in other words.' The doctor looked at him. 'You had best go on without me,' he said, gesturing at the cathedral. 'Looks like I've some candles to light before dinner.'

Pedro could see he wished to minimise time spent with the duke. 'You don't trust him, do you?'

'I trust men to look after their own interests. All I know is that if Veii surrenders to Spinther and is well treated, it'll be devilish hard to make the case for fighting on.'

'You'd best light a candle and pray that they don't, then.'

Back in the duke's cave-like court, Pedro complimented Veii's natural defences. The duke could not have been prouder if he himself had laid out the city alongside the Tarquins. 'These walls have not failed yet. Concordians may make rivers dance uphill, but with the sea behind us, there's no danger of us being outflanked.'

'Past performance is no indicator of future earnings,' interrupted a booming voice.

Duke Grimani's genial mask slipped momentarily. 'Ah – I was about to send for you to help me welcome your paesano, but I needn't have worried. Nothing south of Concord escapes Salvatore Bombelli.' He turned back to Pedro. 'His power is something uncanny. We may not have haruspices to interpret sheep entrails in my court but I fear we will always need men who can commune with Mammon.'

It had been some time since Pedro had seen any of Fabbro's

sons. The three of them here – Salvatore, the heir apparent, Costanzo the youngest and Guido, one of the twins – represented the richest financial institution in Etruria after Ariminum's Basilica. None of them looked like bankers; Salvatore looked and sounded like a sailor, Costanzo still looked the dandy, and Guido – Guido was a positive monk.

'Are the rest of you here too, Salvatore?'

'What, all us Bombelli together in a town about to be surrounded?' Costanzo wagged his finger. 'You know our papa taught us better than that. Like Etruria's rivers, we Bombelli are everywhere.' The brothers were scattered through Europa, in Byzant, Francia and Aragon, now Guido and his twin Gasparo had left Ariminum. Fabbro's death had left Salvatore head of the family, with the twins next in line; Costanzo was the youngest and the nearest in age to Pedro. He was the only son who had initially resisted becoming a merchant, and as Fabbro wasn't the type to stop his children doing what they loved – in inconstant times, diversification made sense – Costanzo was indulged. Alas, his vices were expensive ones, and when poetry failed to pay, the siren call of coin-counting drew him back to the fold. He retained the long hair, fine clothes and louche habits of the *bon vivant*, but his youthful experiences proved a surprisingly prudent investment, for a facility with fine phrases is always useful to a salesman, and his contacts soon led to lucrative contracts with Etruria's leading families, that upper tier his rough-hewn father never quite managed to breach.

'We've been eager to see this young fellow for quite a while,' Salvatore announced. 'Pedro – or I should say, *Maestro Vanzetti* – is our last hope of returning to Rasenna and of avenging our father.' He caught Pedro in a bearhug. 'What did you do with the little Pedro then – eat him?'

Salvatore was sociable as his father, if not nearly as diplomatic. Where Fabbro had cajoled and bargained with the world,

Salvatore barged through. Fabbro's death confirmed Salvatore's position as head of the family firm; after Rasenna was lost, the Bombelli Family banco became a truly rootless venture – and a whole world of profits opened to it.

Guido was always pale and hollow-cheeked, but he looked even more gaunt, Pedro thought. He had never before seen him without his twin, but some instinct prompted him not to remark on it now. Neither had ever flirted with other trades; banking had been their sole obsession since they were boys. Guido might be less effusive in his greeting than Salvatore and Costanzo, but he was never very warm; all that mattered was that the Bombelli were here. Pedro's great fear had been that they would find some accommodation with the Concordians – they were businessmen, after all, and for all their swagger they were conservative risk-averse investors.

When Pedro finished telling them about the situation in the city of towers, Guido cleared his throat solemnly and said, 'Things have moved on in Ariminum too. The revolution—'

'—that's what they're calling it,' said Costanzo. 'Sounds better than *coup*, I suppose.'

'Whatever they're calling it,' Guido continued calmly, 'it was soon settled. When the Consilium barricaded themselves in the Basilica, the Moor took the harbour and the arsenal – God knows how.'

'I know,' Pedro said quietly. 'The arsenalotti gave it to him.'

'Look at the dark horse,' Costanzo said.

Guido nodded slowly. 'That explains it. The arsenal is Ariminum's real heart.'

'I suppose the Consilium tripped over themselves to betray each other?'

Guido regarded Pedro carefully. 'I see you've dealt with them before. The Moor said yes to everyone, and when the Basilica's doors were opened – well, they learned what his word was worth.'

'In the Basilica!' the duke exclaimed, then reflectively, 'I suppose that temple was long defiled by moneylenders. No offence, Signore—'

'None taken,' said Salvatore graciously. 'Our work's not holy, only necessary.'

'In any case,' Guido continued, 'I escaped, but Gasparo didn't. He was strung up with the rest of the Consilium.'

'I'm so sorry,' Pedro exclaimed.

'We've all suffered,' said Salvatore stoutly.

This was the time to reveal what he'd discovered at the summit. 'The Moor's made a deal with Concord,' he announced.

Salvatore didn't look remotely surprised. 'Of course. Akka's far away. He wears the corna as long as Concord allows it. But we can discuss this over dinner. Come back to my apartment and we'll make you presentable. You can't dine with a duke dressed like a brick mason.'

Back in Salvatore's apartment, Costanzo sheepishly presented a purple velvet suit. 'Byzantine. I'm terribly sorry about the cut. It's two years old.'

Pedro assured Costanzo that he'd never worn anything as fine; his father would have greatly admired the exquisite tailoring. As he dressed, he remarked to Salvatore that his relations with the duke seemed somewhat strained.

'You picked up on that?' said Costanzo dryly.

'It's the stress,' said Salvatore. 'Grimani is a man used to solving his money problems by fiat.'

Pedro looked around the lavish surrounding, 'Money problems?'

'Yes. One would think a people with a cornucopia like the Cagligarian Isles would have few, but prudence is like any muscle. It atrophies if it's not used. The duke's appetites and the indolence of his subjects have both grown over time. When he discovered there was a limit to the amount he could levy and remain popular, he debased the coinage. Then he began to confiscate the estates of wealthier citizens. Of course he distributed a fraction to the Small People so no one protested, but now that he has to pay for things that have been neglected, trivialities like defence, all the fat sheep are gone.'

'And so he has to deal with you. How indebted is he?'

'He's the most ostentatious pauper you're ever likely to meet. Twenty thousand soldi.'

'*Merda*. Where did you even get that kind of money to lend?'

'My dear boy, that is the simplest thing in the world. A rich man's stool reeks like ours, but every man considers his debt perfume. I sold it on to investors in the form of five-hundred-soldi bonds, thus raising the cash and pocketing a substantial commission. We want the League to succeed, but it's profit that makes our chimney smoke.'

'Don't try to explain that to Grimani,' said Costanzo gleefully. 'He thinks it immoral that we make him pay interest.'

'If it's high, I'm sure you have reason,' said Pedro. 'What is your opinion of Veii's prospects?'

'Oh, it's not like that at all. I just have to cover my arse,' Salvatore laughed. 'The duke gives me a hard time, but as you see, he knows how to treat his guests.'

Pedro reflected how far the Bombelli had come from Rasenna, and the contrast between these extravagant apartments and the joyous anarchy of Tower Bombelli. He remembered tripping over bolts of cloth, hitting his head on the camphor pomades that hung from the counting room's ceiling. He remembered Fabbro fretting over his scales and rapping orders to his sons while Maddalena offered advice on everything. Sweet memories. At last, Pedro ventured onto the subject that had been on his mind since they met. 'Salvatore, your father and I didn't always agree, especially towards the end, but above all else he cared about family. He would rather have seen the Bombelli beggared and united than the richest family in Etruria and hating each other.'

Warmth drained from the banker's smile. 'And I would rather he was alive. That woman is dead to me,' he said simply.

'We would have looked after her,' Costanzo said, 'but she connived with a foreign dog to kill our father.'

'You don't know that—'

'We know she stole our patrimony,' said Guido, 'and for that alone, she deserves a traitor's death.'

Salvatore's face darkened further. 'You find that funny, Pedro?'

'No, I was laughing at myself. When you declared against Concord, I took it as a sign that our chances were decent. Now I realise it's just your Rasenneisi blood that makes you willing to back a loser.'

'Our motivations don't matter any more,' said Guido. 'Only money matters from here on. Without credit, no city eats and no army marches.'

The long table was carpeted with a menagerie of meats and fresh fruit, and there was enough wine to dizzy an army. A new set of candles burned their hearts out as servants danced around the guests and fiddlers clawed the silence away. The four elders who represented Veii's four lower hills sat with Doctor Ferruccio, Pedro and the Bombelli brothers, but they ate and drank little. Their silent presence was required whenever Duke Grimani wanted to impress upon foreigners that his reign was stable. In spite of all the effort, there was a strained quality to the air. It takes practise to make guests at ease, and being a tyrant – aside from the moral implications – can make one an awkward host.

Grimani began with a toast. 'My *deepest* condolences for the loss of your brother.' He tipped his glass towards Guido. 'You must feel the loss most keenly.'

Guido solemnly raised his glass. 'To Gasparo Bombelli!'

'I'm just surprised that he couldn't buy his way out,' Grimani remarked as he sat down.

The talk moved swiftly on to developments north and south, and the inevitable discussion of that great mystery that even the most penetrating couldn't unravel – how things had come to this pass.

'Etruria has but one problem and that is the Etrurians. The people of this land of ours are loyal to the flag of their home town and nothing else.'

The duke repeated the cliché as though it was a great profundity, but Ferruccio could not agree. 'You speak as if your only objection to the First Apprentice's ambition is that you are not him – have you ever considered that our very disunity is an asset? Etruria is cosmopolitan, and variety is more than the spice of life: it's a curb to tyranny. Each state's government and customs exist in close competition with others. Of course there are arguments to the contrary: united, we would be military stronger, less vulnerable to invasion, and yes, yes, all true – but all the same, we would be reduced.'

'How dull it would be to constantly agree,' Costanzo laughed.

Salvatore was coolly analytical about the brewing conflict. 'Say what you will about the Concordians, they know how to plan inter-generationally. Papa always said it's the only way to get anything done. Our banco didn't grow in one lifetime, and Papa wouldn't have been the man he was without *his* papa's capital behind him. My bet is Captain Giovanni's bridge was just one step in a strategy conceived long ago, maybe even as far back as Bernoulli's day.'

'They didn't plan for Rasenna to revolt,' the duke said pointedly.

'No, but a plan like this isn't overthrown by one setback.'

Ferruccio paused in his mastication to remark, 'They're as dogged as their bloody machines.'

'The good doctor has trouble understanding such unity of purpose. Salerno is a democracy.' The duke looked around brightly. He considered himself rather a wit, but this was more a consequence of being surrounded by terrorised sycophants than any quickness of intellect.

'Better than a tyranny,' Ferruccio growled.

The duke's smile vanished. 'Veii is a republic, like Rasenna.'

Salvatore had also had enough of Grimani's patronising attitude. 'Come, Duke, you may not wear a corna, but Veii is your kingdom.'

The duke was unwilling to concede the point in front of his subjects and temporised, 'It's true my family are influential voices – what of it? A select group rule in Ariminum, in Rasenna, in Concord – the only difference is that we do not require foreigners to believe its hypocrisies. Our citizens are content. Ask them.' He turned to the row of elders. 'Isn't that so, Marsuppini?'

'Entirely contented,' said the magnate without looking up from his plate.

'You see! Whilst it is true that they have sacrificed a degree of freedom for stability, they have the maturity to know a republic ruled by the Small People would soon vote itself into ruin. Dictatorship is the best solution in this imperfect world. All revolutionaries say their revolution is the last, but the momentum that brings them about carries them to excess, and that makes reaction inevitable and presently a fresh revolution is necessary. My people have chosen to get off that wearying carousel. I'm surprised that a son of Fabbro Bombelli doesn't acknowledge their wisdom – but delude yourself, by all means, if it makes you happy.'

'My father was no tyrant.'

'But somehow your sister is. I'm not sure I understand the distinction.'

What remained of the meal was a tense affair, as was the week that followed.

As Pedro explained his drawings to the Veian masons and black-smiths, he saw in the tight lips that mouthed thanks and felt in their weak handshakes that it was not just the Concordians who held Rasenneisi engineers in suspicion. He was free with his knowledge, but such profligacy makes the miserly wary and before long certain voices started to whisper to Duke Grimani that Pedro Vanzetti was a new Girolamo Bernoulli come amongst them. Had not the *Stupor Mundi* been contemptuous of the Guild traditions in his youth? Had not his hand been open before he made a fist?

It wasn't just guildsmen who showered them with hostile looks. The Small People did their bit. *Didn't they know*, Pedro wondered, *that he was here to help?* This, he realised with a start, was how it must have been for Giovanni when he first came to Rasenna.

As Pedro outlined his suggestions to the duke, the notary kept a running total of the costs. The duke agreed to his key suggestions – the earthworks and diverting the Albula – but his other ideas were dismissed out of hand. It was becoming clear that the Bombelli were but one of the bancos to whom Grimani was indebted.

Although he wasn't prepared to pay for it, the duke still craved assurance. 'What say you, Maestro Vanzetti – shall we survive the coming storm?'

He answered cautiously, 'It depends on how badly Concord wants Veii. I've left some of my best people to help you prepare. You've a fighting chance, unless you are surrounded.'

Pedro suggested two well-stocked and well-armed batteries, one either side of the harbour mouth, to insure against naval incursions, but Grimani assured him that would be taking things too far. 'We have our navy, after all.'

'You have a few slave galleys – that's nothing compared to Ariminum's, and when you add in Concord's firepower, the contest is even more unequal. As soon as the Moor has Ariminum stable – by which I mean sufficiently terrified – he'll set off down the Adriatic. Between the Concordian legions and the Golden Fleet, Veii'll be pretty stuck.'

'They may have taken Rasenna without blood, but Veii will cost them dearer,' the duke bluffed stoutly. Such protestations were expected from him, but Pedro prayed it wouldn't come to the test.

He was not sorry to say goodbye to Veii at the end of the week. A posse of butteri mounted on stocky Tolfetano horses were waiting east of the city to escort Ferruccio home. Pedro wondered aloud how they had crossed the Albula without getting wet.

'Oh, we have our ways. That other riddle's still gnawing at you, ain't it?'

Pedro smiled at the old man's astuteness. 'Engineers are circumspect by necessity. Even in the brief time we were there, Veii's population was swelling – all those trains of exiles carrying a hundred different flags . . . Towns small and large are fleeing before the Grand Legion like a plague. They think Veii's the place to make a stand. But they are—'

'—desperate,' Ferruccio finished soberly.

'Yes. Something's gnawing at you too, Doctor.'

He stared at the river, 'I'm just worried that this is nothing more than a gambit to give Grimani a better negotiating position when Concord comes knocking. Veii have hitherto remained studiously neutral in Etrurian squabbles. They took no part in Tagliacozzo, remember.'

'—unlike certain rash neighbours of theirs. The hour's late. We must start trusting each other.'

'I suppose we must.' He clapped Pedro's back so hard he nearly fell from his saddle. 'I hope to see you down the trail, Maestro. Must you really go back? What's the point of returning to a city held by the enemy? Whatever its shortcomings, the first battle will be fought in Veii.'

'You're wrong, Doctor. The battle is already under way, in Rasenna.'

CHAPTER 5

The Colossus, by some miracle, still stood, but all that remained of the Molè was rubble. A boy in rags little better than a mendicant's stood by the great statue's base.

Next to him, taking instruction, was the finely dressed chairman of the Opera del Duomo. His quill ceased scratching momentarily as he inclined his head. '—and the statue?'

The boy turned to study it. The Etruscan motto carved in its base was still legible, but the sword the Angel of Reason held aloft was shattered. Its face was distorted as if by a palsy. The fire had gouged the bronze deep, painting the newly mottled surface with a carbon patina. 'Melt it down.'

'Oh surely not, First Apprentice!' the chairman exclaimed. 'The damage is only superficial; we could easily restore it – we could relocate it in front of the Collegio.'

'Concord is done with idols,' the boy said in tones that brooked no contradiction. 'We shall need every ounce of the metal before long.'

On the way down from the windy mount he passed one child after another; the fanciulli all wore the same fervent expressions on their face, the same red bands on their arms they had donned the day that he had renounced the Red. Now they hauled stone up to the mount, working until they collapsed, and their mothers and fathers, who had by now joined the daily procession, stepped over them, oblivious to the deaths of their sons and daughters. There was no time to stop.

The children were in the thrall of a king in their image – but they were deceived, for he was nothing like them. He was nothing like *anyone*.

The gondolier pushed along the canal while his unkempt young passenger sat quietly mediating. Torbidda begrudged the trip to the Collegio dei Consoli, though he knew it was necessary. For a few months more he must keep the consuls as tightly leashed as the fanciulli. Afterwards, they could all go to hell together. It seemed a lifetime ago since he'd last considered abstract political questions; his days now were full of masons, glassblowers, iconographers and goldsmiths, and treks to dusty quarries near the coast looking for fine-grained stone. The craftsmen found the First Apprentice precise, cold and demanding – but not one of them could hear him screaming for help. He, the boy called Torbidda, had some awareness still, though his limbs and tongue were controlled by another power, ageless, pitiless. But the coffin-lid was getting heavier each day.

The Darkness cast its pall over everything his eyes regarded. He was no longer a boy trying to survive but a carrier of corruption like a Lazar. He had no bell to warn people away. He remembered everything – his mother's betrayal, Agrippina's duplicity, Leto's loyalty, the rote-learned lessons and formulae, and the hard-won magic words he'd used to open the Molè – but all colour had been leached from those memories. They were husks. To say *I am Torbidda* now would be sophistry. In the Guildhalls, Examiner Varro had taught them the principles of logic: lies that deny truth are harmless, he'd said; it's the lies that *distort* truth that are poisonous.

His memories were intact, but stripped of their emotion they no longer made *sense*. He remembered the terrible day he had entered the Guild. He remembered his dread of the Examiners, of the other children, of never seeing his mother again – and how those fears had vanished when he had received his name: Sixty.

It was the first beautiful thing he had ever owned. *Sixty* had so many facets: it was not a prime, though the two adjacent numbers were, as were three of its twelve factors. It was the smallest number divisible by one through six. Squared, it was three thousand and sixty, the number of seconds in an hour. More: it was the fifteenth trump card of that deck his mother used when she thought he was sleeping. The wailing mendicants who roamed the Depths rattled rosaries with sixty beads. The dread faded to nothing as he lost himself in its myriad aspects.

Before he knew it, the shearing was over and he had jumped the Guild's hurdles and become a candidate. To win the yellow he had to step over Agrippina's corpse. That final hurdle was steep.

Then there had been the months wasted in the Molè's library looking for the means to outshine Girolamo Bernoulli, the sun. He learned . . . *nothing*. The Babylonians, those marvellous astrologers, had believed sixty a firmer base than the decimal. Their king Nebuchadnezzar had built a statue sixty cubits tall, which he commanded the Jews to worship – and the Jews' god promptly struck him mad for it. What else? Isaac was sixty when his son Esau was born, with Jacob grasping at his heel. Sixty men of Israel, valiant and expert in war, guarded the bed of Solomon, that king whose temple was sixty cubits wide and tall.

It was all nonsense and trivia: the piled detritus of history, the absurd fancies of theology.

He remembered the other terrible day, when he had finally tested himself against the *Stupor Mundi* – the wonder of the world, Bernoulli himself. There was another shearing and his beautiful name broke into fractions after he lost not just the contest but himself.

He remembered his fear growing as the pod descended, and at the same time he remembered his hunger to consume the boy, the expectation of the Darkness he descended into. He was both hunter and hunted, the petrified hare leaping over the contato and the hawk diving to break its back. He was within and without of his body. He was the boy shrinking from the pit and the slavering, obscene beast within. His last physical memory was the agony of being consumed; after that he was nothing but a voyeur, experiencing only second-hand sensations. The Darkness' carnal satisfaction was intense as it fed on fresh meat at last, as – at last – it regained a foothold in the world of men.

Most likely none of it was real. Most likely he had broken under the strain of being the last Apprentice, had gone insane. A philosopher should not multiply explanations. And yet . . . the Darkness's purpose was clear. The occupation of his body was simply the first step. He was a bridge by which Bernoulli could reach his ultimate object: the Handmaid's child. The worst was knowing that he had made himself that bridge. And even had his usurper allowed him a voice, how could he – the boy who had sacrificed all he loved to ambition – object?

Attendance was high at the general assembly of the Collegio dei Consoli – as was anxiety. Rumours and theories circled the concentric rows of the chamber. This was a very different gathering of Guild leaders to the one that had met just a few months ago. Then, the First Apprentice had been politically isolated and had been maintaining control only by the authority of his rank – and when that failed, by the assassination of his critics. Now he had a power-base that was legion, comprising the young and the poor. He had won over the mob by eulogising Fra Norcino and pillorying Girolamo Bernoulli, and the consuls, looking to their own self-preservation, needed to know *why*. Was this just a ploy, or the beginning of a new stage of Concord's revolution?

Torbidda did not keep them waiting.

'Consuls, only those who have been candidates for Apprenticeship are allowed to sit in this august body. So one way to see this

– the way we tend to – is that the Collegio is composed of the best of the best. A more realistic view is that the Collegio is composed of failures. That is my view, and therefore, I am reopening the Guild's rolls to the nobility.'

Protests erupted from all circles, but Torbidda's head swivelled to his right and lit on a round, red-faced round man with a half-eaten sack of yellow apples in his lap. He was leaning towards his neighbour and whispering.

'Please, Consul Fuscus, be so good as to share your opinion with all of your colleagues.'

Numitor Fuscus, one of Consul Corvis' allies, had been lucky to escape the purge when Corvis fell. He was an Empiricist of the old school and suspicious of all innovation. Though he was an outspoken opponent of Leto Spinther, he was well aware that questioning the First Apprentice in public had generally proved to be fatal. Now his usually hooded eyes became round as pennies and his flushed cheeks paled.

When he began to stutter, Torbidda interrupted, 'Come, Consul – if any hour called for boldness, this is it. Speak your mind. In this chamber, we do not censure candour.'

That was demonstrably untrue, but the challenge had the desired effect and Fuscus threw down his half-eaten apple and stood. 'Very well, First Apprentice. I believe that your proposal is contrary to everything Bernoulli believed in. Even if we could trust the nobility to share power – and we cannot – they lack competence for the job.'

Hear-hears told the consul that the majority agreed with him, and he ended with stentorian resolve, 'Bernoulli built a state devoted to Reason and the rigour of Natural Philosophy, not the spurious claims of pedigree. Let us stay true to that vision.'

'You will, I trust, allow that the First Apprentice knows the mind of Bernoulli better than you?' Torbidda started, his voice suspiously calm. 'He believed in *expedience*. He excluded the nobility from government in Forty-Seven because it was expedient – but circumstances change. I am privileged and burdened with knowledge you are not, a little of it esoteric and wonderful, but most wearingly dull. And amongst the latter is the true state of our finances. Brothers, they are grim. I see your doubtful faces and I hear you asking: how could we, who have Nature on a leash, have empty vaults? How did we arrive at this pass? Who is to blame? Some of you have heard me defame Bernoulli's name to the fanciulli and doubtless thought it a clever ruse. I tell you: I meant every word. I tell you the Guild has made of Bernoulli a false idol. We call him the Supreme Architect, but he built his empire on weak foundations. With our native talent and skill, we could have let the world come to Concord and attained a lasting hegemony, built peacefully and gradually. But Bernoulli was a man in a hurry, and plunder and violent confrontation were his methods. For a time, they worked, and the appropriated fortune of the Curia funded our legions. As long as the empire was expanding, the fact that the tumult of Re-formation destroyed Concord's tax-base did not matter, for we acquired vassals aplenty and whenever we needed to pay for new projects, more legions, bigger war machines, we simply squeezed them.'

The consuls listened silently to this blasphemy with a mixture of indignation and confusion, appalled to hear the First Apprentice, of all people, insulting Bernoulli so casually.

He appeared not to notice. 'Since Rasenna destroyed the Twelfth Legion, all of Etruria had been in a state of rebellion. This has wounded our pride, and broken our finances. We need capital – so where shall we find it? There's no one to tax – no one with money, anyway. Most of the nobility are impoverished. The smarter families renounced their names and joined the Guild – families such as yours, Consul Fuscus. What are we to do, then? Fleece ourselves? And when we are all sheared, what then?'

Numitor Fuscus touched his neck nervously.

'Therefore I move again that we open the rolls. If you're worried that every wretch will be allowed in, don't be; only those with something to offer will be welcomed. Not every noble took the route yours did, Consul. A few went into trade and not only maintained their fortunes but acquired greater ones – Malapert Omodeo is one such—'

Torbidda's spell wavered as the rows began to mutter. Malapert Omodeo: a notorious name, a name regarded with special hostility by nobles and engineers alike. The Guild might exclude nobles from all important positions, but it respected expertise and ability. Omodeo had run one of the most productive mines in the Rhine Lands and had used his direct access to the mint and his foreknowledge of Concordian plans to invade the Dalmatian Pass to speculate on grain prices – the fortune he made off the back of the ensuing disaster was enough to buy sanctuary in Byzant.

Consul Fuscus gave voice to the common feeling when he spat, 'That traitor!'

Torbidda moved to silence the mutters of agreement. 'Consul Fuscus, you know very well that Omodeo fled only because he feared the Guild would appropriate his fortune – surely that is prudence, not treachery – surely we would each have done the same. We have need of prudent men. I wish to invite him back into the fold. Does anyone object?'

The consuls took the prudent course – silence – and once they passed the motion, Torbidda left the assembly. The chamber quickly emptied, until Numitor and half a dozen of his supporters were alone.

'The First Apprentice may be insane, but he is cunning as ever,' he told them. 'You know what this is, don't you? He hasn't forgiven us for giving Corvis power. It's bad enough he ignores the Collegio; now he wants to dilute what little influence we have left by planting enemies in our midst. With the Collegio warring with itself, he can pursue his mad schemes unopposed.'

'We can do nothing,' said one consul disconsolately, 'but bide our time.'

'Oh, I think we can do more than that,' said Numitor serenely. 'Concord's never lacked ambitious soldiers. We simply have to recruit a few.'

Deep in the chambers beneath the Guild Halls, the blind man stared at his reflection. What he saw in it, only God – or some power equally omniscient – knew. His ears pricked up as feet splashed through a puddle and he felt the torch's warmth on his face. 'Where have you been, my King?'

'Busy.'

'Why do you waste time with these parliaments? Are you a king or no?'

'These days kings must pretend not to be. I need the Collegio's support to buy the materials to build my temple.'

The First Apprentice stopped as he saw the warped mirror Fra Norcino crouched over. 'You got that in the Drawing Room.'

'What of it?'

'You cannot go about in the Guild Halls! The fanciulli are devoted to me only because they believe me your heir.'

Norcino chuckled at that. 'The times are hysterical. There's nothing so remarkable about a dead man walking – you above all should appreciate that.'

'Just take more care. I need the fanciulli as much as I need the Collegio.'

The blind man leaned closer to the mirror, his foul breath misting the parabolic lake of its surface. 'I care nothing for your temple.'

'If you could see the foundations, you'd care.'

'I'm blind. Did you forget?' said Norcino. He was used to Herods and their mania for building; they might be useful tools, but they were also tiresome.

The boy turned away. 'We have each our part to play, Astrologer. Mine is to build towers.'

'You'd be better off concentrating on finding the Handmaid.'

'I think you overestimate this girl. My body's previous incumbent wasn't a total fool. He did not notice anything remarkable about her when he guarded her prison.'

'Until she burned that prison!' Norcino spat. 'Do you imagine this Handmaid will lie docile on your altar? The Madonna has been waiting longer than you for the Wave's return. She did not choose someone meek and mild to be her successor.' He walked to the edge of the puddle and pointed to the other side. 'The Contessa is a warrior.'

The boy took his position. 'I can fight.'

'Show me.'

This time Norcino did not restrain himself; he did not like the sneering, cynical creature that had returned from the pit and wished to remind it of the mortal pain to which it was now subject. Of course, it was he who had persuaded Torbidda into the pit in the first place. The boy, whoever he was, had fought well, coolly receiving blows and returning them, not surrendering ground. The water droplets hung about them in a mist.

'I wrung the secret of Water Style out of the buio in my last incarnation,' he said with lofty hauteur.

'Indeed? How subtle of you. Alas, the Jinn are not so easily frightened,' said Norcino, and he began flipping end-over-end in a circle. All the boy could do was turn with him and keep his guard up – but suddenly Norcino was gone. Then a column of dust snaked through the pillars and a punch rattled his jaw. He turned groggily. Another gust passed by and this time he found himself face-down in the pool with dust settling on his back.

He got to his feet, soaked and bleeding from lip and nose, his arm dead at the shoulder. 'I can't counter it. How did you—?'

'Now you know: the Wind too has its secrets. I did not hold back so that you would realise how badly you need my help. The boy you supplanted had some humility. You have none, and it is a terrible weakness. Water awaits the enemy, adapts itself and eats the enemy's strength. Wind is equally powerful, but it is a force that consumes itself. To defeat the Handmaid, you'll need both your right and your left hand.'

'But who would school the Handmaid in this art?' the boy asked disingenuously. 'Ah . . . your brother. He is quite the nuisance.'

'He is an *infidel*! When the Sacred Fire burned away our mortality we swore never to directly interfere in mortal affairs; we would only *influence*.'

'Seems to me you've both exceeded your brief.'

Doubt darkened Norcino's face 'I —I—' he started, then, 'I do what's necessary. He broke the covenant first.'

'Tell yourself whatever tale pleases you, Astrologer' – the boy limped back to the start position – 'but for now, show me what I need to know.'

CHAPTER 6

The evening had leached the last of the day's warmth. The stranger loosened his purse and asked, 'How much is that?'

Bocca was genuinely touched to hear these words. He'd prospered during Rasenna's boom, but those days were long gone. 'Six,' he said, then added, 'You can't be a Rasenneisi.'

'I've just come from Veii.' Though the stranger's jaw was buried in a scarf and his eyes were concealed by an overhanging hood his youth was evident – but it was not a problem: Bocca's policy was to serve anyone who paid cash. 'I make a point to drink in the Lion's Fountain whenever I stop in Rasenna,' said the stranger, before sheepishly adding, 'Maybe I've had too much already, but wasn't your establishment on the other side of the river?'

Bocca welcomed any opportunity to air his grievances, but he checked first that no condottieri were sleeping in the corners of the piazzetta. 'We relocated after the Night of Black Towers.'

The stranger matched his confidential whisper. 'I heard about that. Nasty business.'

'Nasty's not the half of it.' Bocca poured a glass for each of them before the stranger could demure. 'Veian, eh? We used to have all sorts in town, but that dried up and those who are still thirsty don't pay their tabs.'

'That's what brings me here,' the stranger said, 'I'm trying to settle a debt with Polo Sorrento. The market's been disrupted lately, but still – a man should honour his debts.'

'I sympathise. But you might have saved yourself the journey.

The farmer's deep in hock to a Concordian thief by the name of Geta.'

'Why doesn't your podesta do something about it?'

'Geta is our podesta. Officially he's answerable to the gonfaloniere and the Signoria, but they're either indebted or terrified of him.'

'Terrible,' the stranger repeated.

The brewer supped his drink. The whole truth was that he was part of that same Signoria; he'd just realised quicker than most the error they'd made backing Geta. After that night the Hawk's Company had shown their true flag: once, they outraged only those women who prostituted themselves, but without the bandieratori towers to restrain them, even respectable women were harassed anew each day. The bandieratori – the remnant left, who now called themselves the Tartaruchi – had retaliated, but the sporadic assassinations of Signoria members and the palazzi that mysteriously burned in the night only made the situation more volatile. Revenge followed reprisal till fear kept the streets – and Bocca's tavern – empty.

'Bad as Geta is, his wife makes him worse. Fabbro, God rest him, spoiled her something awful.'

'You don't mean Bombelli's daughter?'

'The same. I suppose you did business with Fabbro? His sons are active in Veii, I believe?'

'Veii, Salerno, the Sicilies – the Bombelli banco has fingers in every city south of Concord, and a few north to boot.'

'Well, I hope they don't expect to be welcomed back. It was Maddalena who urged Geta to persecute the families of those who'd gone underground. She's always been a handful, but Geta encourages her; he finds it amusing to let her harangue the Signoria.'

The stranger raised the glass, but did not drink.

'What's the matter?' said Bocca, and started back when the stranger let it drop to the ground. 'You'll pay for the g—'

Half a dozen figures dropped from the sky and he sat back down slowly. 'What is this? I'm just an innocent tavern keeper—'

'No one's innocent in Rasenna.' Pedro pulled back his hood. 'We want a name. Which family's going to be hit tonight? Take another drink if it helps jog your memory.'

'But how would I know? I'm just a —'

'You're just a dead man if you don't talk. You're Master of the Vintners' Guild and one of the Signoria that elected Geta, and that alone is treason as far as the rest are concerned.'

Bocca reached for the bottle. 'The Strozzi.'

'And they say good service is a thing of the past. I'm going to be a regular from now on. All you have to do is keep your ears open.'

'I won't be party to murder.'

The flagmen, silent till now, began laughing.

'A bit late to acquire scruples, Bocca,' said Pedro, gesturing to the shadows. 'You condemned every one of these men when you permitted their towers to burn. The real Signoria has condemned you. This is your only chance to earn a reprieve. Why don't you think of it as paying off your tab?'

If Rasenna was a city half-dead, then the northside was where the bodies were buried. It was a graveyard of tall black tombstones where black webs of burnt wool drifted like wraiths. After the destruction of Giovanni's bridge, the only way across the Irenicon was the Midnight Road. Since it led directly to Tartarus, only the well-armed, the brave or the foolhardy used it. On the Night of Black Towers the bandieratori and their partisans had retreated to the borough of the Guilds of Fire, before vanishing entirely.

But this rigor mortis was only superficial. In the *sottosuolo*, the vast maze-like necropolis underneath Tartarus, the turbulent heart of Rasenna beat yet.

Uggeri Galati and the rest of the soldiers were waiting impatiently when Pedro returned from the Lion's Fountain.

'You get a name?'

'Strozzi. Just get them out of their tower – don't start anything.'

'I don't tell you how to do your job, Vanzetti. Flags up, bandieratori.'

Pedro peered into the waters that flowed around the rock he was standing on. Down at these lowest depths of the *sottosuolo* there were few places to stand with any degree of safety: a false step would carry him swiftly away. The glow-globes made little impression on the darkness or on the cold, that adamantine kind that permeates places that have never been kissed by the sun.

He crouched and took a sample.

Since going underground, the Irenicon was off-limits. Uggeri said they had more pressing worries than water levels, but Pedro didn't like feeling blind. Testing the Irenicon's levels was more besides a way to monitor Concord's activities; it was a ritual. So he'd began monitoring the subterranean river that snaked through the depths of the *sottosuolo* untouched by the troubles of the sun-drowned world.

'So, what did you make of Veii, Pedro?'

Isabella, the little Reverend Mother, often accompanied him on his descents. She said she liked to pray beside the river. He didn't believe it was just that, but he appreciated the company. She sat now on the rocky riverbank, looking down at him.

'Well-positioned, and eminently defensible if the duke takes my advice. It's a place we could make a stand.'

'You tell that to Uggeri?'

'I tried to – he said he'd done enough retreating already, all the while giving me that stare. You know the one.'

'He's not really angry at you,' she said softly. In their cramped confines it was impossible to avoid conflict, or intimacy. 'The Contessa left him in charge of Tower Scaligeri. He blames himself.'

Pedro turned around. 'And I don't?' His irritation turned to alarm when she stood suddenly, an awed look on her face. 'What is it?'

He turned and saw it too: a buio was 'walking' along the river's surface. It disappeared into a ravine, then fell apart and reassembled as it went over a string of rapids. They watched silently until it disappeared.

'What do you think it was?'

'A scout,' she said with certainty, and sure enough, the river's surface was soon full of buio, a great herd swaying as it passed by, the figures sometimes merging with each other, sometimes pulling away, but always going forward.

'Looks like a pilgrimage.'

'Or a migration,' he suggested. 'Perhaps the Irenicon is returning to normal.'

'All rivers have buio, whether you can see them or not. Without buio, a river is dead.'

'Salvatore Bombelli said the First Apprentice is rebuilding the Molè. You think that's what's driving them out? Nothing's shown up in the samples so far.'

She looked at him sternly. 'You don't imagine your tools are more sensitive than the buio?' She was about to say more, but suddenly stopped; one of the buio was standing apart from the herd, looking at them.

Pedro swallowed. 'Is that—?'

'Go to him.'

Debris from fallen rocks formed stepping stones and he leaped from one to the other till he was facing the buio. The rest of the herd continued to pour by, indifferent.

Pedro heard his voice trembling as he asked, 'Giovanni?'

The voice that answered was not one but many, and he did not *hear* it; it blossomed in his mind like an inspiration. '*I bring news of great joy: this day a king is born.*'

On the climb up they were silent, both thinking that whatever Sofia now faced, she was facing alone. The Tartaruchi at least had each other, for emotional and physical support, heart and head. That alone made the hub – the large domed chamber from where all the tunnels seemed to originate – habitable, though the air was moist with a slow-dripping rot that infused everything: the broth they ate, the clothes they wore, the torn flag that hung over them.

This was not the banner that Rasenna had united behind for the last three years but the Scaligeri black and gold. It was scorched by fire and stained by blood, but the Golden Lion was tainted with something altogether worse: failure. The newly united town had been tested and found wanting, and now the survivors fell back on old verities. Every remnant soldier had a new map of the city to learn, for there was streetside, there was topside and now there was downside – the map of downside kept changing because every new exit brought new risk.

The *sottosuolo* stretched under the Irenicon, giving them access to the south – although it had been too dangerous at first; it was easy to get trapped in big open spaces like Piazza Luna, and many southern families were collaborating – it was traditional to side with those from the same side of the Irenicon, and that hadn't changed much. Having flags fighting with Geta was intended to make his rule look less alien, and make the Tartaruchi's resistance against Concord's agent look less like patriotic insurgence and more like civil war. But Rasenna's oldest towers had deep basements with escape tunnels, some connecting with their neighbours, and breaking into this ancient network had expanded the Tartaruchi's reach, giving them the ability to appear in any quarter of the city at any time.

These collaborators, the traitor towers, were the Tartaruchi's first target, but tonight's mission was not one of revenge but rescue: the Strozzi family had been proscribed not for any crime, but simply because they were rich.

'Uggeri's not back?'

'Not yet, Reverend Mother,' said Sister Carmella coldly. 'We ought to be out there with him.' The Sisterhood visited the *sottosuolo* often; they were cooks and nurses as well as company for tired and dirty tunnellers.

'Uggeri doesn't want you,' said Pedro. After the Night of Black Towers, the baptistery and its orphanage – by mutual consent of the warring parties – had been left untouched: better to keep the nuns ostensibly neutral and in reserve, in case things got really bad. On that much at least, Pedro and Uggeri agreed.

'Oh, doesn't he? Where is he, then?'

'I'm here.' Uggeri and his bandieratori looked as bedraggled as the family they shepherded into the cavern.

'You're wounded,' said Carmella, leaping up.

'It's nothing. See to Alfredo's leg. They got him good.'

'Where are the others?' said Pedro. Two dozen men had left; barely a score had returned.

'Where do you think?' Uggeri growled.

Uggeri always placed himself on the dangerous edge of every mission so he was fighting for his life night after night, as if daring Death to do his worst. More often than not, it was Sister Carmella who bandaged his wounds and listened to his complaints about Pedro's timidity. She had grown up in the tower next to Hog Galati's rundown pile, and as Hog habitually left his family hungry while he lost at cards, Carmella had often been sent across to offer a meal to his two boys. Hog and his eldest son had died in the uprising, leaving Uggeri an orphan – that was another thing they had in common.

'Don't act like a hero, Uggeri,' said Isabella. 'You went looking for a fight and because of that, four men are dead.'

'He's bleeding and you're blaming him?' said Carmella incredulously. 'At least he's doing something besides praying.'

'Stay out of this, Carmella,' said Uggeri, staring hard at Isabella. 'Listen here, little Sister, we've all been waiting for months for a miracle from Maestro Vanzetti, but he's been too busy visiting cities he obviously deems better bets. Until he comes up with something we have to fight, and that means flags will tear.'

'I'm not going to take responsibility if you can't control yourself,' shouted Pedro.

By the time the shouting died down, Carmella had stormed off and the three Strozzi children were crying. Uggeri was unapologetic, but Carmella soon regretted her angry words and came back to apologise to Isabella. She couldn't find her anywhere.

Geta burst into the chamber. '*Amore*?'

The room was empty and he was more than a little drunk. 'Ah, you want me to look for you?' He left the two glasses and bottle on the table and looked behind the door, then into a wardrobe, then behind the dressing screen. Then he sat down. He could see several other possibilities, but his enthusiasm for the game was gone.

He poured himself some wine and announced, 'I surrender.'

He raised the glass to his lips then slowly – *slowly* – placed it back down and repeated, 'I said I surrender.' The cold edge of the blade touched his skin, soft as a breeze. 'Maddalena warned me to expect a social call at some point. Sister Isabella, isn't it? No need to ask how you got in; I've heard what a preternaturally wonderful water-stylist you are. The Apprentices call it an art, but

I call it unfair. I can't abide unfairness. That's why I made certain we'd be on a fair footing when we met. Despite appearances, I have a knife to your neck too. He's a loyal fellow, is Sempronio – not too bright, but good with a blade – and his sole duty is to burn the orphanage should I get what's coming to me.'

The hand that held the knife trembled.

'If you're quick you might save one or two – are you prepared to sacrifice the rest? It's a nasty way to die, is fire. Maddalena told me how you lost your family.' Geta felt the knife removed. 'I was so very sorry to hear it.'

Isabella whispered, 'I didn't "lose" them. They were assassinated.'

'Dead's dead. By the time I finish my drink. I hope sincerely – not for my sake, you understand, but for those little dears – to find myself alone. I trust you understand me?'

There was no answer. Geta swallowed the wine in one gulp then turned, pulling his sword free. The window was empty, but for a flag flapping above it. 'Yes, I think you do.'

The door opened suddenly and Geta swung round, his sword knocking the glass he'd just emptied onto the floor.

'I heard voices,' said Maddalena. She entered and carefully circled the broken glass.

Geta sheathed his sword and sat back down. He reached for the second glass and filled it. 'Don't worry, *amore*. There're no whores hiding under my bed. I had a visitor, but she was a little too young, even for me.'

'I told you she'd come.'

'And I told her I had an arsonist on call – the dear child actually believed me. You certainly know the weaknesses of your *paesani*.'

'And my podesta's.' She kissed his neck and slid her hand down his shirt to tangle her fingers in his chest hair.

Geta returned her caresses, and his hand slid from her waist to her belly – and there stopped. 'Ah,' he said, removing his hand.

Though their wedding had been only only a few months ago, Maddalena's bump had grown large. He drained his glass. 'Forgive me, *amore*, but you know I can't see you in this condition.'

Maddalena stood up and said indignantly, 'You're drinking to much.'

He poured another. 'Helps me sleep. Hard to rest easy wondering who might pop through that window next.'

'You're scared of Uggeri?'

She was aiming to wound, so he answered with an equanimity that he knew would annoy her. 'On the contrary. That contest I would welcome – it'll settle things once and for all. When I win, we can finally rule in peace – if it pleases the First Apprentice, that is.'

'For the last time, I forbid you to give up Rasenna without a fight!'

'For the last time, this town doesn't have any fight left. You can be imperious as you like with the natives but when the legions come knocking, believe me, servility is our best defence.'

'You're a coward.'

'Don't worry, you're perfectly safe. All General Spinther wants from Rasenna is quietude on his way south. He needs someone who can guarantee that and I'm willing to bet he'll leave me in charge. We're old friends.'

'You're gambling with the life of your unborn son,' Maddalena hissed and stomped back to the doorway.

'*Amore*, we've discussed this,' he cried. 'It's a good bet.' But she was gone, slamming the door behind her. 'That woman,' he said philosophically and wondered how to sneak out the whore under the bed without his wife noticing. His flag was sufficiently soiled already.

CHAPTER 7

The winds that scattered the dunes fell silent at dusk and uncanny black-bellied clouds crept silently from the west until the emerging stars were shrouded. The first drop fell before midnight and sands that had not seen rain for a generation were deluged. Sleepers awoke to the sound of the bone-dry rooftops of Akka being battered, and the percussive waves of thunder drowned the celebratory clackers and rejoicing. Streets became rushing streams.

It ceased, as abruptly as it had begun, and the sand absorbed the puddles so thoroughly that it might have been a dream. Befuddled harbour gulls drifted over the city as white-cloaked angels of death bearing torches marched through the streets. The Lazars hammered on doors; any not immediately opened were broken down. They searched every Ebionite home; they ransacked boats moored in the harbour; they overturned merchant caravans about to embark across the Sands. Sentinels lined the walls as usual, but tonight the enemy they sought was within.

The sinister flocks invaded every district bar one.

A single Lazar silently prowled the Butchers' Quarter, bearing a bundle instead of a torch. Puddles remained between the cobbles to reflect the moonlight. Not all the detritus of the day's work had been washed away, and the smell of bad meat and old clots started to penetrate his mask. He stopped at a stall that fronted one of the abattoirs and listened; through the thick wooden door he could hear huffing oxen and hectoring goats. The lock looked intact in the darkness and he nearly passed on. *Nearly*. When he touched the lock gently, it fell in two.

Drawing his axe, he pushed the door open and stepped inside.

'Bleat and I'll leave you hanging on a hook with the lambs.'

The blade pressed deep in his neck, expertly placed beside the carotid. He was trembling from the blood pounding to his brain. 'It's me,' he whispered.

Sofia pulled the knife away. In the shafts of white light piercing the roof, her face was pale, though glistening with sweat. Her hair hung down in damp straggles.

Fulk searched the darkness behind her and saw – there between the stalls of beasts patiently awaiting slaughter – the little manger. How he knew the child within was smiling, he could not have explained. He knew little of childbirth except that it was a deadly business that required an officiating midwife. 'Are you all right?'

'All right?' she said sardonically. 'Hell, I'm blessed amongst women.' But it was true: she had been dreading the litany of horrors new mothers suffered – cracked skin, weak back, swollen legs – but she felt nothing. Her body was hers again. Seeing his confusion, she explained, 'My pain comes later.'

'Can you walk?'

'Where's Levi?'

'He put up a fight, but they have him.'

'And Arik?'

'They . . . got him too.'

'How long have I?'

'A few hours at best. They're moving from the walls inwards. Stay here and you'll be discovered by dawn.'

A short sob escaped her as she considered the reality of her situation. 'I'll go down flag in hand,' she promised.

There was a soft answering sob from the manger – just an infant's cry, nothing more – but Fulk felt some hidden string within him plucked. The purity of it cleansed this wretched place, made it holy.

'If you die, your child dies,' he said unwrapping his bundle. 'You have to trust me, Contessa.'

She was confused, exhausted, terrified. He grabbed her shoulder as he would one of his brethren. 'Stay strong, and put this on.'

The search parties in the street and the sentinels manning the citadel's ramparts were looking for something out of the ordinary and so paid no attention to the boyish knight trailing the Grand Master, or the bundle he cradled so tightly in his arms. The citadel's lower floors would be empty at this hour, so Fulk led her down to the workshop and lifted lids till he found a coffin without an occupant. She had always respected his courage, but when he lifted the coffin down to the slope with a single heave, she realised how physically strong he was too.

He looked at her, waiting.

'Are you *pazzo*?'

'I said you'd have to trust me.'

While she climbed in, grumbling, Fulk found a small plank that he deemed suitable and placed it beside her. The baby looked up at him. He was the most beautiful thing Fulk had ever seen. He hastened to brief Sofia before he began to weep. 'You'll be underground for a good minute – it'll be bumpy, but don't worry; there's no space to overturn. Then you'll feel the ground below you go and there'll be a sudden drop and a big splash. I have to nail this tight because after the drop, you'll be submerged, all right? There'll be enough air to bring you up again. As soon as you feel the coffin return to the surface, break the lid open.'

'I can do that.'

He removed his gloves to hammer in the nails, then leaned in, holding up a scar-mottled index finger. 'There's a riptide –

it'll take you miles out if you let it. It's too strong to fight, so just start paddling north – that's the side the moon will be on. Once you're free of the current, row to shore, but don't tarry on the beach. There are dogs, and bandits worse than dogs, all looking for cast-ups. I'll try and keep the search parties away as long as—'

He froze as the baby grabbed his finger.

'It's fine,' she said.

Fulk jerked his hand away. 'He shouldn't touch me!'

'His name's Iscanno, and he can't get sick – not that way.'

'You can't be sure,' he said. But he knew she was right. Like any Lazar, he was accustomed to discreet looks of superstition from men, flinching sympathy from women and unconcealed horror from children – but Iscanno smiled at him with the steady eyes of a sage.

'What's his grip like?'

'Strong.'

'Thank you, Fulk – for tonight, for everything. I won't forget.'

'Just don't forget to start paddling. Get away from Akka as quick as you can. There's nothing here but death.'

He hammered the lid shut, banged three times for luck and heaved the coffin onto the slope. 'God's speed,' he muttered as it began to slide. It vanished as soon as it hit the water, and he felt a wave of desolation. He was a master of pain, but this new keen note threatened to unman him. He bent to pick up his gloves.

'I've been looking all over for you.'

Fulk pulled his gloves on and nodded at Basilius. 'Too bad I'm not the one you're looking for. If we don't find that Etrurian whore, the queen will throw us both in the Sea of Filth – or worse. Come. There's a nest of places she could be hiding in the Butchers' Quarter.'

Sofia was entombed in the bracing smell of fresh-cut cedar. There was no light, only Iscanno's warm breath on her neck and a cascade of noises. Her sense of smell and sound and touch were all she had to rely on as her little vessel sped through the narrow tunnel, carried on rapid waters. She waited for the drop – was that it? That? How long had it been? It felt an age . . .

Suddenly her heart hit her ribs and she knew she was falling.

whumpf

There was a great blow as they struck the water and her shoulder hit the lid so hard she feared it would burst open. She could still feel Iscanno's breath against her skin, but now there was cold trickling water too. The coffin slowed as buoyancy reasserted itself, then there was another surge as it shot upwards. She had time to consider a single terrible thought – what if it surfaced face-down? – before new sounds grabbed her attention: a bawling gull, lapping waves, a tolling bell. She pulled her fist back as far as it could go and—

'Ugh!'

The only thing that broke was the skin on her knuckle. Fulk had sealed the lid too securely. Every moment took them further out as the current's tendrils caught them and started pulling them already. She heard the gull land on the lid. It paced about this strange floating fish, pecking its wooden belly.

'Yah!'

The coffin's lid flew off, sending the gull flapping skywards, squawking its outrage.

She gasped to see how far away Akka already was and reached for the paddle. It was still dark, but the band of watery orange light beyond the city heralded the morning. The dead were discharged frequently enough into the *Lordemare* not to be a novelty, but if anyone happened to be watching from Akka's battlements, their attention could be drawn to the coffin suddenly bearing north. She prayed that every eye still turned inwards.

By the time she escaped the current, she was shattered. The

first spark of dawn gave her the spirit to finish the job – that, and the knowledge that she'd just become very visible.

When she felt the coffin bottom catching, she climbed out awkwardly, carrying Iscanno. She fell, but managed to hold him clear of the shallow water as she picked herself up and waded to dry sand. She threw herself down, breathing hard, looking around: the last time she been in this situation, scavengers had attacked. Even so, she couldn't move. She watched the empty coffin being carried out to sea again and wondered where it would wash up. Etruria? She might have done better to have gone to sleep, allow herself to perish quietly and be buried in the soil of her motherland, instead of prolonging the inevitable in this hellhole – but no. She wrenched herself out of her mawkish fantasy. Iscanno depended on her to be strong. *Up, you spoiled brat.* She could hear the Reverend Mother's croak and pulled herself to her feet. *As long as you can breathe, you can fight.*

The forsaken shore on which she had washed up was north of Akka's Harbour; any traders who failed to make it to the city's gates before curfew camped here. There were a few isolated dying campfires and as she came closer she could hear the sighs and moans of waking camels. She doubted she'd be able to steal one without being discovered – the Sown lived in fear of tribal banditry – but even so, she was looking about for a likely target when she saw the silhouette of a man riding towards her.

'Ho there!'

There was nowhere to flee, so Sofia prepared to fight, all the while praying she would not need to. She was still dressed as a Lazar and this close to Akka the queen's men were not molested without consequence.

The stranger pulled his white horse short. 'Why is your hand on your weapon, Mistress? Do you not recognise me?'

It took her a moment, then, '. . . Abdel? What are you doing here?'

'The Grand Master entrusted me to wait for you here and' – the Moorish slave hopped down – 'to present you with this clumsy creature. Dressed as you are, a horse will be less conspicuous than a camel.' He patted a bundle tied to the saddle. 'There is a change of clothing here – a simple shift and veil – and bread and water. I would have taken more, but it would have been conspicuous. All the Sown are suspects until you are found.'

Sofia nearly cried with gratitude, but instead she hugged him hard and kissed him. 'Tell Fulk I can never repay his kindness.'

'Repay him by taking yourself far away,' Abdel said sadly. 'An evil time is come to Akka.'

CHAPTER 8

The sky of bleached cobalt was tyrannised by the patient white sun that reflected, dazzling, off the sand crystals. She rode with Iscanno tied to her chest, as she'd seen the Ebionite women in Akka do, and covered by the white cloak, until she stopped to rest by a cluster of tall speckled rocks. Iscanno was happy to be unbound while she changed into the Ebionite clothes and buried the uniform. She covered the disturbed sand with stones, though she knew it wouldn't fool any decent tracker. She kept the axe. She watered the mare first, then herself, taking care to ration her own sips from the waterskin.

As she fed Iscanno, Sofia looked about to see what effect the monsoon had had – but she could see nothing.

The Sands had swallowed every drop of the torrential downpour. Disappointed, she lay down in the shade – and was thrilled to discover a small lizard hiding under the rocks. Down its back were stripes of vivid yellow, the colour of the crocuses of the Rasenneisi contato. So life was possible here.

She feared to sleep too long, and after a few hours of uneasy dozing she set off again. She rode until dark, when a lonely tamarisk bush served as kindling for a fire too small to warm her but large enough to scare away potential scavengers. The night was bitterly cold, and she hugged Iscanno close as she prayed for the sun to hurry back and thaw out her bones.

A few hours later, she was cursing its heat.

The Kerak Malregard sat on the summit of a hill whose hard-edged lines proclaimed it obviously manmade. The kerak dominated the eastern border of Esdraelon Plain, overseeing the Akkan border. Though the Guiscards made bold claim to rule beyond the dry bowl of Galilee, this was the true limit of Akkan power. Further east were the badlands, where no merchant caravan willingly ventured.

Kerak Malregard was the keystone of a ring of garrisons surrounding the city. The keraks might be architecturally unimaginative, but they served their purpose. If the Lazars were to patrol Akka's hinterland effectively, they needed well-provisioned redoubts at the end of each day's march where they could rest and regroup, or to retreat to if met by a superior force. The outermost garrison ring had been abandoned for years: some of the keraks had been buried by the Sands and others had been claimed by whichever tribe was locally dominant. But the inner rings remained in active use; they were sufficiently well maintained and equipped to cool the ardour of any ambitious nasi. The tribes were more likely to try to sneak around the forts than attack them, but then they had to contend with the increasing probability of being outflanked, and the closer to Akka they got, the greater the danger.

Besides a garrison of queen's men, Sofia knew the Malregard had deep, full cisterns. She might go there now, beg sanctuary, and drink her fill of cool water – and that too was death, and so she rode on and prayed that no one was looking her way.

In another hour the valley was flooded with a windless heat that shimmered like oil on water. She'd been moving gradually downhill, and now there were small signs of the downpour – the song of invisible birds and the constant merry chirp of crickets. Her mare grew stupid, often stumbling, and Iscanno was uncomfortable under the scarf, but she dared not expose him to the sun. The suspicion that a more experienced traveller would have found water by now was galling, but she sucked on a pebble and ignored it.

The further east she travelled, the less certain she was of the wisdom of her course. She was reconsidering her limited options when they came to a patch of black stumps that once must have been a copse of trees. Ahead lay a patch of grass, lush, green and perfectly round, and her horse broke into a trot. With difficulty, she held the panting animal back.

The grass was no apparition, but she peered closely and soon discerned a slightly darker tone to the surrounding sand, as though the rains had not fully soaked through. It made a great circle, forty braccia across. None of the tree stumps were within its circumference. She knew a camel would be savvier about the snares of the Sands than her poor mare; absent an animal's instincts, she must trust her gut. Something was off. She led the protesting horse around, only to be faced with another grass patch, and yet another, up ahead. There were dozens now, and it was increasingly hard leading her dehydrated beast around each of these temptations. She was concentrating so hard on the circles that by the time she noticed a red flower in their path, it was too late: the mare had thrust her head forward and gobbled it.

'*Avanti!*' she cried, and dug her heels in, forcing the mare into a gallop. Behind her she heard the explosion and felt the sand scatter as the Jinni burst from its trap. She pulled her veil tighter around her face and leaned forward, urging the mare on, though she had no idea if the Jinni *could* be outrun. The miniature storm swept by and Sofia felt herself lifted from the saddle. Still she kept hold of the reins and then – a miracle! – she felt the storm's hold weaken and she sank back onto the mare's back. Perhaps this type of Jinn was restricted to a certain radius?

But she had no time to rejoice before the panicked horse tripped over one of the tree stumps and tumbled to the ground. Sofia landed on her back, protecting Iscanno, and she pressed his face to her body, covering him with her arms and keeping her own eyes shut till the screaming wind had died away and the rain of sand particles subsided.

Warily, she shook off the shallow layer of sand covering her legs. Iscanno emerged smiling from the folds of the scarf and she kissed him with relief. A few braccia ahead, the now thoroughly disorientated horse was back on its legs, shaking her head, flicking the sand from ears and tail. She looked about foolishly, then neighed contentedly at finding herself right beside one of the lush grass patches. Sofia looked down: they too were sitting on discoloured sand. She leaped up and ran for the tree stump the horse had tripped over.

The horse was at last able to satisfy her hunger – but no sooner had she bent her head to nibble the inviting grass than the green centre capsized.

Sofia already had her axe out. She would not look back, though she heard the mare whinny despairingly as dark sand churning like mud dragged her down. Feeling the sands flowing round her feet, Sofia leaped. The axe sank into the dead wood and she kept tight hold of the handle even as the sand sucked at her feet.

A final scream made her turn at last, but the horse was gone. In its place a great pit had opened and from its bowels a dozen pale green tendrils were whirling around wildly like blind maggots. A blast of hot air poured out: the stench of musty vegetation and putrid meat. Sofia pulled herself up until she could grab the stump, balancing on her side so as not to crush Iscanno. She gasped, still trying to catch her breath, when one of the tendrils brushed by her heel. Before she could pull her foot away it had wrapped itself round her ankle and started tugging. She held on tight, but the dead stump was being yanked from the sand. Now only one thick root remained – and other tendrils were writhing up the slope towards her, either to help their brother, or to steal his feast. Either way, she and Iscanno were in touble . . .

She untied the sling and rolled Iscanno out of the dark circle, then yanked her axe free and struck the tentacle hard. It felt like chopping through an old carrot. Immediately the writhing worm shrivelled away, bleeding colourless sap. Sofia scrambled out of the circle and picked up Iscanno, while the tendrils, moving more slowly now, meticulously searched the slope before sinking back disappointed into the centre.

Then – slowly, as though a great set of lungs were inflating underneath – the sand level rose again.

Grand Master Fulk and Seneschal Basilius knelt in front of the empty throne while the queen circled them menacingly, swinging her royal baton.

'I used to think Lazars' minds rotted slower than your bodies. Now I'm certain it's the opposite: there is certainly no other explanation for how you can have let a heavily pregnant girl *escape*!'

'She and the mercenary must have been planning this for months,' said Fulk calmly.

'I only decided to give her to Concord days ago . . .'

Before Fulk could point out that her attitude to rivals was no secret, Basilius interjected, 'She's alone – that's the key thing. Without a man's protection she'll not last long in the Sands.'

The queen gave him a withering look. 'She is more than a woman: she is a *queen* and therefore not to be underestimated. She couldn't have done this without the connivance of the Sown. I'll wager she plans to take sanctuary with the lizard-eaters.'

'She has nothing. Why would the—?'

'For bounty, you fool! The nesi'im are credulous, like all great braggarts. Who knows what she'll promise? Who knows how she could inflame them?'

'Mother, you're being paranoid—'

She swung the baton and Fulk only narrowly avoided the blow.

'And *you* are being over-familiar, Grand Master!' She threw herself down on the throne and waved dismissal. 'You're also wasting time with these feeble excuses. Get a search party together – *now!*'

Fulk's anger at this public rebuke showed only in the abrupt manner he strode out. The queen rubbed her eyes in frustration. Presently she looked up to find Basilius, kneeling still. 'Have your ears finally fallen off?' she shouted. 'I said "*Dismissed*"!'

'Be patient with this old soldier.' Basilius began to rise. 'I'm not as spry as I was.'

Suddenly curious, the queen climbed down from her throne and tenderly took his gloved hand to assist him. 'I sometimes forget how long you've served me, Basilius, and how loyally.'

'It is I who must beg pardon.'

The old bastard wants something. The queen flicked her head to dismiss her attendant slaves. 'My dear fellow, for what?'

'You spoke of loyalty – that loyalty has stayed my tongue till now, but I am at last compelled to speak. You see the labour with which I rise from my knees?'

Her maternal smile vanished. 'Pain is a Lazar's lot.'

'That it is,' he agreed. 'Did you see the Grand Master struggle?'

'Fulk's a young man,' she said impatiently.

'That he is. Did you hear his voice?'

'. . . I attended to what he said, not how.'

'His rasp's gone.'

'What of it?' she said, now very aware of the seneschal's painful croak.

'Our condition does not ebb and flow, Majesty. It has but one trajectory: downwards.'

'I see that you are ambitious as well as loyal, Seneschal. Happily for you, I esteem both qualities. Tell me now – with less tiresome circumvention if you please – what exactly you are implying.'

The masks on the walls were alive with gaping mouths and blinking eyes that said and saw nothing. Fulk was standing in the Ancestor Room. It was longer than he remembered – indeed, it stretched to infinity. He was altered too, his condition more advanced, and each breath was a painful gasp. Sofia walked down the stairs towards him, beautiful in a white gown and veil.

'She looks every bit the queen,' leered a voice behind him. Fulk wanted to ask the patriarch where he had come from, but a muted hammering was coming from the flagstones beneath their feet and the cleric was obviously impatient to begin the ceremony. 'Contessa, take your place before they get here!'

He officiated the rite quickly, though the hammering became so loud that he had to shout. '. . . I now pronounce you king and queen,' he cried, and handed Sofia the mace. She lifted her veil and said, 'Now show me yours.' The slabs covering the crypt below trembled.

Scabs and bits of hair came with his helmet as Fulk pulled it off. He handed it over to the patriarch, who took down a mask from the wall and replaced it with Fulk's. 'Now that you're a real Guiscard,' he said as he handed over the new mask, 'you may kiss the bride.'

He looked down and when he saw it was Catrina's face, he dropped it.

'Infidel!' the mask screamed as it fell to the ground. 'You have deceived your queen!'

The rapping finally woke him. He'd slept only a couple of hours after having searched all day, until the queen finally gave it up as fruitless. He leaped quickly off his slab and put on his mask and surcoat before unbolting his door to find Basilius standing there, axe in hand. He was flanked by old Gustav, a knight who was a positive Methuselah by Lazar standards.

'Come, Brother. We have more work tonight.' Basilius turned and knocked on the next door without further explanation. Fulk pushed his way through the corridor of sleepy knights. 'What work?'

The dipping flares of the torches dazzled the eyes as whispers and rumours filled the corridor. The air was tense with expectation. Fulk, too concerned that Sofia had been found to worry about the lack of deference, stepped to the head of the line alongside Basilius, leading the train of marching men, though he knew not where they were headed. Amongst the stomp of boots on stone he couldn't tell whether his questions had gone unheard or were being ignored. They passed through the coffin-lined workshop and finally reached the training hall, where the queen stood upon a closed coffin. In the flickering red torchlight, her eyes sparkled like a jackal. She bestowed a proud smile on Fulk as he entered.

A chill of fear shook him he saw the bloodied body of Sofia's servant, Abdel, tied to a pillar. Could he have talked?

The patriarch stood nearby, pale and frightened. He'd obviously been witness to the torture.

'Grand Master, I had the seneschal rally the men because there's no time to lose.'

'Are we under attack?' he asked. If they were, surely they should not be congregating in the bowels of the city like a coven.

'No – I've decided to make one last search. The Etrurian whore *must* be hiding in the Ebionite Quarter.'

Fulk's mind raced as he thought about those dark slums. Was it possible that Sofia had returned? Surely not. 'How do you know?'

'Reason: the Contessa has experienced the Sands' cruelty. She fled my palace to save her life, so she would not flee the city, even if she could find a way out. That would be exchanging one death for another. Therefore she's hiding amongst our own, a canker in our bosom. We know Arik betrayed us, so she *must* have corrupted other servants. This one' – she gestured casually at Abdel's corpse – 'revealed nothing. But time is short, so we are forced to more extreme measures. We shall make the Contessa's protectors reveal her. We will show the Sown that they may live amongst us but they remain strangers. This night you and your men will slaughter every newborn Ebionite within Akka's walls.'

The fresh recruits and young journeymen, who were still outside of the discontented circle that orbited Basilius, turned automatically to Fulk. They did not love the Ebionites, but, infidel or no, there was a great difference between the bandits of the Sands and unarmed townsfolk.

Fulk in turn looked to the patriarch for support. 'But – but— That would be criminal. Children, Chrysoberges—?'

The patriarch nodded sympathetically, but said calmly, 'It is harsh, but the germane question is: is it *necessary*? Necessity does not admit of sin. The Contessa, we know, means to undermine the people of God. Given that, killing the apostates who shelter her would be a pious act.'

Disgusted, Fulk turned back to his mother. 'Consider the tribes, then. They little care for the Sown, but this would demand vengeance – it would raise up a storm that could swallow us.'

'You've always given them too much credit, Fulk. Such emotion is absent from the souls of those animals.'

Fulk looked around helplessly. The chain of command was too strong for those whose vows were still fresh to give voice to their doubts. The implacable masks of his men returned his stare silently. He knew better than to look for pity from Basilius, so he turned to old Gustav. 'You know this is madness. There are poor Marians down there as well as Ebionites, living side by side. We won't be able to tell them apart in the darkness.'

Before the old knight could say anything, Basilius answered, 'We need not try.' Then louder, so every doubter could hear, 'If it crawls and cannot speak, you will kill it as you would a snake. God will know his own.'

Catrina stamped her foot on the coffin. 'I know you all to be loyal sons of Akka. This night's work will go hard, even on such stout hearts as yours. Think of the masks of your ancestors and take strength knowing that Lazars not yet born will revere your example, even as you yourselves revere your forefathers' sacrifice. God's work is never easy. The path is narrow. You must blind your eyes and deafen your ears to pleas of false charity. Those slain tonight are saved from a life of sin and their souls in perdition will sing thanks to the axes that delivered them.'

She leaped from the podium into the cheering crowd that parted before her.

'Deus lo Volt! Deus lo Volt!' The thundering repetition of that sentiment was its own argument, convincing many silent vacillators that it was their own judgement that was awry.

The chanting surrounded Fulk and echoed through the arches. He had to shout to make himself heard. 'Stop!'

The chanting died away and Queen Catrina stopped, but did not turn. 'Yes, Grand Master?'

'She's not in Akka.'

Still not turning, her voice trembling, the queen asked, 'You're certain?'

There was no other sound in the chamber but the fugitive night wind dodging between the pillars and rush of water plunging underground. 'I helped her escape.'

A tremor of appalled wonder rolled through the ranks. They pulled away from him like sheep panicking at the storm's first peal. Basilius cleared his throat, breaking the horrified silence. 'The Grand Master is lying. He's no traitor, merely soft. He's willing to sacrifice his honour with a lie because he thinks this cull would hurt you.'

The expectant knights nodded unconsciously. *Yes, surely that was it. Surely.*

She turned at last. 'Is that so, Grand Master?'

Fulk strove to speak clearly so that all would hear. 'I believe this massacre would be rash as well as wicked – but no, it's the truth. Rather than let you sell her to Concord, I warned her.'

Basilius's men went for their axes, but just as swiftly one young knight stepped in front of Fulk. The Contessa had ministered to him during last year's Day of the Dead, and he could not stand by. 'Please – let's everyone remain calm. The Grand Master would not do such a thing idly. Your Majesty—'

'Drop your weapon,' the queen commanded the knight and his axe came clattering down immediately.

'Which lie shall we believe? By your admission you have deceived us – so why should we believe you now?'

Fulk removed his mask. 'Because your son is healed.'

She screamed – a terrible cry of betrayal and grief.

The young leper who had just defended his Grand Master took up his axe and backed away as from something infectious. The rest of the Lazars took a step back, moving as one, their grips tightening on their weapons: old and young, united once again.

Fulk's face was that of a handsome – unsullied – young man.

'All of you, listen.' Fulk looked around the circle widening around him. 'Something wonderful has happened. The Contessa's son is come to dispel corruption.' His voice failed as he saw in their eyes the reproach that he felt for himself. They looked at him like a thief caught out, a shirker, a *coward*. The circumstances of his fall did not matter. He had done the unforgivable: he had tainted their sacrifice.

'You silly boy,' the queen said, chidingly, 'she has come to *corrupt*. You have betrayed your queen and – worse – your brothers.'

'And God Almighty!' exclaimed the patriarch. 'O most wicked apostasy, what the Lord hath corrupted, no man or woman may purify. I know not what sorcery unwove your righteous scars but your soul, once so perfect, is now irredeemably mired.'

'Congratulations, Grand Master Basilius,' said the queen, her rage barely contained. 'You have just been promoted. Take this traitor before your men and flay his clean new pelt from his bones. He shall be punished later.'

It took several of them to wrestle Fulk to the ground and bind him. 'Let's see if I can't improve on perfection,' Gustav said, and kicked him in the jaw.

'We'll take the city in quarters. Teams of twenty,' said Basilius giddily, eager to consecrate his promotion with a sanguinary effusion. The journeymen stamped and bellowed 'Deus lo Volt!' in a kind of hysteria, as though by sheer volume they could purge themselves of all taint of loyalty to their betrayer.

The queen guffawed. 'You preposterous man, I was *bluffing*. What good is a pile of dead babies to me? I want only one. No, you must take to the Sands: not a vulture drops from the sky without some toothless old shepherd noticing it. If the Contessa is dead, I want proof. If she's not, I want her found. I'll show her the strength it takes to be a queen.'

She climbed back onto the coffin. 'Lazars, your honour is soiled. Only blood can blot out the stain. *Thou shalt not suffer a witch to live*. Be on guard; harden your hearts to false weakness. If my son can be seduced, then anyone is vulnerable – even Oltremare herself, unless you are strong. It is your queen who asks. How do you answer?'

'*Deus lo Volt!*' they cried, '*Deus lo Volt!*'

CHAPTER 9

The earth-fallen clouds waltzed along the horizon, obliterating scrub and stone and whatever else they touched. Arik had shown her a variety of Jinn: some, like the *zar* she'd encountered, were little more than dust-devils, barely sentient but vicious as animals. but these were of the higher order: great whales of the desert. At this remove, Sofia could admire their beauty, but she was not in the mood. 'Damn you,' she whispered.

Her curse was directed not at the Jinn, but at the mare that had taken her water into her grave. With no water, she had no hope. Soon the winds would be stripping her desiccated corpse to a yellowed pile of bones. It would have been better to have been swallowed than to suffer death by thirst. Delirium hovered, and a hateful voice whispered that it was fitting that it ended this way. She'd been dying of thirst since Giovanni left her . . .

'*Ahhwah!*'

Iscanno's sudden cry punctured her stupor, reminding her it would not be her bones alone. She couldn't just lie here and wait for death to find her. John Acuto and the Doc had both fought to their very last breath. But how to fight a desert? The rolling dunes were heaving waves; the curvilinear crests, ripples; the scattered sand, spume. It couldn't be beaten any more than the sea could, or the wind.

Sofia stopped in her tracks. You *couldn't*, so you *didn't* . . . Ezra had taught her that the best sailors made an ally of the wind. She would have to go with it, without reservation or fear, in order to touch that power. Those demi-gods who'd so violently occupied

Jerusalem and who now guarded it so jealously were kin in some sense to the buio – so was it insane to challenge a great Jinni? What would stop it from unwrapping her flesh like peeling a ripe orange? Why, nothing – except that nothing in nature killed for pleasure. That was Man's special vice.

She trekked towards the hilltop where the behemoths circled each other, carving the dunes by their passage. These were truly vast, sky-reaching things, and she was making for the largest of them, but the distance was deceptive, and an hour's walk had brought her little closer – but still its howl filled everything, rattling her teeth, penetrating her body. Iscanno wailed, but she could not hear him.

'Forgive me, *amore*,' she told him. 'I fear this monster is our only hope.'

She climbed the dune and saw at last its full majesty. Its spinning surface was unstable, shifting bands of red, pale yellow and blue soot and crystalline white that sparkled in the sun, as many shades as the Sands themselves possessed. It scalded the yellow air. Most terrifying was the contrast between its narrow base and the breadth of its uppermost reaches – like a mad acrobat spinning on one finger. Like the Wave, it was touched by the sickness that had got into the world, and like the Wave, it looked practically unstoppable.

'Hey!' she hollered, 'hey! You!'

A blast of hot air nearly knocked her from her feet. She had its attention. 'I'm not afraid of you!' she lied. 'You can tear me up or suck the breath right out of me – but this is my son! I see you recognise him.'

The pace of the storm's spinning perceptibly slowed.

'He's here to make things better. You know it shouldn't be this way and he can fix it. But not if he dies out here. I'm asking for help.'

The cone of whirling sand began retreating.

'Wait—'

Suddenly it collapsed, like a great tree falling toward her, impossible to outrun. All she could do was cover her face, bury Iscanno's head in her breast and cry *Madonna!* as the roar enveloped her. She was powerless to resist as she felt her feet leave the ground and she was borne up into a cloud of hostile winds studded with tiny shredded diamonds, each fighting for the privilege of flaying her. Her headdress was ripped open and the sand-saturated air battered her face.

Hush.

The assault ceased and the stillness of night cocooned her. The scream remained, but it was a muted echo, miles away. With her eyes still shut, she reached out and felt the void. The air which moments ago was furnace-hot was delightfully cool now. The rumble of thunder was now more like the soothing throb of the tide. Iscanno laughed in delight, and when she opened her eyes she saw his were open already. They were in the belly of the Jinni, and Iscanno gurgled as balls of blue fiery strings drifted about them. All was calm. The air flowed over them. Only the streaking stars above revealed the speed at which they travelled. She was too tired to be amazed, but not too tired to rejoice that the Jinn at least were not amongst her enemies. That was enough. She gave herself to sleep, certain that she could only wake somewhere better.

CHAPTER 10

Sand shifted, thinned and was gone, leaving them in the crepuscular embrace of dusk. They'd spent the better part of a day travelling.

She uncovered Iscanno and batted their clothes free of dust, and laughed when she realised where the Jinni had let them down. The burial ground was at the bottom of a steep-sided wadi. It must have known that dead humans were buried here. Death was almost certain, but to have it confirmed like this . . . She laughed again. Crying would only spill precious water. She turned her back to the dark band on the horizon, knowing too well what it signified. A month ago the Sirocco, a wave of turbulent hot air straight from Barbary, had filled Akka's streets with a braccia of sand that the Ebionites had spent days cleaning away. The unconscious monsters of nature were powerful as any Jinni, and they would not heed her pleading.

The craggy sides of the wadi threw weird shadows in the evening light. The overlapping rock walls were gouged with deep holes like eyes and broken-toothed grins. The Sown of Akka reserved Jerusalem's sacred name for prayer, using other names in conversation, and she remembered one: *Golgotha*, the place of the skull. Arik had once joked that even the dead were territorial in the Sands. She wondered now if he had been serious. She shuddered at the memory of the last time she had been in such proximity to the dead – but the fevered atmosphere of All Souls was absent from this solemn place. Iscanno murmured in his sleep and she cooed softly and reminded herself this was no time to indulge in fancies. She had to find shelter before the Sirocco hit.

The higher caves would be safer from scavengers but the only chance of finding water would be in the lower ones, and that was urgent. She was about to try one when scattered pebbles falling warned her that she was not alone. The sound, echoing in the narrow pass, was impossible to place. Slowly she removed her headdress and crouched. She searched by touch for a rock the right size, all the while straining to see if something was lurking between the pillars ahead, or behind her, or above.

She was looking up when one of the skulls blinked – just a momententary yellow wink of light – and it was all too quickly gone, extinguished or covered. There were more scattered pebbles, and ghostly laughter, but this time they were close enough to place. Whatever was coming for her was still hidden in the forest of pillars ahead, but she forced herself to look up, straining her night vision to the utmost.

There.

It was not as obvious this time, just the reflection of an unsteady light on the cave ceiling, and she only caught it because she was looking so hard.

As she searched the slope for a route, she heard a throaty rumble that collapsed into scattered yelps and huffs, and a dog pack – large striped shoulders and snapping salivating jaws – came padding between the pillars. Their shining eyes saw her and they froze, their dry laughter dying. The largest dog appeared to be taken by surprise, judging by the sharp howl that erupted from his throat and snapped his head back.

She bolted, and the dogs followed her, scrambling up the initially gentle incline. She could climb better than most Rasenneisi – well, she could once – but there was no firm footing on the loose pebbles and she had only one hand free. She could prevent herself falling, but not from scraping her legs. She felt the wetness of her blood on the night air and the dogs smelled its heat. It drove them to frenzy and a jaw snapped shut just behind her heel. She kicked back and the beast yelped and scrabbled on the loose stone until it tumbled back through the pack. Its long howl was interrupted every time it bounced. It finally ended when the dog hit the wadi floor.

Another – the big one – came at her; it was surer-footed, this one. She let it get close before releasing the sling. First there was the hollow *doitt* of stone on skull, then it fell silently though the air and landed beside the other dog that was wheezing through broken ribs. She climbed to another ledge. Crouching there, she searched the darkness for another stone.

The dogs were wary now, and the climb too steep. Besides, they had to attend to their fallen brothers. Sofia listened to the ripping of flesh and the snarls as the pack fought for the choicest meat.

Though the escalade was close to vertical, the uneven rock-face afforded plenty of purchase to climb, though she was breathing hard before she got to the cave-mouth. Iscanno murmured plaintively in his sleep, but thankfully didn't wake. She peered into the darkness. The light was a mere flickering, a star's reflection in a well – then it disappeared. The choice was stark: follow, or be lost. She stepped inside, and discovered that the cave was pleasantly warm, and that it led downwards: so well-chosen for defensibility. The ceiling was low and she had to crouch as she proceeded into the earth's bowels. Whispering winds from tunnels on either side suggested there were other routes, but she did not stray, and at last her fidelity was rewarded with another glimpse of the light, dipping and blinking like a firefly. It was just a glimpse, but it gave her hope.

Gradually she was able to stand again, and proceeded on tiptoe. She worried about jolting Iscanno awake and making him cry out, so when the light came to rest, she put him down and pulled up her head scarf, arranging it so that only her eyes showed, before slowly approaching. She heard whispering voices: a man and a boy. Her Ebionite was good enough now that she could understand most of it.

'If the nasi caught you, he'd have you disembowelled. Why were you sticking your head out anyway?'

'I heard something.'

'Dogs barking is all. You want to betray us with that light?' The question was punctuated by a thump.

The boy stifled a sob. 'It's dark. I thought it might be a Jinni.'

'You're too old to be scared of the dark, Jabari.' The man sounded unsympathetic. 'A true Sicarii ain't frightened of nothing. Darkness is his ally.' He swayed his light – a burning wick in a ceramic tray of oil – as though demonstrating his mastery of the dark.

Sofia stepped out of the shadows. Before he dropped the light, she had time to see he was a heavyset brute with downward-sloping eyes and prominent lower teeth. Next to him was a boy of eight or nine with a freshly bloodied nose.

Darkness fell with the ring of a dagger whipping out of its sheath; that glimpse had been enough for Sofia to gauge the distance.

She took two long strides and leaped, kicked herself off the wall. Her knee slammed into his jaw and she felt some teeth cave. She landed and picked up the lamp and pulled the wick straight. Her knee hurt. The light flickered into life. The dagger's edge was under her chin.

She pulled her scarf down to show her face. 'You wouldn't hurt a woman, would you?'

The boy was unsmiling, resolute. She was about to throw the oil into his face when Iscanno cried out. The boy's eyes widened and he tucked his dagger back in his belt. Sofia reached for the knife that the older man had dropped and turned to find the boy holding Iscanno and tickling him. He was laughing with delight, and so was Iscanno.

'He likes you.'

'What's his name?' the boy asked brightly.

'Iscanno – and yours?'

As Jabari led her deeper into the cave, Sofia realised how lucky she had been so far. Without a guide she would have certainly become lost. Perhaps the Madonna was looking out for her.

Presently she heard the sound of animated argument.

'I did not call you a fool, Yūsuf – I said it would be foolish to take Mik la Nan at his word.'

'A Sicarii's duty is to cut those throats I decide need cutting,' a quarrelsome voice spat back, 'and since your throat-cutting days are behind you, Bakhbukh, your place is to advise me, not irritate like a camel-tick.'

'I am trying.' This voice was deep, and filled with controlled passion. 'Since no one else will tell you the truth, I must—'

'Jabari, you little fool!' The other voice cut across as the boy walked into the clearing. 'Who bloodied your nose? A Jinni who dislikes little beggars?'

There were sniggers at that, and by way of answer, Jabari looked back the way he had come. The laughter fell away as Sofia appeared.

The cavern smelled of sweat and decline. Its domed ceiling was shrouded in smoke, and not even the braziers burning around the curved walls managed to penetrate the darkness. A natural outcrop gave the cavern a second rocky tier and without a word Jabari scrambled up into this viewing gallery and took his place amongst dozens of gaunt, silently staring boys.

Around a pit of glowing embers sat the circle of grim debaters. All faced – with varying degrees of deference and resentment – a bare-chested youth with manic red-rimmed eyes. He had a sharp nose and an equally sharp chin, covered in a grand unkempt beard which served more to emphasise his youth than the gravitas to which he aspired. His wiry strong arms tapered to delicate wrists wrapped in black rags. He wore a baggy loincloth high around his waist, tied with an old leather belt from which hung a handsome curved dagger.

Now he placed his hand on its pommel and glared. 'Woe onto thee, stranger, to have discovered the lair of the Sicarii.'

His was the petulant voice then. She'd seen a similar dagger before. She looked him over for a moment, then glanced around the circle. They were all scared and chary, obviously waiting for the bearded one's lead. Only one retained his composure: a large man with a wizened face shaped like a cashew nut. His chin was covered in grey stubble, his forehead by wrinkles. He was sitting on the opposite side of the circle. He was not very old, but compared to the rest he was the venerable elder. He looked calmly back at her, then took a date from the bowl in his lap and chewed it meditatively, waiting to see what happened.

The bearded one, embarrassed that the stranger was neither impressed nor cowed, tried again. 'Who art thou? It is Yūsuf of the Sicarii who asks.'

That too failed to amaze, but then the stranger pulled down the scarf and it was the Sicarii who gasped at the sight of a foreigner – *and* a female, at that.

'Since you ask so nicely, my name is Sofia Scaligeri, Contessa of Rasenna – but that is a country far from here. All that matters is that I am an enemy of Catrina Guiscard.'

'Her spy, more like,' said Yūsuf, regaining confidence. 'How did you find us? Where's Zayid?'

'The big bully? He'll be along presently.'

'Where is he?'

She shrugged. 'Flat out, where I left him.'

The elder who'd been chewing dates spoke up now. 'Zayid bloodied Jabari's nose?'

Sofia recognised the voice: he was the one who had been trying to change Yūsuf's mind. 'And I bloodied his.'

'What does *that* matter, Bakhbukh!' Yūsuf hissed. 'I'm sure the little criminal gave him cause. What matters is that this trespasser—'

'—is but a poor woman. We ought to offer hospitality,' Bakhbukh said.

Yūsuf angrily replied, 'The Sicarii are not bound by tribal law!'

While they argued, Sofia handed Iscanno up to Jabari. The boy took the baby willingly. 'There seems to be a misunderstanding.' she interrupted. 'There's a sandstorm coming up from the south. This is my cave now. Keep your voices down and I'll let you stay for the duration.'

Yūsuf broke the ensuing silence with a dry laugh. 'The winds have deranged this foreign whore. We have no food to spare for lunatics.' He tapped the shoulder of a fierce-looking fellow with hawk eyebrows. 'The Jinn and the jackals can fight over her.'

Sofia let him come close. When he grabbed for her, he caught only her scarf. She leaned away from him and let him come free, then a precise kick under his jaw clamped his teeth shut on his tongue. He staggered back and as three others jumped up, Sofia ran at the staggering man and used his body as a ramp to propel her towards the trio. The first she struck in the chest, a Water-Style kick that sent him flying into the other two; he landed amidst their sprawled bodies.

Yūsuf pushed another at her. This one, seeing she could fight, was warier, and came with his blade drawn. It whipped close to her neck, back then forth, and the second time he swiped she jabbed her fingers into his arm, just above the elbow. He yelped and dropped the dagger. Gamely he tried to land a blow with his remaining arm, but she blocked it easily. Her attention was now on the rest of the circle of men advancing on either flank.

She had to end this before someone got seriously hurt.

She caught his arm as it shot past her ear again and as she twisted him round there was a wrenching sound. When she let go, he bowed low, weighed down by two now-useless arms. She dropped him with an elbow between his shoulder blades and took a step back as pairs of men advanced on either side of his body. Stepping back, she ran into the fellow with the eyebrows whom she had left sprawled earlier. He'd recovered enough to grab her left leg, but she kicked her heel back without turning.

The four men in front of her picked that moment to charge.

'Stop!'

Yūsuf bounded over the low flames of the fire and landed with his dagger drawn. 'Nothing holy could have survived the Sands. I know not which you are, Jinni or witch, but I will show you why Sicarii steel is feared.'

As his men drew back, Sofia risked a glance back. Up on their perch, Jabari and Iscanno were laughing together and quite ignoring the mêlée .

She snatched up one of the Sicarii daggers as Yūsuf rushed for her and their blades made blue sparks in the gloom as they clashed. Sofia made a sudden twist to break the clench, but she lost her balance as she came free. She kept her blade up, but his came down with such force that she dropped hers.

Yūsuf's red-rimmed, sleepy eyes came alive with an animal lust as his blade shimmered in the glow of the cinders.

He struck like a scorpion, and her heightened senses felt the air being sliced and the catch of ripped silk as the blade brushed by her breast, just an eyelash away from her skin. Until now her only experience of Air Style was seeing Arik fight. It was direct where Water Style was evasive, brutal where Water Style was precise: a dance of explosive punches and sudden shifts of ground.

But now was not the time for study. It was all she could do to avoid his slashes, but she knew better than to meet them head-on and instead parried them away from her body.

Slash. Parry. And again. And again.

Too late to block this one; avoid it.

She tilted so far back that she had to steady herself against the ground with one hand. Dexterously Yūsuf twirled his dagger. With teeth bared in triumph and both hands on the grip, he brought it down.

Sofia *pushed*, and her torso responded like a whipcord, rising towards the falling blade. Her hands met with a mighty clap.

Yūsuf's blade was trapped in-between palms immovable as granite slabs.

His grin melted into astonishment as Sofia turned her wrists slightly. As his knife dropped, she leaped. Yūsuf had enough wit to block the roundhouse kick at the last moment, but he was on the defensive now, retreating, which was what she wanted. She lashed out, another big showy kick, and Yūsuf stepped back to avoid it – straight onto the smouldering cinders of the firepit. There was the hiss of frying flesh and an agonised screech and Yūsuf hopped backwards, lost his balance and fell on his backside. He rolled out of the circle and kept rolling until his loincloth was no longer smoking.

While Yūsuf's howls turned to whimpers, Sofia glanced at the half-dozen men who had remained sitting. They were waiting apparently for Bakhbukh to speak. The groaning men behind her were huddled together too, and waiting for orders.

'We can do this all night,' she addressed Bakhbukh, 'and maybe one of these boys will get lucky and kill me. But that will help no one except she who styles herself Queen of the Sands.'

An abashed Yūsuf took his place in the circle, and asked, 'You would claim that title, I suppose?'

She turned to him. 'I told you, my home is far from here. As long as she lives, my boy is in peril. You've seen me fight, Yūsuf of the Sicarii. Ask yourself, do you want me *with* you or *against* you?'

Iscanno – who had been perfectly quiet through all the commotion – now began to wail hungrily, and without waiting for Yūsuf's decision, Sofia turned her back on the circle. The men parted before her as she leaped gracefully up to Jabari's shelf, took Iscanno and began feeding him.

Some of the Sicarii were wondering how this stranger had managed to find a lair that had been secure for generations; others were wondering how she fought so well. Yūsuf was pondering something more personal: how exactly this affected him. He wanted to order his men to rush her, but he was canny enough to know that order might not be obeyed – and how bad that would be for him. Some invisible barrier had shifted. It wasn't her fierce determination, but the vulnerable cry of her child that had done it. A furtive glance at Bakhbukh confirmed his fear; the stubborn old fool was smiling.

'Lo,' Yūsuf announced with great solemnity, 'this is a great day in our struggle with the interlopers. When even the queen's own people turn against her, can our victory be delayed much longer? This poor woman has not the wit to demand sanctuary, nor as a *franj* has she any right to expect it, but yet I bestow it. Never let it be said that I do not reward the bearers of good news.'

He had addressed his men, but Sofia nodded her acknowledgment. She would not have to fight tonight. It was enough.

CHAPTER 11

It was the dregs of the campaigning season, and in any other year, the legionaries' boots would be keeping the dust from settling on the Europan Front as they patrolled Concord's northern borders. The dying days of summer would resound with the cheering clash of arms and the evenings would echo to the groan of anguished barbarians. Instead, the only quarrels were the musical contests of those larks that had not found mates.

Though Europa was silent, there was no question of leaving the Rhine Lands unoccupied, lest the Frankish tribes forget their squabbles and regain territory dearly bought with Concordian blood. The mines had never been more important; since the Rasenneisi had demonstrated the military use of annunciators, a new model, designed expressly for aerial bombardment, had been rolling off Concord's assembly lines by the hundreds. Without a steady flow of metal to the capital, that torrent would slow to a trickle.

There was another reason – beside iron – to protect their flanks: a second front would doom all hope of success in the coming campaign in Etruria. The prospect of a large Byzantine push worried Leto much more than Frankish raids, though his concerns had lessened after his spies discovered why the armies on the eastern side of the Dalmatian March had been so abnormally courteous of late. Apparently, Prince Andronikos had done Concord the enormous favour of getting himself killed in some sordid adventure in the border territories. The purple throne remained empty, though there were several contenders circling.

Until a new prince was established, Leto could safely turn his back to finish his great project, the conquest of Etruria. Even so, he persuaded the First Apprentice to leave three legions behind. The other six were combined into one great host.

The columns marched by Concord without stopping for honours or respite – other than the Praetorian Guard, only a small unit of reserves was permitted into the capital – and halted at Rasenna.

Many of the legionaries had lost friends in the last siege of the City of Towers, and they were looking forward to seeing the red flags lining its battlements dragged though the muck; that would be sweet indeed. They waited for the order to begin the investment, confident in their strength. It was true, these battlements were the same ones that had rebuffed the Twelfth – but that was two years ago, and the Grand Legion was not commanded by a fool.

Anticipation pervaded the ranks but the order never came. Instead, Leto rode up to the north wall holding the green banner of Concord. He stopped within arrow-range and waited. Presently, a small hidden door beside the main gate creaked open and a man in a gaudy uniform emerged carrying a Rasenneisi banner. He marched up to the general and saluted.

'I received your invitation,' said Leto. 'You always land on your feet, don't you?'

Geta bowed in acknowledgment. 'That's what soldiers do.'

'And traitors.'

Geta threw his head back and laughed. 'You were sharpening a pike for me. I'd no choice but to leave Concord. You'll be glad that I sought exile here. I've become terribly popular with the natives.'

'Is that down to your charm or the silver you stole before you left?'

'Equal, I'd say – anyway, it was money well spent. You don't want to be stuck here, fighting a beaten city, do you? Not with summer marching on, not when there's a real challenge, like Veii, waiting for you. I can grant you safe passage south and all I ask is to be confirmed in my position.'

'Town drunk?'

Geta merrily shook his banner. 'Gonfaloniere, silly.'

'So, you'll grant me safe passage bought with my silver? *Madonna*, but you have gall. Here's my counter: surrender Rasenna as you promised in your letter, and I'll consider letting you keep your head, never mind your job.'

'Don't test me, Spinther. You know what I'm liable to do when pushed into a corner.'

'You're already in a corner. You're not *universally* popular with the natives, are you? Certainly not with the sons of Fabbro Bombelli. They've declared your election fraudulent.'

'It was fairly bought. My erstwhile brothers-in-law are exiled, so their opinions are irrelevant. They are contesting our late gonfaloniere's estate with my wife too, but that's a tedious family matter. I took office with the Signoria's consent. Doing so without civil war was no easy matter.'

'I'm sure, but perception matters. You bought this hovel's poor excuse for a government, but the Bombelli's endless credit moulds opinion everywhere south of the Irenicon. Rightfully or not, you and your gentle wife are seen as usurpers. You've no choice but to work for me.'

Geta lowered his banner with amiable resignation. 'True enough.'

Leto watched as the battlement banners lowered in emulation and were replaced with Concordian blue. When he looked back he saw something even more satisfying: Geta kneeling, his head bowed, his hands held up in supplication. 'The City of Towers is yours. Treat her gently.'

He would have relished running the scoundrel through, but

instead he dismounted and held out his hand. 'On behalf of the First Apprentice of Concord, I accept your surrender.' Geta rose grinning from his knees and stood looking down on Leto. 'Glad you've decided to be the bigger man.'

'Thank Torbidda, not me. I wished to make an example of Rasenna – and you. He would not hear of unnecessary delay.'

'I'm happy wisdom prevailed,' Geta said equably as he signalled to the walls, 'but heartbroken to stand so low in your eyes. I shall endeavour to rise.'

Leto watched impatiently as the heavy gate slowly lifted. 'Just give me a bed and I'll be on my way.'

Geta turned back and said awkwardly, 'Our gate is open, but I advise not entering till tomorrow.'

Leto's scowl deepened. 'Why?'

'No trickery,' Geta protested. 'It's just that things are never simple in the City of Towers. Before I routed my opposition, they managed to destroy that splendid bridge we had built. Stay calm – it's a problem your engineers can swiftly solve. Look at it as practise for the coming campaign. They'll have a pontoon ready by morning; you'll march over and on your way.'

Leto slowly exhaled. 'Fine, but we'll bivouac within the walls tonight.'

'That might be unwise—'

'How's that?' snapped Leto, thoroughly frustrated.

'The north side of Rasenna wasn't for sale, so I was forced to pursue a scorched-earth strategy.'

'So it lacks amenities. Do these men look like they're used to soft sheets?'

Geta could feign only so much humility. 'Yes, I know what a tough lot your legionaries are. I'm more worried about our pest infestation.'

Leto sighed. He'd been expecting something like this. 'The opposition's gone underground?'

'Literally. If the legionaries were to find themselves under attack in the night, I fear that that they'd—'

'—leave the other half ruined too. I daresay you're right. If I send my pontonniers to ford the Irenicon, can you at least guarantee their safety? Or is that asking too much?'

'Not at all.'

'Fine then,' said Leto remounting. 'Next time you capture a city, Geta—'

'Yes, General?'

'*Capture it*, will you?'

The ladder creaked as Pedro climbed and he marvelled at the thought that he'd raced up these rungs as a small boy. Lifting the trapdoor, he found himself looking at a lead-lined hammer about to drop.

'Jacques, it's me!'

The maimed giant lowered his arm and glanced around. Uggeri was standing at the window, looking down towards the river. 'How did you find me?'

'A guess. There's no better view of Piazza Luna than Tower Vanzetti.'

Flocks of shining annunciators flew back and forth over the Irenicon trailing strong silver filaments that sparkled like dew-doused silk. The deep foundations of Rasenna's bridge hadn't been fully destroyed in the explosion and the engineers were making use of them to bolster their pontoon.

'What're you up to?'

'Just thinking about the old days. This is where you made the Golden Lion banner for the Doc, remember?'

Pedro refused to be distracted. 'The old days. I remember the first time you came here. You broke my nose and thrashed the place.'

'You didn't beg. I admired you for that. It's hard to be brave, but breaking things? That's easy. I miss it, if I'm honest. Jacques here used to create wondrous things with his hands. Then they were cut off. The tools you gave him aren't fit for making things, but that's not what times like these call for. You put us in this position, Vanzetti. If you lost the nerve to fight, I'm sorry but—'

'I sent your men home.'

'You wouldn't dare.' Uggeri picked up a small mirror and flashed a signal. It was not returned, neither from the topside positions nor from the alleyways surrounding the piazza. He smashed the mirror on the floor and shouted, 'What gives you the right—?'

'—to stop you destroying Rasenna? I'm gonfaloniere, in the absence of a legitimate Signoria, anyway' – he took a breath – 'and you're my podesta. That means you can't just break things when you feel like it. You need to think.'

'I have done. The more of Geta's cronies we kill, the less power he has. All we have to do is keep up the pressure.'

Pedro sighed. 'Geta doesn't *need* Rasenneisi support any more. He has Concord's. The Grand Legion is here. We're done.'

'You want us to run off to Veii like whipped dogs.' said Uggeri. 'Our fathers weren't alike, you know. Yours was a decent skin, mine was a cur. But they both died fighting for Rasenna's freedom. What would they say if they could hear you?'

'We have to let go of Rasenna if we want to save it.'

Jacques took a step towards Uggeri, but Pedro held up a hand to stop him. 'Do you recall what Doc said when he gave you that banner?'

'He said we stand together or fall together.' Uggeri stared at the mirror fragments, breathing hard. 'Don't talk to me like I'm a child.'

'Then grow up. Geta made the legions camp outside expressly to avoid an incident.'

'Exactly why we should do something to embarrass him.'

'In this case, he's right. The legionaries would be delighted to settle the score. They'd leave this side of town worse than the north.'

'We can hide.'

'Yes – while they massacre our mothers and grandmothers and brothers and sisters.'

Uggeri turned back to the window.

'Are you coming?'

'No. I want to know what it's like to let an army march over you.'

Pedro was about to ask Jacques the same question, but he had already turned his back. It was plain the Hammer belonged to Uggeri now.

The Grand Legion entered Rasenna cheering, but the acclamation soon faded away. The charred and broken northside towers made the legionaries brood on old sins – and each of them had many. When they crossed the swaying pontoon, they found the south side of Rasenna less desolate but no more welcoming. They knew they were trampling a fresh grave, and so they ignored the rictus grins of the pale patricians and hastened to escape the empty piazza.

Geta escorted Leto to the south gate. Before he left, Geta begged for a few battalions from him. 'Flushing out the Tartaruchi – stupid name! – will cost lives,' he explained.

'Doubtless it will,' Leto said with equanimity. 'Why should they be my legionaries' lives? You have mercenaries at your disposal.' The Hawk's Company, what was left of it, might be led by a Concordian, but Leto for one had not forgotten Tagliacozzo; even though Concordian arms had triumphed over John Acuto's coalition that day, it had been a close-run thing. 'Those dogs sold their lives a hundred times over. It's about time someone took them up on it.'

CHAPTER 12

It was too early for snow. The pale flakes carried on the chill wind at their backs were ash. Though Leto rode in the middle of the vanguard, the horses in front of him had already turned the path into mud, and the black mire reflected the column of smoke that was all that remained of the nameless town behind them.

The Grand Legion was an iron river of well-drilled men and broken beasts. Taming truly wild things, Leto reflected, was well-nigh impossible; no matter how servile they might act, their hearts remained defiant. Once, Concord could approach any town and be sure of allies inside; sure that ambition was a stronger instinct than patriotism; sure that if the headman did not open the gates, the next man would; sure that there was no treachery to which a man would not stoop if he could call himself king or dux or doge or gonfaloniere . . .

Then one slip undid years of patient work: Rasenna showed that resistance *was* possible, and even though it was now once more degraded, the memory of the City of Towers' defiance endured. Even the weakest towns now believed they could preserve their independence if only they could muster a convincing defence. Leto had left a string of hamlets broken and burning as a forthright answer to this misapprehension. It had been necessary. Each day the green leaves faded a little more; each day the cold wind crept south faster than they could. Like Rasenna, Veii was a frontier, and it had to be taken if the advance were to continue. If it did not quickly surrender, he must break off the campaign till spring, and Torbidda would never countenance such a delay.

The road to Veii was in ill repair and interrupted by brooks, streams, and finally rivers. To maintain their pace, Leto ordered the big wagons carrying the large cannon and material for siege-engines left behind; they could be sent for a week later, perhaps two. It was a gamble – the sort that came naturally to Geta, the sort at which Leto's cautious sensibility rebelled – but he recognised the necessity. His scouts reported that Veii was making preparations – if they got there before that work was sufficiently advanced, it was unlikely that the Duke of Veii would risk a trial of arms. Leto took consolation in the fact that the Veians had always previously chosen discretion over valour: Duke Grimani had stood apart from John Acuto's coalition, though the field of Tagliacozzo bordered his dominions.

Leto had more to worry about besides the shortening days. Ordinarily, a campaigning general could rely on the unsleeping intelligences of the three Apprentices attending to the flow of men and equipment and foreseeing the many sundry complications that inevitably plagued marching men. That as much as their remarkable war-engines was why Concordian armies most often won. But Torbidda's attentions were divided between building this damn tower and recapturing Rasenna's elusive Contessa Scaligeri – neither of which Leto deemed as pressing – which left his man Scaevola to worry about details Concordian quartermasters had never before had to concern themselves with.

A horn blew somewhere ahead and Leto rode to the front of the vanguard to see a Veian herald. When Leto saw the man was bearing the peacock flag of the Grimani Family rather than the wolf of Veii, his mood brightened. He had forgotten what an advantage it was to have such craven foes.

The salt plains of Volsinii were hardly scenic, but the small coastal town was within Veii's sphere of influence and the perfect place for Duke Grimani to discreetly meet the Concordian general.

The duke believed in diversification: there was no doubt Maestro Vanzetti's improvements made it possible for Veii to withstand a long siege – but surely it would be better if they could avoid that trial altogether? He hoped to sound out General Spinther's intentions, perhaps even make a deal. But just in case Spinther was planning to take a shortcut, he brought a large bodyguard and four elders to demonstrate the eternal loyalty of Veii's population to the Family Grimani.

Leto brought only Quartermaster Scaevola and a centurion. Now that the Duke beheld his adversary face to face, he realised any theatrics were unnecessary; he was a little annoyed that he had chosen such a remote venue. Etruria was quailing before a mere boy – still, at least he had an audience to appreciate the spell he was about to weave upon the inexperienced youth.

'General Spinther,' he began, 'I am so glad to finally meet you, so I can ask in person the question that has been tormenting me: What lies have our mutual enemies told you that would prompt Concord to march against Veii, a city that has always been a friend?'

'Veii took part in the summit at Ariminum,' Leto pointed out. 'That's hardly an act of friendship.'

'Hardly an act of war either. It's true that I was foolish enough to send my son to the summit – but only to urge the other powers to be patient. And for my peacemaking, he was assassinated by parties unknown. The Ariminumese insist it was an accident, but that's—'

'—not what we are here to discuss.'

The duke was taken aback. 'Now listen, son, that's a poor attitude to begin a negotiation—'

'We're not negotiating,' Leto said. 'You know you cannot stand against us.'

'I know nothing of the sort. Indeed, I seem to recall Rasenna sent your legions packing not too long ago.'

Leto sighed. Explaining what an outlier was wouldn't help. In his previous dealings with barbarians, Leto had noticed that brute logic made brutes intransigent. 'That city is now fallen,' he said. 'The First Apprentice aspires to a *Renovatio Imperii* from which all Etruria would profit. Concord's demands are reasonable: the right to tax fish and salt, the right to collect tolls and customs, the right to appoint certain officials to oversee—'

'Yes, yes, the same Regalian Rights that every vaunting would-be conqueror from the north has ever demanded.' The duke felt wrong-footed: he'd come expecting a generous bribe in exchange for neutrality and safe passage through his lands, but instead this pup was expecting him to lick his feet in front of his countrymen. 'Sophistry will not avail you, boy. I patronise enough court-philosophers to know one can disguise anything as Reason.'

'Then it is not Reason,' said Leto with cold fury. 'What if our ancestors had been this obstinate? Had they not banded together in federation, every Etruscan city would have fallen one by one to the ravenous Romans. We must follow their examples and see beyond our petty differences. I offer more than an olive branch: I offer membership of the greatest league since the Etruscan Empire. The First Apprentice has begun to rebuild the Molè. He wishes it to be a monument for *all* Etrurians, a symbol of the titanic works we can achieve when we forget ourselves and think and act as a corporate body.'

'A gilded chain is still a chain.'

Leto realised that Reason was wasted on this one. 'Have you ever studied a peacock closely, Grimani? Its feet are mired in caked shit that mocks the display in which it prides.'

'Meaning what?'

'That the worst fools are those who think themselves wise. You are right about one thing at least: words are the wrong tools to convince the likes of you.'

The duke signalled to his bodyguard that the meeting was over. 'You'll find us ready, Spinther.'

As the dust of the duke's horses engulfed them, Leto said to the man standing behind him, 'What do you think, Scaevola?'

'He must think he has a chance.'

Leto suppressed a smile. 'Has Rasenna discouraged even you?'

'Perish the thought, General. It's only that our engines will be delayed.'

A quartermaster should be cautious, but Scaevola was cursed with such ill luck that risk-avoidance had become his religion. His first error was to be born minor nobility, his family lands far from the capital, where the Concordian contato met the coast. His parents were too reactionary to let an obviously intelligent child train as an engineer, and too poor to send him to a Rasenneisi bandieratori studio, and as a result he entered the army with no advantages – a handicap which spurred him to hard work.

His appearance was no help: his great flapping ears were the most insistent crimson, and his large nose lumpen, and while a smile might have made these features endearing, his cracked lips were perpetually frowning over his sums. This unhappy combination might have attracted the mockery of the young engineers who surrounded Leto, but in truth, Scaevola's foolish appearance had been Fortune's one favour: no one had ever taken him seriously enough to want him assassinated. Over a long career of dogged service he had earned steady promotions, but in such crawling increments that no one ever really noticed, until, to the wonder of all, he had attained a rank of which any man could be proud – though how galling to be grey-haired amongst boys and adolescents. He was condescended to by the engineers, distrusted by the nobles and flat-out despised by the foot soldiers, who would have preferred daily scourging to the tyranny of his fastidious parsimony.

Many officers had used Scaevola to aid their own rise within the ranks, but the first man to truly *see* his qualities was Leto. The First Apprentice's last friend had become suspicious of Wunderkinder – he knew better than anyone the ruin left in the wake of their wild leaps and intricate schemes. Away from Concord, things were simpler. There was no art to War. It was butchery, pure and simple. Brilliant stratagems rarely won the day; most of the time it was simply a matter of grit, drudge and application, of showing up on the right day, of making sure the horses were shod, that the men were fed and marching in the right direction.

Attention to such routine matters was Scaevola's gift. The other reason Leto trusted him was that he was universally reviled – the stiletto of an ambitious subordinate was ever an occupational hazard for a Concordian general, but if Leto were ever assassinated, the quartermaster would lose everything: his rank, his fortune and probably his life.

Scaevola did not see it in these stark terms. He had always won promotion by default, but being shown actual favour had changed his life. His fellow officers, perhaps a little jealous, might mock his hound-like fidelity, but he loved his general as a freed bondsman loved his liberator.

'If they use that time to shore up their walls, gather provisions, well . . .' He looked at his master with concern. 'General, you know I do not voice doubts idly. My loyalty obliges me to attend to the facts, however unpleasant, however bothersome. Veii's natural defences are such that even an incompetent resistance would delay us. What if Grimani does all he's threatened?'

His hero didn't disappoint. 'Then we'll make him pay for it.'

The night after the Grand Legion passed through Rasenna, the pontoon was cut from its moorings. No one attempted any replacement, so the only way north was once again via the Midnight Road.

Geta's soldiers crossed in force. Their mission was to move the orphans south, 'for their protection', and they came armed with kindling and oil. They found the baptistery empty.

No announcement was made but all knew that the war had entered a new, more brutal phase.

Geta entered the bedchamber where Maddalena was confined with the morning sickness that had long outstayed its welcome. 'How are you feeling, *amore*?'

'Duped,' she said grumpily. 'I thought it was called morning sickness because it didn't last beyond noon.' She had chased away her servants hours ago and was surprised to find herself genuinely happy to see him. 'Good day at work, Husband?'

'You don't want to know,' said Geta, uncorking a bottle and pouring two glasses.

'Actually, knowing whether victory is imminent or if my tower is about to collapse is of immense concern to me,' Maddalena said snippily. 'Whatever goes on in the world outside our bedchamber, we promised never to lie to each other.'

'I said that?' He raised his eyebrows as she glowered at him, then gave in.'Well, I'm not hiding anything, *amore*, I promise you that. It's just that my mother taught me to be silent when there's nothing to boast of. We discovered three new holes today.'

'That many!' She sat up abruptly. 'What did you do?'

'I must give Vanzetti his due: he knows how to set a trap. The dogs I sent down weren't smart enough to spot them.'

'What about your men?'

He sniffed. 'They're not much better. The first chap actually volunteered – he was a real bruiser, more muscles than brain, but he wasn't gone more than a minute before he came racing back out, screaming at the top of his voice. Couldn't really blame him, as he was followed by a stampede of braccia-long sewer rats.'

'Charming.'

'Well, I can see the funny side of it now,' he admitted, 'but it wasn't an ideal start to the day. No more volunteers were forthcoming, so I set a fire in the entrance and blocked it off with heavy rocks.'

'Why don't you do that every time? There can't be much air down there.'

'It stinks like a Lazar barracks, but Vanzetti's obviously taken precautions against suffocation.'

'Well, we've always known he's not stupid.' Pointing out the obvious always cheered her up.

'The second tunnel we found is a good example of the bastard's ingenuity: the first man down failed to come up, so I sent another – and then Giorgio reappeared; claimed he'd seen no one else down there, and said that the tunnel sloped downwards until it ended in water. Not that I believed him, of course – they'll say anything to stop me keep sending them down – but in the end I went myself.'

'Well, that accounts for the smell.' Maddalena wrinkled her nose at him and he raised his glass to her. 'But what if something had happened? What would happen to *me*?'

'Don't worry, *amore* – I don't make a habit of leading from the front, I promise you. It's just so damn frustrating. Well, Giorgio was right, there *was* a pool – but no sight of the missing Marco, the first chap, so I held my breath and dived in. The tunnel went down a bit more, then it rose upwards again. I found a set of legs blocking the way up and managed to pull Marco free – nearly suffocated myself, mind, but I got him out in the end.' He sighed. 'Might as well have saved myself the effort. I dragged him back to the other side where I'd left my lamp and as soon as I got him out of the water I could see the poor sod'd been garrotted as soon as he stuck his head out.'

Maddalena's eyes were wide. 'So what did you do?'

'What could I do? Nothing to do but blow up the tunnel-mouth. That took a fair bit of powder . . .'

'What about the third?' Maddalena was stroking his arm now, transfixed. She'd been bored silly all day and even if her gallant knight was being shown up by Pedro Vanzetti's superior planning, it was diverting to hear about. There was also a part of her – she was still Rasenneisi, after all – that cheered for every strip Uggeri's men tore from the foreigners' flag.

'The third was this long, sheer drop. You remember Bastiano? The one who looks like a choirboy until he opens his foul little mouth? We lowered him down on a rope and when he shouted up that there was a second hole I ordered him to investigate.' He sighed. 'Of course I did. What else could I have done?''

'And?' she said impatiently, prodding him in the arm.

'We dragged him up screaming: he'd been stabbed in the crotch with a broken flag-stick. Guess he'll not have to worry about losing that lovely singing voice, eh? Anyway, that was it for me: I decided I'd rather be drinking with my lovely wife – then, to cap off a perfect day, we got into a running battle through Tartarus on the way home and lost another man somewhere in the ruins. All we found for our troubles was a boy with a sling, he couldn't have been more than six. So we stuck him on a stick for the birds to dine upon and crossed the Midnight Road whistling jauntily. *Cin Cin!*' He took a long drink and belched heartily. He smiled down at her. 'You know you're right. It is good to share.'

Maddalena wasn't amused. 'You can't give up the north.'

'If they want that wasteland, let them have it. I'm a soldier, not a pest exterminator.'

'This is Rasenna. If you show weakness, they'll overrun us.'

He yawned. '*Tranquillo, amore.* You're quite safe. I may not be able to get at them, but it works both ways. I've spent enough time in trenches to know that time's on our side. There're no laurels down there, just foot-rot and the flux. Vanzetti is holding Uggeri Galati back – he wants a glorious death—'

'—and my head on a stick—'

'Exactly, my little dove, and a lovely head it is too. So all we have to do is to sit tight, all nice and dry and fed on the high ground, and wait for the rat to come out of his hole.'

Maddalena was about to say that sounded awfully like being used as bait, but Geta had lifted his feet onto the bed and was already snoring.

CHAPTER 13

Sofia spent the next few nights anticipating an ambush that never came. She wondered whether Yūsuf was resigned to her presence, or if he simply could not persuade his men to abandon the concept of tribal hospitality. The old man, Bakhbukh, his chief counsellor, saw that she was fed, but otherwise she was left alone on her perch and treated like a bad-tempered animal that had decided to nest in their cave.

The children were more generous, following Jabari's example. They were all orphans, and they quickly recognised a fellow reject. The tribespeople were called lizard-eaters for good reason: their favourite delicacy was the little gecko they called *dhaab*, which they roasted in its scaly skin. The child who caught it got the head, but they would give her the tiny liver and sweetbreads and the end of the tail, to make her milk rich for Iscanno. Lizards aside, Yūsuf's operation was familiar to Sofia, for she'd been part of a condottieri band herself. Lacking the blood-ties that united normal tribes of the Sands, he relied on the promise of plunder to keep his men together, though competition for the few spice caravans that still risked the Sands was fierce as southern tribes like the Napthtali made their presence felt.

The cell she had happened upon was the hub, but there were more Sicarii units scattered in the hills of the badlands, for they were seen as enemies of the land and could not concentrate their forces. Yūsuf preferred the security of seclusion; he would occasionally allow Bakhbukh to travel between them, but more often he would force his deputies to come to him. Unlike the other tribes, who found safety and growth in their webs of marriage alliances, the Sicarii remained friendless, and were so used to betrayal that suspicion had become habitual. Like the Lazars, they had put themselves beyond normal society, living among the bones of the dead and the scavenging dogs as they did. Some tribes believed the Sicarii had made themselves *traif*, an unclean people to be shunned.

In the absence of booty, Yūsuf tried to inspire with promises of future greatness, insisting that they were the vanguard of a new Radinate – but no one attended to his hectoring. It was plain that his words were nothing more than an attempt to justify his thievery. His fighting skill was unquestioned, but technique was less prized than being lucky, and lucky was one thing, the Sicarii had decided in the secret councils of their minds, that Yūsuf was not. His hold might have been strong once, but it was slipping now, still, Sofia saw no challengers rising. It was a poor crown if no one was attempting to steal it.

After his nightly harangue, Yūsuf would stalk off, leaving his angry, demoralised crew in peace to sit around the fire listening to Bakhbukh's stories of Judas Maccabee and the first Sicarii. Bakhbukh had aching joints and haunted eyes, but when he told his tales, all weariness left him and his whole being was possessed by whatever hero he was singing about. The evening was never complete without his songs of the Golden Age and the marvellous deeds of meliks like Aaron al Rashid.

This night was different.

Yūsuf's theme was the Naphtali's incursion. Their presence was creating tensions, and not just with the Sicarii. Mik la Nan had invited Yūsuf to meet to discuss boundaries, and he was keen to go.

'We might even make an alliance – we could take back our wells from the Benjaminites and our pastures from the Zebulun.'

'I say again: this is foolish,' Bakhbukh grumbled.

'What else can you say, old man? Can you challenge me to my face or only whisper? I cannot defeat a witch, but I can defeat a base-born slave like you.'

When Yūsuf was done blustering, Bakhbukh asked pointedly, 'Why does he wish to meet alone?'

'How should I know? Perhaps he's surrounded by meddling old fools who think they know better than their nasi.'

'Why you?' Sofia interrupted from her perch. 'That's the question you should be asking, Yūsuf. The Sicarii are weak.'

Before Yūsuf could complain that only those within the circle were allowed to speak, Bakhbukh said, 'Mik la Nan says that every other tribe has made an accommodation with the foreigners.'

'The Napthtali are as foreign to me as the *franj*,' said one of the circle haughtily.

'We're Ebionites. That's all that matters,' snapped Yūsuf. 'And this is none of her concern!'

But Bakhbukh was intrigued. 'What does the Contessa say?'

'I say that sons inherit their father's weaknesses as well as their strengths. Yūsuf ben Uriah is making the same mistake that Uriah ben Sinan made.'

'What do you know of my father?' Yūsuf said indignantly.

'What all the Sands knows. That he was a brave warrior, but foolhardy to sit unarmed with an enemy who could only benefit from his death.'

'He was betrayed by a bitch with no honour! I will not hear him called a fool—'

'The world is wicked. He should have expected it.'

Yūsuf threw a cutting glance at Bakhbukh. 'Perhaps he was badly advised.'

'That same bitch,' Sofia continued, 'has welcomed Mik la Nan into her domain, on the condition that he brings her your head.'

'What concern of yours is my head? I have given you a roof

under which to suckle your whelp, more than many would these days—'

'—so much the worse for the cause of Ebionite hospitality. I don't care a fig for your head; the only head I care about is my son's. His safety is bound up with the Sicarii, and so long as they are led by one who will not listen to wise counsel, he is in peril.'

Yūsuf stood with dignity. 'I sit here to dispense justice and to listen to my peers. I have heard what *my men* have had to say. Now I will take counsel with God.' He strode out, and took the tension with him. No one objected when Sofia climbed down and joined the circle.

'You mustn't be offended by Yūsuf,' said Bakhbukh. 'He is capable of many things – but sustained thought is not amongst them.'

'He's not scared of Mik la Nan.'

'He ought to be.' Bakhbukh held his hands close to the fire. 'The first time I heard of Mik la Nan, he was still young, nasi of nothing much but his family tent. One of his camels went missing.'

Sofia was not the only person listening intently.

'Now, Napthtali camels do not *go missing*. They are stolen – and in that case, the proper way of it was to make a formal protest at the next tribal assembly and, if judgement went his way, he would be compensated.'

'Was he?'

'Mik la Nan made his own judgement. He rode through the valleys to the left and right of his lands and crippled his neighbours' herds: three-score camels good for nothing but the cooking pot next morning. The Cat, as he became known soon after, neither knew nor cared which family was guilty. There are no secrets in the Sands and no deed is done without consultation. In his eyes, the family who had sat by and done nothing while his property was stolen was as guilty as the family who had stolen it. His message was twofold: that you must make war on the Cat's enemies or be counted as one yourself. The second message, which the Napthtali later made known throughout the Empty Quarter, was that any slight would be paid back tenfold.'

'He overreacted,' Zayid growled.

'You were never a shepherd, were you? The Cat understood what others did not. The stolen camel was a test. A weak response would have led to more predation. From then on, his flock was inviolate.'

He paused, and then added softly, 'And since then I have often wondered if a violent act that brings peace can truly be considered wicked, or if servility that invites war can be considered moral.'

Sofia asked, 'If the Cat conquered the Empty Quarter so easily, what's to stop him conquering the Sands? He's not scared of the Sicarii.'

Bakhbukh snorted at the thought. 'He did not come to conquer. The drought has simply pushed him north along with all the other wild things.'

'Perhaps the offer is genuine,' said Zayid, 'and he'll come alone to the parley.'

'He would need no help to best a boy like Yūsuf.'

'Yet Yūsuf will go,' Sofia said.

'One cannot keep a fool from his foolishness,' said Omar, one of the older Sicarii.

'So maybe it is for the best,' said another, Abdo. 'We've suffered under his foolishness for too long. Time enough he suffered.'

Sofia leaped to her feet. 'Where are your heads? If Yūsuf's taken, how long will these caves remain secure?'

'He would never betray us,' Bakhbukh thundered. 'If you hadn't embarrassed him, you mischievous foreigner, he wouldn't be trying to prove his courage so foolishly.'

Sofia could see saw how much he cared for Yūsuf. 'If you're

right, Bakhbukh, then the Sicarii name will be for ever disgraced for letting your nasi be captured.'

The anger left him and he said, 'That's true. I should stop him.'

'You'll do no such thing,' she said sternly. 'We need tasty bait to catch the Cat.'

CHAPTER 14

The kerak erupted from the hilltop, silhouetted against a cold-red evening sky interrupted only by an anaemic streak of cloud.

Usually the tribesmen avoided such forts, but the old nasi rode purposefully towards it, leading his own camel, and another besides, through an arid gorge carpeted with black slates that overlapped like scales. The prisoner sitting bound on the beast trailing behind his was already irritable, but when he saw their destination, he became positively agitated. 'If you don't release me, I swear—'

Mik la Nan flicked his stick against the camel's flank. 'You're in no position to make threats or promises. Kindly shut up.'

'The Sands will know you for a traitor if you give Yūsuf ben Uriah to the *franj*—'

'*Give you*? Perish that thought,' said the nasi. 'I will *sell you*, and for a good deal of silver. And do not lecture me on treachery: it's your foolish alliance with the Byzantine lord that has stirred up the blood of that witch in Akka.'

'Prince Andronikos might have succeeded.'

'Aye, and had he won Akka's throne, his first act would have been to send for reinforcements from the Purple City and blot the Sicarii out for good. What became of him after he fled Akka?'

'He sought to bring his bad luck to me.'

The sound of the camels' movement echoed oddly in the gorge and Mik la Nan glanced behind, then up at the cliff-face. 'You denied him sanctuary?'

'He never reached our caves,' said Yūsuf guardedly.

The nasi fixed his prisoner with his one good eye. 'You cut his throat before he could – or more likely, had one of your men cut it. What a fool you are, Yūsuf ben Uriah. You sought to mollify the queen with a corpse. A cat is much happier – and you must take my word on this – with something it can torture a while. Now be still, before I use my stick on you!'

Yūsuf fell silent – perhaps cowed, perhaps considering Mik la Nan's analysis, perhaps merely sulking.

Mik la Nan was on edge; he pressed the camels to a brisker pace, only to come to a sudden stop as a row of riders appeared as if from nowhere, blocking his way.

'Are these not your men?' Yūsuf whispered. He might have hoped to save his skin by betraying the Sicarii to the queen, but the thought of being captured by another nasi was truly worrying.

'Have you no eyes?' said Mik la Nan. 'They're yours.'

'My men!' cried Yūsuf. 'Why – so they are! Alas for you,' he said mockingly. 'I wonder what the Gad would pay for the mangy pelt of an old cat?'

'You'll never know!' the nasi said, thrusting a palm into Yūsuf's chest; the touch sent Yūsuf flying out of the saddle as Mik la Nan stuck his stick into his belt, pulled out a massive curved sword and twirled it aloft to the rhythm of a shrill wailing call – 'Illa – illa – illa!' – that urged the camels into a gallop.

'God's beard,' exclaimed Bakhbukh. 'He means for us to kill him!'

'I could take him down with a stone,' said Sofia. She was dressed like a Sicarii, with her face and hair covered by a black scarf.

'You wouldn't get close. His Air Style is sublime. No, this is blade-work. Sicarii, ready! He'll kill some of us, but numbers will prevail.'

There was a terrible lingering note as a dozen swords were drawn.

'Stand down!' she ordered. 'Make a gap.'

'Contessa, honour demands—'

'Make a gap!' she commanded, and the line duly parted for both camels. She dropped from her saddle and caught hold of the harness of Mik la Nan's riderless camel as it passed her, then swung herself up into the saddle and yanked the reins free. The nasi looked around in surprise, then swung for her, but she ducked and pulled ahead as he swerved to avoid the great mound of quarried rocks, probably left over from the kerak's construction, at the gorge's exit. Sofia knew she could never outrace such an experienced rider, so she took that out of the equation.

The beasts collided with a terrific *whumpp* and tumbled to the sand, their legs turning in the air like the spines of a broken fan. Dust rendered them invisible, but their disappointed groans echoed around the gorge. When it cleared, their riders were standing facing each other.

'Finally!' he laughed, 'a Sicarii with balls.'

Sofia said nothing but took her dagger from her belt, held it up – and threw it down.

He casually followed suit. 'Don't think you've just gained an advantage, boy.'

He padded around her, his feet tensing and untensing in the abstracted manner of a tomcat stalking a mouse.

She backed towards the rock pile as the Sicarii looked on uneasily. Mik la Nan was a renowned warrior. The Contessa was a *franj* – and worse, a woman. Brave as she was, she could not survive the contest. Yet she bore their flag, and so, against all hope, they hoped.

Mik la Nan lost himself in his warm-up ritual, waving his arms in circles and rolling his head till his neck cracked – then, without warning he slid forward, his feet dragging dust, his palms flat, wrists together.

But she was ready for it. She knocked the blow aside with a

gentle swipe, gathering up all its thrust as she did, then releasing it against the old man's chest, sending him sprawling backwards. But he kept his balance and grinned at the masked stranger as he pulled up his sleeves. 'Water Style?' he remarked. 'You're no Ebionite.'

Suddenly he was beside her, punching out, his arms straight, like pistons, again and again. He used his long sleeves to disguise his intentions, just as the Reverend Mother had, and Sofia surrendered ground, climbing backwards up the mound, diverting some blows and avoiding some, but many – too many – she had to block directly. The hammer-blows shook her. He was the most adept Ebionite she'd yet fought – a natural, like Doc – and she recognised that this was Air Style at its full protean potency. And it was lethal.

But Mik la Nan was accustomed to winning, and his offensive, powerful as it was, allowed no room for defence. She kept backing away until she had learned his rhythm, then she darted in and let him run into her knee. A deft undercut pushed through the tangle of his braided beard and she felt his teeth rattle.

He went with the blow, turning in the air and landing on his feet, still fit to fight, but much warier now. 'Who *are* you?'

Sofia kept up her guard, praying that he would tire and knowing he wouldn't. He was harnessing the wind so adeptly that his attack was costing him hardly any energy. In this arid land it was hard to counter wind with water. She would have to slow him down some other way.

By this time Yūsuf – bitter and chagrined that no one had thought to unbind him – had joined his Sicarii. Now he saw who was fighting for their honour.

Mik la Nan kept pace as she leaped backwards, gradually ascending the little ziggurat of rocks, but there was no reprieve for her here. She paused to knock a pair of small boulders at him and as he dodged one, his fist exploded the other. She reached the top and a moment later, he was beside her.

Before he got his balance, she attacked.

The nasi responded to the onslaught coolly, weaving and blocking, never giving ground, waiting for an opening, and when her volley ended, his sleeves whipped by her face like a scythe. She pulled her head back, but he caught her scarf.

She flicked her hair out of her eyes and glared at him.

The old nasi looked dumbly at her, then the scarf in his hand.

She wouldn't get another chance. Her foot exploded into his midriff and the onlooking Sicarii gasped as Mik la Nan tumbled down the other side of the rock mound. Before he hit the ground, she was in mid-air, her knee squarely aimed for his head. He braced his feet and at the last moment jumped aside – but there had been no time to look before leaping and he rammed into the base of the rockpile with such force that it began to collapse.

Before he could be crushed, Sofia pulled him aside, and when the dust cleared, they lay panting on their backs, turned towards one another, staring.

'The Etrurian princess,' he croaked. 'So you learned what Catrina's protection was worth. I'm glad you took my advice to flee Akka.'

'Yes, indeed. It was a miracle that I managed it without a husband.'

'I didn't know you could take care of yourself. Forgive me.'

Sofia imagined that was the best thanks she would get from the proud old man, but she was wrong.

'I have news of your friend,' he said softly.

'Arik?'

'The queen blamed him for your escape – not without cause, I suppose. He was beheaded. Be glad he died before she discovered you had turned her son against her too. She would have tortured him most cruelly.'

Sofia looked at him in silence.

He saw reproach in her eyes. 'What should I have done? Protested, and shared his fate? I have my own children to look after and I will do whatever it takes to make sure the Napthtali are welcome in this land.'

'Even be a slave for that witch.'

'Even that,' he said coldly. 'I let you speak to me so because your grief is fresh. I too grieve to see the sons of Uriah brought low, but they both made poor choices.'

'Arik had no choice!'

'Perhaps not. Perhaps others are equally constrained. You might remember that before you call me a slave again.' He looked back at the Sicarii. 'Now what?'

She shook herself to attention. 'We will not detain you. The alliance you offered Yūsuf—'

'—a ruse to lure a fool.'

'Obviously. What if it wasn't? Together we could be a real threat to the Oltremarines,' she said. 'While Catrina sits on her throne there can be no peace.'

'Peace is a flower, and few grow in the desert. I have no interest in childish dreams, or in helping you get revenge. Still, I am pleased the Sicarii have found a better leader.'

'I'm not their leader,' she said, handing him back his blade.

He took it with a bow. 'If you say so. I shall await word of your exploits, Princess.'

'I shall endeavour to make them newsworthy.'

As he rode away, she walked back slowly to the bemused Sicarii. They were preparing to leave – all but Yūsuf.

'You let him get away?' he squawked. 'The ransom we might have had!'

'Sicarii don't prey on Ebionites any more.'

'Who are you to say what the Sicarii do and do not?'

Sofia ignored him and addressed the rest. 'Does the darkness terrify you? Where are you scurrying, Sicarii?'

'Home,' said Bakhbukh. 'The hour is late.'

'So it is. We must act accordingly. You saw how Mik la Nan trussed up your nasi like a calf. Even as you hung back and let a woman fight for your honour, you must have heard his laughter. We won't be taken seriously until we show we *are* serious. I mean to take that kerak.'

'Impossible,' said Yūsuf.

'I come from a city of towers, the smallest of which would dwarf that pile. I can scale those walls.'

'A keen strategist you are,' he mocked. 'You'd risk these men to capture a pile of rocks on a hill. And if you succeed, what would it profit us?'

'Its cistern is deep,' Bakhbukh remarked. 'There's that.'

'It's an Akkan boot on Ebionite necks,' Sofia said hotly.

Bakhbukh sighed deeply. 'Contessa, Yūsuf is right. You're asking us to be party to self-slaughter. Even if you climb like a lizard, you will surely be noticed.'

'Then your slings must pick them off faster.'

'And when you reach the top, how will you hold off an entire Lazar battalion?'

'I need only take out the night watch and let down a rope. Enough talk. Come if you're coming.' With that, she turned her back and stalked off.

The Sicarii looked at one another doubtfully. 'At last,' said Yūsuf, glowing with vindication, 'you can all see the manner of lunatic she is.'

The Guiscard flag hung limply from the battlements, weakly illuminated by a brazier, around which the night watch were gathered. Sofia prayed they were sharing a bottle too.

The tower seemed to grow organically from the rocks, but this was an illusion created by the glacis, a man-made slope created to ensure no besieging force could make use of any blind spots. For a Rasenneisi, it provided a handy platform to sprint up. It was more recent than the tower itself, and its clean masonry afforded little purchase, but she reached the curving walls before gravity reasserted itself.

She'd persuaded the Sicarii with her confidence, but the truth was she had not climbed in an age. Still, there is nothing as inspiring as mortal danger, and she was soon close enough to the parapet to hear the soldiers' lethargic muttering. They had little reason to be on high alert; siege-craft held little appeal for the tribes, whose idea of war was a sandstorm: sudden, unstoppable, and soon over.

This was no time to begin doubting herself, but still she wondered, if she was spotted now, could the Sicarii slings protect her? It was dark, and they might as easily strike armour.

Someone approached the edge, humming a ditty, and she swung herself underneath a section of battlement projecting further than the rest and held her breath. The soldier vomited casually over the side, then returned to the fire and teasing voices. Sofia found herself looking up into the top storey of the tower through a machicolation on the underside of the battlement. She hauled herself up for a better look, then dropped back down. There were two knights absorbed in dice; the older one's hoarse laughter suggested that he was winning. The machicolation was narrow, designed for dropping stones or burning oil on attackers, but Sofia was slender enough to squeeze through.

She started to count to three – but on *two*, one of the bricks she was hanging from came loose—

Sofia gripped her surviving handhold fiercely and felt around with her toes until she found a putlog hole. With relief she secured herself, then looked up, searching for her next handhold – and found a Lazar helmet staring down at her through the hole in the battlement. She threw the brick at it, then leaped up and wrapped both arms around his neck before he could recover, before scrabbling over his body and pulling him down into the hole even as she rose.

The other Lazar knight was still hunkered over his dice, looking on incredulously, shocked into stillness. Suddenly the one she had climbed over gripped her foot in his desperate efforts not to fall. Sofia turned and snatched the axe from the motionless Lazar's belt and raised it as though she were going to sever the fingers grasping her ankle. The man released his grip – and screamed all the way down to the ground. Before the rock silenced him, Sofia had turned and hurled the axe at the second knight. She didn't have time to aim; she prayed he hadn't moved yet.

He hadn't.

She pulled the heavy table on which they'd been dicing over the trapdoor to stop anyone coming up from below before pulling the axe out of the older Lazar's skull. Then, without daring to pause lest her nerve fail, she climbed the ladder to the battlements.

As she flung open the upper trapdoor, an axe struck it. She leaped back, hurled her own axe and hit nothing, but managed to survey her opponents: there were four of them, and they were backing away, obviously assuming she had company. A moment passed before they realised she was alone, but those seconds were all Sofia needed. Before they could rush her, she leaped for the brazier and knocked it into them. Sparks and cinders went everywhere. One of the knights caught the full impact and fell, already burning, over the side. While the one in the middle danced about, trying to bat out his flaming cloak, the other two hurled their light axes at Sofia. She avoided the first by ducking, and the second passed her by and slammed into the base of the flagpole.

She leaped up, in between the crenellations, and reached for the flagpole. Bracing the base of it with her foot, she pulled it sharply towards her – and it snapped, the sudden release making her lose balance and fall. She rolled over and got to her feet, already testing the weapon in her hand. The spilled fire divided the circle between them. Just as the middle knight succeeded in putting out his burning cloak, a stone struck the exposed flesh at the back of his neck and he dropped with a dismal groan. The other two leaped back in alarm.

Seeing her chance, Sofia leaped over the flames . . .

They didn't stand a chance.

Only when they had all gone over the edge did Sofia notice her flag had caught fire. Rather than throwing it aside, she leaped back up onto the crenellations and waved it wildly, as if to ward off the night's darkness, screaming, '*Avanti! Avanti!*'

The word might have meant nothing to the Ebionites, but they knew what courage was.

When dawn came, the kerak was in Sicarii hands. The victorious warriors prostrated themselves, facing south, and prayed, while Sofia watched them with frank envy. These were people for whom doubt was impossible. The adrenalin from the fight was ebbing now, and she marvelled at the danger she had thrown herself into. In her desire to revenge Arik, had she forgotten Iscanno?

No; it was just that her heart had always been quicker than her mind. She had felt it before, but she had only begun to understand when she heard about Arik's death: this wasn't a fight she was beginning. It was a war in which she must succeed, or die. And to win it, all of her – her *experience*, her *skill*, her *passion*, her *faith* – was required. It was a terrible vocation, but somehow it didn't daunt her; perhaps it was easier to give oneself wholeheartedly to a cause in strange climes? Here in the desert there was poverty, pain and privations aplenty, but there was also perfect freedom.

Take it, a voice within her urged.

Old Bakhbukh saw her and bounded over, crying exultantly, 'Join us, Contessa!'

'It wouldn't be right. I am Marian.'

'Words are hollow things. You feel the sun's heat, don't you? Then your erroneous theology is irrelevant, and it is egoism to think your prejudices matter. What you believe counts not a fig compared to what you *do*. Come, pray with us.'

Bakhbukh led and as she added her voice to the responses, she considered why of all the world's women, God had chosen her. There was no lack of virginal nuns in the world – but He hadn't chosen someone tender and mild. Instead, he chose an impious brawler, and a Rasenneisi to boot, the most quarrelsome race in Etruria. Such was the tool He needed: a soldier, not a saint, and one who could bear His son and raise an army to protect him. This was the Handmaid the times called for.

Afterwards, while Yūsuf and the rest plundered the kerak, she and Bakhbukh sat looking south.

'No offence, but why do you pray facing Jerusalem?' she asked. 'It didn't exactly make me fall to my knees in awe when I saw it.'

He laughed. 'What you saw was just a rock. You cannot *see* Jerusalem – it is not a city, it is wherever God is. And He is restless. Tomorrow we will face east.'

Sofia looked south a while, remembering the abandoned city and the Jinn that swarmed restlessly over it.

'Somewhere out there,' said Bakhbukh, 'a lunatic preacher is wandering the land. His madness affords him protection, for no one other could wander the land unarmed and live long. A moon ago, he predicted rain, and he was mocked by all the nesi'im for it. They said he was stirring up the tribes to folly, but when the rains came, even they began to listen. I heard him myself and I believe he is a holy man – as well as a lunatic. It is conventional for preachers to call themselves John the Baptist or Elijah, but he says he is the one who knows the old names – the *true* names.

The Old Man defeated the army of Gog some forty years ago, so that would make him a veritable Methuselah.'

'But what does he preach?'

'He says the Prophetess has returned to free her people.' He turned to her. 'They will say you are She, you do know that, don't you?'

'Then he must be mad.'

'The Prophetess returned in the body of an infidel!' He laughed at the absurdity. 'I can't wait to hear the Rabbis explain that!' When Bakhbukh saw her grave face, he apologised. 'I meant no offence.'

'I know, but there's something you must know: Arik ben Uriah is dead.'

He turned suddenly cold. 'What is that to me?'

'Are you not Issachar?' She had been with the Sicarii long enough to know the question was more than impolite; the bandits' code of *omerta* meant they never enquired into or mentioned each other's origins. It was the only way that men whose tribes were feuding might live together.

With an abrupt sag of his shoulders, Bakhbukh's frigid dignity departed, leaving only a sad old man. 'I was Uriah ben Sinan's counsellor – the one who advised him to take the queen's peace offer seriously.'

Sofia knew she ought to leave it there. But . . . 'That was foolish.'

He looked at her a while. 'I remember my arguments very well. I told Uriah that the Akkans had long since ceased to be invaders – they acted just like a tribe, demanding tribute, throwing around their weight. I told him that the tribes quarrel ceaselessly, but peace is possible when both sides perceive their own weakness. The Akkans could continue to act belligerently in this land as long as regular reinforcements kept coming from their motherland – but Crusade died a generation ago. I told him – and I truly believed this – that the queen had finally realised that *this* was her home, so she must treat us not as adversaries but neighbours. I was wrong. Uriah's death and what happened subsequently to the Issachar' – he threw a handful of sand in the air – 'was my fault.'

'More foolishness. The queen is to blame.'

He was too proud to agree. 'Only a fool blames a snake for biting his heel. I was Uriah's counsellor, and it was my responsibility to see beyond stratagems, to argue convincingly. Alas, I was capable only of the latter. Yūsuf is foolhardy and vain, but after I failed his father, how could I abandon him?'

'You abandoned Arik readily enough.'

'He abandoned his own people!'

'Because Yūsuf was preparing to kill him.'

'Better that than the shame of serving the one who killed his father.' Bakhbukh rose stiffly. 'I am sorry that Arik died an outcast, but it was in accordance with the Law.'

CHAPTER 15

The Doc had taught Sofia how to handle the flag. His patient way of unravelling foes was another lesson, and one she now drew upon to devise arguments to convince the Sicarii that they had the means to defeat Catrina's tyranny.

Yūsuf, ensconced once more in his fireside throne, was back to his old self. 'God gave us a great victory, but He does not suffer wilful fools.'

'That was not a "great victory". It was a good start.'

'Any nasi foolish enough to attack the cities of the *franj* has destroyed himself along with his people,' said Bakhbukh sullenly.

'I don't propose storming Akka.'

'What then?'

'Cut their hamstrings. Make overland trade impossible,' she said. 'Cut their cities off from each other as completely as they've separated the tribes—'

Yūsuf slapped his thigh theatrically. 'She is brave, but she remains a foreigner, does she not?' He gestured up to the shelf where Jabari and the other children were listening raptly to the adults' debate. 'These dreams might sway the young ones, Contessa, but this is a council of men. What separated the tribes is the tribesmen. You cannot bat your eyelashes and unite us.'

'Not yet I can't. First we must make the name Sicarii glorious again.'

Bakhbukh chuckled. 'I wondered why you did not let Mik la Nan get crushed. You want his help.'

'The Napthtali are big enough to start an inter-tribal war – or they can be the core around which our army is formed.'

'That scoundrel will not be swayed by patriotism,' Yūsuf assured her.

'What about glory, then?'

Yūsuf glared at the thoughtful faces around the fire. 'Are you being taken in by this sorcerous witch? Unity is a children's tale – a rallying cry, nothing more.'

'I come from a country where the people considered unity a base coin. Now they are slaves, united in bondage. They call us homeless beggars, but that is to our advantage, is it not? Catrina must defend her cities, her forts, her convoys – what have we to defend? Rocks? She hides behind fragile walls. The limitless Sands conceal us. We can be like the Jinn and fly on the desert winds.'

Early morning, and the main cave was empty. Sofia was sitting on the shelf with Jabari, now her constant companion, and the other children, watching the last lazy wisp from the extinguished fire and thinking about the tales Bakhbukh had told last night. The debate had prompted him to recite the story of how the Old Man of the Mountain had almost beaten the *franj*, and how, when a greater threat threatened to destroy the land, he forged an alliance with the *franj* to save it.

Her ruminations were disturbed by Jabari tugging at her sleeve. He pointed to a furtive pair of hands clambering for a grip on the edge of their perch, and she recoiled when Yūsuf's bearded face appeared.

'May I join you?'

'By all means,' she said, quickly covering her breast. She had no inhibitions around the others, but the unworldly piety Yūsuf affected made her uneasy.

'What a pleasant nest you've built! A woman's touch can work such wonders.'

Jabari glared at Yusuf like a cornered cat.

'Boy, you're being a nuisance to our guest.' Yūsuf was still at pains to pretend that Sofia was here by his permission. 'Go and play.'

Jabari waited for Sofia's nodded assent before he left the perch.

Yūsuf watched him go benevolently, then turned to her. 'Jabari's father was a fisherman. The drought that swallowed Galilee took him too. We discovered the lad nursing the corpse of his baby brother and took him under our wing.' He smiled. 'You see, we are not total jackals.'

Sofia nodded noncommittally. She had heard a different version from Jabari.

'I came to say all's ready. We ride out in an hour.'

'You're still sceptical about my strategy.'

'I don't doubt your sincerity.' He made a face. 'You seek to hurt the *franj* by hurting their property. It's hard for me to know if it'll work for I myself care nothing for material possessions.'

Yūsuf's appetite for loot was no secret; it was as fierce as any condottiere's. But Sofia played along. 'What would you suggest?'

'No tribe can hope to breach Akka's walls, but one Sicarii with a knife can enter the city at will. Send a new knife every night, each with a new target.'

'Such tactics would only make the Small People rally round the throne. I want to isolate Catrina.'

'Yes, and you want to unite the tribes!' Yūsuf scoffed. 'I tell you it would be easier to herd the Gaderene swine.'

'The Old Man did it.'

'The Old Man had no tribe. He came from nowhere and disappeared without a trace. Don't believe Bakhbukh's bedtime stories – trust me, he sometimes gets it wrong.'

'Time will tell.'

Yūsuf let Iscanno tug his beard for a while, then said casually,

'Tell me, Contessa: how *did* you and this fine fellow survive the Sands?'

'I knew one who knew the Sands as mariners know the sea. He taught me your language too.'

'One of the Sown?'

After Bakhbukh's reaction Sofia had decided that it was probably best not to mention Arik, but the desire to wipe away Yūsuf's cloying smile was overwhelming. 'Your brother,' she said softly.

'I have no brothers,' he stammered.

'You did your best to see to that, and finally it's true. Arik's dead.'

He gawped, visibly grief-stricken, before pride reasserted itself and he growled, 'So perish traitors.'

'He was fighting to survive, as you are doing.'

'I fight to restore the Radinate and I live like a beggar to do so, while that traitor grew fat at the queen's tit.' He slipped off the shelf, muttering, 'Be ready, or we leave without you.'

Sofia stayed her tongue as he walked out. Telling him that his men would not leave without her might be the truth, but Yūsuf probably wasn't ready for that.

The Akkan convoy trundled through the spare expanse of the Jezreel Valley, riding in an almost square formation of six rows of five – long trails presented too tempting a target to those always watching in the hills. Their dust cloud trailed immensely behind them. Their destination was deep in the Wilderness of Paran, far to the south, and their path was obstructed by a ridge of Mount Carmel jutting inland. There were other, more roundabout routes, but the Wadi Aruna which sliced through the ridge was the most direct. In ordinary times they might not have risked it, but they had a long journey ahead of them and they needed to make haste.

As the cliff's shadow fell across the first caravan, shrill cries made them all look up, then over their shoulders.

The bandits came pouring down the side of the foothills, mounted on camels and screaming, '*Illa – illa – illa!*'

There was no room to turn back, nor any point in doing so, nor had they time to count how many bandits were behind them – but it hardly mattered. They were on their own, and their best chance was to get deep into the wadi and find a narrow pass at which they could make their stand.

The Sicarii were not about to let such a rich prize escape. Soon they were riding alongside the convoy, their slings spinning – then suddenly the caravans slowed and parted, revealing what was concealed in the centre: a troop of mounted Lazars.

'Every man for himself,' cried Sofia, and the Sicarii took fright and scattered into the wadi's depths.

Basilius, gleeful that his ruse had worked, led the chase, crying, 'Follow me, Lazars!' even as a hefty stone from a sling bounced ineffectually off his armour.

The wadi divided, and though some of the Sicarii went straight, the majority veered left, closely followed by Basilius, who found himself riding though a steep, narrow ravine. Just as he started to get claustrophobic, the ravine opened out into a large arena-like space. His men, following close behind, watched in amazement as the Sicarii abandoned their camels and started clambering up the sides of the cliffs on ropes lowered from each side.

Basilius chortled and whipped out his throwing axes. 'Target practise, lads,' he called.

As his men's laughter echoed through the arena, Basilius noticed something uncanny: the space was dotted with five immense circles of lush grass. The abandoned Sicarii camels had also noticed, and the Grand Master's glow of triumph faded in an instant.

As the animals crossed onto the grass, each circle buckled and transformed into a sinking vortex. Where the grass and horses vanished, spindly plant limbs exploded and Basilius watched, frozen with fear, as one of his men was lifted from his saddle by two tendrils and pulled apart before his eyes. Persuaded that it was wise to be elsewhere, Basilius whipped his horse into a gallop. He guessed the way behind would be blocked by Sicarii bandits – he didn't even bother to look behind to confirm that, or to see if any of his men were following him. Most of them weren't: they were ripped to pieces or swallowed before they had begun to realise the horrific threat they were facing.

Only a handful of Lazars managed to brave the flailing forest of death and survive to tell the tale in Akka.

The driver's nose was bloodied, but he did not flinch. 'I was simply providing for my family.'

Sofia and her gang were still aloft, waiting till the ground was stable before descending to join the rest of the Sicarii who were already busy stripping the caravans, hooting joyously as they smashed barrels of the prohibited wine, drunk on vainglory. Bakhbukh sat watching uneasily. Yūsuf had evidently sampled some of the loot and was simply drunk.

'I did not ask for your justifications.' He tapped his riding stick against his leg, irritated by the man's bravery. 'I asked if you took silver from those who make an idol of the Prophetess. The question is simple. Yes or no?'

'I don't understand politics, master.'

Yūsuf said sympathetically, 'That is irrelevant. Your actions have ramifications, whether you committed them in ignorance or not. I am the leader of the Sicarii – the renewer of the Radinate – and so I am burdened with terrible responsibility. I have one final question for you: which hand committed this crime against God's people?'

The prisoner made a half-hearted attempt to bolt, but Zayid held him down as Yūsuf, trembling with righteous anger, cried,

'Tell me which hand or I'll take both – and your family will suffer the same fate!'

'I need both to work, master! If I cannot do my job, my family will starve. I'll give you anything—'

'Anything I want, I'll take. Choose!'

The man broke down and proffered his shaking right hand.

'What is this?' Sofia was covered in dust from the chase and weary from the climb.

'A trial.'

'He's a driver. That's no crime. Set him free.'

When Zayid dropped his sword, Yūsuf barked, 'Pick that up. They are collaborators.'

As greatly as the Sicarii loved plunder, they loved argumentation more, and raised voices drew them like molasses draws flies.

'So you've already passed sentence?' Sofia said scornfully. 'Some trial.' Then, so that everyone could hear, she said, 'Akka and all the Oltremarine cities are full of Ebionites who survive by working with the *franj*. Will you punish them too?'

'If they are guilty – yes!'

'Then you're a fool.' She glowered at Zayid until he released the driver. She helped him stand, then turned back to Yūsuf, 'I've known people like you all my life: always making examples of other people, never being one. I was that way once, until someone taught me better.'

'It *is* the Law, Contessa.'

'Bakhbukh, punish this man and you persuade ten like him to seek Catrina's protection. Pardon him, and you recruit his family and friends. We have an army of potential allies in the cities of Oltremare. Give Catrina sleepless nights and she'll drive them to us with her cruelty. This is how we'll win.'

'The Law is the Law,' Yūsuf repeated.

Bakhbukh looked between Yūsuf and Sofia, and sighed. 'Then the Law . . . is wrong.'

Yūsuf threw down his knife in disgust and stalked off.

Sofia turned to the driver. 'Who do you work for?'

'Baron Masoir.'

'Don't lie to me, fellow. I saved your life.'

'It's true, I swear! His widow, Melisende Ibelin, is running the business since Masoir was—' He stopped and cast a wary look at Bakhbukh and the other Sicarii, then said simply, 'Since the baron died.'

'I want you to relay a message to your mistress, my friend. Tell her that Baron Masoir was not killed by Sicarii. Tell her that as long as Catrina sits on the throne, no caravan from Akka will be safe. Tell her it's time to choose.'

The caravans had been picked clean and the Sicarii were mounting up on their reserve mounts when Yūsuf returned and announced, 'I have meditated and communed with God and I have decided that the Contessa is correct: for the time being we must bend in order to win the people to our righteous cause. When we have Akka – then will be the time to ensure that the Law is observed with due rigour.'

After allowing the embarrassed silence to continue for an agonised minute, Sofia said, 'Thou art most sage, O Nasi,' and tapped her camel forward.

As the Sicarii followed her, Yūsuf wondered whether he'd just won or lost.

CHAPTER 16

Half a dozen younger Lazars had gathered outside the door of the throne room to eavesdrop on their beloved Grand Master being on the receiving end of a verbal evisceration for once.

'A fool: that's what I look like. I look like *you*, Grand Master. Is that acceptable?'

'If I may say in my defence—'

'You may *not*. This isn't the Haute Cour. I want no more silly adventures. Find out where they are.'

'With respect, the Sicarii lairs have been secret for years—'

'We have thousands of Ebionites in Akka. Someone must know something. Get out there and encourage them to be good citizens. Well? What're you waiting for?'

'About the – your – the prisoner's sentencing,' Basilius stuttered. 'Have you set a date?'

The patriarch looked on, secretly amused at the Grand Master's blundering. As long as Fulk lived, Basilius could not feel secure in his position, but in his anxiety he quite failed to appreciate the queen's dilemma. Traitor or no, Fulk remained a Guiscard. Killing Guiscards was not unprecedented, but it was not something to which she wished her subjects to grow accustomed.

'When I do, Grand Master, you'll be the first to know – now *get out*! What the devil you smiling at, Chrysoberges?'

'Forgive me – a nervous twitch. You do know that if this disruption continues, Majesty, we won't be able to celebrate All Souls?'

'As you value your head, *never* say that again. That is the debt we owe our ancestors and I will not betray my subjects – the living *or* the dead.'

'Of course, forgive me,' he said quickly. 'It's just that – if you will permit me to observe – the new Grand Master lacks Fulk's guile.'

'I told you never to mention that name again.'

Basilius was missing more than that, and they both knew it. Some of the longer-serving brothers had deeper scars too, wounds that left them as hollow as the Empty Quarter; these strange ones rallied round the new Grand Master.

'What the Grand Master lacks is *men*. We need an army capable of finishing the job. What of my uncle's successor? This base-born charioteer chap?'

'By all accounts Prince Jorge secured the Purple Throne with surprisingly little red. The question is: will he come if you send for him?'

'He is my vassal,' she said crossly.

'It pleases the Byzantines' vanity to claim to be part of our holy enterprise. They recognise our lordship because it costs them nothing to do so. Whether and what they will pay for that privilege is a question—'

'You and your endless questions. Let me pose you this: is Akka not the first city of Oltremare? Am I not its queen? I well remember the mace's weight when first I took it up. This little prince will come when I call and he'll help me crush this rabble. Then we'll give Akka a Day of the Dead for the ages.'

As attacks on Akka's trade caravans escalated, the merchants petitioned the throne for protection. They argued that it was the queen's duty to keep the trade-routes safe – what else were they paying taxes for? Catrina duly committed her Lazars to guarding the convoys, but in return she demanded a larger percentage of their profits. Some initially baulked at this opportunistic extortion, but when their caravans returned empty – or failed to return at all – they bowed to the inevitable.

Just as Sofia had intended, the Lazars' new duties meant their attention was divided and the merchants' operating costs were increasing almost weekly. She changed the Sicarii's focus to the keraks. Swift communication between the forts had always been one of their strengths, but now it became a weakness as the news of one successful Sicarii strike followed hard on the heels of another. Sofia kept up the tension by sending scouts in several directions each day, so that each garrison became certain they were next. When darkness fell, the Sicarii filled the hills with noises, so the whole garrison would pass the night in a state of high alert, every eye fixed on the Sands. A week of sleepless nights made the men worthless when the real attack finally came.

As they took kerak after kerak, Sofia came to know the men she fought with, and they her. The Sicarii trusted this strange queen come amongst them more than they ever would an Ebionite woman, though it was not Sofia's martial prowess or her beauty that created this confidence. It was Iscanno. No singing angels surrounded his manger and no halo surrounded his smiling face. His laugh was sweet – but all babies' laughs are sweet. It was love, and it emanated from him like warmth from a forge. The homesick looked at him and remembered home. The guilt-ridden heard his gurgle and remembered that they were once innocent. In a cruel world, perfect virtue is priceless. Sofia's boy-child was a prodigy of love, and his mastery grew day by day until the cave of the assassins positively glowed with it.

For years the other tribes had treated the Sicarii as pests, like the jackals or the east winds, but mostly they ignored them because they made themselves a nuisance primarily to the *franj*. They could not, however ignore the circle of black towers surrounding Akka and no longer in Lazar hands. The Zebulun were the first tribe to seek alliance. They hated the queen as much as any, but the real draw was the booty the Sicarii were winning. The Zebulun, though famous metalworkers, were not numerous, but it was a good start.

One day a strange hawk shadowed them as they returned from a raid. Bakhbukh lured it down, and found a message attached to its leg.

'The Benjaminites want to talk,' he announced.

'What they want is our spoils. Where were they when—?'

'Yūsuf,' said Bakhbukh, 'I understand that you're wary after Mik la Nan's trickery, but things are different now. The Old Man is currently under the protection of the Benjaminites – it is he who has advised their nasi to join us.'

'Nothing has changed,' said Yūsuf haughtily. 'We are still the vanguard of the Radinate.'

'You've smothered that flame trying to protect it.' Sofia's patience with his pretensions was exhausted. 'We've had it easy so far, but the Akkans won't lie back while we ruin their livelihoods. I'm not looking for martyrdom. Of course we must enlist the other tribes. Tell them we will come, Bakhbukh.'

Bakhbukh would once have spent hours trying to change Yūsuf's mind – now he simply did as Sofia instructed.

A hundred unfriendly eyes followed Bakhbukh, Yūsuf and Sofia as they walked through the camp towards the great tent of Roe de Nail, nasi of the Benjaminite tribe. They lived in the shadow of Mount Gerizim, and their territory was Samaria, south of the badlands – the reason for their conflict with the migrating Naphtali.

Bakhbukh pointed to the overlooking cliffs. 'Up there, Contessa, is the Cave of the Old Man.'

Yūsuf said mockingly, 'Every rabbit hole in this land claims some association with the Old Man. He would have had to have lived three hundred years and been exceedingly fond of travel to have spent a single night in even half of them.'

Roe de Nail did not rise from his pillow to greet them. He was rotund and soft-skinned, and his silks were as fine as those that adorned his fifty wives. 'We have heard tell of your exploits, Contessa, but you must not assume the Benjaminites are unskilled in war,' he said, and indicated his scimitar. 'Here is my famous blade. It has killed fifty-seven men – nineteen Gad, five Issachar and one Zebulun, and the rest Napthtali.'

Sofia believed the inventory, but not that he'd been wielding it at the time. 'Any Akkans?'

'Oh, I do not count the infidels. I know what you are thinking: why is such a warrior willing to join our little rebellion? I will tell you that when I heard of you stirring up the sand like a Jinni my first instinct was to hunt you down, but the Old Man advised me otherwise.'

Sofia could see Roe de Nail was immensely proud to have the preacher under his protection.

'He says a great change is at hand, and that all the faithful should lend their strength to it. The Napthtali dogs have not approached you? I'm not surprised. They are an impious lot, interested only in stealing land.'

'They are no different from any tribe,' said Bakhbukh, irritated by the nasi's pomposity. 'Did not the Benjaminites come from the Ein Gedi? Was it not once Benjaminites doing the displacing?'

Despite Roe de Nail's bluster, his men could certainly fight. As the tribal coalition numbers swelled, so their reach expanded. Sofia's ultimate ambition was to attract the Napthtali, and after each successful raid she waited for an embassy, growing more and more frustrated when none came.

Finally she concluded that they must do something Mik la Nan could not ignore.

The Kerak Malregard was the closest to Akka they had ventured. It was on a different scale to any of the keraks they had tackled hitherto. It had a large garrison, and stores to feed them – oil tanks and water cisterns, grain, and a windmill to grind it. If any tribe ever had the audacity – or the technical wherewithal – to attempt to besiege it, its dual walls provided multiple firing positions to make life very unpleasant for those trying to get in.

Although Bakhbukh cautioned that it was premature, he still went along with Sofia's plan. Yūsuf took part for different reasons. He was painfully conscious that the more successful raids Sofia led, the more his authority dwindled.

The men of the Zebulun let their torches in the hills be seen, their commotion designed to draw the attention of the sentries while the Sicarii scaled the eastern wall. While Bakhbukh and Zayid silently dispatched the guards who stayed at their posts, Sofia and Yūsuf threw ropes across the void to the inner wall, then covered them while two of their Sicarii climbed across. Meanwhile, the Benjaminites launched an oil-pot attack on the western gate.

All was going to plan until the Sicarii reached the top of the wall and found there were no sentries – instead, sitting at their ease and watching them, was a Napthtali tribesman – one of the pair Sofia had last seen in Akka's Haute Cour.

'Put your dagger away, Contessa. The Cat begs an audience with you.'

Yūsuf, Bakhbukh and Zayid followed Sofia down the stairway to the bailey. Mik la Nan's men lined the walls of the courtyard, cradling armfuls of booty. Sofia had often seen the Sicarii in a similar state after a victory: some were sleeping, some boasting and some were affecting indifference to their fresh wounds while determinedly chewing wads of khat.

The Cat stood in the centre, dividing up the spoils – food and carpets, and arms – while the things they had no use for were thrown into a pile, to burn with the defenders' bodies.

After Mik la Nan put a torch to the great pile, he turned to

Sofia and presented her with a silk scarf. 'Contessa – this would make a splendid veil.'

'Too bad I don't need one. Are you ready to join us?'

'I took the kerak for two reasons,' he said calmly. 'To show the Sands I am not afraid of the *franj* either, and to persuade you of your folly.'

'The queen's using you, Mik la Nan.'

'I prefer to have no master, but I am a reasonable man. When the Winds chased me here I understood I must either find some accommodation with her or fight her. I chose the former because she is too powerful. For you, it's different. You are a stranger in this land. The tribe that follows you is no tribe at all.'

'I lead the Sicarii,' Yūsuf protested, 'and they are the vanguard of the Radinate—'

'I have nothing against thievery; it's an honest living,' said the Cat, 'but hypocrisy I cannot abide.' He turned back to Sofia. 'You have nothing to lose, but I am father to the Napthtali. Of course I will raid Catrina's caravans, just as I raid the other tribes, but what you want, Contessa, is war.'

'Do you shrink from it?'

'You are too thin, Contessa, but tolerably pretty for a *franj*. These boys will do anything to prove their bravery to a fair maiden, but I am old and such games will not work on me. My dear, I do not shrink from suicide, I run from it. In a hundred years, we could not challenge Akka.'

Sofia had spent enough hours in the Palazzo dei Signori to know the sound of a man who does not believe his own arguments. The Cat really wanted her to persuade the doubters in his tribe. 'I have no quarrel with the Akkans,' she said. 'The queen has many enemies within the city. If we show them she is weak, they'll kill her for us.'

'Or she'll kill them first – she has a gift for smelling out disloyalty, and much practise. And even if you are successful, what would we have gained?'

'A life better than mere survival. There are some in Akka who know they can profit by working with the tribes, but Catrina means only to grind you down' – Sofia picked up a handful of sand – 'to *this*.' She held her fist and let it drain, speaking loud enough for all the Napthtali to hear. 'Tell me that is not so, you who have looked her in the eye.'

The Cat could not deny it. 'Even if the Napthtali joined with you, our combined strength would still be insufficient. We would need the Gad too, but the Gad will not fight with the Benjaminites, and my Napthtali will not fight with the Gad.'

'Your quarrels are hurting the Ebionites.'

'I said *I* am reasonable. I never claimed my people were.'

'With your quarrels, you hand the queen the stick to beat you. No sooner did you enter the Sands than she sought to exacerbate the feud between you and the Gad.'

'That is not Sicarii business,' the Cat growled. 'Be careful, Contessa. Even Catrina knows better than to get involved with Ebionite matters.'

'Is that what you do when a fight erupts between two Naphtali? Stand aside?'

'No. I settle it.'

'Why do they listen to you? It's none of your business.'

'They listen because I am their nasi,' he said with kingly resolution, 'but alas, no man has the authority to make peace between nesi'im.'

Bakhbukh had been listening to the fractious exchange with growing despair, but at these words he suddenly perked up. 'There is one.'

CHAPTER 17

The charge that the Crusaders who captured Byzant – home to a hundred peoples and the best part of the world's wealth – were themselves captured by its court, is not without foundation. While Byzant's new princes kept the mob amused with races, the same old bureaucrats ensured that continuity prevailed. Oltremare's territory had never been greater, but its poles pulled apart. When Akka lost Jerusalem, its claim to pre-eminence over Byzant lost all credibility.

Byzant, a Study in Purple
by Count Titus Tremellius Pomptinus

The streets were thronged as if it were a Holy Day, and the clackers of Akka made rickety ovation to welcome the Byzantines. The army's large square banner was the richest Tyrian purple and its sharp streamers coiled like a nest of serpents. The two-headed eagle threaded in gold came alive as it bellied with a rare breath of fresh wind from the Sea of Filth. The Northerners carried their long kite-shaped shields over their shoulders. Their armour incorporated jointed metal scales and padded leather, and the coloured sashes revealed rank; those of the high officers were threaded with golden script. Many concealed their faces in ring-mail – but not young Prince Jorge. The Byzantine autokrator drove the quadriga with such ease that most onlookers did not recognise the skill required to control four feisty horses at once.

Although Akka was nominally Oltremare's imperial capital, it had long ceased to think of itself as such: everything that mattered came from Byzant, and everyone: politicians, actors, orators, and of course athletes.

Jorge entered the city gates like a conqueror, hardly slowing despite the pressing throng that roared his praise. He scattered coins and stopped to kiss children and women young and old. He knew how to delight them, and he left them wanting more as he cracked his whip and flew off to cries of, 'Jorge! Prince Jorge!'

Most men who came to the Purple Throne were strangers to all but the queen and a few chosen courtiers. Prince Jorge, however, had been famous throughout Oltremare long before his accession. He made a quick circuit of the city, going down to the docks then through the packed bazaar, diving through the narrow streets with abandon, to the applause of the Sown and poor Marians alike, cheering him from the upper storeys of the tenements and flinging coloured paper and rice. The beggars roared their approval even as they dived out of the way. Finally he circled the citadel and came to a stop in the palace courtyard.

Only then did the jostling courtiers get a proper look at him. As he leaped down, his long-sleeved vest of metal scales rippled and clanked. The lamellae were made alternately of lacquered iron and gilded bronze. Manikelians – splint armour – wrapped his forearms and legs in protective metal: formidable, but not bulky enough to slow him down. His crown, though handsomely gilded and inlaid with precious gems, was similarly practical: thick enough to withstand a blow, with no vulnerable opening in the centre.

And if his armour failed to deter, his exkoubitores were fierce enough to daunt any would-be assassin.

The autokrator was supposed to remain neutral in the rivalry of the racing teams beloved of the rabble, but Jorge's partisanship was obvious in his lush green cloak fastened at his right shoulder with a gaudy dolphin brooch. The green advertised his affiliation in the hippodrome and the dolphin his success there. If any doubts remained, the golden whip in his belt confirmed that here was an Imperator of the Quadriga as well as the battle-field.

His every gesture revealed energy and enthusiasm, and all remarked on how different the young hero was to the boorish Prince Andronikos, who had come to Akka to browbeat and overthrow his niece. The queen's ladies swooned over Jorge's entourage of young bloods, all, like him, heroes of the tracks, and many of them gamblers too, who'd won their fortunes there. The rumours surrounding Jorge's ascent added an irresistible hint of danger.

Grand Master Basilius and Patriarch Chrysoberges ran to the queen to warn her what to expect. Basilius described the strength of the expeditionary force, while the patriarch breathlessly reported that the young prince had brought an army of bureaucrats too.

'Whatever for, I wonder?' But before Catrina could speculate further, the man himself was announced.

'Queen Catrina, I came as soon as I received your summons.'

'I'm unused to such fidelity in my northern subjects,' the queen said dryly.

There was no chink in the young man's confident smile as he dropped to his knee. 'You shall find me in every respect loyal.'

'Forgive my scepticism, Prince Jorge, but I heard similar protestations from your predecessor.'

'Forgive my boldness, Majesty, but your uncle lacked the essential skill to be a prince.'

Catrina looked amused. 'What skill, pray, is that?'

'How to recognise a queen, of course.'

'How to recognise a queen . . .' She turned to the patriarch. 'I like *that*.' Then she returned her gaze to the prince. 'Tell me, how do you like Akka?'

'Since I was a boy I have heard of its glories.'

She noted the evasion and said only, 'I hope we live up to the stories.'

He smiled blandly. 'I'm here to assist you with this tribal trouble you've been having, but also to make peace between us.'

'Are we at war with Byzant?' She looked askance at the Grand Master. 'I was not aware of this, Grand Master – surely I should have been informed of such a thing?'

Her ladies tittered, but Jorge answered seriously, 'For decades the energy of our two cities has been wasted in futile rivalry. Empires do not fall at once: they bifurcate, then splinter into a thousand shards until there is nothing left but a rabble of warring states where once was a family, happy and united.'

Catrina looked at him speculatively before asking, 'And how do your propose to mend this state of affairs?'

'If you will publicly endorse me, I will recognise Akka's suzerainty over Byzant.'

'*Recognise?*'

There was a sharp intake of breath from the patriarch, and the prince at once corrected himself.

'Excuse me – I meant, of course, *reaffirm.*'

'You ask a lot,' the queen said. 'Remind me: what branch of the Guiscards do you come from?'

'An obscure one,' he answered without embarrassment. 'I was born in the wilds of Thrace, far from the purple. I do not regret my obscurity.'

The queen's curiosity was piqued. 'Why not?'

'Forgive me – I'll say no more.'

'I beg you, Prince Jorge, you've begun wonderfully. Do not fail at this jump.' She gestured around at her court as she added, 'We've too much secrecy in Akka already, so I command you: speak freely.'

His habitual smile reasserted itself. 'How can I disobey such a command? As soon as your late uncle ascended to the throne, he applied the time-honoured medicine to all close relatives. I escaped the catgut only because I was barely considered noble.'

'Ha! So you did not expect to be a prince – what did you expect to be?'

'You must not laugh, but all I ever wanted was to ride . . .'

So began Jorge's tale of his ascendancy to the purple. Besides his ample charm, he was an able storyteller, and like all Thracians, he knew horses. At first he had put that knowledge to use gambling at the chariot races, but before long, he realised he could earn far more actually riding the quadriga through the blood-soaked dust.

'The crowd called me the Prince of Green. They were the first to crown me,' he said modestly. 'They applauded my luck – but the true secret of my success was simply that I was a judge of horseflesh and ran the best stable in the city, I had the pick of the right four horses for any particular day.'

The queen's handmaids were not alone as they listened, rapt, to Jorge's frank confessions, how he'd revelled in the adulation, the taste of strange women, the cold music of silver and gold—

'Alas, winning races is just part of a champion's duties' he said. Since the army was restricted from entering the city, ambitious nobles had to make soldiers of the mob. They pitted the Blue and Green factions against each other and armed them with cudgels and blades. As a champion, Jorge found himself unwillingly dragged into these street-fights. He always did what he had to, but never let himself be carried away with the mob – these were just shadow-battles, after all. Knowing that no matter how good an athlete, he would never be more than a pawn without military standing, he determined to acquire some with the same singleminded resolve that had made him a champion.

He laughed wryly. 'You will be unsurprised to hear, Majesty, that the hippodrome is a playground compared to the army.

Rivalry chokes the ranks. The higher echelons have always been the preserve of the aristocracy, and I fear my popularity with the rabble was, if anything, a discommendation.'

The queen, a little surprised by his candour, gestured for him to continue.

'The Dalmatian March is Byzant's most dangerous frontier, but as that was where Prince Andronikos had made his court, that was where I went. I sold my stable and trophies to buy a posting – though my modest fortune was enough only to make me a kentarchos, a piddling rank, I treated it as a foothold.'

Jorge might have done his duty fighting the interloping Concordians, but courage was common on the March, which meant preferment was as far away as ever – until he realised that the quality that had made his fortune in the hippodrome – judgement – was as rare there as everywhere else. 'Your uncle found organising things a terrific bore and so he was delighted to find someone willing to do it for him. He made me Master of the Camp, in charge of keeping the army fed, armed and battle-ready. There were many more prestigious positions, but none more influential, for every archēgētēs and kentarchos and tourmarchēs relies on the camp master.'

The queen was clearly enjoying herself. 'And when my uncle obligingly got himself killed here—?'

'I was always fast off the mark, Majesty. I called in my debts and rode in strength for Byzant. Two houses, alike in viciousness and ensconced in their respective townhouses, had turned the grand boulevards and piazzas of the Purple City into a battlefield, bringing religious observances, trade, and even the Games to an abrupt halt. Each of the rivals promised to restore order – but that turned out to be something only I could deliver. Faced with my hardened fighters, their respective followings melted away, the church first, then the nobility, and at last sense prevailed.'

He smiled, and at last Catrina could see the young man's back-

bone of steel. 'The rival factions came and begged me for help
– what could I do? Of course I had to be magnanimous, so I bade
them publicly embrace and forswear further in-fighting. When
the mobs in the streets clamoured that I be made a *real* prince,
the bureaucrats that keep Byzant running – they are nothing if
not practical – duly crowned me. I had to think of my people,
first and foremost, and the pain they had suffered . . .'

Which was why Prince Jorge's first act was to put out the eyes
of the rival contenders for the throne, a skilful application of
mercy and cruelty that confirmed their excellent choice to the
Byzantines.

'I can only agree,' said the queen. 'So we're not *that* related. I
can't say I'm heartbroken about that. Family has proved such a
disappointment.'

'I have heard,' said Jorge, discreetly lowering his voice, 'of your
son's infidelity. Unworthy as I am, I offer myself as a replacement.'

'I was blind, as only a mother can be. Alas, his outer corruption was nothing compared to the inner. Your words are some
comfort to my grief. Come, let me embrace you then, as a son.'

The young prince, who had not quailed before the Concordian
cavalry or the rioting mobs in the hippodrome, mastered himself
and rose to his feet. He took her hand and lowered his head to
kiss it, but then paused and sniffed it instead, as if inhaling an
odour of sanctity. Suddenly the queen grabbed the hair at the
back of his head and pulled him towards her. She kissed him,
slowly, ravenously, and Jorge responded, first from chivalrous
duty then from awakened passion. Courtiers looked elsewhere in
mute mortification until finally the patriarch cleared his throat
and the queen broke away.

She broke away with a dejected moan. 'I believe we'll get on
famously, my little prince.'

'I earnestly hope so.' Jorge schooled himself to remain still, not to wipe his mouth. 'While our clerks parse the details of our new affiliation, you must consider me at your service.'

He bowed and left, at the head of his retinue and his exkoubitores, and behind them followed a trail of admirers that had been hovering impatiently outside the throne room.

'The bumptious rogue doesn't just overstep the bounds of decency,' the patriarch complained. 'He *leaps* them! Your grief at your son's treachery is natural, but he preys upon it.'

'I'll consider myself warned,' the queen laughed. 'And you, Grand Master. Do you too disapprove of this gay young knight?'

'He is a base flatterer,' Basilius growled. 'He comes to bolster his position, not help us.'

'Yes – isn't it wonderful?'

When Basilius looked askance, the queen said, 'We're in no position to bolster *anything*, but it's vital that our enemies *and* our allies think we are. If Byzant knew our true weakness, believe me, tradition would not keep them bound to us.'

'He did offer his service,' the patriarch remarked.

'Yes, he did. One that free with promises can never expect them to be taken seriously. We will make what use of him we can, while we can.'

CHAPTER 18

. . . and bribery is not considered disgraceful, but common sense. The Byzantines understand that they are buying time, not loyalty – tribal alliances, even the most successful, rarely last longer than a single campaigning season. The fact that Byzant has weathered centuries proves that setting barbarians against barbarians is a sound policy to prevent encirclement. A favourite tactic is to present one chief with a mansion in the capital and wait for his rivals to petition for similar honours. A barbarian out of the saddle is soon domesticated.

Byzant, a Study in Purple
by Count Titus Tremellius Pomptinus

A long mirror faced Fulk's cell. The queen had it placed there to remind him of his betrayal. He tried not to look at it, but this morning he woke and found a young man standing before it, attentively grooming himself. He looked like he did a lot of that, dressed as he was somewhere between a soldier and a dandy. He spotted Fulk in the reflection and spun around with an open smile.

'Good morning! I apologise for dropping in unannounced. I am—'

'Please. I may be locked in a hole, but I did not grow up here, Prince Jorge. How did you get in here?'

'One of the few boons of fame is that perfect strangers desperately want you to like them. The guard was most obliging.'

'What brings you here?'

'I came to Akka for your mother's blessing,' Jorge answered.

'I mean what you brings you *here*. I should think a famous charioteer could find better company—'

'I seek to know the whereabouts of a man, a Northerner like me who was a member of the Order of Saint Lazarus.'

'You had best ask a Lazar then. I'm a whole man, as you can see.'

'I tried, but the Grand Master says he remembers no Lazar by the name of Stephanos.' He paused to watch Fulk's reaction, then went on, 'but then I gather that Basilius has only recently taken office.' When Fulk remained tight-lipped, Jorge stood up. 'Well, I can see you're very busy. I won't take up any more of your time.'

'He remembers him all right,' Fulk said at last. 'Stephanos was seneschal before Basilius. That was about—'

'Ten years ago,' said Jorge. 'I expect he's dead now.'

Fulk saw the foreigner earnestly wished to be contradicted. 'So you've come all the way from the Purple City? Stephanos used to tell stories about it. He said he'd bring me to see the hippodrome one day. That . . . wasn't to be.'

'He's dead then.'

After Jorge was quiet a spell, Fulk said, 'I can tell you about him if you'd—'

'I'd be very grateful.'

Fulk looked up at the sliver of daylight that was allowed to penetrate his cell. He didn't need to cast his mind back. 'He wasn't born into death like most of us – you know that, of course. So he had to work hard to acquire the skills the rest of us learn from boyhood. He never did master the axe, but he was always an excellent horseman and he built up an impressive stable.'

'A gentle old fellow called Gustav showed it to me – you have some excellent animals, some really splendid form.'

'They're nothing like they were. We were still using heavy Europans when he came. He thought that foolish, since knights no longer wear all the iron they did in the time of Tancred. He introduced lighter, hardier animals, horses with better stamina for the Sands.'

'Ebionite breeds. How did he get their cooperation?

'He was a stranger, and he had no blood-grudges. He knew enough about horses to win the respect of the nesi'im – no easy thing in itself – and he had the tact to keep them happy.' Fulk turned away from the window. 'He taught me many things.'

'What happened?'

'Like I said, he kept the tribes happy. The queen prefers them set against each other and she got her way. I only realised how skilfully Stephanos had kept the peace when I saw how quickly things fell apart. By the time I became Grand Master, the days of tribal councils and talking grievances through were long gone. Bridges take time to build. Burning them can be the work of a day.'

'I meant, what happened to Stephanos?'

'What always happens when someone disagrees with her.'

'I heard,' said Jorge, straining to keep his voice level, 'that a Sicarii assassin killed him.'

Fulk glanced over the neighbouring cells to see if anyone was listening. 'That's the story certainly,' he agreed, his voice lowered. 'But I've hunted Sicarii for years. For all the noise they make, they've never been especially skilful at concealment. Whoever got to Stephanos would have had to get close. He'd never let his guard down to a stranger.'

Jorge took that in silence.

Finally, Fulk asked, 'May I ask how you knew him?'

'I competed against him in the hippodrome.'

'Stephanos was a quadriga racer? I never knew.'

'He taught me everything. I think he liked me because I was a decent judge of form and had my eyes on something bigger than racing, just as he did. He always regretted being born too late for the great Crusade. He said there were no great fights left, just wall-building. Then he contracted leprosy. Before he left for Akka, he said to me, "You don't choose your Crusade, it chooses you."'

In the silence that followed, they remembered their mutual friend. Presently, Jorge unpinned a medal from his chest. 'I've taken many prizes in the hippodrome, but the medal I'm proudest of is the one I won in Dalmatia.'

Fulk caught it and looked at it. It was an eagle with two equally fierce heads.

'Byzant is surrounded by enemies. It had to learn to look east and west at once. Stephanos died because he forgot that.'

Fulk rattled his chains wryly. 'I guess I did too. I won't be here much longer. The queen is queasy about executing family, but she'll let herself be persuaded eventually. Here, take this.' In Fulk's hand beside the medal was a ring. 'Stephanos gave me that when I became a journeyman. He was a good man; I'd like to think there's someone left who remembers his name.'

'I'll remember two good men,' Jorge said. 'Can I give you anything in return?'

'The truth: why did you really come to Akka? You don't need the queen to bless your accession.'

Jorge levelled a hard stare at him. 'My predecessor met his end here. I wanted to know if I need to watch my back.'

'I don't believe that either. You knew Prince Andronikos. A fool like that was always going to get himself killed sooner or later.'

'He was a fool, but it wasn't mere power-lust that made him try to take over Akka. A war is coming – one that will make your disputes with the tribes look like schoolboy quarrels. I don't expect help from Akka, but its weakness is a vulnerability the enemy could exploit. Concord has already tried the Dalmatian March and been rebuffed. The logical next step is to establish a foothold here.'

'So,' said Fulk, 'you're here to study our form.'

CHAPTER 19

Roe de Nail agreed with undignified haste to Bakhbukh's plan: hosting a tribal council in his territory brought prestige to the Benjaminite. The nesi'im of those tribes who had already joined the Sicarii answered the invitation. So did those who had not.

'Intolerable!' Yūsuf exploded. He'd been sulking since he learned that the Sicarii alone were excluded from the Nesi'im Council. 'I start a fire and those scoundrels take credit for it!'

They sat a few yards away from the circle of chieftains, watching, along with those around every other fire, the men who were deciding their fate. 'Tranquillo,' said Sofia, though she would have preferred to be in that war council too. 'All that's important is that the Napthtali join us.'

'My God, you're naïve, woman.' It especially irritated Yūsuf that Bakhbukh – who was widely respected as a fair-minded counsellor – had been invited to chair the council. Sofia didn't envy Bakhbukh. Each of the nesi'im would be trying to dominate and petty arguments were inevitable. His job was preventing knives being drawn.

'The Old Man has kept his promise to return when his people needed him. Our fathers' fathers made a promise that we would follow him when he needed us.'

'Do as you wish, Roe de Nail. I consider myself bound only by the promises I make,' said Mik la Nan. 'I've not come for womanly talk of prophecy. I've come to find an arrangement whereby the tribes can live together.'

'Yes,' the nasi of the Gad agreed, 'why should I submit to some nameless beggar who claims to be the Old Man? Most likely he is just another pious idiot.'

Mik la Nan nodded. 'There are many of those.'

Roe de Nail took any slur on the Old Man as a slur on him. 'God's beard, you Southerners are an irreligious brood.'

'In desperate times people cling to desperate hopes. My whole life I have had ragged prophets telling me my duty is to overthrow the Oltremarines. But my duty is to the Napthtali. We are strong because we travel with the wind and not against it.'

'Are you afraid of a fight?'

'Do you take me for a man who flees from trifles? Once the Napthtali called the Empty Quarter home, but a generation ago something barren was born in the heart of it, something inimical to man. The Sands are hungry and they creep further north each year. Graveyards are left along the Plain of Sharon where rich towns were once scattered, and as we fled like panicked kine the dead came claiming their inheritance: cannibal ghouls clawing up graves; Jinn in the pleasing form of girls tempting shepherds into the darkness. Nature's hand turned against us. We were no longer welcome, and so we came here.'

Bakhbukh cleared his throat mildly and the old nasi said more equably, 'That has created tensions. Let us resolve them. I did not come north to fight. I came here to live, and similarly I have come here to your tent, Roe de Nail, to make the peace, not to be dragged into a foolish war. What would be the point of raising an army to throw against the walls of Akka?'

When none of the nesi'im spoke, Mik la Nan stood. 'Come then, and let us see what this Old Man of yours has to say.'

*

While the nesi'im went up to the Old Man's cave, their men waited. There would be war; that was certain. The question was with whom. Yūsuf stomped off in a sulk again. Sofia stayed and watched Jabari as the children of the various tribes played with each other. They had yet to inherit their fathers' quarrels.

After a few hours, the children drifted back to their mothers' tents and Sofia began to get anxious. She took Iscanno from Jabari and went for a walk, though she kept one eye on the cave overhead. She caught occasional glimpses of the Benjaminite women, shadowy creatures whose long veils reminded her of the buio. The gulf between them and her was wider than the Sands.

She jumped when a voice from nowhere whispered, 'You have wrought wonders, Contessa!'

She looked about and found Yūsuf, lying on his back beside one of the Benjaminites' plundered carriages. He was whirling a camel-stick in the air, trying to swat the swirling flies. Evidently Roe de Nail had been remiss in completely destroying the wine he'd captured, for Yūsuf had smelled it out.

'I bog frogovness. I hop today can be a new bargaining for us.'

Sofia didn't like the sound of that 'us', but perhaps, in his oafish way, Yūsuf was trying to be conciliatory.

'We fought back to back,' she said. 'There's nothing to forgive.'

'We footed on the wrong start. I treated you monstrously. I failed as a host, a grave sin for an Ebionite. The trials of my youth, my struggles to hold together the Sicarii against impossible odds don't excuse my behaviour.'

Sofia wasn't interested in his maudlin justifications. 'Victory will hold the Sicarii together now.'

'No. It's not just the successes you have given me. It's you, Contessa. They *believe* now. You don't know how hard I tried to hammer faith into their thick heads. Then you show up – suddenly the blind see and the lame walk.'

'They just needed something better to fight for than silver.'

'You are an enchantress sent by God to aid me.' He jumped to his feet and grabbed her hand. 'With your skill and my name, we shall do great deeds.'

She gently extricated her hand. 'I think you're a little tired.'

'Sleep?' He waved his stick defiantly like a scimitar. 'While Jerusalem remains occupied by devils, while that carbuncle of Akka remains to be excised? Never! Don't you see? God sent you to be my right hand in renewing the Radinate. Marry me, Contessa – your disgrace will vanish like the dew at morning.'

'My disgrace?'

'Come,' he said with a wheedling smile, 'your condition is shameful. Your son remains nameless.' He laid his hand on Iscanno's head. 'Give him a father. Give yourself a husband with a proud lineage. After we push the interlopers into the sea, I will acclaim your son as my heir. I offer a name, and a crown to go with it!'

Sofia slapped his hand away. 'I need no man to walk before me, *or* to fight my battles.'

'Is there a problem?'

'It's none of your business, Bakhbukh,' Yūsuf hissed. 'Go and attend to your new masters.'

'No. Stay and hear,' Sofia said. 'Know this, Yūsuf ben Sinan. If I let you call yourself nasi of the Sicarii another day, it is because it suits my purposes. Your men are mine now. I bring what you never did, never could: I bring victory. But were it otherwise, were I a poor widow, or that fallen woman you took me for when I first entered your caves, I'd sooner die than marry a worm like you.'

Yūsuf raised his stick in fury, but Bakhbukh yanked it from his hand and snapped it in two. 'Do not disgrace yourself.'

'It's you who are disgraced, turning lapdog to this Jezebel!' Yūsuf strode into the darkness, away from the humiliating laughter.

'I think the wedding's off, Bakhbukh.'

'Thank goodness. I haven't a thing to wear. By the way, the Old Man has made the peace.'

'Really?'

'Yes. And he wishes to bless your child.'

As Sofia made her way up the path to the cave, she wondered what to expect: some exotic warlord, an Ebionite John Acuto with a rusted scimitar? The last thing she expected was the wizened old face smiling at her.

It was Ezra. Alive.

'I thought you were drowned!'

'No such luck.' He set down the book he was leafing through, but did not approach. Sofia wanted to embrace him but was stayed by a feeling of foreboding, and her anger. She had grown up in the tower of a man who always knew what was best for her, and who manipulated her accordingly. Now Ezra had deceived her, let her believe he was dead, let her—

'I would have come for you in Akka, Sofia,' he said softly, as if tracking her thoughts, 'but I had to prepare your path.'

'It doesn't matter,' she said lightly, 'whatever tall tale you told the nesi'im, they believed it. Thank you.'

'I told them naught but the truth.' He looked at Iscanno, his eyes wide. 'I told them that your child was the crucible of all our hopes. May I?'

'Of course.'

He took Iscanno with trembling hands, whispered a blessing and kissed him. 'To be Handmaid is a strange calling.'

'I'm mother to a child older than the world – strange hardly covers it. Who are you, Ezra? Really? The Old Man, or just an old sailor who talks too much?'

He handed Iscanno back, grinning. 'I can't be both?'

'Don't get cute. Our meeting in Ariminum wasn't accidental, was it?'

'No. I had to save you from Bernoulli.'

'He's dead.'

'Such a trifle will not stop the likes of him. Like a good philosopher, I see you are sceptical. I shall be a good philosopher too, and start at first principles.'

He stared at the fire a while, and then sighed. 'An age ago, there were three brothers. They were the greatest astrologers in a city famous for astrology. Its name is now forgotten, but once its commandments were carved in granite. They worshipped fire, but their true idol was equilibrium. Though they made sacrifices to *Ohura Mazda*, they believed that *druj* – the Darkness – was necessary. When they imagined perfection, they imagined a balanced scale, a sand-clock resting on its side, a boat on becalmed waters, a desert where the wind does not stir the smallest grain. This arid philosophy pinned them like dried butterflies, but they were content. Then came a terrible day when they stumbled upon the music of the firmament—'

'Why terrible?' Sofia interrupted.

Ezra looked at her for a moment, and then said, 'Perfection is most fragile when it cannot admit new ideas. The universe was *pulsing*. They expected an endless stability, but in fact it was a great wave; its millennial passage washes exhaustion from the land and animates all things. All was change! There were ages when the all-pervading Darkness encroached on one last flickering candle, followed by ages of luminance when the Darkness was reduced to a maggot lurking beside the hot vents of the deep. Perfection? This was *chaos*. It could not be so.'

Words are small things, but Sofia had heard snatches of this wild song before. 'And yet it is.'

'They recoiled from it. If God made this song, then He could not be God. The brothers resolved to compose a harmony congenial to their own conception: three wise men, reforming an irrational world. They suffered fire to make their flesh incorruptible – and that was their fall, Sofia, though they knew it not then. For another worm had conquered them, and it persuaded them, with praise and promises, that their vocation was to stand immortal watch until God's progeny next arrived . . .' His voice trailed off, then he whispered, 'and then to hasten to the court of a king – a mortal potentate who could do what must be done—'

Before he had finished, Sofia had leaped up to interpose her body – and a dagger – between him and Iscanno.

He regarded her steadily, sadly. 'Had I wished to kill you, Contessa, or the babe, I have had numerous opportunities. Even now, you couldn't stop me.'

'Try me!'

'If you wish to use that knife, I won't prevent you. It would be just. Just as Cain and Nimrod and Herod and Bernoulli are one, so all Handmaids are one. In trespassing against Her, I trespassed against you.'

'Why didn't you tell me before?'

'I'm *old*.' The strength had drained from his voice. 'I am so old I scarcely know my part any more – and yet, old as I am, beside you I'm a child. The Handmaid's burden is eternal, no less that God's. Each Handmaid must go to Jerusalem – that much I knew – and so I brought you across the water. But nothing is as it should be: Jerusalem is lost, the Wind and Waters are disturbed and the Darkness is stronger now than ever it has been. The moment Iscanno was born, I felt it – and so did the Darkness. For the first time in centuries its tendrils recoiled – if only momentarily – from the world. O, it is anxious. It knows its time is short.'

Sofia dropped the dagger and sank to the ground, weeping for a child slain a thousand years ago. 'Saints preserve me,' she sobbed.

Ezra would have wept too, but having gone this far he quietly continued, turning the pages of the book mechanically as he spoke. 'Herod's soldiers carried out their work for me. It looked like butchery, not justice, but I concealed my doubts from my brothers – as though my doubts could be more shameful than the slaughter we had instigated. We went our separate ways to wander the old paths and wait for the wheel to turn once more. One *falls* in love, but disenchantment comes as slowly as shedding skin. I roamed the darkening world, mile upon mile, year upon year, and strove to convince myself that all was as it should be. A hundred doubts became one certainty: that far from *creating* balance, we had destroyed it. I saw a world grow old. I saw winters that outstayed their course.'

He sighed again, a sound with decades of dust in it. 'History shambled on. The Prophetess' disciples forged a grand empire and I stumbled through battlefields that had consumed armies, through cities whose walls had been breached by plague and civil discord. The truth was undeniable: in the turmoil of history there is an equilibrium which we, like ants building a nest in the foundation of a great temple, had been too small to perceive. I took myself to the desert and found a cave that had been occupied, centuries ago, by one of the Prophetess' disciples. After Her death, he had retreated from the world, to pray – or perhaps, like me, merely to hide. The tribes said he lived there still.'

Despite her anger, Sofia was curious. 'Was he . . . like you and your brothers?'

'No – there are others like us, but he was just a man. His dried-out corpse was covered in a thin blanket and he wore a hair shirt. I looked upon those bony fingers clasped in prayer with envy, then I fled my body in disgust, throwing my soul into the stars as of old. With the strokes of a drowning man, I swam beyond the several worlds belonging to our sun and – right out there! – I saw it: the Darkness, grown vast and powerful, a great cresting wave of filth about to drown the world and replace the song with one universal scream of pain. Before I could flee, my youngest brother found me. He called me apostate – an enemy of the Light

– and tried to bind me so that the Darkness could complete its work.'

Ezra stopped leafing through the book, pausing not to study the page, but his hands.

'I awoke bloodied by fratricide as well as infanticide, and in that age in which I slept, the world had turned. The Radinate had waxed and, as all empires must, it had waned. I looked about and found my companion's blanket and shirt and skin had quite rotted away. Since the saint had so obligingly let me sleep, I decided to bury what was left of him, but under his bones I found a book. The leather binding had rotted, but the pages were miraculously preserved. It was a compendium of the lore of that ancient people now called Ebionites. After the Temple fell, fortune-hunters sought the Covenant in vain, for *this* was the Covenant. I read it with humble heart and realised that God had been whispering to the Ebionites as he whispered to me – he whispered to all peoples, but only those few who hear are his Chosen Peoples. For many years, I stayed in the cave and pondered my crimes. In that time, the people – shepherds first, later nesi'im – came and sought my advice. They assumed I was the old saint and I did not contradict them. I liked pretending to be someone good. They told me of the warlike strangers who had come, as all men come eventually, seeking Jerusalem. The *franj* were bold and barbarous, simple tools for the Darkness to manipulate. The Handmaid's return was nigh and, knowing that Jerusalem would call her as it had her predecessors, I taught the Ebionite nesi'im arts to repel the *franj*.' The wind hooped through the hollows of the caves. Sofia fancied she saw faint pride on his face – but perhaps it was just an old scar, caught by the flickering fire.

'I had some success before the Darkness took notice and unleashed a storm from the steppe to punish my treachery. I forged a coalition of *franj* and Ebionite and led them against the hordes of Gog, and we were victorious – though such a victory I pray never again to behold. I crawled out from under the dead and came back here to my cave. My body was beaten, punctured, bruised, nearly ruined, but the book was like cool water. One morning, some decades later, I heard a bird singing at the mouth of my cave and when I emerged, it flew away. I searched the empty sky and saw the sun rise, and I knew that somewhere the Handmaid was born. So I took me to sea, where I could commune with the world's winds, and they led me to you.'

Sofia walked over to him, kicked aside his book and carefully spat in his face. 'So that I could give you that. Now why don't you pay your debt to the devil for Jesus' death and die.'

'Handmaid,' he cried as she walked out into the night, 'you *need* me.'

'Aye, like I need a Lazar's kiss. Peddle your stories to the lizard-eaters but keep away from me and my boy. I've got what I need from you already.'

When Sofia came down from the cave, she found the camp in joyful uproar. The laughter trailed off when she appeared and a pregnant silence rushed into the vacuum – and Sofia saw that the nesi'im had told their followers what the Old Man had said, and saw how well Ezra had cast his spell. A great collective dream had possessed the Ebionites: a warrior queen had once purged this land of invaders and now it could happen again.

One after another the tribesmen stood and touched their fore-heads and hearts. Ignoring their salute, she walked straight for the tent covered in dried camelskins and decorated with ibex horns. It was the least ostentatious nesi'im tent, and the ragged men sleeping around the entrance did not salute her when they woke.

Sofia demanded entry, and when they refused, she began to shout.

The Cat was merely amused when he came to see what the disturbance was. 'Come in, Contessa.'

She entered and threw herself down on a pillow. The old nasi stood over her, peering down at Iscanno. 'So, this is your boy? By Solomon's beard, he is ugly.'

Sofia didn't take offence; the Ebionite custom was to protect children from the Evil Eye with dispraise.

'That Old Man is a remarkable fellow. Do you know what he said? He said that you are the Occluded One returned. He said that Akka is an empty ossuary that a strong wind will scatter. He said we are that wind.'

'He's a fraud.'

Mik la Nan did not look in the least bit surprised. 'So? It's a useful lie. The other nasi believe it, or they pretend to, and that's what matters. Your Sicarii have conventions that allow men of different tribes to live together, do they not? We nesi'im are no different.'

'I won't let you fight under false pretences, Mik la Nan. If you join me, you may die.'

'And if I do not, I will die also. A few years later – and without the joy of cutting down my enemy today, *be'ezrat HaShem*.'

'I tell you again: my quarrel is not against the Akkans. I just want to topple Catrina.'

'And I have come to believe it might be possible. That – not some old fool's tales or a dusty word like Radinate – that is why I'll fight for you.'

They talked into the night as the sickle moon sank behind the hill mourned by choirs of foxes, and when the sun came the foxes' place had been taken by the little birds who sweetly hailed that daily miracle of the cold earth becoming warm.

Before she left, Sofia asked, 'What would you do if you ruled this land? Would you rebuild the Temple?'

Mik la Nan took a long time to answer her. At last he said,

'Countless kings have thought that in capturing Jerusalem they captured God. The Temple is gone. God remains. The Winds played upon the mountain before Man. Now that Man is gone, they have returned. Why should God find the prayers of the Jinn less pleasing than ours? He has the power to disperse them, but He does not. My people are slow learners, but we have learned to live without temples at last. No, I will not rebuild it.'

CHAPTER 20

> The Jebusites lined the walls with the blind and lame and the Israelites took it for a threat of what would befall them if they attacked the city, but they were undaunted for their king was the Lord's favourite, and only when David was old and out of favour did he understand that the Jebusites were trying to warn him how the city, the city he had made his capital, scourged the covetous.
>
> *2 Samuel 7*

'My word, but it's hot, isn't it? Hot, I say. Yes, it certainly is hot. Now, about this heat . . .'

East of Akka, the Esdraelon Plain erupted into an uninspiring set of rolling hills. The Byzantine prince had volunteered to accompany a scouting party into the badlands, but all his attempts to strike up conversation with his travel companions were as barren as the landscape. Some of them would have loved to hear the Prince of Green's stories from the Hippodrome, but they knew too well that Basilius would disapprove.

Jorge finally could bear it no longer. 'You might be wearing a mask, Grand Master, but it's obvious you've been frowning since we left Akka. If I have offended—'

'You were free – very free – with the queen.'

'Oh. That.'

'*That*,' said Basilius, 'is a dangerous game.'

'Bah! Byzant is full of such women. A little defiance leaves them wet as Etruria.'

'She is not as other women you have known. She is a desert queen: the Sands have shorn her softness.'

'I'll submit to many indignities, but not a lecture on women from a pious virgin.' He slapped his horse's neck. 'Simple creatures are happiest with a confident rider. Too much freedom and they grow proud.'

Basilius suddenly grabbed Jorge's arm.

'Unhand me!' he snarled.

'Be still and look!' He pointed to a spot where the gentle curve of the hill's crest was broken by several vertical juttings.

'It's just a ruined Etruscan temple,' Jorge said. 'Thrace and Anatolia are littered with them—'

'*Look*, I said.' Basilius pointed to the tallest pillar. At the top sat a man, silhouetted so they could tell nothing about him except that he possessed a vast beard.

'Oh,' said Jorge breezily, 'an anchorite.' His confidence dwindled as he noticed the Lazars slowing to a stop. 'Don't tell me these mad bastards scare you too?'

'We've heard whisperings' – Basilius' voice was hushed, awed – 'that the Old Man wanders the land again.'

'Truly you have grown feeble under that woman!' Jorge galloped off laughing.

Basilius ordered the rest to stay where they were. When he caught up with the prince, the anchorite was climbing down the pillar, as nimble as a gerbil.

'Old Man indeed.'

Basilius ignored Jorge's sarcasm. 'This is a Sicarii.'

'Let's see what he wants before we kill him, then.'

Basilius's axe was drawn before the bearded man had dropped to the ground before them. 'I know you.'

'And I you.' Yūsuf pulled out his blade and dropped it at their feet. 'I came to talk.'

Jorge pushed Basilius aside. 'And we're here to listen.'

Yūsuf drew himself up proudly. 'Long have the Sicarii plagued your people. Still longer have you plagued mine.'

'The Sicarii plague the Ebionites worse than we do,' said Basilius scornfully.

'That's a lie you spread to sow dissension among God's People!' Yūsuf took a breath, and then continued smoothly, 'You kill us and we kill you and there is in this a balance. Now there has come amongst us a woman.' He ran his hair though his knotted hair and looked about wildly. 'She is a harlot who defiles my caves by her presence, who like a Jinni has stirred my men to foolishness.'

'They are easily stirred. The keraks will be easily retaken, if that's worrying you.'

'The captured towers,' said Yūsuf with withering scorn, 'are a means to an end.'

'What end?' said Jorge.

'To impress the Napthtali. The first step to alliance.'

'This fool got too much sun on his perch,' Basilius scoffed. 'The nesi'im could never agree.'

Yūsuf did not react angrily, for he saw that the Byzantine understood his import. 'But what if they did?' He let the question hang a while. 'Such an alliance will not be easily defeated. My people, chosen though we are, are also given to following false prophets. One calling himself the Old Man has convinced them that she is the Prophetess herself, returned to rid the land of corruption.'

'Of us, in other words,' said Basilius. 'Is that not the prediction?'

'Of course it is absurd,' Yūsuf continued, unabashed, 'for how could a *franj* be the Renewer?'

'Enough,' Jorge exclaimed. 'What a perverse land this is. The dead command the living, and the women, men. You waste time exchanging childish tales. Reason as men, if you still remember how.'

'Mock all you like, Byzantine. If this troublemaker succeeds, we all lose. More than any, I wish to push you infidels into the sea, someday. I've proceeded slowly and my men have mistaken prudence for cowardice. She cares only for her bastard but she's leading my people over the precipice. Should I let them?'

'No indeed,' said Jorge with understanding. 'You've shown true vision. I understand how difficult this must be.'

Yūsuf smiled with pathetic gratitude. 'The tribes have gathered in a place where they cannot readily disperse. If I tell you where to find them, promise me—'

'We shall break up their gathering with a minimum of casualties. Only the ringleaders—'

Yūsuf cut him off. 'You may kill as many as you like, but the woman is mine.'

'My word on that. Now, where are they?'

The queen stood on the palace battlements looking out to the Sands while Basilius reported the meeting, and the plan he had formulated.

She hardly seemed to be listening, until she interrupted. 'So you want to force a confrontation.' After the débâcle in Wadi Aruna, she was more sceptical of his ability than she cared to admit. 'Out in the Sands, the lizard-eaters will make you pay dearly.'

'We can do it without much blood,' Prince Jorge assured her.

'What makes you think that is a consideration?' she snapped.

He realised from the venom that something was awry. 'I am a stranger here. If I have I done something to offend—?'

'Yes, perhaps our quaint manners are to blame. In Byzant I suppose you allow unsupervised foreigners to explore your dungeons, to interrogate prisoners as they see fit. Did you think my men so incompetent that I wouldn't find out, or did you not care?'

Jorge had half-suspected that he was under surveillance since coming to Akka, and he recovered smoothly. 'Forgive me. I should have gone through the correct channels. I was curious to see what manner of creature would betray the most sacred of bonds.'

'Disgusting, isn't he?' she said, somewhat mollified. 'There's no better evidence of the time's distemper than a son rebelling against his mother. I am still trying to devise an apt punishment.'

'If you need someone to hold the axe—' Basilius interjected.

Catrina turned around slowly, 'That will be all, Grand Master.'

Jorge took the opportunity to push the ring hanging around his neck out of sight under his vest. Basilius retreated, leaving an awkward silence.

Jorge sought to dispel it. 'The desert is very beautiful.'

'Do you find? It bores me terribly.'

'Come then,' he purred, 'let's look upon the sea instead.' He offered his hand as she climbed onto the ramparts. They circumnavigated the sleeping city until the unsleeping activity of the harbour and shipyard lay below them. Shipwrights streamed over the skeletal ships like busy ants who'd had second thoughts about the corpse they'd just flayed. The fleet being brought to life required miles of rope, fields of canvas and endless supplies of dry wood, and Ariminumese, Byzantine and Sicilian galleys loaded to the rails clogged the harbour. The lantern ships were whales, surrounded by the darting dark fish that were the xebecs.

With their shallow draft, the xebecs, tarred black as the gondolas that clogged Ariminum's canals, could cross reefs the lantern could never dare. They were long and low, a hundred and twenty piedi stem to stern, with a distinctive forward-raking main mast from which green pennants lolled like a dragon's forked tongue. They had two long curved yards, with sails furled tight to them. With twenty-five oars each side, they glided so effortlessly that one could forget the sweating men responsible.

'It will be a magnificent fleet. I caught a glimpse of those lanterns the other day.'

The queen raised her eyebrows as she realised that the prince's lap of honour had not been entirely for show. 'You're very kind – but I could not afford a "magnificent fleet". That is at best a simulacrum of one. If they were forced to fight, the only place my flagships' lamps would lead is the seabed. On closer inspection you'll find they are antiques.'

'I prefer a mature beauty.'

She touched his face gently. 'You're a good boy, but desist from flattery for a moment. I'm happy to listen to sweet lies but there are times when hard truths must be faced.'

Jorge's seductive smile vanished. 'My eyes are open, as are yours. Whatever its fighting ability, that fleet tells me you realise the great dangers we face.'

'The Sicarii?'

'You're joking! I mean Concord, of course. We have to bring the fight to Etruria, before they bring it here.'

'Oh,' she cried in amusement, 'what an imagination the young possess! Is that why you brought this vast army, to compel me to join you in arms?'

'On the contrary, they are a gift.'

The queen stiffened. 'Thank you, but I cannot accept.'

Jorge was taken aback to be refused. 'I can't persuade you to reconsider?'

'Concord isn't going to venture across the water, and I'm certainly not going to Etruria. My family left that sodden land behind long ago – and good riddance. I am building a navy so I don't *have* to fight. Don't look so glum, dear boy. I'm not angry. Once we put down this rebellion, you shall have the confirmation you came here for.'

Jorge smiled politely, wondering what exactly the queen was playing at. They both knew he didn't give a damn about her endorsement.

A shadow was skulking through the tents on the outskirts of the Benjaminite camp. In the centre Roe de Nail had made a huge bonfire which threw a staggering dome of light against the stars. The skulker froze as he came unexpectedly upon Bakhbukh and Sofia, whispering together by the dim light of a dying fire on the perimeter.

'Yūsuf! There you are.'

'I was praying,' he blurted in panic. 'On the mountain, praying.'

'We were discussing,' Sofia said, 'how to deal with Mik la Nan. He'll seek to dominate the council of war.'

'And Roe de Nail's no match for him,' said Bakhbukh. 'What's your opinion?'

'My opinion,' said Yūsuf, 'is that it is unseemly for old men to gossip in the shadows with young women. I put my faith in God, not stratagems. You would do well to do likewise,' he said, and stalked off.

Bakhbukh watched him go and grief choked his voice when finally he spoke. 'This is the second time you've used him for bait.'

'Even fools have their uses.'

'Promise me one thing, Contessa: it will be my knife that ends him.'

There was a tense silence as the queen told them Prince Jorge's offer. Basilius said nothing, thinking it over. Finally the patriarch asked, 'Is it wise to refuse? We *are* short of men.'

She slapped his bearded face and he cowered like a whipped dog. 'This *gift* is a measure of contempt, you idiot! What kind of queen would I be if I allowed an army of foreigners to bed down in my capital? Akka would be a garrison; I, a vassal.'

With all the skill of a seasoned courtier, the patriarch changed tack. 'The bumptious rogue pretends he cannot afford a weak kingdom at his flank, when really he seeks the same thing your uncle did.'

'My throne,' she hissed. 'Grand Master?'

Basilius knew what she had in mind. 'I can make sure the Byzantines take the brunt.'

'Some of your Lazars must be sacrificed if he's not to suspect treachery,' said the patriarch.

'That is nothing. We consider our blood already spilled. We shall overwhelm their high places with numbers. The Sands will be quietened, Byzant humbled, Akka's authority confirmed.' Basilius took a moment to calm down. 'What say you, Majesty?'

'I say you're not quite the blunt instrument I thought.'

The day of battle is generally, but for a few hours of fantastic vividness, duller than most. Aside from marching, it is a day of waiting, manoeuvring, checking arms, keeping horses watered, rechecking arms, and more waiting still. Inevitably and endlessly the soldiers talk of battles fought, anything to remind themselves that survival is possible. Their officers, in terms more elevated, do likewise.

In the command tent, Jorge was telling the Grand Master of his part in the destruction of Concord's Ninth Legion, though Basilius was so tense that he scarcely attended. He had persuaded Jorge to take only his elite troops on the raid, leaving the main body camped outside Akka, 'to protect the city'. The queen would seize his men after Prince Jorge's heroic death was confirmed..

When Jorge had finished his tale, he asked, as if out of nowhere, 'Who did you replace as Seneschal?'

'A Northerner like you,' Basilius answered without thinking, 'slain by a Sicarii blade, ironically.'

'Why is that ironic?'

'He was something of an Ebionite lover.' Suddenly Basilius started laughing. 'One of us might be dead tomorrow, so there's no harm telling the truth, is there? We Lazars don't have the luxury of waiting to be promoted, and he was in my way, so – well, you get the idea.' He slapped Jorge's back. 'Ha! You look as though you've seen a Jinni. Don't be anxious; we'll do fine today. It's one thing for a woman to sit on a throne,' he added, 'but at the head of an army? Our victory is assured.'

Yūsuf had revealed that the tribal confederation was going to attack the Kerak de Chartres – which was far to the south – today. The plan was to fall on the undefended encampment left behind, which would both expose the Contessa as a false prophet and destroy Roe de Nail's prestige in one fell swoop. A nasi who could not even protect his wives seldom ruled long. The inevitable recrimination would fracture the fragile tribal alliance.

Jorge was not enthused. 'It's a clever scheme, but it does not seem—'

'— chivalrous? You may have use for such fine notions at home but the Sands punish the deluded harshly. I've planned everything to the last detail.'

Jorge smiled despite himself, 'One thing I learned in the hippodrome was that no matter how well prepared you are, loose half a dozen chariots on a track and not even God knows what'll happen. The love of strangers gets pretty tasteless after a while, but the beast turning left when you want him to go right, or a wheel coming off? Ah, that's when you know you're alive!'

Beneath his helmet, Basilius smiled to himself as he clapped the prince on the back. 'Oh, I'm confident that there'll be a few surprises today, Prince,' he promised warmly.

CHAPTER 21

Black, half-fallen towers cast porous shadows as dawn broke over the northside. Isabella danced through the enclosed garden, going through her sets obsessively. She had not slept peacefully since the abomination had first invaded her dreams; she'd become accustomed now to waking grinding her teeth. She could not sleep; she could not pray; only Water Style calmed her.

Her trance was interrupted by an urgent pounding on the baptistery's bronze door that didn't stop until she had pushed it fully open.

'You know you can't be seen topside. What if you were spotted?'

'This can't wait,' said Pedro. 'Remember you said the buio were more sensitive than my instruments? You were right – I've only now picked up what had them spooked.'

'You'd best come in.'

Pedro emptied his satchel on the floor beside the font and grabbed a scroll. He unrolled a chart of measurements – daily, weekly and monthly. She could barely follow him in his excitement as he pointed out the trends. Then he dived into the pile on the floor and pulled out a small book with a calfskin cover. 'This is Giovanni's journal,' he said, brandishing it. 'I saved it when we fled Tartarus. It's mostly Wave theory – too complicated for me, if I'm honest. Bernoulli used acoustics to torture the buio, and this describes how. It's a dissection of sorts. There's an essential binding agent in water – Bernoulli called it *aether*. He didn't know where it came from, just its power. His Molè was a great mill that spilled water into its smallest parts. He realised that water without aether would collapse, leading to a chain-reaction, and that would—'

'—cause a Wave.'

'I assumed that the First Apprentice was building another Molè because he meant to send another Wave, but it's worse than that – much worse. The subterranean river gives a purer sample than the Irenicon. It seems the aether level has been static for at least a thousand years.'

'Since Mary's son died.'

'I can only speak to what I've measured,' Pedro said doggedly. 'Up till now, the aether's been low – that's not bad in itself; it *should* rise and fall. There are waves throughout all nature – our breath, the tides, solar cycles, and so with aether. When levels are high, there's harmony. When they are low, there's not. But we've been living through a lull that's gone on centuries too long. The question left is this: what's the source of the aether, and what's the source of obstruction?'

'It's not God, if that's what you're afraid to ask. It's us. What Bernoulli called aether is the medium God speaks through. We generate it when the Handmaid's son inspires us.'

Pedro was wary of such talk. 'All I know is such prolonged stasis is unnatural. I'm afraid that the Wave has been flat for so long that we've reached a critical point where it can't restart. I think that's what the First Apprentice wants. Whatever he's building doesn't just extract the aether. It destroys it. That's what my readings seem to show anyway.'

'It can't be allowed,' Isabella said gravely.

'What can we do? We can barely keep alive.'

'We ourselves? Nothing. Only Sofia can win this war. All we can do is help her.'

The atmosphere in the hub was more tense than usual; the leaders of the Tartaruchi all knew what Pedro was going to say.

Their numbers had dwindled significantly: besides Geta's toll, infections and flux had carried off many more.

But only Uggeri objected. 'The Contessa left us one charge: to protect Rasenna.'

'If Sofia were here, she'd see the same thing the rest of us do,' Pedro insisted. 'Rasenna is lost. There's no shame in a strategic retreat. We'll return—'

'The motto of all exiles.'

'Uggeri, the Signoria is controlled by a Concordian. Our towers are fallen. Giovanni's bridge is gone. The only flags flying above our heads are the Hawk's Company's and Concord's. If Rasenna exists anywhere, it's down here. The next city Concord needs to conquer is Veii – that's the front where what remains of the Southern League should be.'

'The *League*,' Uggeri sneered. 'If you'd made them understand in Ariminum, we wouldn't be in this mess.'

'We all wish things had turned out differently,' Isabella said softly. 'I'm staying.'

'*Idiota!*' Pedro's anger surprised everybody. 'You want to get yourself killed, don't you? You think it'll prove something to Maddalena.'

'You give me too much credit. I'm not that complicated, Vanzetti. I just want to strangle that whore.'

'Then you're the one betraying Sofia and I'm not going to waste my breath arguing. Anyone else?'

The hulking figure at the back of the cavern stood up. He had to crouch as he lumbered to Uggeri's side. Pedro knew Jacques was certain in his choice. 'I guess we all know where we're supposed to be.'

The meeting broke up as everyone else went to make preparations for the move. Despite Pedro's brave face, most assumed they would never return.

*

When Maddalena stepped into the banquet hall, the feast was prepared and there at the top of the table sat—

She almost screamed, but she managed to hold off and quickly recovered her composure.

'Pedro! It's customary to wait for the head of household,' she said sliding into a chair next to him. 'If we don't practise manners in the breach, what's the use? Never mind. Here you are, in my house. You were always so good at prediction – tell me, what would happen if I dropped this glass?'

'Servants and guards would come running and we would not get to talk. I came because of the love our fathers bore each other. Fabbro and I didn't always agree, but I never doubted his patriotism. I know he never guessed what Geta *was* till it was too late. Neither, I believe, did you. You were like my sister once and it hurts to see you degraded.'

'This,' she looked about theatrically, 'is hardly squalor. Uggeri sent you to plead his case, I suppose?'

'No. He sees only one resolution to this. I came at the behest of your brothers.' This was a lie, but one he could justify if it led to reconciliation.

'They're alive, then? I wrote to each of them, offering the freedom of Rasenna, and heard nothing—'

'Salvatore recognises the Tartaruchi as Rasenna's legitimate authority and will not treat with Geta – or you, so long as you're attached to him. They know you're in his power.'

'*I'm* the one being manipulated? Ha! My brothers have made you a pawn. They expected to wander Europa profiteering, building private fortunes in places where commercial acumen consists of bartering chickens for sheep, and then return to divide the Bombelli estate and leave me a puny dowry. How tragic that things did not work out as they hoped. Tell me, Pedro, you who are *so* logical, why I should let myself be beggared? Because of the accident of my sex?'

'They merely seek to revenge your father, to rescue you from his murderer—'

'Uggeri murdered my father,' she hissed.

'Uggeri is hot-headed, but he would never—'

'You'd be more convincing if his bandieratori weren't proving such efficient assassins. The Signori hardly dares meet for fear of their knives. I can't say I liked Polo Sorrento much, but he didn't deserve to be thrown from his tower. '

'He was a collaborator.'

'As am I apparently.' She drummed her sharp fingers lightly upon her round stomach. 'So I must expect the same fate. Is that why you came? Where's your knife concealed?'

'I've come to give you an out. We're abandoning Rasenna. I'm asking you to come south with us and—'

CHRRrasssshh!

The shattering glass stopped him short.

Maddalena pulled back her chair and stood. 'Run – and if you escape, give my brothers my love. Tell them I'll burn what's left of Rasenna before I let them take it.'

Isabella found Carmella sitting in the baptistery chapel sewing a torn flag. A gentle rain pattered on the stained-glass window, melting the colours into each other.

Carmella looked up. 'So, finally decided our fate, have you?'

'Yes, we've decided. Uggeri's staying. You'll go south with Pedro.'

'And you?'

'Duty calls me elsewhere. I need someone strong to look after the orphans and the other sisters – that's you, Sister.'

Carmella threw down the flag. 'Find another slave. I won't serve.'

'You made a vow to obey, and I am head of this order—'

'This order's home is here. We're not mendicants. If you

want to run, fine, you can run. But you leave behind the Sister-hood.'

After Carmella's pretty little speech, Isabella looked around to see no one was at the door, then said quietly, 'When you entered this order, you offered up your virginity to the Madonna.'

The novice blushed. 'Don't try to besmirch my honour because you're abandoning yours. Your predecessors never ran from danger.'

'It's hopeless.'

'This is home!'

'I mean your scheme is hopeless. Uggeri's heart belongs to another—'

'You little *bitch*!'

Hissing like a feral cat, Carmella threw herself at Isabella, whose arms remained hanging by her sides as her body weaved out of the shredding path of Carmella's claws until she retreated out into the garden and danced in a circle around the little orange trees. Enraged, Carmella followed her blindly. Isabella crouched, bracing her legs for the right moment, letting her get close. Carmella made a wild swipe, tipping too far to sustain balance – it was a fault she had never been able to correct – and Isabella sprang over an orange tree and landed behind her. A simple jab to the back of the legs brought Carmella to her knees. Isabella pushed her face into the cold mud and kept her there until she feared the girl might suffocate.

Carmella picked herself up, panting. Her face was black but for her teeth and staring eyes. 'Uggeri just works for the Contessa. That's all there is too it.'

'Oh, you blind fool! I don't mean *Sofia*. Uggeri loves *Maddalena* – he always has! Why else would a soldier choose to stay in such a hopeless situation? There's no reason, as you well know. It's the same reason you wish to stay.'

The blind fury left Carmella's face, but the hate remained. 'What does a little girl know about love?'

Isabella saw she was not to be dissuaded. 'We each have our role to play. Perhaps yours is here. Uggeri's like you, Carmella: he's his own worst enemy. Don't let him destroy himself.'

'All right, everyone ready? Final check.'

The tunnel went deep under the Irenicon; it would come up far south of the city walls. Pedro went round to shake hands with those that were staying. There were many more than he would have liked.

He stopped in front of Uggeri and Jacques. 'Most likely we won't ever see each other again. If we're successful at Veii, we'll take back the captured territory. I don't know what our chances are, but I do know it won't be done quickly. Help us. The longer you *stay alive* and make their lives hell, the better.'

'Good to feel needed,' said Uggeri dryly. 'We'll try our damnedest, and if we can't, we'll take as many as we can with us to hell.' They embraced awkwardly. 'Tell Sofia—'

'I know. I will. Keep your flag up.'

As they set off, Pedro saw that Rosa Sorrento was shepherding the orphans; that Isabella and Carmella were both standing to one side.

'*Madonna!* You too?'

'No, just Carmella. I'm leaving, but I'm not going with you.'

It took Pedro a moment to understand her meaning. He was furious. 'That's a fool's errand! You'll be killed before you reach the Wastes. Even if you get into Concord, what can you do?'

'The prime mover in all this is—'

'Isabella! You can't defeat a First Apprentice!'

'Sofia did. If any Etrurian can stop him, it's me. I owe it to Sofia, and to all the Reverend Mothers before me to try.'

'We don't even know if Sofia's still alive!'

'The buio told you she was and I believe it and so do you, if only you'd bring yourself to admit it.'

'So you'll sacrifice yourself to buy time, is that the idea? Sofia wouldn't hear of it. We *need* you. The road south won't be friendly territory – plenty of towns between here and Veii will be eager to curry favour with Concord.'

'You have the bandieratori. I'm sorry, Pedro. I must try.'

CHAPTER 22

While he was waiting in his tent for the dispatch, Leto spent a frustrating morning working on Torbidda's Bouncing Bridge idea from their Guild Hall days. After his first few attempts he'd begun to suspect the solution would always be beyond him, but still he persisted, until he'd convinced himself it really was impossible. He put it to one side with an oath and brooded. He had been liverish all day. He was annoyed by the dull mosquitoes he must continually swat and because he knew they were nothing to the swarms his troops must soon face. The Albula had too many tributaries to count. Around Veii, the land began to get marshy.

Seeking to avoid those unhealthy conditions, he had made Volsinii his base. It was further north than he would have preferred, but the choice was popular with the officers: the coastal air was salubrious, the fish delicious, the women cheap. Above all, for the first time since leaving Concord, they felt *wanted*. For years Volsinii had paid Veii tribute with salt and slaves. Now the city fathers had not merely surrendered to the Concordians; they had welcomed them, offering shelter, scouts and soldiers.

But while helpful neighbours were all very well, he knew it would take considerably more to overcome Veii's formidable defences.

The officers dreaded bringing the general dispatches from Veii. The news was always bad. Scaevola drew the short straw – he always did.

'I promised Torbidda a swift result, Scaevola, yet here we are, fretting over supplies – as though we were the ones under siege.'

There was no need to search for the reason; it was obvious. A city not encircled is not truly besieged. Though his legion had stopped supplies reaching the city from the north, the blockade was ineffective so long as Veii's harbour remained open. The Veian Navy might be antique, but it controlled the Albulian Estuary very effectively. Captured deserters had confirmed that Rasenna engineers had schooled the Veians in tactics to frustrate the Concordian diggers – but that too had been pretty obvious.

Veii was a city of small hills atop one large hill. Any army attacking it must go uphill – except now, before they even reached that first hill, they would have to cross a new river that had been created by diverting a tributary of the Albula. Veian archers complicated any attempt to ford the new moat. The archers' attentions were divided by having the pontonniers working under makeshift shelters, and at three locations, and on the fifth day, one team had made it across. A robust charge might have ended it there and then, but the Veians sent only a battalion of slaves to meet the Concordian Stormguard. The slaves fought fiercely, but were overcome when the second pontoon was completed.

Even with the third pontoon in place, securing the captured bank was a bloody task, and one that presented new difficulties when done: the steep hill facing them was interrupted by several plateaus. The first was defended by a rather uneven wall of boulders. The Concordian centurions, unimpressed, decided without consulting the general that it could be taken with sheer numbers, and raising a terrible cry of '*Bernoulli!*', they charged.

The boulders the Veians crouched behind were settled so that a mere nudge would start them rolling. They shattered the Concordians' line and rolled down to the base camp, where they wrecked men and machines indiscriminately. The push was abandoned entirely when one capricious boulder smashed the central pontoon and sent a battalion of reinforcements to their deaths. Hours later, another attempt was made, and it failed in like manner. The captured bank became the new front: a sea of mud precariously vulnerable to being entirely overrun.

That night brought fresh terrors. Instead of boulders, wheels of fiery death – great barbed metal wheels stuffed with burning straw – burst into the Concordian lines in successive waves, supplemented by raining oil-pots, that not only kept the fires burning, but successfully banished sleep. The Concordians prayed for morning, and when it came they discovered what horrors the darkness had concealed: men burnt alive in their tents or drowned in the muddy banks, and the stagnant moat laden with the bodies of those soldiers who'd sought refuge from the fire in its water. It would have been much simpler if Leto could commit all his men – but diversionary sallies against the main legion camp on the other side of the moat made that impossible. They were sporadic and half-hearted, but effective in their aim: to prevent him from concentrating his forces.

The start of every siege was a moment of immense importance. If the city folk could be terrified sufficiently by the initial assault they would often capitulate without further resistance. That had failed here; now it would be entirely a question of stamina.

'Investments are deceptive affairs, Scaevola. For all the variety of the Veians' defences and our machines, only one weapon counts: hunger. A limited blockade only creates privations for the Small People; we cannot win until famine gnaws higher. It's galling to be stalemated by an enemy one does not respect, but failing tactics must be abandoned.'

'Quite right, General.' Scaevola waited breathlessly to hear the inspired plan his hero had devised to break the impasse.

'Saddle my horse.'

Leto would have preferred to travel alone, but knowing what a prize he'd make, he took a dozen men – eleven swords, one gunner – enough to scare off opportunistic bandits, not enough to slow progress.

It was late when they arrived in Rasenna; with some fresh horses, food and rest, they could reach Concord before the end of the following day. His men were stationed with the Hawk's Company and he was escorted to the gonfaloniere's residence. Geta had made his court in one of Piazza Luna's larger palazzi after the mansion's previous owner had been charged – on somewhat doubtful evidence – with collaborating with the Tartaruchi.

Leto found little to admire in the decorations of the banqueting hall except for an oversized chessboard which must have been carved during one of Etruria's fleeting enthusiasms for the Crusade. The white pieces were Lazar knights of ivory, bravely facing the scimitars and turbans of the swarthy Radinate horde, fashioned in this case from black horn.

The nightly bacchanal was under way and a few cowed patricians sat between their drunken gonfaloniere and his glum wife.

'General Spinther, I declare! Seems like only yesterday that I waved you off, yet here you are again! Did you return my tear-stained handkerchief? Join us, join us. You must be quite worn out by army rations and rough living. How goes the war?'

'Slowly.'

'I should say so!' Geta turned to Maddalena, 'He predicted Veii would fall in few weeks.'

'Don't gloat, *amore*. It's common.' As Maddalena's womb had grown round, her sense of humour had suffered. 'I'm sure the little chap's trying his best.'

Leto bristled at the condescension. 'And who are you, Signora?'

'I don't believe you've met my wife yet, General.'

'So this is the Bombelli girl? I wonder, if I had betrayed my own people, if I would find the setbacks of my only allies so amusing. Do you wonder, dear lady, why the siege is protracted? It's not courage keeping Veii going; it's your brothers' deep pockets.'

Geta had warned Maddalena to be polite. Her smile was fixed. 'I am but a trifling woman. What would I know of such things?'

'Nothing, I suppose. Well, let me tell you that those damned speculators are a worse plague than the condottieri. They hear my armies marching sooner than everyone else, and send agents ahead to buy grain.'

'Isn't that legal?' she said coolly.

'Oh, of course – they are *very* careful. And when they can't get reliable information, they spread lies, and the price goes up all the same. I wonder that you leap to their defence. They seem to think you stole their birthright.'

The Rasenneisi patricians at the table suddenly looked away and started tucking into the food.

'You think you know me,' Maddalena snarled. 'Well, my husband told me all about you—'

'Maddalena . . .'

'Did he now?' said Leto, affably.

'Yes! He told me that Spinther was once a noble name. *You* sold *your* birthright for a number.'

'Should I have stayed constant like your husband? Why such a model of fidelity is hated by all parties – his former allies most of all – I can't begin to imagine.'

Maddalena glared at her husband. 'Are you going to tolerate this boy's impertinence?'

Geta shrugged. 'He has a point *amore*. Tell me, Spinther, how *do* you propose to break the impasse?'

'That's between me and the First Apprentice.'

'Hasn't the little fellow found God? What's he going to do, pray to Saint Eco?'

'That act is for the Small People.'

'Pretty convincing, from what I hear.' Geta tutted, the disappointed parent. 'But even so, what's he going to tell you that you don't already know? You simply need to convince Veians that the cost of resisting will be far worse than the cost of capitulation. Your trouble is that they aren't scared.'

'And how shall I remedy that?'

'Why, scare them, of course!'

'How simple,' said Leto. 'Why didn't I think of that?'

Geta ignored the sarcasm. 'You need to show initiative, lad! That's what your father would have done.'

Leto pretended not to be intrigued. 'I suppose you're going to pretend you were friends.'

'Friends? *Dio*, no – Manius Spinther was my superior, and I never forgave him for it. It was way back in the fifties, on the Frankish front—'

'Save it, Geta. I'm not interested in tall tales. My father was a Concordian officer who did his duty.'

'He showed initiative when it was necessary, and *that* is what the men responded to. Didn't you learn *anything* from me?'

'Not to employ drunks.'

As Geta toasted his adversary's riposte, Maddalena said suddenly, 'Have you found the Contessa?'

Leto couldn't see any point being mysterious. 'The Queen of Oltremare ought to have sent her to us, but as yet she has not arrived. What about that rat infestation, Geta? Have you eradicated it?'

'Not yet,' Geta conceded. 'I'll show you my progress tomorrow, if you can spare an hour before you leave.'

With his guard trailing behind them, Leto followed Geta through the emptiness of Piazza Luna to the river. He wondered vaguely why Geta was wearing armour; perhaps he planned to see them off with full honours. Perhaps he thought to return to grace by such gestures. If so he was sorely mistaken.

Then Leto saw it: 'My pontoon . . .'

Geta was amused at his childish pout, but he stifled a guffaw with a cough.

'Destroyed soon after you left,' he said soberly. 'A sorry sight indeed.'

'Is this your progress?'

'No, but it illustrates the problem with the Tartaruchi; they can attack when and where they want, then disappear underground where we can't pursue.'

'Frustrating, I imagine.' Leto was uninterested; he was eager to get on.

'Terribly. Well, I finally realised I just had to block the bolt-holes and find the right bait to lure them out.'

Leto began to see how isolated they were. Just them and the river. 'Geta . . .'

'The little thug in charge is spoiling for a fight. He wouldn't miss a chance to assassinate the Commander of the Grand Legion. The Tartaruchi hears everything, but just to be sure, we've been spreading the news in the taverns and whorehouses ever since you arrived.'

In every direction Leto looked, he could see surly young men bearing black flags emerging from the alleyways. The unfeigned panic of his men drew the bandieratori on.

'I hope you've brought some stout hearts, Spinther. This *will* get hot!'

'You reckless fool—'

'Have you forgotten how to use a blade?'

When Leto unsheathed his sword, he laughed. 'Good lad! You're not dead yet! Ready, boys: ring a rosy round your beloved general!' He pushed the gunner beside Leto and ordered, 'Hold your fire till it's needed, there's a good fellow.'

He turned back as the half-circle tightened around them like a noose. There were some thirty of them, boys mostly, but capable-looking. 'Come on, you pigeon-livered curs!' he shouted. 'Let's have at it!'

He stopped shouting abruptly when Uggeri stepped forward.

'So you've finally come for that duel, boy? Be warned, this isn't my first.'

Uggeri held his banner so tightly that his knuckles stood out. 'I'd love to, but a friend of mind has a greater claim.' He withdrew into the ranks and a giant shadow stepped forward. His neck and shoulders ran into one arch of muscle. His face was grim. To Leto, snatching glimpses between his ring of bodyguards, it looked as though he was holding two massive hammers; it took him a moment to realise that in fact the hammers were connected to his forelimbs: they *were* his hands.

'Ah, *le Roi*. You've become quite the artist with your new tools.' This wasn't idle praise; Geta had become well acquainted with Jacques's handiwork. 'What's the matter? You don't enjoy flattery? Cat got your tongue?'

Geta wished to madden the giant before he attacked, but for all the effect his taunting was having he might have been deaf as well as dumb. Seeing this, he abandoned caution and dashed forward, his sword drawn back.

Jacques waited calmly, and when the thrust came, he batted it carelessly aside. The other hammer punched a dent in Geta's chestplate and sent him flying. He landed awkwardly and rolled – and sat up to see Jacques bearing down on him.

Bewildered to find no sword in his hand, Geta looked around. The blade caught the sun and twinkled – just out of reach – and he leaped for it just as Jacques's hammer crushed the cobblestone he'd been sitting on seconds before. He stumbled to his feet and risked a glance over the heads of the watching bandieratori.

No, not yet.

He ducked a blow meant to stave in his head and neatly stabbed the giant's deltoid. He went down to the bone, and twisted the blade as he pulled it free. 'Stings, eh?'

With a contemptuous swipe, Jacques broke the blade in two.

Geta lost his footing, and though the blow rattled his arm to numbness, he managed to hold on to the hilt of his broken sword. 'Barbarian!' he cried. 'That was *Damascene* steel – you never forged such a weapon in your life!' And so saying, he plunged the blade-stump into Jacques' kneecap.

A strange animal sound filled the piazza and Geta scrambled to his feet with the roaring giant limping behind, his death-dealing arms swinging like a capsizing windmill. Geta ran towards the inner circle and pushed his way in until he faced the cannoneer, who was holding his weapon with shaking arms. Geta dived to one side, crying, 'Fire!'

Jacques presented such a massive target that even a hasty shot couldn't miss, and though Uggeri shouted, 'Watch out!' he was already far too late.

The hammer knocked the gunner's head sideway with a crack nearly as loud as the cannon's report. For a moment Jacques remained erect, his arms still swinging, then he exhaled a little cloud into the cold morning and crashed to his knees.

Leto, stepping forward, said, 'What an extraordinarily chivalric display.' He swiped his blade, neat as a surgeon, across the giant's throat and Jacques' head rolled back as a torrent of blood bathed his torso and legs. He stared into the kingless kingdom of the clouds as his giant heart hammered its last.

Leto stepped back from the spreading puddle in disgust. 'What's next, a joust?'

'A massacre,' said Geta, 'I hope.'

'*Forza Rasenna!*' Uggeri shouted as he led the charge.

The circle reformed and Geta dived inside, shouting gaily, 'Protect your general, lads!'

An impact – *whoomph!* – and a collective groan. The circle

swayed backwards, then forwards. The world became very small: half-uttered oaths and screams, the press of men, toes trodden upon, fresh sweat. The sudden warmth of blood or piss splashing legs and arms – please, Madonna, not yours – and the *whoop whoop whoop* of the flags doing their deadly work. The circle buckling, the gaps widening; the faces of the snarling bandieratori crying for their blood—

—and in another world, a horn sounded.

The pressure on the centre immediately relented. The bandieratori backed off and turned. Leto didn't know what was happening, only that he wasn't dead and second chances in battle are rare. He pushed his way through the protecting circle and plunged his sword into the spine of a bandieratoro whose attention was elsewhere; his men finally got the idea and did likewise.

The bandieratori retreated slowly, and now Leto saw why: the bandieratori were themselves encircled.

He had always considered Geta a lucky fool whose successes were due to dash rather than intelligence, but he was impressed at the Hawk's Company's cunning deployment. They advanced in three curved rows: the first consisted of a dozen men, widely spread; the second had some thirty men; the third row had yet more.

A Concordian battalion faced with encirclement would have massed to break through at one spot, but the bandieratori had made an art of fragmentary fighting. Uggeri didn't need to give the order; it was always each man for himself. Some bandieratori made it through the first row's gaps, only to be struck down by the second. Very few even got to see the third row.

Uggeri himself was one of the few who defeated the odds and escaped the piazza. It only cost him an ear and a nasty arm wound. He dived into familiar alleys, suddenly so confusing. That blood-trail was reflecting slivers of sunlight – where was it coming from? Oh, *him*. He doubled back a little and tore a piece from his shredded flag, all the while listening for footsteps, and tied off his arm before climbing into an empty statue niche. The condottiere raced by without noticing him, intent on the trail, slowing as he came to the next corner. He turned abruptly, just in time to see the stick, but not quick enough to avoid it.

Uggeri jumped down and raced on, heading for a nearby bolt-hole. The bleeding . . . he couldn't go on much longer. *Grazia Madonna*, it was close, just around this corner . . .

Suddenly he stopped and threw himself against the alley wall, forcing himself to breath. His mind was fogged with recrimination, guilt and anger, but he made himself *think* – about how Geta had drawn them out in a way that ensured none would escape.

He peeked round the corner. Yes, there is was, a final gauntlet: a trio of waiting hawks. He guessed that every exit in the south would be similarly guarded. If anyone did manage to escape Piazza Luna, none would make it back underground. He needed to find an empty tower to hide in until dark.

He found his way to Tower Vanzetti by a winding route and from the upper storey, where looms once wove proud flags, he watched as the day's dead were thrown into the Irenicon. The last time he'd stood here, he told Pedro that he wanted to see what defeat looked like. That wish had been answered.

CHAPTER 23

And Lucifer brought Her to Jerusalem, and set Her on a pinnacle of the temple, and said unto Her, If thou be the Handmaid of God, cast thyself down from hence . . .

Barabbas 4

The furiously burning bonfires made the men's faces red as devils. Each tribe had its own circle. Largest and noisiest was the Naphtali's. Their nasi stalked around the flames to the martial beat of the drum declaiming,

> *Sing of triumph dearly bought*
> *Sing how the dread Napthtali fought*
> *Sing how with valour rarely seen.*
> *They chased the scoundrel Byzantine,*
> *On gilded chariot through the gorge*
> *And laughed to see the famed Prince Jorge*
> *Flee the dreaded Cat. 'Today,' quoth he,*
> *'The Lord has willed us victory.'*

Sofia wandered smiling between the circles talking to the men, praising their bravery, letting Iscanno be passed around like a trophy, laughing at their jokes. She felt like screaming.

Sofia caught the Cat's gleeful eye as he concluded the tale, telling how the Napthtali had raced to the Sicarii's aid and found their allies had destroyed the Lazars almost to a man. She had presented Mik La Nan with the blade that killed Basilius and now he proffered it to the moon like a talisman.

> *Heads piked, bodies stacked, Sicarii slaughter,*
> *Bloodily had the Contessa wrought her*
> *Vengeance. Here's the dreaded knife*
> *With which she ended the worthless life*
> *Of a false and base Grand Master,*
> *Who led the infidel to disaster.*
> *Today the faithful celebrate*
> *The rebirth of the Radinate.*

Nauseated by the bombast, Sofia retreated from the fire. She came upon Bakhbukh, sitting alone in the shadows, staring into nothing. His hands were still bloody. He had got his wish and perhaps now he was realising that he'd ended the bloodline he'd once sworn to serve.

She left him alone with his grief.

She too had gone too far. The 'heat of battle' was a weasel phrase offering no excuse, no absolution. She'd been hunted for so long that being the one *inspiring* fear for once had been irresistible – but the rush of victory had soon passed and she knew that those anguished, accusing wounds would be waiting when she closed her eyes tonight, including the face of one young Lazar whose voice she had recognised when he had begged her for mercy. She had bandaged the boy's wounds on the night of All Souls, just a year ago. He had cried and pleaded, but there could be no exceptions.

Just beyond their campfires, the cold eyes of the feral dogs shone like jewels. The Darkness was watching her, even here, even now. She turned and looked up at the cave of the Old Man.

Ezra's words came back to her: '*Such a victory I pray to never again behold.*' He'd confessed the full truth – even though he must have known how she'd react. Now she knew why: he'd been warning her that the Darkness was most dangerous when one believed one's cause was righteous. She thought back now to her first meeting with him, at the dock in Ariminum – she had been trying to escape after discovering John Acuto's part in the rape of Gubbio. How self-righteous she'd been – and where was John Acuto now, in Heaven, or the other place? When the toll was totted up, how much did his final hour count for: one moment of mad idealism against a life of cynical betrayal and avarice. What was the rate of conversion in that exchange?

Ezra was exactly as she'd left him, huddled over his book in the cave. Without looking up, he asked, 'Did you win?'

'I thought that book told you everything.'

He looked up. 'I see it was a glorious victory. Those are always the most terrible,' he said. 'You heard my confession, Sofia. There was never such a sin as mine, but there has never been such atonement either. I'm not asking for forgiveness. I must earn that yet. For both of us, a great trial remains.'

'Iscanno is bound to suffer most. You said I needed you, Ezra. For what?'

'It will be easier to show you.'

She told Bakhbukh that she would be gone a while and left Jabari in charge of Iscanno. Bakhbukh nodded numbly and did not enquire where she was going.

The Benjaminite territory was close to Jerusalem, but it would always have been easy to find: all they had to do was follow the wind. They rode to a mountain in Emmaus just west of the city. Ezra was a nimble climber, but the higher they got, the more the wind assailed them.

At the summit, he let her get her breath back. The winds enmeshed the distant city like coiling yellow serpents, now howling, now painfully screeching. They were on the very border of that storm. Patient birds of prey hovered overhead, borne on the updrafts that tumbled her hair. Sofia kicked a stone over the edge experimentally and it floated in mid-air for a moment before tumbling down.

She had to shout to be heard. 'Does it ever stop?'

'It blows as men do: fitfully, and without rules. It's a small part of a great wave. You've touched it before, but mere awareness is not enough. The battle is won, but to win the war you must go further. You mastered your fears in Rasenna, but fear has myriad forms. When Iscanno was born it stole back into you.'

'It's not wrong to care for my son.'

'Of course not – but *fear* helps neither of you.'

He pointed to the city. 'That was the mountain to which Man ascended and He descended, where both could walk together. David took it from the Jebusites and Solomon built a temple. It was an embassy in a land ruled by another king. *Bet Yahweh*, the Ebionites called it: God's House. Like all embassies, it acquired secrets. Solomon employed three hundred attendants to guard them and keep the lamps burning, and whenever an attendant died, his son took over. Purity became their idol: clean food, clean hands, clean feet – and hearts too tired to love. They became as blind as the Jebusites from whom David took the mountain. The Temple was destroyed and rebuilt and destroyed again, and all that was left were three hundred ghosts enslaved by their rituals. In times of war, the embassy is burned and the ambassador who does not flee is killed.'

'Without the Temple then, God is homeless?'

'A vagabond God for a race of wanderers,' he shouted back, and the wind howled in sympathy and dowsed them in blinding sand. 'But even Solomon's temple was never anything more than a simulacrum of the *true* Temple. God is the Temple. Vainly Our soul searches for Him, in books and caves and grottos and mountaintops – everywhere but *within*. He is closer to us than our own jugular vein. The Jinn knew that. They chased out the ghosts, so they could wait for the Messiah too.' He took a step to the edge and looked back at her.

She knew what he was asking, 'I can't.'

'Look!' Ezra pointed to the birds. 'They don't experience air as we do, Sofia. It's *thick* as water for them. You are sceptical, but tell me, do you control the ocean with Water Style?'

'. . . no . . . It's more like I control *myself*. I allow its flow to become mine.'

'Exactly: magicians don't decide what spells erupt from their wands, any more than kings decide when to go to war. Wind and Water, the same power that moves them. They are one: realise that and you can enlist their aid. You think you are not falling now? All of us are falling at the same rate through time. Trust in God.'

'So He can betray me like He did the Madonna?' she screamed.

'He didn't betray Her.' Slowly he began to tip forward into the wind and empty space.

'He never told Her what was in store.'

He was tilting forward until now he was almost horizontal, yet supported by nothing.

'All He has are prayers, same as the rest of us. Abraham didn't know the future when he brought his boy up to the Mount.'

She stepped to the edge, feeling the wind buffet her. Her eyes watered and she wiped them angrily. 'I don't give a damn about Abraham's son,' she cried, and leaped—

They found a niche a little down from the summit protected from the gusts. Ezra made a fire and brewed up some tea which he sweetened with a lump of greasy honey. Sofia drank it gratefully and watched him. He sat leafing through his book as though nothing extraordinary had happened that day. She had thrown herself off the summit, and the Wind had caught her.

'How did I do it?'

'Water Style and Air Style are different names for the same discipline,' he said placidly. 'The little you needed to know about The Wind I taught you when we sailed from Ariminum.'

'You only taught me to sail, Ezra. Mik la Nan nearly killed me with his Air Style when we fought.'

'That is because you didn't know you *knew*. You see how the mind hobbles us?'

She supped her tea thoughtfully. 'Why does God need a Handmaid to fight His battles anyway? If He can be born and born again, He can do anything.'

'I fear you will never make a philosopher,' he said mildly. 'That does not follow at all. Like all mortals, you overestimate God's strength. There was no "Let there be Light". The world had to be made like every other thing, and like any masterpiece, it required several iterations. No one would look at this chaotic universe and guess that it had sprung from mathematical perfection. His first essay was a family of perfect forms. Within fractions of the first moment, the crystalline vessels shattered. They were too perfect. The universe *had* to love its Creator. It tore itself apart to do so and became this fertile universe of division and flux. Its heartbeat was the Wave. He saw that it was better. To be fit for such an inconstant world, men must be free to love, free to err, free to change. After that titanic act of foundation, He slept for an age and when He awoke, the Darkness had crept into Creation.'

'From where?'

'God had to remove Himself from the world to make room for life. In that vacuum, we were made, but so was an emptiness. Nature has a horror of the vacuum, because the vacuum *is* horror. We were born together: Man and this shadow.'

'Why not just start over then, return to the perfect forms?'

'I told you: God is weak. Through a dark glass, He looks on our world. Once every millennium, He waxes strong enough to create – not a universe, but a single life imbued with His essence. A wave is composed of drops of water, after all, and one of those drops is the first mover.'

Sofia thought of the love Iscanno made her feel, and that he inspired in others. 'That's all there is to it?' It seemed inadequate.

'All it takes to change the world is one voice speaking the truth. Once in an aeon, someone comes who says what God *is*, loud enough that everybody can hear. The Wave forces change. The Messiah is a genius of love. It's hard to love, but for Him, the first steps come easy. He struggles on higher planes. His reward is to wrestle with the most difficult problems, problems the rest of us fail to notice.'

'Is there hope? What does the book say?'

'It's irrelevant. This is only history's first draft.' He showed her a page on which the text rippled, like the crest on a flag in the wind, words and letters constantly rearranging. 'Our lives are blank pages, our blood is the ink. The author strives to keep up. We surprise Him as much as ourselves. History's not a prison, it's a dance.'

'The pages are running out,' she observed.

'Yes. Iscanno is the new Covenant, and the Darkness knows it. It has never been stronger. Mary's son was to free us by his sacrifice, but before conquering death, He was to harrow Hell. Devils must be culled, evil pruned, or wicked weeds break through. The First Apprentice is but a puppet of Bernoulli's ghost, but the ghost is just another puppet. Urgently, like a ravening wolf, the Darkness seeks Iscanno – it is dethroned if the Messiah attains the age of Reason.'

'Then why don't I just hide him? Go deep into the Sands and lose myself – I can survive here now.'

'There's nowhere it would not find you. The Darkness doesn't want a fair fight. I fear that at this year's Day of the Dead the guests will outstay their welcome and take Akka as they once

215

took Jerusalem. O, if I was Joshua I would halt the sun's passage and let Iscanno grow to be a man, but I'm not that strong. Night is coming, and we must not fear the Dark. Now hurry and finish your tea. The Wind appears to have got its second wind and you need more practise.'

CHAPTER 24

The *Spira Mirabilis* is perfection, a thing terrifying to imperfect creatures. We see clearly in the nautilus shell that the spiral is not a
living thing. Its trail is the dead things life leaves in its wake. Its
beauty is that of the charnel pit.

The Maxims of Bernoulli, collected
by Count Titus Tremellius Pomptinus

The Etruscan town of Concordia was founded in a deep valley.
Old Town was a relic of that older Concord, as were the soaring
aqueducts that collided with the foothills of Monte Nero. Once,
the aqueducts were the tallest man-made structures in Concord,
but after the Re-formation, a second Concord of steel and marble
completed that canopy. That city of broad avenues and canals was
the realm of philosophers who learned never to look down, never
to consider the squalid denizens of Old Town who toiled in a
choking mist of coal and on whose back was built an empire. The
philosophers' eyes were ever on Monte Nero, the linked towers
of the Guild that girded it, and the leaning triple towers that
capped it.

It was the first thing that struck Leto when he laid his eyes on
his home. He paused a while in the Wastes to take it in before
riding on. He still remembered the first time he'd ever seen Concord: on the occasion of his father's Triumph. Then, the mountain
had been crowned by the Molè. He'd been raised in the military
camps of the north and had never before seen anything so glorious as the Molè – or the city, or the crowds who chanted, 'Hail

Imperator!' and cheered for the hero Manius Spinther. His father had ridden through the streets in a quadriga, showered with rose petals and crowned with oak, his solemn face daubed red like the god of war. Try as he might, Leto remembered little else about the man as vividly as that day. The only other memory that came close was the day he was killed.

The assassins had scattered in panic and left his corpse squirming in the mud. Leto fearfully pulled his cloak aside and looked upon his father's blood-caked visage, and there he saw something he'd never before seen on his father's face: terror.

As Concord was segregated within, so it was without. The wall surrounding the city was a perfect circle – it might have been rendered on a colossal lathe. The massive stones were water-blade-smooth, and laid together so seamlessly that not even a daub of moss had ever found purchase there. Surrounding the wall was a dry moat formed by the slopes of the valley. This recession was bridged by the Ponte Bernoulliana.

As Leto crossed it, he reflected that there had been other, smaller, bridges once – before Concord became a city that treated all the world as antagonists. Under the engineers the other bridges were allowed to fall into disrepair, their gates welded shut and bricked up.

Every officer with any ambition made a point of visiting the Piazzetta Bocca della Verità whenever he was in Concord, and Leto was no exception. The Mouth of Truth was an efficient way to gauge the public mood. There wasn't much fresh material – a sense of humour is a dangerous thing during a pious upheaval, so the city's wits lay low. Instead of poems, there was the same graffito that was repeated everywhere these days: a Herod's Sword on a rising sun, with the motto: *Her Kingdom Come*. Eventually, he did find one new rhyme. Its theme was uncomfortably close to home:

It will take time, there's no doubt,
To civilise the barbaric south.
And we've been patient, but how much longer
Will it take? They're weak. We're stronger.
Rome did not burn in a day,
But why so long to vanquish Veii?
Our faith is strong in General Spinther.
. . . he'd better get it done by winter.

It wasn't a denunciation, exactly, but the threat was clear enough – not that he required such pathetic doggerel to tell him his neck was on the line and he brooded on it as he walked through the Guild Halls. Teaching had still not resumed since the Emergency. It was eerie, walking these empty halls – and then to find Torbidda in the Drawing Room, bent over his desk . . . The sense of *déjà vu* left him speechless.

'You look as though you've seen a ghost, Leto. I pray it's not as bad as all that.'

Leto was feeling insecure, so he began with a subject that had always proved agreeable in the past. But anecdotes about the blunders of mutual acquaintances didn't interest Torbidda today, so instead he started to describe his brush with death in Rasenna – but that too failed to penetrate the First Apprentice's indifference.

'Torbidda? Are you hearing me? He used me as *bait*.'

Torbidda looked at him blankly. 'It worked. What else matters?'

Leto was taken aback momentarily. '*I* command your legions.'

'But lately not very well. If Veii was not taking so absurdly long, perhaps I'd agree that Geta took an unacceptable risk. As it is, I begin to wonder if new blood might accomplish what you cannot.'

Leto stiffly drew his blade and knelt. 'If you want my sword, you need only ask.'

'Must you resort to melodrama every time I state the facts? Veii is an important test. All Etruria is watching. If we succeed there, the memory of Rasenna's defiance will be washed away, and with it all hope. While hope remains, we're vulnerable. No matter how grand the Grand Legion, a united Etruria could field a larger army.'

'A united Etruria is a contradiction in terms,' said Leto irritably.

'And ours,' said Torbidda mildly, 'is an age of prodigies.'

Leto flinched. There it was again: that mocking sarcasm, so unlike the boy who had been his steadfast comrade in the Guild Halls. When Cadet Sixty meant something, he said it outright, bluntly, with no dissimulation. Lately Leto had the impression that Torbidda was secretly laughing at the world. He kept the frustration from his voice,

'So I'm told, First Apprentice. Speaking of which, I'm having no more luck than you in getting that bouncing bridge to work. It's the harmonics, I think—'

Torbidda cut him off, saying impatiently, 'It served its purpose. I have no time to waste on such trivialities.'

Leto took a breath and tried again. 'What about Numitor Fuscus? Is he still causing a fuss?'

'For the moment, his faction is reserving their righteous indignation for Malapert Omodeo, the mint master.'

All of the new moneyed breed with whom Torbidda had flooded the Collegio dei Consoli were objects of suspicion to the engineers and those nobles – the majority – who lacked the funds to buy a consulship, and Omodeo was by far the most prominent of them.

'I'm not surprised,' Leto said, trying to hide his disapproval, but still Torbidda picked up on it.

'I told the Collegio that it were better if neither side had recourse to the dark art of banking, but since our enemies have the Bombelli brothers, we must have Omodeo. You, above all, understand that we need the money.'

'I do.'

'Oh Madonna! Spit it out, Leto.'

'War brings out the worst in man, and the worst men. Malapert Omodeo is a faithless profiteer, the lowest of a low breed. He got rich on a war that killed Concordians.'

'Hypocrite!' he chortled. 'Our empire *exists* because of wars that killed Concordians. Omodeo is a means to an end, just like the rest of the Collegio. If any consul gets too vocal in his loyal opposition I can always inspire the fanciulli to have a bonfire of politicians. Make them see that.'

'You're not coming?'

'I have better things to do than listen to those fools chatter.'

'Torbidda, be careful. Fanatics are a dangerous weapon. What if they discover Norcino's alive? We ought to have killed him when we pretended to. I say this as your friend: he's influencing you for the worse. You can't see how much you're changed. You're not yourself lately.'

'That's called growing up, my friend,' he said, picking up his quill and dipping it into the ink jar.

Leto understood that he was dismissed. As soon as he turned his back, the insidious smile vanished from the First Apprentice's face, to be replaced by a look of desperation. His hand began to shake, blotting his drawing with ink. He grabbed it savagely with his other hand and pounded it savagely against the desk until the pen fell from his grip. A strangled '*Leto!*' escaped the contested tongue.

Leto had just reached the door. He turned back urgently. 'I'm here, Torbidda!'

The First Apprentice was leaning over the desk like one who'd been mauled. He had survived the mutiny and was back in command 'Yes, why is that? The consuls are waiting.'

Leto clicked his heels and slammed the door behind him.

The vestibule of the Collegio was thronged with consuls filing into the chamber. In the middle of this river was an island formed by a neat young man surrounded by consuls eager as hatchlings. As they gabbed into each ear, his lively blue eyes roved about and stopped only when they fell on Leto.

Leto sized him up as he approached. Malapert Omodeo was about ten years older than him, and while Geta's generation had lost themselves in an endless circle of debauchery and conspiracy, the next generation of nobles had accepted their lot and found ways to survive and even prosper. Leto had expected Omodeo to have taken up Byzantine fashions during his exile, but he was a clean-shaven man with close-cropped hair who dressed like a high-ranking servant: dark, simple, neat as a parcel. His winning smile never failed, even when insulted – which, since his return from Byzant, was often. They called him Speculator, Usurer, Traitor, and he smiled with the knowledge that the future belonged to those alchemists who could invariably make from one piece of silver two hundred of gold.

'An honour to finally meet you, General.'

'Forgive me, Signor, but I cannot say the same.'

'You too, Spinther?' Omodeo pouted, mockingly. 'I expected principled scorn from the rest of these unworldly worthies, but not from you. I did what I had to do to survive, just like your forefathers.'

'My forefathers joined the Guild because they believed in Bernoulli.'

'That, and to protect their estates, to have influence, to *count*. I sought the same thing, but I took another route.'

'And it led you here, right back to where you started.'

'Which means we are on the same side now. A general who shows up to battle alone looks rather foolish, so I beg you to remember, when next you see your Grand Legion assembled, who's paying for it.'

'I will – and you should remember that you're a temporary expedient. When the war is done, we'll once again have steady revenues from our vassals.'

'Perhaps . . . but the ambitions of States have a way of expanding. I'm confident that I can make myself useful whatever the circumstances.'

Before Leto could respond, the bell summoned them inside.

Leto was used to addressing mechanically cheering soldiers and he found himself struggling to complete his report over the sardonic jeering of the chamber. He did note that Omodeo and his supporters were not part of the noisy opposition, which was centred on the consul known as the Circle, Numitor Fuscus.

Consul Fuscus was nosily listening eating his way through a bag of apples, making an exhibition of his inattention to the general's address. The apples were not just props but ammunition, for whenever a speaker made a point that he disagreed with, he would shift on his fleshy buttocks and release a great rumbling fart that echoed round the chamber like a cannon's report.

His bowels might be eloquent, but the consul himself was an indifferent speaker. His weapons of choice were bribery and threats, a combination that in his skilled hands had proved as persuasive as the most inspiring oratory. He was a backbench whisperer, one who represented the Old Guard, the conservatives who wanted a return to traditional Guild values – by which they meant the straightforward Empiricism of Bernoulli's immediate successors. His opposition to Torbidda was muted in comparison to that of Consul Corvis, which was not unsurprising, as he had achieved prominence only after Corvis' execution. Of course he would tread carefully, to avoid suffering the same fate.

Leto broke away from his prepared remarks to challenge him. 'I answer to the First Apprentice, not you, Consul Fuscus, and he has complete confidence in my command.'

The consul replied through a mouthful of apple, 'So you say, but it would be nice to hear it *from him*. It would be nice to hear *anything* from him – but alas, we are not *worthy* of his time. He spends his days in consultation with the Opera del Duomo.'

Consul Fuscus looked away from Leto and addressed the chamber. 'I fear that in the First Apprentice's absence we are reduced to interpreting his actions like soothsayers deciphering sheep-guts. Surely the fact that the First Apprentice allows *this* incompetent to keep the baton reveals his total indifference to the war effort—?'

Leto had never had much time for the Collegio, and he listened with increasing irritation to this annoying man playing to the crowd. This wasn't about Veii. The animosity between the Fuscus and Spinther families spanned generations, but Leto had fired the feud with new blood when he'd killed the consul's niece and nephew in the Guild Hall.

Then Malapert Omodeo jumped up to defend Leto, and that was the final insult. Leto was about to leave in disgust when a passing notary dropped his papers. As he bent to pick them up, he surreptitiously passed Leto a note.

After the assembly broke up, Leto went out to the Collegio balcony – and was met there with the broad expanse of Numitor Fuscus' back. He was leaning over the balustrade, admiring the gargantuan green banner that hung below it over the impressive view of the empty Piazza dei Collegio and the broad canal that led to it, one of many that stretched from Monte Nero in every direction like the strands of a spider's web.

He turned around and grinned at Leto. 'You're not used to the

Collegio, General Spinther. We seem to take bites out of each other, but it's all theatre, I promise you. You mustn't take our rhetoric seriously. Apple?'

Leto caught it and took a bite. 'I don't take you seriously at all. You were of Consul Corvis' party once. You would do well to remember his fate.'

'Funny thing, you mentioning that. I have been meditating upon that very thing.' He turned back and pointed. 'There – you see that? That is the podium on which Corvis was flayed, at the orders of your one-time friend.'

'Torbidda remains my friend, Consul.'

'Such fidelity! You must be the most singular Cadet in the history of the Guild Halls. I do appreciate the risk I take in approaching you, but I believe your patriotism will outweigh your emotional attachments. Our families have long vied against each other, but I am willing to leave that in the past, for the sake of Concord. Don't pretend you have no qualms about letting that rat Malapert Omodeo into the Collegio, and don't pretend'– he gestured towards Monte Nero – 'that you enjoyed the First Apprentice's conversion either. This daily spectacle of children dying is as vulgar as a Miracle Play. Is this what our great Reformation has become? There's only so much suffering people will bear.'

'That is what you don't understand, Consul: they're *glad* to suffer. If you're expecting rebellion, you'll be disappointed.'

'The *last* thing I want is a rebellion,' said Fuscus hastily. 'What we need is a *revolution*.'

Leto had little patience for the word-parsing of parliamentarians. 'There's a distinction?'

'My dear boy, there is a *world* of a difference. Rebellion is a spasm, like vomiting. Revolution is born of Reason and calculation by men who have something to lose. The suffering people I refer to are our peers: it's the powerful who challenge tyrants. The poor, having never tasted the fine wine of liberty, are content to quaff the weak beer of stability. Free a serf and he will take up his chains again within a generation. We who have known power, on the other hand, are inured to its glamour. We can act in unison, assured that all of us are inspired by a disinterested patriotism.'

Leto did not bother to conceal his scepticism, but he let the consul continue.

'Your friend, to put it simply, is on the wrong side of history. After the Curia, the Apprentices were necessary transition figures – now they have outlived their use. That's clear to all now that a lunatic has risen to the red.'

That was going too far. 'You call it lunacy,' said Leto, 'but Torbidda was chosen as First Apprentice for reasons that are beyond you and me. His understanding is not given to the rest of us. Consider this, Consul: Bernoulli expanded the empire to limits we can barely protect today, and he did it with more than technology. He did it because Concord *believed* in him. Faith wins wars, and Torbidda knows that. His seduction of the fanciulli wasn't just some gambit: look at the miracles they are working on a daily basis.'

'Aye – and to what end?' the consul said bitterly. 'Your *friend* cares about this Sangrail to the exclusion of all else, even the war. When it is done, mark my words, he will set Concord on fire the better to light it up.'

'You ask me to believe that it's patriotism that animates you, but you forget I was made in the Guild Hall – I recognise the stink of ambition. Be careful, lest yours leads you to that podium.' He tore up the note and threw it over the balcony. 'I will not speak of this, but do not ask me again to betray my friend. Good day, Consul.'

Leto climbed Monte Nero, taking the same dusted path as the fanciulli. The stone stairway he had climbed on the day of his induction had been worn smooth by the daily passage of that army of zealots. Despite his promise of discretion, he considered as he climbed whether he should tell Torbidda of the consul's plotting, but decided in the end to leave it – another round of purges would only weaken Concord, and this was a time when it needed all its strength.

The Grand Legion was vying against Veii, a nation sustained by bondsmen. He had little sympathy for the slaves, but the effeminacy it implied in their masters disgusted him – and it bothered him that Torbidda was intent on making Concord into such place – the fanciulli might be enslaved by fear of God rather than the whip, but a slave was a slave nonetheless.

The stink that assailed him when he reached the summit reminded him that architecture is no pure art but one where the gross and sublime lie together: the foundations had been plastered with dung and urine to keep the masonry moist and workable. Overhead, the tripod's form was already clear: it was as if a great diseased insect of unknown origin had alighted on the mount and was waiting there to die. Scaffolding erupted out of the bricks like wildflowers on a mountaintop; workers in that great crown of thorns did not have to be admonished not to look down.

The First Apprentice, standing at the very centre of the mount, spotted him and waved Leto on. After his moment of weakness, he was eager to flaunt his control to the captured soul within him. 'Think, Leto, how terrible it will be when this tower goes unpunished. No censuring thunderbolt, no purging flood, just . . . silence. The ego of the race will not bear it. Is it not marvellous?'

The Angel of Reason had been dismembered and rendered down. The stone base had been split into great fragments, and the motto was now illegible.

'Marvellous . . .'

'I've known you long enough to know when something's irking you.'

'It *is* marvellous, Torbidda – but can't it wait? We have finite resources. Would we not be better delaying construction to concentrate on the war? Once we win, there will be time—'

'Time is *short*! Winter is almost upon us and yet still Veii remains uncracked.'

'I'm pushing as hard as I can,' said Leto unhappily, tired of repeating himself.

'Perhaps you've been pushing in the wrong direction. I want you to go to Ariminum and tell the Moor that it's time for him to pick a side.'

It was a moment before Leto realised what he meant. 'What if he decides to stick with Catrina? He's in a good spot.'

'You saw the relish with which he strangled the procurator.'

'What of it?' said Leto coolly. He was beginning to to dislike both Torbidda's new didacticism and his un-Torbidda-like loquacity.

'For some men, pride is a stronger spur than greed. As long as the Moor holds Ariminum in Catrina's name he knows he's a slave, even if the leash is very long. Tell him we'll recognise him as doge if he'll allow us the use of the Ariminumese fleet.'

'You're right.' Leto was already savouring the moment. 'It's just what's needed to break the deadlock at Veii—'

'No – you're going to Akka. Queen Catrina has decided to keep the Scaligeri girl. The fleet's presence in her harbour will change her mind. And if it doesn't, you'll just have to use other means.'

'I do understand the propaganda value of bringing the Scaligeri line to an end, but just to be clear, Torbidda: you're talking about starting another war.'

'War must come to Oltremare,' he said serenely.

'Of course I agree, but must it come immediately? Akka's not the power it was, but I know from personal experience that

Byzant is as terrible as it ever was. Opening a second front right now would be imprudent, to put it mildly—'

'You can take Akka before the Byzantines can reinforce it. Fortune is won by the bold, is it not?'

This was uncomfortably close to Geta's prescription, and Leto said angrily, 'What's lost by first using the fleet against Veii?'

'Time, Leto, *time!* You measure in seasons, but my scale is wider. This moment has been coming for centuries, so should I miss it just so I can knock down walls that must surely fall a few days later?'

Leto looked at him, bemused. 'Torbidda, I don't understand what the greatest power in Etruria can possibly have to fear from one girl?'

Torbidda stared at him then, a quart of pity, a pint of contempt in his look. 'Next to her, our power is wind-borne dust. Next to her, all this is *nothing*. She is the edge of history and behind her is a wave that can overcome us, if we let her set foot on Etruria again.'

Leto put a steadying hand on Torbidda's shoulder. 'I think you're worrying about nothing. Most likely she's dead in the Oltremarine desert.'

'If she was dead, I'd know it!'

'How?'

'The way I know it's night or day.' Torbidda pushed his hand away. '*Ack!* I might as well describe red to a blind man. Being First means I don't have to explain. *Ever.* Find her, Leto – because I say find her.'

'I'm not an Apprentice,' Leto said coldly, 'and I never sought that honour. I *know* you're privy to secrets I am not, but *surely* it is common sense—'

'I've heard enough! Do as I say, or I'll find someone else who will follow my orders! You have presumed on our friendship for too long. I need soldiers willing to take risks – and for all his faults,

Lord Geta knows when that's necessary. You see that mob down there? They're carrying stones of such weight that their bones are deforming. It is not Reason that makes men toil till their bodies collapse! When Varro made us dissect the human heart he never told us of the power of dreams. I've shown them my dream, and I've let them *share* it. I'm asking you now to dream a little too.'

Leto straightened his uniform and tried to maintain his composure. He had always been instinctively wary of this kind of Naturalist nonsense, but to hear it spouting from Torbidda's mouth was shocking. The exhausted young bodies scattered dead and dying across Monte Nero's cold, sharp stones were like a parody of the Guild Hall's annual cull, hardly any cause for celebration.

Torbidda's new talkativeness disturbed him too: he'd never been one to chatter or share. Other Cadets and Consuls bragged and joked, told stories, related plans – but Torbidda was silent. He listened and pondered, and when the time came to act, he knew the right course; that was how he'd navigated the crises of his youth with the world against him and come out on top.

'Besides, Veii can be made to surrender by other means,' said Torbidda with his new smile. 'Shall I tell you why Bernoulli's legions were so successful? *Fear.* No town wanted to be another Rasenna or Gubbio. After we sent the Waves, the other towns got into line. Etruria's memory is short. A fresh example is overdue.'

Leto had been growing more and more appalled at Torbidda's plans, but this idea made him forget all his reservations. 'Make it Rasenna!' he exclaimed with sudden inspiration. 'What better place to destroy than the city that destroyed the Twelfth?'

'You're really angry with Geta, aren't you?' Torbidda laughed. He turned his back. 'You'll need men if the Moor proves less than agreeable. Ready the reserves to go to Ariminum tomorrow.'

'Is it safe to remove them from the capital?'

'I have an army of maniacs at my command. I'll survive.'

'Where are you going?' Leto asked, eager to get on now.

Without turning, Torbidda answered, 'To the Wastes, of course. I must prepare Rasenna's lesson.'

CHAPTER 25

When Pedro left Veii after organising its defences, they gave him a trumpet chorus, in recognition of his service. Even so, he doubted that Duke Grimani would welcome a group of Rasenneisi exiles into his already crowded city, which was no doubt already suffering privations due to the siege. But Doctor Ferruccio had promised a posse of butteri to escort them to Salerno, so he sent the rest of his party across the Albula.

Pedro was able to gain entry only because the siege was undergoing a lull while the Concordians were busy constructing a vast ramp up the rolling hills, a massive task that involved shifting thousands of tons of earth and stone. When it was done, they would be able to roll their siege-engines right up to the wall.

He expected to find the duke atop the walls, seeing that his men were ready for the coming storm, but a much-amused Captain of the Guard instead pointed Pedro to the stables. The duke's long argus-eyed cloak stood out brilliantly amidst the dun straw and leather-garbed stablehands.

'Maestro Vanzetti! About time you gave up on Rasenna. Good blood after bad, I say. Come, let me show my latest acquisition. Beautiful, ain't she? Apullian – look at those legs! I tell you, I'm confident that victory's in the bag.'

Pedro soon realised he was talking not about the siege but the Palio di Veii, the annual race in the horseshoe-shaped piazza at the heart of the city. Each borough had a jockey and mount to represent its honour.

The duke, noticing his expression, grinned. 'My condolences, Maestro Vanzetti. I discern that you are one of those unfortunate youths who take life far too seriously. As you shall see, we implemented your advice – well, those parts we could afford. The layered blockade has done well: it's sufficed to delay the Concordians, which is all that is necessary. They can't prolong a siege into winter.'

Grimani's complacent speech was punctuated by – and somewhat undercut by – the groaning parade of stretchers carried past the stables. But he ignored them, patted the skittish horses and told Pedro to take his time surveying the walls before turning away to consult with his jockey. Pedro saw with a sinking heart that Doctor Ferruccio had been completely right. Grimani was resisting only so he could cut a better deal. After a few weeks, he'd hammer out a pact with the Concordians and solemnly promise not to interfere while the Grand Legion continued south.

Later, when Pedro was shown into the Castello, he found Salvatore Bombelli and the duke in heated argument. Without a trace of embarrassment, Grimani broke away to enquire about his review.

Pedro paused before speaking. Candour would not be appreciated, he guessed: it would either wound or anger this peacock, and neither would help. In the end, he said simply, 'Satisfactory, on the whole.'

Grimani beamed. 'I'm happy you are happy, for this is only the most recent occasion Rasenna and Veii have cooperated.' The duke clapped Pedro on the back and said expansively, 'Your late gonfaloniere was an excellent friend to Veii – a great customer of our alum – and a man who knew his place. I grieve for his sons, who have forgotten the base roots from which they sprang. But the young are loyal to profit only; their fidelity is as transient as the price of silver. They rush across the peninsula chasing deals, exchanging, changing. I will not go as far as the Curia and say it is *sinful*, but it *is* unnatural, this wringing coin from coin.'

Pedro had no idea how to respond – these barbs were clearly aimed at Salvatore, not him.

But the head of the Bombelli Family was not to be cowed by innuendo.

'I understand completely, Duke Grimani,' he said smoothly. 'I am often obliged to deal with those I would rather not. If my company ever grows too onerous, you could stop borrowing my money – and of course, there's always the option of paying your debts, or even the interest on it.'

Pedro feared Grimani was about to order Salvatore beheaded, but the tension was dispelled with a round of insincere laughter from all sides.

'We dine at eight,' the duke announced shortly, and left the chamber.

As before, Salvatore insisted that Pedro accompanied him to his quarters to prepare. 'That profligate Costanzo has left behind quite a wardrobe,' he said with a laugh.

'So where is he?'

'Oh, I sent him and Guido down to Salerno. It never hurts to spread one's assets. I was going to go with them, but when I heard you were on the way I decided to hang back.'

Pedro waited a beat, then asked, 'Have you any word of the Contessa, Salvatore?'

'Indirectly. The Tarentines trade horses with Akka in exchange for spices. The traffic's usually pretty constant, but in recent months, hardly any ships have come from Oltremare.'

'What is it, a rebellion?'

'More like a civil war,' he said with a sniff. 'The Tarentines have been hearing Queen Catrina's side of it, of course, but it's clear she's hard-pressed. She's even been building herself a fleet.'

Pedro looked surprised. 'Why would she need one?'

'That *is* the question.' He gave a generous tip to the attendant standing guard at the door and closed it behind him. 'Well, how do you like my chambers?'

Pedro was confused: the rooms were barely furnished. There were no carpets, no tapestries, no paintings – it was all oddly austere, especially for a successful banking house. Even in Rasenna, Fabbro and his children had surrounded themselves in luxury.

Then he understood. 'Going somewhere?'

'Soon as I can.'

'Not staying for the race?'

'I only like to gamble when there's an excellent chance of winning. Veii's doomed, and Papa always said a viper's most dangerous in its death-throes.'

'Would Grimani really betray the League?'

'Come, Pedro, you're not a boy any more. A king must at least pretend his actions are honourable – but no such chains bind a republic's first citizen. He and his fellows need only convince themselves that a thing is *expedient* and that gives them leave to stoop to any crime, and not even furtively, but with pride. Right now, Grimani's still in denial, but the siege has begun to bite. He'll be trying to buy his way back into Concord's favour soon enough, and I have no doubt he'll use us as honey.'

Pedro did not need much convincing that their host might betray them. 'Like father, like son, I guess. Do you think Spinther will go for it?'

'No,' Salvatore said, 'the Concordians don't want Veii; they just want its assets – the colonies, and the Albula's waterways. But we'll be dead before Grimani figures that out.'

'When are you leaving?'

Salvatore looked around the empty suite of rooms. 'This very night. I delayed only so I could warn you.'

CHAPTER 26

For years the Wastes had been slowly expanding, but lately the pace of infection had increased, and now the autumn crocuses of the Rasenneisi contato sickened wherever its dust settled. Isabella stopped at the threshold, paralysed by a terror greater than any she'd known. The night Tower Vaccarelli had burned was nothing compared to this. Behind her was home; ahead was a silence no bird could out-sing. She'd needed no map to get here: like the pole draws the needle's eye, so the awful hum at Concord's heart summoned her. Wherever Sofia was, she must feel it too, Isabella realised. Distance was nothing to power this potent.

Pedro might be right, that she wasn't strong or skilful enough, but what she needed now was neither strength nor skill, but *Grace*.

With a whispered prayer she crossed into the shadows. She could see Concord's high walls in the distance and as dusk came on, the glow-globes painted the grand structures of the new city with blue light, and from that pulsing mist arose the great black mountain. Some rot had exposed Monte Nero's skeleton and now a great tripod arose from a web of scaffolding. Each leg was a colossal buttress that caught the last of the day's light before the sun sank behind the northern mountains. Whatever sorcery had supported them while they were being built, they now supported each other.

There was the source of the maddening song.

'Where goest thou, little bird?'

Isabella turned to see a man squatting in the shredded shadow of a dead tree that she had just walked by. He blended perfectly with the rotten wood. His skin was chapped with scars and burns and liver spots, and the rags he wore were recognisably those of a mendicant. He looked at her through empty eye sockets and smiled as he raised a bloody hand in greeting. 'Delightful to *see* you again.'

'We haven't—' she began, but the words died in her mouth as she saw he was missing a thumb. She drew back in alarm, holding her forearm. 'You!' The scar his fingers had burned had never truly healed.

'Silly bird, you're in no danger – not from me, anyway.' Before him lay a buzzard with its ribcage prised open; he went back to pulling it apart, explaining, 'I'm looking for my brother. He's been hiding from me for – oh, for centuries now. But I'm catching up. What would you say if I advised you that there is nothing for you in Concord but *pain*?'

'I'd say, get behind me, Satan.'

'You've mistaken me for someone else,' he said. 'Him, perhaps?'

Still in the distance but walking towards them was a boy, a little older than Isabella. He was dressed in rags, some yellow, some orange, some red.

'Alas,' the blind man whispered, 'too late to fly now.' His unseeing gaze followed her as she walked towards the boy.

The wind raised a wave of choking dust and the boy's body shifted like a mirage. Could it be—? Was this the *same boy* who had played such havoc during the siege in Rasenna, the one who'd calmly riddled Doc Bardini with arrows and escaped before the Wave came? He'd worn yellow then, but that was a superficial difference.

But no, this was not the same boy; this was not a boy at all. He was a shell, and Isabella could see the abomination that was his true form.

'Brave to face me, Sister. Brave but foolish.'

'That one,' Isabella gestured to the mendicant behind her, 'is too blind to see your intentions, but I *see* you.'

'You ought to thank me. I will stay that wheel of suffering to which the absentee landlord you call *God* has bound you.'

'And in so doing, kill hope.'

'There's no greater torture than hope. I am your liberator. I will teach Man to call me God. It will be an easy task, for we are alike in so many ways. When Men anger me, I send a flood to punish them. You, fortunate child, are the first to hear my good news. I shall make you my Evangelist.'

He was the Deceiver and there was no point listening to his lies. 'I'd rather be your executioner!' She leaped, crossing the distance between them in a moment, and he raised his hand like a bishop giving benediction, blocking her kick. He skidded backwards. His body was unnaturally rigid as his feet dragged the dirt. He had barely settled before she was spinning towards him, and again he blocked her. She rebounded with a second kick, followed by a cascade of battering fists. Her onslaught was furious, fluid and unremitting. The dust raised made the air cloudy and he calmly retreated into the murk.

'Is the Handmaid as inept as you?' he asked conversationally. 'This will be easier than I expected. You're getting tired. Why don't you go to sleep?'

His voice was honey-seductive, but she resisted. 'Because I see *you*. You may have deceived all of Concord, that blind priest, even that boy whose skin you wear, but I see *you*.'

Her words penetrated and for a moment his serene expression faltered and a twist of doubt made his face spasm. His right arm began trembling. His other hand restrained it. 'Down!' he commanded, speaking not to Isabella, but to someone else, partially present.

Isabella chose that moment to strike. A jab to the neck made his chin dip involuntarily and with her other hand she dragged her nails across his brow, then leaped out of reach.

His fist burst suddenly out from the dust, but rather than block it, she avoided his touch as something vile.

'You're beginning to vex— Aaahh!' he screamed as the blood from his brow hit his eyes.

Isabella had been waiting. She slammed her knee into his bent-over face and he swung wildly, stumbling back. She caught his wrist as it passed and punched him in the kidney – a blow that would have made any normal opponent collapse.

He just laughed.

She grabbed the arm with her other hand too, and turned a standing somersault, never releasing her grip. The tendons of his shoulder joint ripped audibly and he bellowed with royal outrage.

A whiplash kick to her chest sent her flying.

Darkness for a second – no – don't black out – don't—

Her tongue was blood-coated. The kick had broken ribs, and every breath was jagged agony, and tasted of over-salted meat.

He stood before her in the swirling dust, his arm limp and backwards, blood streaming down his waxy face. He writhed unnaturally, and she saw the sickeningly pale skin between its black iron scales.

'Worm, I *see* you,' she cried.

With demonic strength, he raised his dislocated arm and it coiled like a trapped serpent until it wriggled back into position. His blood-bathed eyes remained closed.

'Child, I see you too,' he crowed.

Isabella awoke with a throbbing pain in her head and a constricting feeling around her chest. She was bound to the base of a massive metal cylinder that narrowed to a spike, exactly beneath the tripod legs on the summit of Monte Nero. The boy stood over her, tightening the manacles that held her wrists. Around the needle's base was a shallow circular pool filled with briny-looking water intermittently blackened by inky slicks.

'I must leave, my King,' said a voice behind the needle.

The boy left off his work and waded towards the speaker. Isabella, listening to their voices as she looked at the water, began to suspect that the unreflective dark liquid was very slowly drifting towards her.

'You are abandoning me, Astrologer.'

'I have an appointment to keep in Jerusalem.'

'There's no need – I'm dispatching Leto to bring her back.'

'The Contessa and her child are invulnerable while my brother is at their side. I will stop his meddling at last.'

'You'll go with the fleet then?'

'There are quicker ways to travel.'

'Very well,' the boy said. 'I owe you thanks.'

'Don't embarrass yourself. I knew what you were when I persuaded Torbidda into your jaws.'

The boy dropped his hand uncertainly. 'Then why did you help me?'

'I believe in Balance. The Messiah needs a devil to tempt him, and if that fails, to crucify him.'

The Astrologer turned and looked at Isabella. 'I'll give the Handmaid your regards, little bird.'

The boy appeared in front of her once more. 'So it appears you weren't the only one who saw through me.'

'*Torbidda*,' she said, looking him in the eye. 'That was your name, wasn't it?'

'His name matters little. I do not expect to be staying long in this vessel. Tell me, do you like my temple? It will soon be complete, but its heart is beating already. Those busy ants beautifying the giant's skin cannot hear it, but they are not my audience. The world those ants think so vast is merely a membrane between heaven and hell, an intermediate stage scarcely noticed by the contesting parties. You and I know the truth, little bird: to them it is *everything*, to us it is merely a bridge. When I erect the rest of the needle, it will be visible to the great unblinking eye for which I built it. I shall emulate cunning Ulysses and put it out! Then blessed blindness shall descend upon the earth like a mist. That foolish astrologer craved sleep, but I've drunk my surfeit of that nightly death. While I was entombed I dreamed of rivers. I mapped them in my last life – a life which seems another dream now. As the Molè was but a shadow of the Beast, so the rivers of Etruria my pedantic tools described are like the superficial veins compared to deep arteries.'

He crouched and scooped up a handful of the strange liquid. 'The *real* rivers of Etruria run deep underground, pulsing life throughout the earth – I could hear them flowing beneath my grave. And O! how I yearned to drink them dry!'

He held his cupped palms up to her face. 'This is *melan*, water unpolluted by God. I have extracted that essence that made the buio such a nuisance. See its purity – *smell* it.'

Isabella gagged, and the boy laughed.

'You think it's unnatural? On the contrary, I wish to return to Nature. I remember when Man was just another filth-encrusted beast, chewing roots in the plains – and then that terrible eye fell on him and suddenly Man's little head, hitherto concerned with nothing more than rutting and eating, was filled with *notions*. Inventions. Art. Argument. The overweening creature stood upright, and every beast shrank from his nakedness. They recognised his unnaturalness – would that they had torn him to pieces. The world would have been spared so much grief.'

'God raised us up,' Isabella said.

'He gave you a thirst that could never be quenched, like a whore teasing beggars. And for it, you slaves *praise* Him! He gave you wit enough to know your flesh is rotting, and for that you *thank* Him. O base, base servility. It was a crime against Nature and in kind it shall be punished. An eye for an eye!'

Isabella strained against her restraints to look him in the eye. 'Take your life back, Torbidda!'

'You cannot move me.'

'Silence, Worm! I'm talking to the boy inside you – can you hear me? Philosophy blinded you! They said you were a number, but you're more than that. The hole in you is *not* God's fault. Only God can fill it.'

'Shut up!' he snarled.

'Break free!' she shouted, and suddenly his expression *changed*. Fear and regret flooded his face, and Isabella realised that the prisoner had heard her and was fighting to escape.

Then his face changed back, twisting in bottomless hate as the two souls warred for one body. The struggle ended suddenly.

The worm had won. His black pupils had over-spilled until his eyes were totally black. He brought the liquid closer to her, raising his palms above her head. 'You must be born again, as I was. God is an infection of the mind. A most radical purge is necessary.'

Isabella closed her eyes and prayed: *Reverend Mother, Lucia, Sofia, be with me now. Madonna, give me Grace.*

'You shall be my prophet, going before me in the world, spreading my good news.'

'I shall die before I do your bidding!'

'Torbidda said that too, before I ate him. I'll tell you what I told him: a little dying is necessary.'

The unexpected coldness was shocking. It snaked through her hair down to her face, and before it invaded her, she knew that Grace had fled the world.

Her tormentor watched his medicine work, musing, 'Now that I recall, it didn't comfort him either.'

CHAPTER 27

The interlocking layers of the Ponte Bernoulli's lapidary gate slid open and spilled the soldiers of the Reserve Legion into the Wastes, heading for Ariminum.

Before the legion came to the mountainous backbone that bisected Etruria, the last caravan of the baggage train turned south towards the Rasenneisi contato. The corporal driving the small covered caravan had precise orders; he was to catch up the rest of the men as soon as he had seen them carried out.

The two foot soldiers in the back of the caravan were eager to rejoin their comrades. Ariminum was not a city to miss. The younger of the pair tried to make conversation with his colleague. 'You were one of Geta's bravos, weren't you?'

The old soldier's hair was grey, and his sun-withered skin was slashed with horizontal wrinkles and vertical scars. 'What's it to you?'

'Only asking. What's he like?'

'The best fighter I've known, and the worst man. After the Apprentice did for that Corvis, Geta abandoned us without a thought. If it hadn't been for the amnesty I'd've hanged for sure. Plenty of me mates did. I'm an old man, but I've one ambition left, and that's to see Geta dangle.'

The younger soldier had been hoping to pass the time listening to a good yarn, not a rant. He tried to change the subject before the veteran got fully into his stride. 'What's she singing for, you reckon?' He looked at the prisoner kneeling opposite them. A pole behind her back connected the steel hoop around her neck to manacles around her ankles.

'Crazies always sing.' The veteran's scowl inverted itself into a leer. 'Pretty, though. Got a look before they put the hood on. Nice young thing. Reckon the corporal will let us—?'

'Being as how he forbade us to even touch her, I'd say not. What're you at?'

'Relax.' The veteran pushed his younger counterpart aside, leaned over and poked a finger under the hood. 'No harm in saying hello— OW!' He pulled back, swearing. 'She bleedin' bit me!'

The other laughed. 'Serves you right, dirty donkey.'

The veteran petulantly punched her and the prisoner gasped until her breath returned, then resumed her sing-song.

He sucked his finger. 'Ought to knock her bloody teeth out. Mad as a mendicant, she is.'

'You ask me, it was that Fra Norcino what drove everyone mad – First Apprentice and all.'

'Naw, sonny, you mark my words. The Apprentice's just *using* them fanciulli to build his new – whatever it is. Soon as it's done, he'll let us at 'em. Seen it a hundred times.'

The caravan stopped at the southern border where only the hardiest scrub was growing. A little further south were the grassy hills of the Rasenneisi contato.

The corporal came round to the back. 'We're here.'

'Here don't look like much,' the veteran commented.

'Ignoramus! This is Montefeltro.'

The young soldier looked around superstitiously. This was the field where, thirty years ago, his grandfather and thousands besides had perished, where Rasenna and her allies had smashed the Concordian host. The ground was an uneven blanket under which a mass of cannon and engines were rudely buried. They would need to tread carefully, lest broken bones beneath the weeds draw fresh blood.

'So?' the veteran didn't like being reprimanded in front of the youngster. 'Bit late for reinforcements, ain't it?'

'So General Spinther said to bring her this far.'

'Don't see the need—'

'Don't you? Well, maybe that's why you're the oldest foot soldier in the legions. Now get her out – and be careful. Don't let her touch you – and before you ask, it's 'cause it's orders is why.'

Grumbling incoherently, the veteran climbed back into the caravan. After some awkward manoeuvring, he managed to disconnect the pole from the girl's ankles and hurried her to her feet. He used the pole to lead her to the caravan's edge – then viciously booted her out.

The corporal swore at him, then added, 'Didn't I say keep hold!'

The veteran leaped down, pleased with himself. 'All this fuss. It's not as if she's a mad dog.'

The young soldier grinned. 'She gave you a good—'

'Shut up!'

'Shut up the both of you.' The corporal grabbed the pole and pulled the prisoner to her feet. He pointed her away from Concord. 'Release her feet and stand back – don't worry, I got her.'

They did as instructed, then the corporal carefully disconnected the pole before backing away himself. All three waited as the girl swayed on the spot, her fingers twitching, moaning.

'Now what, Corp? She going to grow roots?'

The sweating corporal jabbed the pole between her shoulder blades and thanked Saint Eco when she took the hint and started walking. They watched her getting smaller for a good quarter of an hour.

'She ain't turning, Corporal.'

'No,' he agreed. 'General Spinther said she wouldn't. Let's go then.'

'Before they start without us,' the veteran said, and slapped his colleague's back. 'Ariminum, here we come!'

As the carriage turned around and set off in pursuit of the legion, the hooded girl didn't deviate from her course, not even when a stale breath from the Wastes whipped the shroud from her head. She danced on, on towards Rasenna.

Isabella was coming home.

Pale flesh, lined red where the skin was creased for the first time. A rotund chest, inflated to bursting point before emitting a shrill cry. By some animal instinct, the infant knew it was in peril. Torbidda tried to stifle the crying. It was so very cold up here on the canals. The guards must be close – he could hear their voices – but the mist rising up from the water – uneasy water, disturbed by the beckoning hands and grasping claws of the buio – made it hard to be sure of anything, even his next step. He stumbled and . . .

. . . was in the Dissection Hall, scalpel in hand.

'I warned you, Cadets,' Agrippina shouted to the class. 'You'd better have your subjects securely restrained.'

She glanced at his bench as she marched by.

'Cadet Sixty, what is that?'

A trembling lamb lay upon the table. She whipped a sheet from a nearby cadaver and covered it. 'Take it away,' she whispered, 'before they smell it.'

Torbidda peeped over her shoulder and saw that his classmates were mostly wolves, though a few were still in the agonising process of shedding their human pelts. At the top of the hall, an old wolf stalked up and down the podium with his shaggy mane dripping wet. 'Homo Homini Lupus!' he howled and the class leaped onto their dissection tables and began eating their subjects.

Over the screams, Agrippina thrust the bundle into this arms. 'Go!'

He ran under a bench and saw a student approaching Agrippina.

'Where is he?' Although the boy was not yet fully wolf, Torbidda shuddered. The voice was his own.

'Who?'

The other Torbidda pinned her wrists with his paws.

'Torbidda, run!' she screamed before her throat was ripped out.

He burst out through the door into the corridors of Guild Hall – although somehow, as he ran, the columns changed to the scaffolds and cranes of a building site.

Now he was on the windy summit of Monte Nero and looming overhead were the legs of the tripod. Disorientated, he stumbled again and dropped the bundle. It rolled to a stop ahead of him and the lamb poked its head out into the cold, then stumbled to its feet. A pathetic shudder ran through its body.

It stood there, defiantly bleating. He tried to tell it to run, but what came from his throat was a low growl. He looked down at his hands: they were great brown wolf paws now. He watched curved ebony claws emerging, panting with fascination. The churning hunger in his gut made him look up.

A young woman – he fancied he knew her smell – had picked up the lamb. 'I lie upon your altar freely,' she said, and again her voice was familiar. She could not outrun his long, loping stride – but she didn't even try.

'Damn you, run!'

He was lying on the dusty wooden floorboards – must've fallen from his stool in his sleep. The candle had burned down and the Drawing Room was inconsistently illuminated by clouded moonlight while the windows were battered by rain and wind. He picked up the stool and placed it by the desk, on which were a dozen schematics he had no memory of drawing. He rubbed his eyes and looked into the dark shadows surrounding him. The nightmare fled from his memory and he did not pursue it.

Suddenly his knees went weak and he stopped himself falling only by clinging to his desk. He remembered *everything*.

The layers peeled off, in reverse order: the little nun and the things he'd done to her; Fra Norcino's farewell; overseeing the tripod's construction; addressing the people. As clear as a cut jewel, he remembered every second of the last few months – but that was the terrifying thing, for *those memories were someone else's.*

The last memory he could claim sole ownership of was dimmer. He recalled descending in the coffin, and his confidence that his strength was equal to whatever lay waiting. After that, a veil covered everything. Do ghosts remember their deaths? He remembered . . .

. . . drowning. Codes long etched into metal enlivened by electric fluid clicked into place. The unsleeping blood-bloated worm that dwelt at the bottom of the pit – from whom even the mad buio fled – was waiting. His eyes opened underwater and cold red eyes stared back hungrily – the eyes of the architect who had fashioned his cathedral into a tomb. The Darkness had invaded him and he had been buried within himself.

Afterwards, the usurper's actions were things he watched from afar as he periodically attempted to break free, like a sleeper trying to kick off suffocating nightmare. Then a courageous girl had addressed him, spoke his name and awakened him from that horrid dream. He was Torbidda again, not Sixty: Torbidda. His hands, his feet, his mind, were his once more. He almost laughed, but a glimpse of himself in a window quelled all mirth. Illuminated by the moon's frigid light, he looked like a corpse incompetently animated by some novice necromancer. The worm was only slumbering. How long before it swallowed him again? He had awakened from a nightmare into a reality that was worse.

It was still raining when he got there – it was always raining in the Depths. Despite the tumult in the rest of Concord, this part of Old Town never changed. He'd once brought Agrippina here on some mad romantic impulse. She'd asked about his mother, and he said she was dead and changed the subject.

He knocked hard – a fair approximation of a praetorian rap, the summons that immediately demanded a response – and his heart pounded as he saw a flickering candle behind the shutters. Sweat covered his brow even though the heavy cloak he wore was saturated by rain.

The door creaked open. 'Oh. It's you. Come in before death catches you,' said a croak from the darkness. 'Clever as you were, you always was daft.'

He stepped in, and the smell of offal cooking on the charcoal fire that was never extinguished was exactly as he remembered. The shifting candlelight, the wind shaking the shutters, the rain trickling down his back, his disorientation with his flesh – it was as though the little hut was a cabin of a ship sailing unquiet seas.

But no, not everything was the same – something was *off*.

'Why've you returned, then? I've naught for you.' She was shrunken like a ham hung too long. Her dried face was squashed between two round apple cheeks. Her hair, what was left of it, was like wiry white steel. Her skin was thin as a film of oil, and a similar greasy colour. A cheap tin Herod's Sword hung from her neck by a leather string.

'Nothing, eh? Well, you always was talkative,' she said. 'Let me put that cloak by the fire—'

She saw among the rags underneath a distinctive red and pulled away as though it had burned her. Torbidda knew it was he who was out of place here.

'I made First, Mother.' He said it with a strange embarrassment, then asked, 'You didn't know?'

Her ignorance wasn't too surprising. The denizens of the Depths had as little notion of Guild politics as they had of the movements of the stars. One First Apprentice was much like the last.

'I had one of my notions, but I don't trust 'em no more.' She shuffled over to a little counter and said, 'I've naught to offer but hard bread and buttermilk. That used to settle you when you was little and dreamt bad.'

On a tilting shelf beside the counter he saw an old Byzantine doll painted in shades of purple. He took it down. It was a wooden Madonna that came apart. Within its womb was another Madonna, and within that another. The final doll – small as a thimble – was the slain baby.

She hacked at the loaf. 'Funny you spotting that. It was your favourite toy.'

'This was how I first conceived of Infinity.'

'Aye, you was one for notions too,' she said with a shrewd look. 'Apprentice . . . so, it's so. Your colour always was red. Hard to get, I expect?'

There was so much he wanted to say, but no terms he could put it in that she would understand. 'It required much labour.'

'More than that, I expect. I expect you've a year's worth of nasty dreams.'

'An infinity. Tonight I dreamed I was carrying a baby by the Grand Canal. Guards were chasing me. It reminded me of a story you once told me.'

'So, that's why you came. To blame your old mother for your troubles.'

'On the contrary. I think you had the right idea.'

She sat down beside him, regarding him suspiciously. 'You was never one for doubting yourself.'

'You gave me to the Guild. I don't blame you for it but they . . . *changed* me. They made me a vessel, but first they made me a killer.'

The old woman laughed suddenly. 'Oh no! They might have expanded your range but you was always a wrong 'un.' She spat phlegm into the fire and wiped her mouth. 'Better than any cat for keeping vermin down, you was. Had to hunt you into the streets or you'd cut them up in here. I expect that's where I got the notion you'd get to the mountaintop if I put you on the track. They goaded you all the way up with promises and praise, no doubt. They told you you was smart, smartest of all – and now you come complaining to me that they tricked you into lying on their altar? Well, I can't say I'm sorry. Ah, you don't like that. I thought philosophers prized truth, but you came here for consoling lies, didn't you?'

'Very well then,' said Torbidda, his voice hard. 'The truth. Who was my father?'

She leaped up and backed away, her hand still clutching the knife. 'An evil wind got you! I ought to have drowned myself, there and then. I knew you was malignant from the start, even before the buio warned me. By the time I got up the courage, it was too late. I was too weak. You're weak too, bastard. We was both vessels, vessels within vessels, and you didn't come to ask me no questions.'

'Why did I come?' he whispered.

She rushed at him with a despairing cry and he fell back from the table and touched the gash on his cheek. 'Stop! What are you doing?'

'What I ought to have!'

She slashed again and this time he caught the blade in his dangling sleeves, wound it round and yanked it from her grip. As he bent to pick it up, she smashed the milk bottle and held the shattered end up. 'Weak, I say! You can't fight what's in you!'

Torbidda's stomach lurched as if he'd been punched hard. If he had come for the truth, that was it. He couldn't fight it. There was no reneging. A colourless pall descended over his eyes. He, the soul that had woken this night, was smothered and evicted by another much stronger, much older. He dropped the knife and smiled at her – and she instantly dropped the bottle and held up her Herod's Sword. 'Madonna protect me!'

The worm slid over the glass shards. 'She can't even protect Herself.'

In the storm, the neighbours claimed to have heard nothing, and by the time the smell became impossible to ignore, the rats had eaten most of her. Then they behaved as all neighbours did in the Depths and stole what was not wholly worthless and burned the rest – amongst the latter was a curious wooden doll that had been smashed into an infinity of splinters.

CHAPTER 28

The sons of Adam agreed to build a Temple to atone
for their father's sin but fell to arguing where to
build it. Brother, thou art not my keeper, Abel
said, Go thou thy way and let me go mine. And it
came to pass that when Cain found Abel on Mount
Moriah laying out foundations at the threshing
place, he rose up and cleaved Abel's head against
a stone in the earth thereof. And the earth opened
its mouth to receive his blood. Then the Lord said
unto Cain, Where is Abel your brother? What have
you done?

Genesis 4

Sofia came hurtling up on a gust and landed neatly beside Ezra.
He did not comment, or even acknowledge her.

'Oh come on! You have to admit that was better.'

He kept looking at a swirling dust cloud on a distant ridge;
Sofia didn't think it looked so remarkable.

He closed the book and gave it to her. 'I must go.'

She suddenly understood that he was deadly serious. 'You
promised to be at my side.'

He turned wearily and faced the south. 'You're on a road that
only Handmaids may travel. I've taught you how to do what's
expected – but hear me. You can be more than God's wetnurse:
you can *change* your role, as I have done. You are preparing to
wrestle the Darkness, but there will come a time when you must

wrestle God. He has made up His mind, but a righteous spirit can make Him relent. You have within you a power more powerful than any Molè, any army or wind or Wave. The love you bear for Iscanno can move mountains.'

The sand-laden gusts that assailed them ebbed momentarily, long enough for Sofia to glimpse the object of Ezra's attention. On the opposite ridge stood a solitary silhouette. The rags tumbling about him made him look like a great crow, vainly beating against the wind.

'That's him? The other—?'

'My brother, yes.'

'I'll fight with you—'

'*You* will protect Iscanno. This is my fight – my remaining act of contrition. I mentioned that we are not the only immortals left. A creature named Befana can tell you what I have not had time to teach you – don't worry about finding her. She'll find you.'

The ragged figure pointed south, towards Jerusalem.

She felt the wind change pitch and shouted, 'You're going to die, aren't you?'

Ezra pointed grimly in the same direction, as if in response. 'Most likely.'

A great sand-spout burst from the chasm that separated them and the ragged figure calmly let it carry him aloft. Ezra dashed forward and leaped from the cliff.

Then the cold wind was upon them and Ezra was carried backwards and was gone.

The wind tried to pry her fingers loose and when that failed, tried to lift the boulder to which she clung. She felt her grip weaken, but then as suddenly as it came, it was gone.

She raised herself up dizzily, the wail still ringing in her ears, and saw the spout, unanchored now, writhing like a serpent towards the ruined city to whatever end Fate ordained.

No one was free – though for a moment Ezra had convinced her otherwise.

He believed that he'd broken his shackles, but they had pulled him away at last. If even immortals were subject to fate's decrees, what hope had she? Once this land was populated by people who considered themselves Chosen because they kept the covenant – but surely it was the covenant that kept them? Every breath, every step, every kiss, every betrayal – these were gestures long-ordained and long-rehearsed, devoid of meaning, like a graveyard language.

The wind carried them swiftly to their appointed end. Ezra floated a hundred braccia in front of Fra Norcino. They had known each other in the world's first spring, had seen Nimrod's tower rise and fall, had cured Nebuchadnezzar's madness, had welcomed the Macedonian conqueror into Babylon – and their implacable hate for each other was vital as summer grass. The Jinn had removed all trace of Herod's false temple from the Mount, all stain of the hand of Man. No temple was necessary; time itself was as holy here, an eternal Sabbath. They would not permit the race of Adam to defile it again.

But the two astrologers had ceased to be men aeons ago. The mile-high wall of airborne sand that surrounded the Mount parted to allow them entry, and instantly reformed. There could only be one victor, for the Jinn too recognised that the Mount was a place of sacrifice.

They landed lightly, each facing the other.

'Brother,' said Ezra.

'We ceased to be brothers when you strayed from the true path.'

'We were deceived! Can you not feel the change? How stale the water, how limp the wind? It was not thus when we were young.'

'We were never meant to intervene directly.'

'Aye, we used proxies: Nimrods, Herods, Bernoullis, just as the Darkness used us.'

'I didn't come to debate, Apostate. I came to end you!' Air ripped as he hurtled through it, but Ezra was ready. Norcino's attack was reckless, savage, frantic, and he countered with his most apollonian Water Style. Norcino switched to Wind to disrupt his rhythm, then both switched to Water together.

The transitions – the result of centuries' practise – were fluid as bird-flight, as gas, as thought, and the power was *dreadful*. Ezra returned his brother's blows with doubled force till the displaced energy made the air around them vibrate, forcing the swirling wind back a few braccia.

In this fight, Norcino's sightless eyes were no impediment – a mere fragment of this contest was physical. The duel to which the Jinn were bearing witness took place on a higher plane.

There was a muffled explosion as the vacuum collapsed. Ezra was momentarily fazed, and Norcino struck a fraction of a second before he recovered, sending him flying towards the fatal wall.

The impact as he first struck the ground knocked the breath out of him and he rolled over and over until his left hand flopped over the threshold. The sand stripped skin, then bone, before he could pull out his wrist and stumble to his feet. The wound was instantly cauterised by the heat, and pain is something immortals learn early to master.

Ezra had gathered his composure before Norcino landed.

Norcino fought with all a madman's certainty, but his defence was weak. After several blows to his chest and midsection, he was smiling through reddened teeth.

Close to desperate, Ezra threw a huge right to shatter that grin – but Norcino slipped by Ezra's lunge and caught him under his chin. He snared him in a vice-like embrace, his legs wrapped round Ezra's waist, his hands resting on his face like a healer.

Ezra's legs buckled as Norcino's thumbs plunged into his eyes and he fell onto his back with the madman still on top, rhythmically pushing his thumbs in like a potter working clay, and all the time whispering: '*I alone was true to the Ahura Mazda, the Light.*'

Ezra wrested his stump free and smashed Norcino's nose with it, and he rolled off with a groan.

As Ezra got to his feet, Norcino giggled. 'I begin to understand: you seek to suffer in her stead.' He bounced up, ready for more. 'Alas, this is just a rehearsal. When I'm done with you, you know I'll find her. I know every grain of every desert. I promise you, I will show her that grief is as boundless as God's love.'

Babylon, Uruk, Tara and Mexico – all the lives Norcino had lived – they were dreams now. The Darkness had made him as deaf as he was blind. He'd simply keep going until Ezra was spent. In this contest, insanity was the deciding advantage.

Ezra whispered a prayer to every wind that owed him a favour and carried Norcino screaming across the threshold. The sand consumed them both in moments and scattered the dust of their bones amongst the exhausted things for which the world has no use.

The Handmaid, watching from afar, knew that her navigator had finally come aground. She opened the book and held it up to the Winds like a feast. The sheaves leaped for freedom and coiled in one long vortex of pages, spiralling on towards Jerusalem, to be consumed by its fire, as finally all things must be consumed.

CHAPTER 29

The old soldier had cause to be disappointed: the enchantment of Ariminumese looking-glasses famously made every brute fancy himself an Adonis and every whore, a Venus, but though he had never been particularly handsome, the veteran suddenly looked so wretched that even the younger soldier remarked upon it.

'Tell the truth, sonny, I *am* a bit peaky.' He shivered with rapture. 'But this establishment cures all ills – Geta told us stories about it. The oldest in the Serenissima, he said. They've got girls from all over.'

'I don't think General Spinther brought us here to enjoy ourselves.'

'Me neither, but he's busy talking to the Moor, ain't he?'

The captain wields absolute power at sea, a position to which even the most vaunting terrestrial tyrant does not aspire. But place that despot on Terra Firma and he is rendered impotent. And if the landlocked captain is sorry to behold, consider the still-more-pitiful condition of the landlocked admiral. After the Consilium gave the Moor command of the Golden Fleet, he was chagrined to realise that he could not indulge in even one of the thousand grudges that his pirate soul cherished for those proper Ariminumese captains who supposedly answered to him. *What use is power*, he asked himself, *when one cannot abuse it?* Such was his bitterness at the Consilium's mendacity that he almost forgot he had come to Ariminum in the first place to dupe them.

Much had changed since the Moor became master of *all* Ariminum. With all checks removed, he swept like fire through the gilded circle. Those captains who displeased him were keel-hauled or hanged; a lucky few escaped with flogging. Though he had no notion of currying favour with the arsenalotti, the purge made him wildly popular. He capped it all by burning the Golden Book, and thereby won their loyalty for ever.

But – O! life's endless surprises! – one can have a surfeit even of power. In winning Ariminum, the Moor discovered he had lost something crucial. Despite the ceaseless activity of the City of Bridges, he could not escape the feeling that he was mired in the doldrums. He would have been happier to sail away from it all, but since power once taken up cannot be safely left down, he sought other time-honoured remedies.

The brothel's lower storeys were given over to an extensive array of bathhouses in the Byzantine manner. While his men enjoyed themselves with the staff upstairs, Leto was sitting uncomfortably in a steam-filled chamber beside a large copper bathtub. He discerned from the empty jugs and full glasses scattered around that the Moor's early dalliance with the local wine had become something of an infatuation.

A bubble broke the surface of the warm, foam covered water and Leto said, 'We had a deal.'

A pair of black lips parted the surface. 'Have I not kept my part?'

'You were to persuade Queen Catrina to deliver the Contessa.'

'I asked her, and while waiting for a response, I've been preparing the fleet and drilling the men.'

'You've been raiding the southern coast.' Leto sniffed in disgust. 'It's like an addiction with you.'

The Moor sat up suddenly, water streaming through his beard like Neptune. His righteous anger would have been more impressive if the foam tufts either side of his head did not make him resemble a carnival devil. 'What's a navy for if not to inspire terror? I think you're being unfair. The more I harass the Black Hand, the less ready they'll be for you.' He lay back and rang a bell. The Moor's ensign appeared, filled his glass, rolled up his trousers and sat on the edge of the bath with his feet in the water, then leaned over and started rubbing some very expensive-smelling perfumed oil into his master's back, which he then proceeded to remove with long slow strokes of the strigil, all the while eyeing Leto like a feline mother.

'I didn't come to watch you wallow in excuses.'

'You must learn to *relax*, General. Life is good! I believe I am being finally corrupted. The local wine is sweet, but nothing compared to the local talent. They play the most wonderful tricks. Come, let me find you an angel to make a man of you.'

'I don't want a whore.'

'Excellent. This establishment offers only courtesans.'

'What's the difference?'

'A courtesan tells jokes – not good ones, of course. But it makes a fellow feel less pathetic if he can tell himself he's paying for wit instead of a fuck. We're all about customer satisfaction here.'

'The only female I'm interested in is the Contessa.'

The Moor exchanged a look with his ensign and sank lower in his bathwater. 'No word as yet.'

'Don't trifle with me. If your queen meant to deliver the child, she's had ample chance.'

'That's true. Khoril's been back and forth several times.'

'What? You mean to say the Queen's *flagship* was here?'

'The *Tancred* sailed but a few days ago at the head of a convoy, all so heavily loaded with supplies that I feared for their safety. Acquiring Ariminum has obviously awakened Catrina's maritime ambitions. She's been buying up wood, hemp and steel. I don't suppose you're planning another advance into the Dalmatian March, because that's where we get our timbers and cordage.

Lately it's all gone direct to Akka. It's damned hard to build when there's nothing to build with. And even if the Golden Fleet were at full capacity, I would struggle to find good men. My crew, once the terror of the Tyrrhenian, have ruined themselves. Some have even sold themselves into bondage.' He glanced sadly at his ensign, then back at Leto. 'Catrina also requested a loan of some of my best arsenalotti. I could hardly refuse without alerting her to our – *ah* – understanding.'

'You could have found a thousand reasons to delay,' said Leto, trying hard to hold on to his temper.

'Aye, and perhaps Khoril might have swallowed them, but she would discern my treachery immediately.'

'*Idiota!* She's already guessed it – she's taking what she can while she can.' Leto stood up.

'Where are you going?'

'To salvage this mess.'

'Surely it'll wait till morning?'

Ignoring the Moor's imprecations, Leto strode through the maze of narrow corridors. His personal guard were nowhere to be seen, but the moans and laughter from behind the lace curtains suggested they were busy. The smell of flesh, sweat and other excretions was nauseating. Damn them all. He wanted only two things: fresh air and reliable allies.

A young soldier emerged from a curtain fixing his belt and froze when he saw the young general approaching.

'Sir!'

Leto ignored his salute, brushing past him.

'Arrogant prick,' muttered the soldier without conviction. He couldn't be mad at anyone right now. He'd just conducted a most satisfactory transaction with a dusky brunette. She swore she was Ebionite, but she was probably from Taranto or some other Black Hand backwater. He didn't mind; they didn't talk much.

He swaggered through the corridor and stopped outside the veteran's room.

When he heard uproarious laughter inside he decided to leave them to it. The old man had picked a pair of giggling Russ twins. It was true: the charms of Ariminum cured all ills. As if to confirm the proverb, the hysteria inside grew louder.

While Leto's men indulged themselves into the next day, the Moor had his ensign give the general a tour of the arsenal – that usually impressed visitors. The shipyard was the marvel of Etruria, but Leto saw only its inefficiencies. The arsenalotti's ships relied on the weakness of men, the fragility of oars and the vagaries of wind. What miracles could be wrought with the power of steel and steam. He dismissed the fantasy; ambitious plans, like Torbidda's wonderful self-forming pontoon, were bootless if they were unrealised when Mars called his disciples to their vocation. One always goes to war with the weapons at hand.

Everyone described Ariminum as changeless – yet this was surely a different city to the one that had hosted the League negotiations. He attributed it at first to the new management, but as the day went on, he detected a note of decay, a sickliness he had not noticed before.

He remarked upon this to the ensign, who said, 'The lagoon we owe so much collects its annual tribute. Plague's a trial to be endured like winter storms or heatwaves in June. Such is the seasonal demand that the undertakers have formed a guild.' He pointed out their gondolas pushing through the mist: they had a distinctive green-burning light on their prow as they herded their coffins along the canals like loggers.

Leto had been pondering the change in Torbidda all day, both his mania about the Contessa, and what Consul Fuscus had intimated. He was motivated by power – that was obvious – but nonetheless, might the consul be right? Perhaps Concord had outgrown the Apprentices. Perhaps they could be shrugged off as easily as the Serenissima had shrugged off the doges.

The sun was setting but the running lights on the rigging of the lantern ships kept the harbour illuminated.

'Admiral on deck,' a voice piped.

'Madonna! You look like you've only just got up.'

'That's because I have.' The Moor had dragged himself out of bed when he'd heard that Leto was issuing orders to *his* arsenalotti. 'Now see here, I did not give you permission to board my ships or— What exactly *are* you doing with them?'

'Upgrades. We're allies, remember?' He stopped an engineer and ordered, 'Install the siphons on the smaller ships. They're more manoeuvrable.'

He turned back to the Moor, and patted him on the arm. 'Don't worry. You'll like what they'll do. I've brought materiel enough for the whole fleet, but I count only twenty galleys.' Leto waited for an explanation. When none was forthcoming, he softly swore. 'So not only did you let her take your supplies, you gave her ships to carry them? Did you ever consider that arming the enemy might be a bad strategy?'

'Bah!' the Moor said, 'six ships. The arsenalotti can shit that many out a week!'

Before their argument could get properly started, it was interrupted by the Moor's secretary tugging on his sleeve.

'Admiral, I recommend the Courtesans' Ward be quarantined.'

'That would cripple our economy, you fool.'

'Yes, but something's – well, something *strange* is happening . . . everyone's *dancing*.'

'That's hardly cause for concern,' the Moor said fondly. 'Those girls know their business.'

By the time the secretary managed to convince the Moor that

this really was something they needed to see, the burning ward reflected in the lagoon like a rising sun. The bridges leading from it were dangerously thronged, for the crowds were *desperate* – not to escape the inferno, but to tell the world about the wonderful music. Happy pushing contests developed, and one bear-keeper spun like a dervish between the couples until he tumbled into the water. He was still dancing as he sank. His bear roared plaintively and wandered loose through the canal banks, dragging his chain and clawing with increasing irritation at the citizens who wanted to dance with him.

'Saints protect us!' the Moor exclaimed. The mariner's horror of plague was deep-seated.

One of the bridges suddenly collapsed, and while the Moor stared, his secretary suddenly suggested, 'We could destroy them all, Admiral – create a firebreak—'

'No, it's too late for quarantine.' The newly arrived ensign's face was blackened with soot, making him look like some ill-judged parody of his master.

'You're sure?' said Leto.

'Can't you hear?' he said with irritation. The din of disordered chiming was growing as ward by ward, the precise language of Ariminum's bells was being rendered into babble.

'We must do *something*,' the secretary insisted.

'My dear fellow,' the Moor said, 'do what you like – but first go and lower the harbour chain.'

'And then?'

'Follow me. Or stay and perish. As you like. I'm going for my ship.'

Foreigners of a romantic bent might have expected the arsen-alotti to perish in the hallowed dockyards their forefathers had toiled in, but they had the same idea as their admiral. More than any, they knew there could be only one outcome when the inferno met that great store of tar, pitch and dry wood. They fled via rooftops and unknown alleys to the harbour and hoisted themselves along the ratlines to the nearest ships.

The admiral leaned over the stern of the *San Barabaso* as it bullied its way through the crowded water. Approximately half the ships had cast off – the navy in good order; the merchant barges chaotically. Those ships that had delayed were already overrun by the dancers.

The Moor looked on the city he had so briefly ruled with melancholy, mixed – he had to admit – with relief. He could track the infection's rapid progress by the spreading blooms of fire. The looms of the Silk Quarter added more fuel.

When Leto joined him at the rail, the Moor said, 'By the way, this sickness – it came from Concord?'

The general had been brooding on that very subject. 'Yes . . .'

The Moor unsheathed his great curved sword calmly. 'Too bad.'

Leto eyed him coldly for a moment before turning back to the flames. 'You were never stupid, Azizi, so you must be still drunk. Why would we burn a city that had so much to offer us?'

Convinced by that simple reasoning, the Moor returned his sword. 'This is the second time I have been dethroned. Evidently it is not God's will that I be a king.'

Leto agreed, and was about to say more when a cry came from the rigging: '*Man overboard!*'

The Moor looked over the bulwark. A red-faced man was paddling towards them, ecstatically panting. The Moor took hold of a long rigging-hook and let the wooden end drop onto the swimmer's head. He sank silently, leaving a dark stain on the water. 'Not one of ours,' he explained.

'No, but that is,' said Leto.

'Admiral, the *Affondatore*,' a ship's boy cried, 'she's – she's *coming* for us!'

One of the lantern ships had turned and was bearing down on them. After the Moor had ordered evasive manoeuvres, he looked about for Leto and found him standing at the newly-installed siphon with a look of glee that would have been normal on the face of any other boy. Suddenly a great stream of green-bordered fire shot forth and brushed over the galleon with a touch soft as a swaying reed. Wherever it touched was washed with white dancing flames. Momentum kept the *Affondatore* going forward, and as it narrowly missed them they could see the crew, burned to skeletons, still dancing, even as their skin melted.

The Moor pulled a boy from the rigging. 'Signal the merchant frigates: they can follow me, or I'll assume they're infected and give them like treatment. What is that marvellous fire, Spinther? It's like the blazing sword that chased our unworthy ancestors from Eden.'

'What an imagination you have. It's just a blend of resin, quick-lime, saltpetre and *naphtha*, a wicked oil that seeps from the ground where the Ebionite tribes roam. Torbidda discovered the recipe in the Molè's archive before it burned.'

The Moor gave his ensign command of the other first-class lantern, the *San Eco*. Together with the *San Barabaso*, they glided into the Adriatic, trailed by a patchwork fleet.

'*Addio*, my City of Bridges,' he sighed.

'When you're done with romantic gestures, find out how many ships and men we have.'

'I won't kill you, Spinther,' said the Moor through his teeth, 'but don't expect me to follow orders.'

'Why ever not?'

'You don't think this' – he nodded to the fast-dwindling flaming harbour – 'changes our relationship rather? To attain the use of *my* fleet, the Apprentice offered me the corna. But look:

the whore of the Adriatic is burnt to the waterline, may she rest in peace. How will you motivate me now?'

'Unless you plan to found another city on the waves,' Leto answered sharply, 'you need a place to dock.'

'What's wrong with Akka?'

'I should have thought that was obvious. Queen Catrina doesn't trust you. You've more reason to fear her than me. I can always use a man like you, but if you return to Akka and give her what's left of Ariminum's fleet, you'll find yourself strung up from the *Tancred's* yardarm. It'll be a popular gesture, I'd guess.'

'Sailors are a jealous breed,' the Moor agreed ruefully. 'So Akka's out.'

'When we go, we'll go to burn it. But first, set sail to Veii.'

'I thought your First Apprentice considered finding the Contessa a matter of urgency?'

'So he does, but – well—' Leto gestured to the burning city. The ash whispered down between the giddy sparks rising from the ruins. 'As you say, this changes things.'

'I see the sense in that,' the Moor said. 'Will your First Apprentice?'

'One doesn't get to wear the red by being stupid. He trusts my judgement.' Leto spoke with such confidence that he almost believed it was true.

CHAPTER 30

Geta leaned over the wall and whistled. 'How long's she been standing there?'

'All day – maybe longer.' The sentry was an old condottiere, bored with his station but unfit for anything better. 'She was there when the sun came up. Didn't think much of it at first – you often get mendicants passing by, on their way to Jerusalem or what have you – only that she's been there so long . . . I didn't recognise her as the little Reverend Mother what baptised my little lad not a year ago, not at first. Soon as did, though, I thought, "Better get the boss". Look at her feet! She's not *right*, is she?'

'No, she's not,' said Geta, and then, more to himself than his companion, 'What does she want?'

The sentry tried for the obvious. 'Us to open the gate?'

'*Cretino!* The Tartaruchi have tunnels under the Irenicon. You don't think they might have ways under the walls? If she wanted to get in, she'd already be in.'

'Reckon I could plug her easy from here,' the eager-to-please sentry volunteered. He loaded a quarrel into his crossbow. 'I practise on the cottontails – not much else to do all day, an' I hates to be idle— Hey!' He glowered at Geta, who had snatched it from him. The quarrel sent up a puff of dust not a braccia from Isabella's raw, bleeding feet, but she didn't appear to notice.

'*Oooh*. Very close,' the sentry said. 'But if you don't mind me saying, you wanna aim high – an' try breathing out when you fire.'

'My good fellow, shut your mouth and open the gate.'

*

When the portcullis was halfway up, Geta ducked under and walked towards Isabella with his usual assertive step. As he got closer, close enough to hear her panting like a tired hound, his hand strayed towards his sword. 'I didn't expect to see you again, Reverend Mother,' he said jovially. 'I heard a worrying rumour that you had gone to visit the First Apprentice.'

His tongue went dry. Isabella looked like a corpse, one that had pulled itself from the pyre half-done. Her skin was a patchwork: where it wasn't horribly sunburnt, it was deathly pale. She swayed towards him and back, like a pendulum both drawn and repelled by Rasenna, the spot upon which her ruined feet bounced wet with blood and pus. Her right hand clawed the air while the other hung awkwardly, her fingernails shreds sticking out of swollen black digits. Her lips had all but vanished, and a quivering black tongue poked lewdly between the sharp bits of teeth remaining.

But it was her stare that held him. Her upper and lower eyelids were both peeled back, revealing protruding, putrid-yellow orbs, her pupils shrunken to empty pinpricks.

She was just a harmless little girl foaming at the mouth, he told himself, ignoring that other voice that was screaming *RETREAT!*

'I see Concord didn't agree with you. Well, the big city's not for everyone . . .' He kept up his smooth stream of patter. 'You're home now and that's what matters. I do hope we can put this late unpleasantness behind us because, quite frankly, I need you, Reverend Mother. My wife is about to give birth. She's quite modern in most respects, but she is *very* conservative when it comes to religion, and she *insists* that he – I'm certain it'll be a boy – be baptised right away.'

She was but a flag-thrust away now. His confident voice continued even as his grip on his sword-hilt tightened. The closer he came, the more agitated Isabella became, panting more rapidly as her fingers started twitching and reaching, now for him, now for the Herod's Sword that still hung round her neck.

She was trying to say something, he thought, but had forgotten the habit of speech, and her uncooperative mouth made weird shapes as strange noises emanated: '*Kuh-Kuh-Kuh*—'

Her once-lithe little body leaned towards him with a kind of yearning, yet her feet stubbornly stayed stamping the same puddles. He could see the grey-white streak of bone through the abused skin of her heels.

Her panting speeded up, 'Kuh-kuo-kuoome-daancee. Coomen-daance! Come daance!'

Geta took a tentative step forward. He held his hands up, as though ready to lead her in a measure. 'I'm told I do an elegant galliard, but is it decent? You're not just a nun, after all, but our Reverend Mother—'

'Ku-cuh-cluh-cluh-sedee-guh-ate—'

Her grasping fingers clawed at each other and she howled despairingly and lurched for him. Geta backed away, drawing his sword – but Isabella did not move towards him again and he realised she was wrestling with herself. One hand was reaching for the Herod's Sword and she looked at him, her round yellow eyes bleeding tears.

'What ails you, Reverend Mother?' he asked softly.

'Close the gate!' Her fingers grasped the Herod's Sword and turned the sharp end towards her throat while the other hand tried to resist it.

'NOW!'

The first hand won the struggle and Geta, horrified, backed hurriedly away from the arterial jets as Isabella did a final pirouette and collapsed to the ground.

He turned and ran and ducked under the portcullis. 'Do as she said,' he shouted. 'Close it!'

The sentry shouted down, 'She weren't right, was she?'

Geta stared through the grating at Isabella's body. 'If any more pilgrims show up coming from the north—'

'Yes, my lord?'

'Plug 'em.'

CHAPTER 31

Once, a doughty fisherman sailing the Sybarite coast came upon one
of Neptune's daughters bathing in a cove. The naiad was modest
as she was beautiful and transformed into a narrow river where
his ship could not follow. The enamoured fisherman sought out
Morgana to make for him a love-potion, but his song of his desire
inspired lust in the sorceress's cold heart. When next the fisherman
spied the naiad, he poured the potion into the cove. Instantly she
transformed into a serpent, licentious as once she was demure. He
was the first victim of her embrace and died protesting his devotion. Nor did Morgana escape punishment: Neptune condemned
her to spin for eternity. Thus Scylla and Charybdis were born from
the wreckage of love.

The Etruscan Annals

A strange armada of scarred warships, merchant barks and frigates of all stripes sailed down the Adriatic like a pilgrimage. The
convoy's need to escape had been too great to allow any taking
stock before embarking, but there were several Ariminumese-
owned shipyards along the coast where they might replenish.
Since water was especially scarce, the Moor sated his thirst on
wine. He grew contemplative watching the star that was once
Ariminum shrinking in the distance and listening to the bells
falling silent one by one.

He was dissatisfied with his crew – there were too many
Ariminumese for his liking. They were perfectly good sailors
– respectful, disciplined, well-drilled, for the most, but he

demanded more than competency of his men: he wanted *greed*. He wanted men who would die before surrendering a prize. He'd left many such men behind in the cinders of the city – he would have regretted it, but he had to admit that most of them were ruined long before Ariminum had burned. Come the hour, he could rely only on himself, and his ensign.

He looked up from his reverie and found the boy-general was in equally sombre mood. The games of chance that obsessed the Moor's men bored him horribly, so he had made the shipwright knock up a chessboard. The sailors gave him a wide berth while he sat at it, silently staring, certain that it was some table of necromancy through which he communed with the infernal.

'May I ask, Spinther, why you never sought the Red?'

'That particular colour makes a great target,' Leto said. 'I prefer mud-splattered battle fatigues myself.'

The Moor was not to be deflected. 'If you will allow me to say so, your friend's desire to capture this girl – well, if it were anyone else, I'd call it *unreasonable*. She did not strike me as worth starting a war over when I met her. Pretty, and spirited certainly, but–'

'Concord has only been defeated twice. The first time the Contessa's grandfather led the army. The destruction of the Twelfth Legion two years ago convinced Etrurians that his granddaughter was made of similar stuff. As long as a Scaligeri lives, they'll keep fighting. Her head on a pike means peace.'

'I see,' the Moor said, though obviously he still didn't. 'Well, I hope your employer is content to wait.'

Leto fell silent. He was tired of defending Torbidda. The Moor was right after all: Torbidda's obsession with Sofia Scaligeri *was* unreasonable – and the plague had come from Concord. He'd caught a glimpse of that Rasenneisi girl before the hood was put on her. Torbidda had just told him to set her loose at Montefeltro – he should have been warned about how infectious she was.

It wasn't the secrecy that irked; it was the sloppiness. People changed, but he could not believe that Torbidda of all people had become careless.

After the convoy passed Pescara, they saw that word of the Serenissima's fall had outpaced them: the burning shipyards told them exactly how the natives were celebrating their unlooked-for freedom.

Still suffering privation, and in no great order, the exiles swept down the long outstretched limb that was Etruria and turned west once the thumb of Taranto was sighted. The Moor said the rock-strewn bays between the Four Fingers were unfit even for pirates, 'And harder to navigate than a wolf's gut.'

'You know the Black Hand well?' Leto asked. When he had brought Veii and Salerno to heel he would have to subdue this wilderness next.

The Moor leaned over the rail so that the cooling spray doused him. 'I hail from Barbary, where the sun is too hot for civilised thought, but the Black Hand gives me nightmares. There is a cave here roundabouts where, the natives say, an immortal crone keeps the four winds and their progeny imprisoned, and when she sleeps they run free. The one I dread most is an errant child of the Ostro. The Libeccio herds before it stampeding squalls, coming sometimes from the west, sometimes from the south. It especially delights in throwing ships against the rocks, and the natives of this hellish land sacrifice to their barbarous idols for shipwrecks. That, General Spinther, is all you need to know about the Black Hand.'

A few hours after they passed the last finger, Leto looked up from his maps and correspondence and demanded to know why they weren't bearing north again.

'Don't meddle in things you don't understand,' the Moor said. 'We go around the Sicilies first. It makes little difference.'

'It means days lost! That's unacceptable – we'll take the Strait of Messina.'

Leto had insisted that the First Apprentice would understand their need to deviate from the plan, but the Moor saw now that he was less certain than he pretended – and he was not surprised. He had heard many things about the First Apprentice, but never that he was forgiving.

But on this front, Spinther *had* to be persuaded otherwise. 'Taking the strait would be folly, General.'

'Do you take me for a novice? It's been used since antiquity—'

'Yes, and any mariner will tell you it has turned into a grave-yard since the Great War. Charybdis has expanded her reach. I'd hesitate to run it with one ship, let alone a fleet. I pray you, do not insist on this.'

The Moor – and his entire crew – waited for Spinther's decision, praying he would see Reason.

'But I do insist, Admiral.'

Only when Leto got his first look at Charybdis did he begin to understand the Moor's doubts – but it was too late; they were committed to this course. He held on to the railing and remembered how the Guild Hall examiners used to talk of the terrible beauty of the spirals. He could see nothing beautiful in the great perpetual vortex, which was caused by the meeting of currents off the coast of the Sicilies and the rocky shoal-ridden shore of Etruria.

Besides the danger these two merciless ladies presented in themselves, each extended her reach with her kin. The nephews of Scylla and the sons of Charybdis made the strait into a lethal gauntlet. The row of craggy black pillars that interrupted the strait at irregular intervals were called the *niponti*, Scylla's nephews, and they concealed ship-murdering reefs beneath a skin of water. They could be run, but each was a roll of the die, for terrible though Charybdis was, the chief terror was her wayward children, the smaller maelstroms that roamed subject to no law – sometimes they vanished for months, only to appear suddenly in routes previously considered safe; such inconstancy meant that even with the most experienced navigator at the tiller there was never any sure passage.

The Moor had made the run before, but still he kept a close watch on his helmsman, who in turn watched the shifting undercurrents as if they were rapid dogs. In any other stretch of shoaling waters, a leadsman would be in the channels, regularly calling the depths, but such caution was impossible here, surrounded as they were by a swarm of vortexes.

The helmsman was all for gambling on an eastern passage, but the Moor insisted that they go by the mother – at least Charybdis was something they could see. He listened to the creaking rigging, feeling her teasing fingers luring them to port, and the *Barabaso*'s protests as the helmsmen yanked her back to starboard.

Unlike most sailors, the Moor was not unduly superstitious, but for once the crew's stories of ghost castles and sirens didn't seem so incredible. He glanced starboard as the *San Eco* entered the next passage over. Behind them, the rest of the fleet were grouped messily in two halves, waiting to follow.

The passage of the lanterns took place in agonised silence, but once through, a spontaneous cheer erupted. When the hurrahs died down, the cry from the forecastle became audible: 'Sail ho! Two points on the larboard bow.'

Tension made the Moor snarl, 'Hush, fool. It's the *Fata Morgana*.' The mirages around the strait were legendary.

Another cry: 'Admiral, the *Eco*'s hailing us.'

He spun around – and saw the problem immediately: the *Eco* was stationary, though her drums commanded ramming speed. Her stern alone moved, turning as if some unseen giant hand had hold of it. On the distant deck, his ensign stood looking back at him.

'She's holding, Admiral – we could throw a line, tow her free—'

'And be dragged to our death along with her? Charybdis' pups don't let go, you know that. Stretch back and pull, you slaves,' he roared, 'before we join them in Hades.'

As the *Barabaso* pulled away, the Moor looked back and raised his hand in a final salute.

On the distant deck, his ensign touched his heart, bowed and bellowed an order they could not hear. Rather than prolong a pointless fight, the ensnared ship raised its oars. In a moment, the maelstrom had sucked her screaming into the silent depths.

CHAPTER 32

The heavily pregnant mistress of Rasenna was taking her passeggiata along the town walls, surveying her dominion with her husband. This pleasant promenade was interrupted when a panting sentry came galloping towards them.

'Another visitor at the north gate, Lord Geta.'

'I gave you your instructions—'

'That you did, an' I was going to plug him, only he didn't come from the north. He came from the east. Add to that, he ain't dancing and – well, he looks pretty rich.'

Maddalena grabbed her husband's arm. 'It is our Marian duty to help the helpless.'

'That it is, *amore*. Lead on, my good man.'

It was obvious that the fellow had been riding all day, though he was foolishly dressed for it. The women and children behind him looked to have embarked upon this journey with even less notice.

The man's finery and his magnificent bay horse would have revealed his wealth had his manners not got there first. 'We are Ariminumese exiles – I demand sanctuary.'

'You look an honest sort,' said Geta. 'Why did they kick you out?'

'All my *paesani* are exiles. The *Serenissima* is no more.' He paused after this statement, not for effect so much but because it was still astounding to him.

'You exaggerate, surely, Signore . . .'

'It is the unadorned truth – a fever swept the islands, followed by a fire that forced me to abandon my palazzo and flee with only my hapless wife and poor children.'

'I'll call you Lot, then,' said Geta. He turned to his wife as Maddalena whispered in his ear. Ever the money-changer's daughter, she had noticed that the mules bearing the man's wan-faced children were also bearing heavy coin bags.

'Where did this fever originate?'

'I'm sure I don't know. My city spread her legs to the entire Adriatic. What does it matter?' The gentleman was obviously unused to being questioned, and now he finally lost his temper. 'It's ridiculous to converse this way. You will open the gate—'

'Our legs don't spread so easily, Signore Lot. I'll open my gate when you convince me there's no danger.'

'But really, how can I guess its origin? We had not the time to pack, let alone time for investigation. Ariminum is accustomed to minor plagues – our too-social sailors bring them back in the holds of their ships – but this dancing fever—'

'*Dancing?*' Geta drew back, placing a protective hand on Maddalena's stomach. 'You've had visitors from Concord recently?'

'Ariminum is the world's bazaar. We consider it a disgrace to shut our gates to *anyone* . . .' The long silence that followed failed to prick anyone's conscience and at last the man admitted, 'Yes, all right. I heard rumours that the Concordian boy general was meeting with the Moor. Look here, will you give us sanctuary or no?'

Geta frowned.

The increasingly desperate Ariminumese suddenly recognised the woman at the gonfaloniere's side. 'Signorina Bombelli?' he exclaimed in relief. 'I worked with your father—'

'I remember,' she said graciously. 'How are you?'

'Honestly? I've had better days. I beseech you, gracious lady, convince your husband to do his Marian duty.'

'Alas, sir, my husband is a perfect tyrant. Perhaps I could sway him if you donated one of those heavy-looking coin-bags to the city.'

'You grasping whore!'

'Oh dear husband,' Maddalena cried, 'what did he call me?'

'Block your ears, my delicate flower. Try another city, Signore Lot!'

'Please – no! I'll pay—'

'Good,' said Geta, trying hard not to lick his lips, 'but I fear the price of admission has gone up. Two bags.'

'To take advantage of us like this—'

'Make that three. Murder these days, inflation.'

Still grumbling, Lot untied three of his bags and lugged them to the gate. Maddalena descended to verify that the silver was genuine, then awkwardly covered the sentry with his crossbow as he hauled the bags inside and slammed the gate shut.

After Maddalena had confirmed the silver's worth, Geta shouted down to the expectant exiles, 'Signore Lot! You may enter—' As the family dismounted, he continued, '—in three days' time. If you and your family haven't turned to salt, Rasenna will welcome you.'

The Ariminumese hurled bitter curses as the city's first couple continued their promenade.

'Was that a bit harsh?' said Geta.

'Would you rather be hospitable and perish? The Reverend Mother warned you keep the gates shut, did she not? You have to look after me and your son.' After a pause, she asked 'What do you think this plague is?'

'Divine punishment for our sins. About time too.'

She began walking faster. 'You oughtn't joke about such things.'

'*Amore*, you should see your face!' He pursued her, laughing, as a bell began to chime somewhere in the ruins north of the Irenicon. 'Come, I'll teach you how to fire a crossbow. Something tells me you might need to know before long.'

CHAPTER 33

Groans of despair filled the corridors of the palace – though the outcome of the Lazars' raid was as yet unknown. This repentance was the rehearsal of Akka's courtiers for the following day. Today – the Day of the Innocents – was for the Akkans a day of parades and marigolds, ablutions and confession extracted by flagellation. For their petrified servants, it was a day of cooking feasts, of nailing down furniture and burying silver and hiding knives. The final stage of Akka's purge was the temporary expulsion of all the Sown, and as the Ebionites streamed out of the city, merchants' caravans rolled in, eager to get home before the fun got under way.

One of these dust-covered caravans belonged to the widow Melisende Ibelin. The Lazar escort had not been enough to prevent her drivers from quitting and so she had led it herself. She, her private guards and the escort were weary. She bid the Lazars thanks and good luck and took herself home to the Palazzo Masoir to board herself in before the coming storm.

The twelve dusty knights did not report to the citadel but marched instead straight for the Haute Cour. No one in the jostling crowds noticed. With most of the Lazars off on the raid and without Fulk's stern eye overseeing security, there was an air of improvisation and chaos to the day.

Patriarch Chrysoberges tried to fill the void, but he was himself too giddy with anticipation to be much help, and he finally gave up all pretence of organisation at the sound of a desolate horn. He rushed to the eastern gate, ready to hail the returning heroes – where a whimper escaped him, for the sight before him was not that of a victorious army.

Old Gustav, now acting head of the Lazars, was riding alongside Jorge's chariot at the head of a much-reduced body of men. As Chrysoberges watched, Gustav saluted Jorge and then rode into the city to deliver his report to the queen. The surviving Lazars followed despondently, filing past the patriarch as he turned and made his way towards the Byzantine camp. He heard Jorge call for attention and joined the press of men gathered round his chariot. The mood was sour: the Byzants had escaped almost certain death thanks to Jorge's stalwart leadership, but it was obvious to the soldiers that the Lazar Grand Master had meant to use them as bait. That Basilius had got himself killed instead was little consolation, and many thought that sacking Akka would be just repayment for the queen's mendacity.

Jorge was more measured, but he made no attempt to hide his bitterness. 'When locusts have eaten all that grows, they needs must eat each other. I beg pardon for dragging you here. We have tarried too long while real enemies trouble our western borders. Rest, tend your wounds, feed your animals, and we shall depart this lazaretto and leave these locusts to their feast.'

The soldiers bounded from thoughts of revenge to homecoming and lustily cheered this unexpected news, even as the patriarch threw himself in front of the prince.

'You cannot go, you cannot,' the patriarch begged him, 'Please – our queen has great need of you.'

'To throw more men on the pyre?' Jorge responded. 'I left them bawling for their mothers, sloshing about in each other's blood and drowning innocent worms beneath the earth. I've paid my tithe, Priest.'

'They will see the Kingdom of Heaven—'

'And never again their wives, their children.'

'This is betrayal!' He leaped up and attempted to grab the reins of the chariot, but the prince promptly kicked him under the chin.

'*Your* queen has taught me well!'

The patriarch fell to the ground and wiped his bloody mouth. 'Foolish boy. When you return to Byzant and find yourself surrounded by rivals and doubters, you'll rue this day. What are you anyway? Nothing but a *jockey* made good. Without her sanction, your rule lacks any credibility—'

'That is the trouble with you courtiers. You mistake the appearance of power with its substance. You may whisper and call me usurper behind my back, but what of it? I need no man's permission to rule, nor any woman's either. A true prince forges his own crown.'

The Lazar's cape was torn and his white robes were dyed grey and brown by the filth of battle. His shield was little more than splinters held together by its frame. 'Your Majesty,' he croaked, falling to one knee.

'Is that you, Gustav?' the queen asked, looking around. 'Where's Basilius?'

'Fallen,' the old knight said simply.

'Alas,' she said perfunctorily, then, 'I see you don't have a basket with a head for me; did the Contessa escape, then?'

'Your Majesty,' he said, 'she won.'

The queen received the calamitous news calmly, with her usual proud bearing, but the gabbling courtiers fell into shocked silence as they struggled to take in this unforeseen reversal.

Minutes passed, and then someone with more loyalty to the queen than truth began, 'Perhaps if we—?' but then fell silent.

Someone else said, 'We did everything possible—' and another agreed, nodding, 'Everything.'

Still the queen merely stared and said nothing, and Gustav got up awkwardly and bowed. 'Majesty, dread of corruption will keep the tribes away from Akka for the duration of All Souls. I'll see the defences are prepared for . . . afterwards.'

As soon as he was gone, Catrina slid bonelessly from her throne and moaned, 'I am alone after all. After all, I am alone.'

As more messengers arrived and the scale of the rout became clear, the queen took to pacing and wringing her hands. She shouted abuse at her attendants, pausing occasionally to beat any of her slaves who came within reach, until finally she dismissed them all.

The Lazar novice had been stationed outside Fulk's cell since Jorge's unscheduled visit. It was dull work, and most of the time he slept. A particularly pleasant dream – in which he was liberating a grateful harem from a wicked nasi – was interrupted by the clatter of twelve knights entering the dungeon.

'We're here for the prisoner,' said their captain in a gruff voice.

'I had no notice of this,' the novice began, 'so I'll need to confirm—'

'Relax, lad,' said Fulk. 'I believe these loyal gentlemen are here in an unofficial capacity.' He had suspected the queen would exploit the annual anarchy of the Day of the Dead to dispose of him in such a way that she could plausibly deny responsibility.

'You're not wrong,' said the knight. The novice hit the bars so hard that he left a dent. Sofia removed her mask, gasping, 'I don't know how you breathe in those things!' She took the unconscious novice's key and opened the cell, then paused uncertainly.

The handsome prisoner she did not recognise turned to her but remained sitting. 'It's me, Sofia.'

'*Fulk?*'

'Aye. Your boy has got some grip.'

Sofia turned back to her colleagues, who could not know what was so marvellous, then back again, and in the same tones of wonder exclaimed, 'But you're *whole!*'

'Yes: crime enough to land me in here.'

'Well, you're free now.'

He didn't move. 'If you mean to betray Akka, best kill me now.'

'I don't want Akka. I only want her.'

'And what of your men?'

'We want peace,' said Bakhbukh.

'Forgive my incredulity, but you've been making war for the last year.'

'You mother has led Akka to the brink of ruin,' Sofia answered, 'as you well know. A true prince preserves the kingdom for the next generation; she has promised Akka to the dead. Tonight they're coming to claim their inheritance.'

'What does that mean?'

'After the masks go on, they won't come off.'

Fulk walked out of the cell, removed his glove and smashed the taunting mirror with his fist. 'How can I help?'

'We brought you a uniform. Keep the Lazars away from the palace – we'll do the rest.'

He looked at it, then kneeled beside the slumped guard. 'If you want them to listen to me, I'll need a mask too.'

While the Byzantines struck camp, Jorge reluctantly went to bid farewell to the queen. He found her in the Ancestor Room. He told his Exkoubitores to stand guard at the stairway to give them some privacy; he guessed Queen Catrina would not take rejection well.

She was staring up at the mask of her grandfather, the infamous Tancred Guiscard. Beneath that cruel face hung the conqueror's broadsword, one of the oversized blades that the first Crusaders had wielded to awe the Ebionites.

It was not just the facial resemblance that brought Jorge up short: with her back bent and hair unkempt, Catrina looked old, haggard, and he could make out her whispering voice: *'I will not sleep. They shall not find me in bed.'*

He cleared his throat and without looking at him she said, 'Gustav told me what happened. I can't imagine what prompted Basilius to stray from the plan.' She turned away from the broadsword.

Jorge sighed inwardly but played along. 'Who can say? The God of War is capricious. It doesn't matter anyway; he paid for it.' He glanced up at the fearsome mask above her.

She caught his glance and explained, 'In times of adversity past glories remind us for what we fight – but do you know what I've just now realised? My city is protected by dead men. Once the Lazars were the dashing vanguard of Akka's army. Now they *are* the army. I did not notice because my enemies had been reduced to scattered bands of thieves I could play off against each other. Now a wind has risen and fused those fragments into an army to dwarf my own. What are our chances?'

'The Ebionites strike hard and fast, then they break apart like waves. Such tactics will not help them take Akka. They'll have to mass: a bold charge would break that wave – but it would be bloody work.'

'A suicide mission? I know just the men for it.'

'The Lazars fought courageously for you today, and they suffered grievously.'

'Tears are wasted on the dead.' She did not bother to hide her contempt. 'The Lazars have sworn to protect Akka. In using them to break the Contessa's army, I will help them keep their vow.'

'Why not make peace – a temporary peace – and regroup?'

'No, Akka's day is done – but not the Guiscards. Our empire is greater than any city. Take me with you to Byzant and there we will reforge the fraying bonds of north and south. Think of it, Jorge: an end to this tiresome vying. You fear Concord. Oltremare can break *that* wave too, but only if it's united. I speak of union and inheritance. You came here to find an ally and to be confirmed ruler of Byzant. Take me with you and you'll return as Crown Prince of all Oltremare.'

'Now and for ever,' said Jorge hesitantly, 'I am your loyal son but—' He stopped short as her hand came to rest on the chain around his neck.

'If I am to be your bride there must be a ring.'

'No,' he said.

She ignored him, and yanked so hard that the chain snapped.

'I said no!' he shouted, and slapped her. She fell against the wall and he prised the ring from her fingers. 'It's time someone taught you what "no" means.'

Before she could begin to weep, he turned his back on her, but a harsh metal clang made him spin around. She had taken Tancred's sword down, but was unable to even lift it. Jorge was chilled by the murderous hate that distorted her face – if she had been a man, his head would be off – but bravado made him sneer. 'It isn't as easy as it looks, is it?' he said mockingly. 'You'll have to do your own lifting from now on.'

The Order of Saint Lazarus had their own Haute Cour, in which even novices and journeymen had a voice. They gathered round the forge next to the citadel's stables. Instead of a judge's gavel, Gustav rapped the blacksmith's hammer on an anvil. He was supposed to choose the speakers, but no one was listening to him. The queen had yet to nominate a new Grand Master and in the absence of a leader, dispute held sway.

Faction was common in Akkan politics – indeed, faction was practically its hallmark – but the Lazars had always been above that. Now they were divided. The knights all knew that Basilius had led them and their allies to disaster. The veterans knew it too, but that sin paled beside Fulk's betrayal.

Into this cacophony, like a spark on dry kindling, walked the disgraced figure many blamed for their current ill fortune. At once axes came out and the circle broke apart into two wings. The younger knights went to Fulk; the veterans clustered around Gustav.

'Akka's in mortal danger,' Fulk said.

'Stranger' – Gustav rapped his anvil – 'only Lazars are allowed to speak here. We are brothers sworn to each other. Who are you?'

Fulk answered the challenge without rancour. 'You know me, friend.'

'Aye: you're that pretended knight revealed a traitor!' Gustav rushed at Fulk, and the entire chamber disintegrated into a mass of heaving bodies and echoed to the clash of steel wielded by men of matched skill and wills of deadly intent.

Fulk turned his axe sideways to block Gustav's downward sweep, but the handle came apart and he leaped back to avoid being sliced. He swung the broadside of his axe into Gustav's mask, smashing it into two. The old man fell back and Fulk lifted his weapon to deliver the death blow – but the sight of the old man's noseless, lipless face stopped him short.

'Ah, that repulses you, does it?' cried Gustav triumphantly. 'Look, Brothers!' he bellowed, 'these scars are my bona fides. Let us see yours, Brother Fulk. Prove that you have suffered.'

The fighting came to a sudden halt. 'Brothers, listen,' Fulk began, 'this doesn't matter. The queen has betrayed Akka—'

'Why are you ashamed? Has the sorcery of that devil's whelp worn off?'

'Show us!' another repeated, and another, and the cry was soon taken up, even by those Lazars who had fought with him.

Fulk looked around. They were a brotherhood of pain and he was now an interloper. He slowly removed his mask. 'You wish to see my face? Then see!' He scooped up a handful of burning coals from the forge and plunged them into his face. The reek of cooking flesh filled the chamber.

The circle drew back. When he removed his gloves, the glowing cinders were still eating away his flesh. His face was now indistinguishable from Gustav's, and his voice was as ragged. 'I promised my life and death to this Order. Who doubts me?'

No one said a word. He fell to his knees beside the water trough and pushed his head under. The water hissed and bubbled.

Gustav knelt beside him and pulled him out. 'Welcome home, Grand Master.'

As chill dawn broke over the city the Lazars split up and went door to door. They had to work fast: they were angels of life as once they had been angels of death. They broke down doors and shouted warnings, that this year the guests meant to stay. Most of the citizens, horrified, ran to warn friends and family, but some, those who craved the freedom a mask conferred on this night, refused to believe the Lazars. Others did not care. These unfortunates had to be dragged from their Ancestor Rooms, but for many, the warning had come too late. Their flesh already belonged to the Dead – and the only remedy was the axe.

CHAPTER 34

More exiles arrived before the second day, and over Signore Lot's shrill protestations, the quarantine was extended. Soon Rasenna was surrounded by a sea of tents and caravans. The wealthy tried to bribe their way in and Lord Geta happily collected their gold, but the gates remained closed.

The dancers took longer to arrive. The first swaying silhouettes were spotted in the distance on the third day. Some stricken by the *Danse Macabre* had exhausted themselves in an hour, but in others the fire smouldered on, and those who had somehow escaped Ariminum's flames were drawn by an insatiable hunger for society to the nearest city: Rasenna, though many perished on the way, drowned in the rivers, froze on the mountain, eaten by wolves or murdered by suspicious farmers.

The exiles did their best to keep the infected away from the refugee camp. Young bravos rode forth to dispatch them at a safe distance; at night they kept fires burning and maintained diligent watch. It worked for a while – but they were not soldiers, and on the third watch of the fifth night the camp was breached.

Rasenna awoke to find itself besieged by hordes of dancers, all battering their fists bloody on her walls.

For want of anything better, Geta had fiddlers and pipers stationed along the battlements. Then he waited for time to do its work and when that got boring, he helped the process along, applauding and shouting, 'Bravo, *amore*! Good shot!'

Maddalena lowered her crossbow with a demure smile. 'Where do you think the plague came from?'

'Ariminum, of course.'

'Yes, it did break out there,' she said patiently.

'Ah,' said Geta catching on. 'You think this dart was shot from a Concordian bow?'

'Worse than that: I think *we* were the intended target. They've never forgiven us, and you didn't help matters by embarrassing Spinther.'

Geta's pride was wounded. 'Truly my stock must be low to treat me so callously after all I've done for them.'

'We must win back their favour.'

'That's easier said.'

'It's that, or kill Leto Spinther.'

The second suggestion dispelled his gloom. 'My dear, you always know the right thing to say. Oh look – there's Lot's wife. Watch this shot . . .'

The restless horses stamped on the cold cobbles and their breath made a low-lying cloud over Piazza Luna. Geta's horse Arête was impatiently waiting. His master was looking fondly on the sleeping city, wondering when he would see it again. Geta couldn't boast that he was leaving Rasenna a better place, but the natives' obstinacy was mostly to blame for that.

An outraged cry burst from the window above and the shutters slammed open. 'It's true! Bastard!'

The men attended to their saddles, grinning that their captain had missed his opportunity to make a quiet exit.

He looked up at his wife. 'Maddalena, don't misunderstand—'

'I understand perfectly. You're cutting your losses—'

'I am devoted to you, our son and Rasenna, and that is why I must leave. The First Apprentice and General Spinther think I'm expendable – you said so yourself. I have to show them they're wrong.'

'What about us?'

'Once I'm secure, I can protect you. Just keep the gates barred and hold tight. Bocca will look after you.'

'That sot! I'll be alone for the birth of our son, for his *baptism*. Uggeri will kill us both.'

'I'm leaving a battalion of Hawks behind, *amore*, more than enough to keep Uggeri underground and the Signoria and the Small People in line. You're in no danger.'

'Go, then! Abandon me with the rest of Rasenna's widows.'

'You won't let me leave without a smile?' he said confidently. His men chuckled when the shutters slammed shut.

He was relieved when the palazzo's door opened and she marched out, prising a ring from her finger. She flung it at him. 'I want it back.'

He caught it and declared, 'I'll think of you whenever I look at it.'

'Just don't pawn it.'

Geta slipped a silver medal from his chest. 'This I won for bravery in Dalmatia.' He considered this a white lie; he'd actually stolen it from the body of a Byzantine soldier. 'I've never known anyone as brave as you.'

She kissed his hand as she took it. He held her chin. 'You *do* understand, don't you? I can do more for us in the south than waiting here for the First Apprentice to dream up more ways to murder us. Besides, the Signoria's coffers are quite empty. These dauntless fellows won't stand going unpaid much longer.' He held up the ring. 'How much do you think it's worth?'

She grinned and slapped Arête's flank. He turned his head and snapped at her viciously, before Geta reigned him in. 'I won't be sorry to see the back of your horse, but if you must go, Lord Geta, go with my love.'

'Then I depart happy. *Andiamo*, Condottieri!'

The heroes mounted and the Hawks rode through Rasenna, leaving heartbreak in their wake. They reached the southern gate and formed up tensely, watching the swaying mass through the portcullis. By now, starvation had done more damage than even the archers on the walls. Some were still moving, lying on their backs, writhing and cycling their legs. A hardy few were dancing still.

'*Avanti!*' cried Geta and the gate was hauled up. Boiling oil cleared a path and archers above and below provided cover. The Hawks' tight formation broke through like a cannon-shot and the portcullis dropped; the few dancers who succeeded in getting close got decapitated or trampled for their efforts.

Back in Piazza Luna, Maddalena looked around at the other abandoned women, knowing all too well the reason for their tears. Brothers, fathers and neighbours who had held their tongues would from today call them whores and traitors.

She cast Geta's medal in a pile of horse dung and spat on it. 'Scorn your tears, Signorinas. A pox on all Concordians, all soldiers, and all men.'

CHAPTER 35

In previous years, the streets of Akka would have been awash with shameless lovers rutting away, and a few brawlers wading amongst them, but today the Dead moved with one mind, isolating the citadel and the palace where the Lazars had regrouped.

The palace barbican faced into the streets. Lazar guards would have stood fast to any earthly enemy, but the sheer wave of rage broke through and quickly flooded the bailey. Above this mayhem, the twelve dusty knights who had released Fulk were seeking entry to the second storey of the palace. Sofia led them to the balcony of the throne room, where they willingly shed their masks. Inside, the tribesmen circled the empty throne with their knives out. On either side hung a pair of Guiscard flags; it emanated awful power still. Behind the chamber's thick doors, they heard panicked voices, urging each other to stand fast.

'God blacken her face,' Mik la Nan swore, 'she's already fled.'

Sofia took down one of the flags. 'I know where.'

As the knights outside were overpowered, their screams were drowned under a bestial baying. The door began to buckle under pounding.

'Go then, Contessa,' said Bakhbukh. 'We shall hold these ghouls.'

Jorge lay bleeding at the foot of the staircases. One of his arm manikelians had been shattered by a blow and his Exkoubitores stood over him, trying to keep his attacker at bay. One tried some fancy swordplay, intending to disarm the queen, but with an effortless sweep of the broadsword she shattered his blade. The next stroke lopped off his head.

The other swordsman froze in terror as a falling blow parted his shoulder from his body. Blood cascaded on the steps about Jorge. His right shoulder was a bleeding mess and he tried to still the trembling in his left hand and raise his sword as the queen turned towards him.

Suddenly, behind her, he saw a young woman dressed in a Lazar uniform, creeping up. At first he doubted his own eyes – but in case she was real, chivalry obliged him to cry warning. 'Stay back – she's possessed,' he croaked.

The stranger didn't retreat but called out, 'Here I am, Catrina!'

'*Catrrrina is hiding inside me.*' The queen turned around. She was wearing the death-mask of Tancred Guiscard. '*She rrrran to me as she did when she was a frrrightened child.*' The growl from the grim face had the rolling tenor of old-fashioned Etrurian. The queen rested her foot on the Exkoubitore's severed head. '*That is my flag thou holdest, lass. Thou seekest to be my mascot bearerrr?*'

'I seek justice. I've no quarrel with you, but Catrina must answer for her crimes.'

'*Crrimes! I am punished forrr mine. Hot chains bind me. Ice burrrns me. Rrrat-spawn gnaw my entrrrails. But only cowards rrrepent. I rrrather weep that I had just one life's worrrth of sin. Would that I had a scorrre, I'd make my name as famous in Hell as Berrrnoulli's!*'

'You've had your turn.'

As Sofia ran toward the queen, Catrina kicked the head with huge force, but Sofia leaped it, landed on her knees and skidded below the queen's great sweeping turn. She struck upwards with her flag, but it was blocked by the crossguard of the broadsword.

'*Not bad, Handmaid. Oh yes, I know what thou arrrt, even if my grrranddaughter does not. Where is thy whelp? I'll purrrge it as I purrged this land of infidels.*'

'I didn't come for you, demon.' She was face to face with the mask. 'I know you can hear me, Catrina!'

Sofia twisted her flag, and the sword fell from the queen's grip, but before she could follow up, she was hurled backwards by a heavy iron fist against the side of her head.

'I hear!' Catrina's voice echoed from behind the death mask. 'Now hear me: you turned my people against me – that I could admire – but to turn a son against his mother? *Unforgivable.*'

'You did that yourself,' Sofia spat.

The queen landed a kick to Sofia's stomach. 'I should not be surprised at Fulk's weakness; after all, all men are traitors. I should congratulate you. To conceive without a man's touch is some trick.' She picked up the sword and hefted it meditatively. '*I think it a capital idea. I'll sneak into my grrranddaughter's womb and teach the worrrld to once again fear the name of Tancrrred Guiscard. Why should Berrrnoulli have all the fun?*'

Jorge made a weak grab for the queen's leg, but she viciously kicked him aside and raised her sword.

'Drop it, Mother.'

'Fulk, stay back!' Sofia cried.

'*No, boy – come. Or dost thou only take orrrders from women? What stamp of weakling did my grranddaughterrr bear?*'

Fulk took down one of the masks. 'Shall I show you?'

'*Yes!*' The queen's body shook as a great baritone laugh boomed out. '*That's the face of my firrrst wife, the poorrr wee thing. Trrry it on; I shall need a consort when I rule again.*'

'Fulk, don't listen – *please*, you're better than her—'

'I know,' he said, and smashed the mask to the ground. The queen roared curses at him as he stalked forward towards her, attacking the rest of the hanging masks with the flat of his axe, smashing plaster and clay left and right.

The queen leaped over Sofia, bellowing, 'You are not my flesh!'

He calmly ducked her swooping sword, came up quickly and buried his axe in the scaled armour between her breasts.

'*Guhha*weaahahh!' Two cries came from one mouth.

As her life slipped away, Tancred's grip on her body loosened. Fulk pried the mask off her face and looked into Catrina's dying eyes as he smashed it to the ground. 'Would that it were so, Mother.'

She reached out for him, but he pulled away from her embrace and she fell to the cold marble floor, her face pierced though by the shards of Tancred's.

The Sown had served the *franj* for so long that they considered themselves inured to shock – but nothing could have prepared them for what awaited them when they returned to clean up after the Akkans' revelry. The Marian population of the city had been dwindling for years, but in one terrible night it had reduced itself by half.

The Lazars could tell themselves that they had saved Akka from itself, but the heaped bodies of the citizens they had sworn to defend told another tale. Like kings of old, the Guiscards had taken their most devoted servants to the grave with them.

CHAPTER 36

The Grand Master set the queen's body on a pyre by the shore. It was a small funeral, with just a few elderly courtiers who remembered when Catrina was younger. One of the mourners was the noblewoman already emerging as Akka's new mistress: Melisende Ibelin. Like the rest of the mourners, she watched the flames warily, as if expecting some sort of fiery resurrection. The patriarch was more emotional than most – he had survived the Day of the Dead only because Fulk had tied him up in the Lazar chapel. Now he had to be restrained again, this time from throwing himself on the pyre.

Melisende pulled back her veil and stepped closer to the fire, where Fulk stood like a sentry. He thanked her for coming.

'I came to shed tears for a friend I lost decades ago, and pay respects to Akka's king.'

'You mistake me, my Lady. A king would not have let it come to this pass.'

'We were all of us in her thrall. You cannot carry all our guilt.'

He kicked a burning log back into the flames. 'Is that not a king's duty?'

One by one, the mourners drifted away. Fulk kept vigil through the night.

From the walls, Sofia watched the dying flames. 'I didn't think it would be right to go.'

Bakhbukh stood next to her. 'No, best leave them to it.'

222

AIDAN HARTE

'The throne is his to take, but he's determined not to. She brought him up to sacrifice himself.'

'It's more than that: there's a part of him – of all the Lazars – that feasts upon itself. It's an evil appetite that can never be sated. They are *traif*, Mistress: injured meat. There's no cure for that malady.'

'Nonsense, Bakhbukh. He's a king, if he'd let himself be.'

'Whatever he calls himself, his men need him. Since the bodies have been gathered up, the Lazars are just drifting round the city like aimless ghosts.'

'What of the nesi'im? Still squabbling over the spoils?'

Bakhbukh cast a stone from the wall meditatively. After a moment he said, 'Mik la Nan takes seriously the charge you've given. Melisende Ibelin and he are practical souls; they'll work together well. Unfortunately, Roe de Nail takes it as an affront that he is not Governor of the Sands. I fear the Benjaminites and Issachar will go to war before long.' He shrugged. 'It's a miracle the peace lasted this long.'

'You're bitter, my friend.'

'Merely heartbroken. When the sons of Uriah ben Sinan did not live to see our victory, how can I call it victory? The Issachar are done and I am responsible. Every grain of the Sands reproaches my incompetence. Mistress, I long to leave.'

The hiss of the tide licking the charring wood woke Fulk and he had to work quickly to remove what remained in the ashes. Her bones were carved from rock that would defy even the Sands, so he had brought a harrier's mallet to smash them. He was setting to work when he saw Sofia approaching.

'Where's Chrysoberges?' she called.

'The patriarch slunk off in the night. Perhaps he's drowned himself.'

'You're back to wearing your mask again? Why? Your wounds are not shameful.'

He looked away in embarrassment. 'After all these years, it's more comfortable.'

She didn't believe him. 'Your men are shaken, Fulk.'

'I know it. We considered ourselves intimate with death, but this—' He swung the hammer. The ribs shattered like delicate ceramic. 'When the fleet's ready, we wish to go with you.'

'You can't prove anything to the dead. I'm going because I must, but I fear success is highly unlikely.'

'What matter? By leaving, we'll let in a new wind.' He swung the hammer again and crushed the skull. 'My mother wanted to make Akka into a necropolis. You stopped her, but she succeeded years ago in making her court a mausoleum, and we, who swore to protect Akka, slept as she did it. We owe you a great debt. The odds are irrelevant.'

'Not to me. If you really want to help, there's a way you could improve them . . .'

He said he would attend to it when this last duty was done. He would accept no help, and when he gashed himself on the splinters, he took that parting cut without complaint. When he looked for his mother's death mask to smash it too, it was gone. Perhaps the sea had taken it.

Captain Khoril wasted little time celebrating the queen's overthrow. He still had a job to do, getting the fleet ready to sail. There were rows of ships tied along the wharfs and the hands were cleaning them out, dumping the bilge-soaked straw and spoilt flour and provisioning with barrels of sweet fresh water and wine, smoked lamb and camel, bags of oranges and dried dates and figs and biscuit. The docks were a playground for the Sicarii orphans. Young Jabari was exploring the lanterns, reconnoîtring their darkest recesses. His fear of the dark retreated whenever he carried Iscanno with him into the depths.

The bulky lanterns were physically impressive, but it was the xebecs, the galleys with which the Radinate had once dominated the Middle Sea, that caught Sofia's eye. Those dating from that heroic era had been made seaworthy again by the borrowed arsenalotti; the more recent vessels were those that still worked the Leviathan coast – Khoril didn't ask their captains whether their work had been trading or raiding – who had voluntarily joined the fleet. He had chased and been chased by them and had a particular respect for these canny sailors. They were another breed of Ebionite entirely, as different from the lizard-eaters as they were from the Sown. The xebecs' chief virtue was their speed – with the weather-gage, they could outrun most ships – and the adaptability of their crews, who were rowers, sailors and soldiers as necessity dictated.

'Ahoy, Captain!'

Khoril looked up from his logbook. 'Welcome aboard the *Tancred*. Is this an inspection?'

'Actually, I'm looking for Jabari. He's purloined my son again.'

'That little lizard-eater has been getting under my men's feet all morning. I told him to go below and check for leaks.' He took a dramatic breath, and Sofia prepared herself for the usual cascade of complaints; she had discovered Khoril's chief delight was delivering bad news. 'I'm afraid there's little metal left to cast cannon for the xebecs.'

'Damn,' she said mildly.

Her lack of disappointment disappointed him. 'Not to worry, there's little room for cannon either side of the waterline anyway. Such nimble vessels are not designed for trading missiles.'

Sofia smiled. 'I imagine that's a form of warfare the Ebionites consider dull.'

'Aye: they much prefer boarding, which is why they are packed to the rails with men who can fight like Jinn.'

'Very good. If you'll excuse me, I'll go and find this stowaway.'

Below decks was another world, of confinement and creaking, pungent woods. As she walked through the empty rowing stalls she wondered yet again what would become of their venture, and whether it was foolish to go looking for a fight when they might stay here in Akka, bolster their defences and hope.

A baby's cry interrupted her dark musings and she rushed to the sound. In the central aisle of the lower deck she found a great black shape crouched over, looking like a great hound. The patriarch had his hands tight about Jabari's neck.

'Get off him!' she cried, and the patriarch released his grip – Jabari didn't gasp for air, or move – and picked up Iscanno. He took the ornate Herod's Sword from around his neck and pressed it to the bawling baby's chest. He wore Catrina's death mask, and it was her voice that spoke, *'It's very simple, Contessa. Your life for his.'*

'If I thought you'd keep your word, I'd do it in a heartbeat.'

'Come, child. You can trust the word of a queen.'

'No, you can't.'

Sofia's sling snapped and the mask shattered. The queen would not have hesitated, but Patriarch Chrysoberges stammered, 'She – she took advantage of me!'

Sofia put out his eye with another pebble, caught Iscanno before he fell and incapacitated the screaming patriarch with a downward kick that broke his leg. His howls attracted the attention of the sailors, and when they saw Jabari, they dragged Chrysoberges up to the deck and threw him into the sea, and they all cheered as the filth clotted his heavy robes and pulled him under.

Sofia stayed below in the gloom and wept. She held Iscanno

to her breast and cradled Jabari's limp body under her arm. Ezra had warned her that the devils had not been culled. The weeds of Hell were breaking loose and there was no corner of the world to hide from them.

The Byzantine expeditionary force, diminished though it was, still raised a large cloud of dust. At its head was Jorge in his four-horsed chariot. Scouts rode up to tell the prince that they had a shadow, and he pulled aside to wait for the lone rider.

'I don't know why you've come, Fulk. I've nothing for you.'

'Not even a sup of water? I'm parched.' He'd managed to catch up by taking a highland route and not stopping.

Jorge threw him a canteen. 'I don't doubt it. Give some to your horse too.'

Jorge's anger was directed not at him so much as Akka and the lives he had wasted coming here; Fulk recognised that. 'We need you,' he said quietly.

'That is nothing to me,' said Jorge coldly. 'The king of lepers ought to know what to do with rotting limbs. I'm severing all ties with Akka before the infection spreads. We'll face Concord alone.'

'That's a losing bet and you know it. You said the Concordians will attack Oltremare where it's weakest. If they take Akka, Byzant won't hold out for long.'

'Akka's reputation may have been a bluff, but Byzant's is well-deserved. My city bestrides two seas: half the world fears it, the other envies it. We have lands from Anatolia to Dalmatia, lands through which rivers yet flow. Our walls have stood a thousand years.'

'And within those walls there are a thousand knights as ambitious as you. When Concordian armies converge from east and west, how long before someone looking to their own future opens the gates? Crises create opportunity – that's why you're here today, after all. Don't make the mistake my mother made. Isolation is a living death. Join us, Jorge. We're sailing for Etruria to bring the fight to the Concordians.'

'I won half my races by letting my competitors exhaust each other. Tell me why I shouldn't let you kill each other and take the spoils?'

'You know the answer very well,' Fulk said removing his mask so that Jorge might see his sincerity. 'You don't choose your Crusade. It chooses you. This is ours, brother.'

PART II

AQUA ALTO

'... the rivers, they shall not overflow thee:
when thou walkest through the fire, thou
shalt not be burned ...'

Isaiah 43:2

CHAPTER 37

On the Origins of Concordian Gothic

If History has a shape, it is the perpetually expanding coil of the *Spira Mirabilis*. Your humble author continually returns to the Molè Bernoulliana's moment of conception, because it too illustrates the recursive principle.[1] Originally the Engineers' Guild consisted of the artisans gathered to build Saint Eco's Basilica. It began to achieve political importance only when its rolls opened to the nobility. These creative souls[2] were tired of dogma and intrigued by the Engineers' novel notions and practical methods. Practised politicians, they fast ascended the Guild's hierarchy.[3] Thanks to their patronage, the Guild soon received its charter.

Prominence was not an unadulterated boon. While Curial sanction gave the Engineers' work public legitimacy, the Cardinals too began to take notice. More comfortable with received wisdom, they looked askance on the Engineers' endless experimentation. They chastised the Guild for 'doing naught but weighing air', and asking questions that Aristotle and Galen had already answered.[4] Intimidated, the Guild pledged to limit its enquiries to mechan-

---

1 The principle so picturesquely expressed in the Bernoulli family motto, *In my end is my beginning.*

2 That these recruits were mostly second sons from lesser families makes it likely that some were men of frustrated ambition looking for alternate avenues to power.

3 Senator Tremellius defended the interlopers: 'Foundation must be dense. Stones closest to God at the summit must be refined. So with the Guild, tiers of rough craftsmen support a school of subtle philosophers.'

4 'The old authorities never mention the unseen forces that I have shown spin and vitiate and illuminate the world,' wrote Bernoulli. 'What other winds and currents did the Ancients fail to discern?'

ical questions. Such toadying ceased soon after Girolamo Bernoulli joined the Guild. An unusually ingenious artisan, he conducted the dissections that made Guild meetings so popular with young intellectuals. Even before building his first bridge, even before the publication of his river maps, his tireless curiosity inspired.[5]

---

5 When Bernoulli emerged as a central actor of the Re-formation, a cluster of critics emerged. The naysayers claimed that when he said, 'Solomon, I have outdone thee!', he was not comparing his Molè to the Solomon's Temple but their sorcery. Both men, they whispered, had enslaved the elements to perform their prodigies.

CHAPTER 38

General Spinther grimly sized up Salerno as the Golden Fleet passed by. Salerno was the only great power in the Black Hand, the only state in Etruria that had wholeheartedly fought alongside John Acuto at Tagliacozzo. Its harbour was wide and deep, but the Salernitan interest in the sea did not extend much beyond fishing and the collection of seaweed for medicinal poultices. The chaotic sprawl which was the actual city nestled in a valley defended by the Buffalo Hump Mountains, down which flowed the antique but still-impressive aqueduct.

From here at least, it looked poorly defended, and that was something, but Leto would have been happier had the admiral been on deck to lend his perspective. The Moor's maudlin singing could be heard from his quarters at all hours of the day and night. Though Charybdis had claimed only three ships in the end – a very acceptable result, in Leto's eyes – the heartbroken admiral did not see it that way.

The Asclepeion had been built by the same Eleatic philosophers who had founded Salerno; those paradoxical Greeks had been duly supplanted by the Etruscans and then, after that empire fell, by a succession of invaders too numerous to list. Throughout, the Asclepeion remained. Northerners called it the Schola Salernitana, but it was more than a place of learning; it was a temple, and the famous apothecary was but one small wing.

It was homely, despite the lack of warmth and the dim light. Hanging bunches of fresh and dried herbs and flowers swayed back and forth in the narrow currents of air let in, just enough to circulate and no more, else it would have been both too cold for Matron Trotula to work and unhealthy for her patients.

She stood now before a statue that looked much like her and cupped the flame till it could support itself against the wind. She had a wide-hipped Grecian figure and strong arms, and olive skin pockmarked by some childhood disease. Her thick, long black hair was streaked with white. Her life had not been easy, but she was not one of those who blamed the world; her face was tranquil as that of the goddess before her.

The winds invaded the apothecary as the door behind her suddenly burst open and someone called out urgently, 'Trotula?'

'*Dio*, Ferruccio, what a din you make!' Her smile vanished when she saw the boy in his arms. She raced to his side and put her hand on him. 'How long has he been sweating like that?'

'He fell ill yesterday, got worse through the night. I got the *grosso* out of him and bled the wound – I would have stopped, but I knew I didn't have the art to save him from those evil leeches—'

'You're old enough to know better than to take a Northerner through the Minturnae.'

'No choice. Grimani's men were pursuing us. I knew they wouldn't risk the marshes.

She parted his eyelids and Pedro's dilated pupils fixed on the statue and then moved to her. He started screaming. She stepped back and swept her instruments from the desktop. 'Put him down.'

They managed to restrain his arms with the leather straps on either side – Trotula's desk often had to double as a surgery table – before Pedro did any damage to himself.

'You *must* save this boy,' Ferrucio said. 'He's vital to the League.'

She gave him an unkind look. 'You know I'll do my best no matter who he is. Now go, let me work.'

'Are you sure I cannot—?'

'Close the door behind you!'

The three-tiered aqueduct was left unrepaired, like most in the south, but it was magnificent nonetheless. 'Salerno may not be wealthy as Ariminum, but we have the sun, the wind and the sea in abundance. The Devil's Bridge offers the best view of our treasure.'

'Why's it called that, Doctor?' Guido Bombelli asked.

'Oh, Guido,' Costanzo scolded, 'can't there be any mysteries left in the world?'

'You're still too much the poet, little brother,' said Guido gravely. 'Knowledge is money.'

Anyone looking from up the Asclepeion's gardens could have seen the three figures walking the top of the aqueduct built into the cliffs, for the setting sun cast giant shadows of them and the aqueduct against the flank of the hump-backed mountains.

Ferruccio chuckled at the sibling rivalry. 'Well, it's no mystery; any Salernitan child could tell you the story. Three hundred years ago, a foolish alchemist asked the devil to make him as great an architect as King Solomon. The next morning, the aqueduct had appeared and the alchemist had vanished.'

Guido exchanged a dubious look with his brother. 'You believe that?'

The doctor chuckled. 'Heavens, no. It's an Etruscan aqueduct – there's an inscription to Emperor Catiline on the keystone of every arch – but it's a sweet story.'

'I wonder,' Guido said meditatively, 'if three hundred years hence, simple folk will say the Concordians made a pact with the devil.'

'Perhaps,' said Ferruccio. 'The difference is, they'd be right. Before he fell ill, your young maestro told me that the rivers in the north are turning queer. Mark my words, there's wickedness afoot in Concord of the like not seen since the days of Bernoulli.'

'Where's Pedro now?' Costanzo asked.

Ferruccio pointed out the Giardino della Minerva surrounding the Asclepeion. 'He's in the best hands I know.' He turned back to the brothers and the subject at hand. 'Look, I know you are businessmen as well as patriots. Our backs are not against the wall just yet. We'll get some help from the rest of the Black Hand – Bari, Brundisium and Taranto are as jealous of their freedom as we are.'

'And Sybaris?'

'What help could those cannibals be against the Grand Legion, Costanzo?'

'Not much I suppose.' The Sybarites were infamously *odd*. 'But the Sicilians won't be much use either,' he added. 'They've troubles of their own.'

'How do you know about that?' Ferruccio asked guardedly.

'I still have contacts. The fishermen who work the Tyrrhenian Sea gossip with their counterparts from the Three Sicilies. Rumour – though admittedly an uncertain guide – suggests the current rebellion is centred in the Port of Syracuse.'

'And not, as is usually the case, in the lemon plantations and vineyards. But you know this already, Doctor,' said Guido. 'They have petitioned you for help.'

Ferruccio did not deny it. 'We threw off our own tyrants; we are not about to prop them up elsewhere. Anyway, the Syracusans have always stood aloof from the mainland. Let them stand alone now.'

Anyone else might think it insane that old grudges mattered more than their common enemy, but the Rasenneisi knew all too well the fierce enmity that could exist between neighbours. The City of Towers had torn itself apart daily – until Captain Giovanni had shown them another way.

'You will find we are sceptical of everything here,' said Ferruccio, 'particularly civilisation. The earth regularly shakes to pieces every tall building south of the River Allia. When Nature is taking her passeggiata, a wise man doffs his cap and stands aside.'

'Yet you ask us to stand with you.'

'I do, Guido, most earnestly.' He stopped short and watched as the sun sank beneath the sea, them turned back. 'Forgive me, but I must cut our own passeggiata short this evening.'

'You're riding out tonight?' said Costanzo eagerly. 'May I come?'

Guido responded before Ferruccio could. 'You want to get yourself captured like Salvatore? Certainly not.'

'Your brother's right,' Ferruccio said, though with more sympathy. 'You're too important. With you two on our side, I have hope yet. We're in your debt.'

'You saved Pedro Vanzetti's life, Doctor,' said Guido with a low bow. 'The debt is ours.'

Costanzo watched the afterglow reflecting off the clouds in silence, thinking about Salvatore, until his brother interjected, '*Grazie Dio*, I thought the old fool would never leave. We need to talk about how we're going to escape.'

'Escape? We've escaped to here.'

'Yes, and while you've been walking Salerno's gardens, smelling the flowers and harassing the nuns, I've been studying her prospects. She's doomed. Do you know how they do business? They don't even have a leader, Costanzo. When they need to decide something, they call an assembly, and the lowest shepherd is given the same attention as the fellow who owns the herd.'

'You prefer dealing with tyrants?'

'It's certainly more efficient.'

'And what of Gasparo? What of Salvatore? We just write them off?'

'I don't deny that our losses have been heavy, but doubling down never solves anything – you know that. The bottom line is that we need to get to the Grand Legion before the Grand Legion gets here.'

Costanzo was amazed. 'Tread carefully, Guido. Our tower has already one traitor too many.'

'Facing the truth is not treachery. Pedro Vanzetti is dying – it might be unpalatable, but that's a fact. With our Chief Engineer gone, what is the League but an army of yesterdays?'

'If you are so doubtful of our chances, why did you allow Salvatore to send us away from Veii?'

'Because Grimani's a fool. If I must be sold, I'd rather be the one negotiating the price. I know what's worrying you. You think General Spinther won't want to talk – but I tell you, he's someone we can do business with. The Concordians look intimidating, but they're nearly as desperate as these fools. Their expenses are massive – just keeping their machines in good repair and their men fed so far from the capital must be costing a large fortune, *every* day, and the further south they come, the worse it will get. They *need* us.'

Guido saw his arguments weren't convincing Costanzo and started getting irritated. 'And just listen to yourself: *our* chances? You can't judge an investment's prospects if you're emotionally involved, you *know* that. Our father taught you your letters and he taught me to read exchange rates tables. While you were off composing rhapsodies on the glories of autumnal trees and virginal bosoms, I was advancing my education. Events have now completed it. As our business has expanded, so the margin for error has narrowed; one misplaced dot could blow away the Bombelli fortune like a feather in a gale.'

'This isn't an investment,' said Costanzo slowly. 'It's our family honour.'

'And what could be more dishonourable for our banco than to

314

be ruptured by a bet any novice could tell was a long shot? You and I control the family's assets in Etruria; we are in an excellent position to seek amnesty, with honourable terms.'

Costanzo grabbed him by the lapels and pushed him right to the edge of the cliff. He held him there, the murderous fall looming up at him.

'Are you mad?' Guido shouted.

Costanzo held him there. 'I may be, and a rash and injudicious poet to boot, but at least I am not a dog. Let me put this in terms you'll understand, Brother. When it comes to honour, the Bombelli Family is in the red. I aim to *clear* our debts, not compound them. If I hear another whisper of this, I'll write you off myself.'

The patient was sleeping. Matron Trotula undid the straps one at a time and applied an oily balm to his wrists. He had worn the skin raw with his struggles. After damping his forehead again, she went to relight the candles that had lost their constant quarrel with the wind.

When she turned back, he was sitting up and staring, as if mesmerised by the statue.

'What do you see?' she asked gently.

Pedro looked at her doubtfully. 'I'm hallucinating.'

'Here's how this works: I do the diagnosing and you get better. What do you see on the statue, Pedro?'

'. . . snakes—'

'Many?'

'No, but it was crawling with them when I was brought in and so was your . . .' He trailed off and she sat beside him, blocking his view of the statue.

'Drink this.'

The steaming pink concoction smelled of apple and wormwood. She mumbled a sing-song prayer as he drank it. It made his eyes water but it cleared his head. He did not enquire about the aftertaste of blood that coated his tongue. She took the empty glass from him and went back to her counter. He watched her back, paying particular attention to her hair – he remembered clearly the writhing snakes, but he saw now they were just white streaks. Slowly, he looked over to the statue and breathed a sigh of relief. They were gone too.

More at ease now, he examined the chamber: a simple domed vault built from red bricks and supported by thick columns, around which wound carved snakes. The whistling wind carried the scents of fresh herbs and blooming flowers from the garden, along with the distant sound of melodic chanting.

The roof was decorated with a mosaic depicting a snake coiling around an upright rod; underneath was the motto, in Low Etruscan: *Eadem Mutata Resurgo*. Pedro was satisfied: his fevered mind must have seen this and dreamed the snakes into reality. He rubbed his aching neck – and felt a string; when he pulled it out from his bedshirt he found a small pouch hanging from it. He sniffed it. Lavender mingled with the smell of old cinders and ash. There was something else, something that rattled.

'Don't open it.'

He dropped the pouch with a guilty look and Trotula sat again beside him and started praying again, moving her callused hands over him.

'With respect, Matron, I think I need to worry more about malaria than the Evil Eye—'

'Is that so? Doctor Ferruccio tell me you're quite the engineer. Some Black Handers consider engineering Concordian sorcery—'

'Because they don't understand it.'

'Exactly. And what do you understand of our traditions? The Eye isn't something cast upon us by jealous neighbours and hunchbacks, it's something we put upon ourselves. Who is

Uggeri? You've been cursing him all night – that's when you're not begging his forgiveness.'

Pedro lay back, looking sombre. 'He's someone I left behind. He wanted to stay, but I shouldn't have let him.'

'I see. How do you feel?'

'Better, I think – unless I'm imagining that singing too?'

'No, that's real,' she said with a laugh. 'This is a school of sorts and the first thing we learn is how to sing together.'

This beautiful place was far removed from the privations of the butteri trail. He was beginning to remember a little of the journey across the Minturnae – at least the part before he'd been attacked by the leech.

'From what I saw of your menfolk, setting bones would be more useful—' He checked himself and apologised. 'I'm sorry, I don't mean to be— What I meant was, thank you for helping me.'

'*Niente*. My work is simple, really. It's about maintaining harmony and restoring it when it is absent.' She took his hand. 'I'll be frank with you: this is but a lull. The worst is coming and you'll need all your strength to fight it. If your spirit is lost in the past, you *will* lose. I will give you what I can to prepare you, but you must match your strength – your *full* strength – against it.'

He stared at her. 'How do you know this?'

'Do you imagine we have studied the humours for centuries and learned nothing? I am a *maghe,* not a tooth-puller. I treat maladies of the spirit.' She saw he had more questions, and said firmly, 'Close your eyes and rest while you can. You may not sleep properly for days once you leave us.'

She did not mention that she would not be sleeping either. The unguents and vapours she was preparing were not just for him. However strong, his spirit alone could not win this fight, and if he lost, she would be lost too.

CHAPTER 39

Black-topped Vesuvius was only twenty miles north of Salerno, but the prevailing winds blew its ash-clouds out to sea. The Ariminumese fleet passed through foul-smelling mists of hot steam and prayed for the evil nipple that smoked so tirelessly and continually belched glowing boulders to stay its wrath. The Moor remained sequestered in his quarters. The closer they got to Veii, the tenser Leto became. A surprise attack was out of the question – it was impossible that such a large fleet could escape attention. Ideally, the Veians would come out to meet them in force . . . but he knew that was unlikely.

His pessimistic expectations were confirmed when they approached the Albulian Estuary and the Veians promptly returned to their moorings and declined to meet them. A cursory look was enough to see the siege had made little progress – he had been right to bring the fleet round to break the stalemate. Torbidda must see that – he *must*.

The Moor at last appeared on deck. He looked grizzled and shaken, but he immediately banished Leto's doubts by neatly blockading the estuary.

Satisfied that all was in hand, Leto took a small barque and sailed north to coordinate the final push with his officers. Volsinii, the town he'd chosen for his base, was a sombre, religious place, home in the main to fishermen and salt-harvesters. He barely recognised the town when he landed – or rather, he recognised it all too well. It had turned into any garrison town, with every soldier drunk and every woman turned whore – and everyone getting what they could while they could.

He was deeply annoyed to hear singing when he approached the command tent, and even more annoyed that no one challenged him. He would have words with Scaevola about this laxity.

'Gangway!' cried a familiar voice, and the tent flap was ripped open. Before he could jump aside, his boots were covered in warm vomit.

'Well met, General!' Geta wiped the slobber from his mouth. 'You discover me, as usual, at a disadvantage. Someday, I will surprise you.'

Leto, disgusted, brushed past him and entered the tent. The circle of officers sitting around the desk hastily removed the wine glasses staining the map before them, staggered to their feet and saluted.

'Gentlemen,' said Leto frostily, handing his gloves to a drunken squire. He caught Scaevola's eye and was not surprised that he was the only officer sober. The quartermaster, immune to Geta's charms, wore a told-you-so smirk. He was looking forward to watching his beloved general rain down dishonourable discharges and demotions. The last thing he expected to hear was: 'Scaevola, report.'

The quartermaster searched amidst his documents while the other officers looked down in embarrassment. 'Let's see – well, we were making good progress on the earthen ramp, but then, shortly after you left for Concord, a plague broke out in the north.'

'I already know about that.'

'Oh, you *do*?' said Geta as he re-entered the tent.

'And though its virulence appears to have limited its spread,' Scaevola continued, 'it has disturbed our supply chain.'

'You'll be delighted to know Rasenna survived it,' Geta remarked sarcastically.

'While remedying those issues,' Scaevola went on, 'the locals have been most accommodating – some of them rather too accommodating. There's been outbreak of Roland's Horn. I've sent for medical supplies from Concord, but they are delayed.'

'On the sunny side of the ledger,' Geta interrupted, 'I'm here, and I've brought my Hawks along.'

'A pack of drunks led by a whoremaster. Our enemies must be quaking,' said Leto. 'Go on, Scaevola.'

'Lord Geta's reinforcements, welcome though they are, have added to the strain on supplies, so I've been organising foraging parties,' Scaevola added hastily. 'What else? An emissary from Syracuse has arrived.'

'Sicily's far from here.'

'They are beset by a slave rebellion; if we assist them in suppressing it, they promise their neutrality.'

'What a surprise. If Syracuse desires Concord's friendship, they must not haggle. The price is the same for everyone: tribute.'

'They're a proud people.'

'Etruria is full of proud people. Send him away,' said Leto impatiently, wondering why Scaevola was stalling. 'Come, man: the matter at hand. I've blockaded Veii's harbour, but from what I saw, the situation is unchanged.'

Before Scaevola could make any excuses, Geta interjected, 'Oh, I wouldn't say that. Your boys have retreated a few miles and lost several hundred to disease – and a good few hundred to the butteri.'

'*Butteri*? North of the Albula? Is this true?'

'They've harried us like the very devil,' Scaevola said lamely. 'They come whooping out of the fog with their damned bolos – well, If you'd seen them . . .'

'Am I hearing this right?' Leto asked. 'The Grand Legion is too frightened of a herd of buffalo-wranglers to take the offensive? And you've been doing – what, precisely? Nothing?'

'Fools rush in,' said Scaevola solemnly.

'I'll consult an almanac if I'm ever short of idiotic proverbs. Right now I'll trouble you for an explanation. We saw off scores of barbarians in Gaul and the Reichlands – so why can't we do the same here?'

'The Rasenneisi engineers have augmented the butteri's weaponry.'

'How exactly?'

When Scaevola began once again searching through his memoranda for the answer, Geta snorted with impatience. 'It would be quicker to show you,' he said.

It was galling to have to admit Geta might be right, but the siege was indeed in jeopardy. The men were bedraggled and the standards were soiled and sagging. At least the horses were still alive, though none could be described as fat. Soon the contato would be completely exhausted, and it didn't require an Alexander to realise that once the army began to eat itself, the campaign was over.

Like most of the denizens of the Black Hand, the butteri had little affection for Veii – they fought now only because they knew they would be next. Once Veii was in Concordian hands the south would be open to the ravages of Spinther's war-machine, and lacking the north's greater wealth, technology and population, they would be able to resist for only so long.

The distinction between condottieri, butteri and bandits was hazy, like everything else in this land of warped air and soaking valleys, But whatever you called them, the butteri, guerrillas by long habit and preference, were skilful and they knew their chief advantage was the ability to choose the time and place for battle. They struck hard, like a flash-flood, burning food-wagons, disabling engines and stealing horses before sinking back into the mist. They seldom stopped to kill – they knew camp-fever would attend to that.

The midnight raids were making the soldiers jumpy and irritable, and Scaevola was getting increasingly frustrated. There were those in the camp who argued for breaking off the siege and dealing quickly with the butteri – and these mutterers were not just the usual hotheads. But that was just what the butteri wanted, Scaevola knew; to send the men off chasing after an enemy who melted away like water would be the worst thing they could do. No, whatever the difficulties, they would proceed methodically: first they would take Veii, then they would deal with Salerno.

'There, General,' said Geta.

The colossal ramp had been constructed close to what remained of a copse of poplars. It had a vast, gentle gradient, up which siege-engines could be rolled. Unfortunately, the engines which should right now be smashing down Veii's walls stood decapitated, lined up in a row at the bottom of the palisade, the row of wooden stakes charred to a point, their legs overgrown with long grass.

Geta waved expansively and explained, 'They were no sooner assembled than those bastards came through and made mayhem with their bolos—'

Leto had seen these weapons in Gaul: there were a variety of different styles but a bolo was basically two balls attached to either end of a piece of chain.

'They're loaded with powder and rigged to blow up when the balls strike each other,' Geta pointed out. 'They may be small, but they're extremely effective. We just don't know what to do.'

'That's obvious: make more towers.'

'Which they'll just destroy,' Geta said. 'Haven't you been listening?'

'It's time *you* listened,' Leto said. He was calmer now. 'The new siege-towers will draw them in, as will the skeleton guard we place on the ground. Put a quarter of your men flat in the tall grass amongst the towers. The rest will wait out of sight in those trees yonder and they'll let the butteri pass – this time. They've come to raid, not fight, so they'll turn tail when they realise the towers *are* defended – and that's when the rest will charge out and block their escape.'

Geta played with the ring on his chain for a bit, then said, 'They'll fight like devils.'

'That's the point. They'll fight where and when we choose. We can stand to lose men. They can't.'

'Funny that it's my men, specifically, we can stand to lose.'

'Not like you to get sentimental, Geta. These condottieri expect to be paid, don't they? I assume you're deep in arrears?' When Geta didn't argue, he continued, 'So better to cull their numbers in an excellent cause before they become nothing more than extra mouths to feed.'

'I won't weep for them, but if I didn't know better, I'd suspect I'm being punished.'

'It's war. All are punished.'

'General Spinther,' said Scaevola, 'it's an excellent plan, but Geta's men are what's left of John Acuto's army.'

'So?'

'At Tagliacozzo they fought *with* the Salernitans – will they fight their former allies?'

Geta and Leto simultaneously erupted in laughter. 'God bless your innocence, Scaevola,' Geta hooted. 'I could set them on *each other* if I had the gold.'

CHAPTER 40

The Peoples of the Black Hand: A Bestiary

As one crosses the River Albula, the impression of travelling into the ante-diluvian past is inescapable.[6] The stretch of contato between Veii and Salerno is a gauntlet of swamps, the slit wrist from which Etruria's eternally-flowing blood bubbles over into a quagmire which has swallowed a hundred armies. This natural barrier as much as native bravery accounts for Salerno's lack of defensive structures.

The Salernitans are a queer hybrid of philosophers and outlaws,[7] famous for three things: their rectitude and their poverty and their longevity. This nation of amateurs is truly Etruria's anomaly. Consider their perversity: they have the sea like the Ariminumese, but they have never subjugated it; they have courage equal to the Rasenneisi, but they have never made an art of war, and they study nature as we Concordians do, but they have never sought to exploit it.

Some ignorant Northerners attributed their poverty to the fact that they have no king, assuming that a kingless state must be a wretched anarchy. In fact, the opposite is true: above all, Salernitans revere the law. We Northerners consider it a matter of commonsense to change our laws according to the mutable conditions of life; to the Salernitans, such inconstancy is anathema. Their law is harsh, but they accommodate themselves to it because they believe that nothing noble comes without sacrifice.

---

6 So it is said. Owing to the author's delicate constitution, he has not made the journey south himself. However, every effort has been made to verify the facts of this survey.

7 Their pedigree is, to put it mildly, inauspicious. They are descendants of Greek philosophers and Etruscan slaves – the foothills of nearby Vesuvius were long a favourite haunt of renegade slaves.

CHAPTER 41

While the counter-attack got under way, Leto had the command tent moved closer to Veii, a signal that he meant to suffer with the ordinary soldier while the siege lasted. Scaevola was in the middle of reporting that everything had gone as planned when a commotion arose. A masterless horse had arrived in the camp. The mare was lathered in sweat and blood and one of her front legs was entangled in frayed wire and a set of bolo balls. Arête was notorious; he would submit to be ridden by none but Geta and was a tyrant to other horses, nipping their flanks and necks and harrying them like a monstrous gadfly. Civilians were singled out for the worst treatment, grooms in particular, and he was ever threatening to snap off the fingers of the unwary.

The ranks parted before the fearsome creature and Scaevola moved in front of Leto, saying, 'Stand back, General. Someone fetch a groom—'

'No, let him come. Where's Geta?'

Arête stamped his hooves on the ground in front of Leto and knelt.

The quartermaster ignored the question. 'They suffered heavy losses before we forced a retreat—'

'Damn it, where's Geta?'

'We don't know,' he admitted. 'The fool gave chase in a fit of enthusiasm.'

Butteri war bands were transient things, hastily assembled, quickly disbanded. They never loitered in numbers too long after raids, especially unsuccessful ones. One by one they mounted up and bid ornate farewells to the old man.

'*Auguri* back at you. Go on then,' Ferruccio said, calmly knotting two ends of a rope. 'I'll take care of this one.'

Geta was on his knees in the cold mud under a desolate old tree with a flaking black bark. The five condottieri who had been captured with him had already been beheaded and the crows were busy feasting on their eyeballs. One singularly well-fed bird – surely their chief? – was not partaking of the tawdry gluttony. It was obviously content to wait, and sat on a branch watching Geta with an intensity he did not appreciate. He had a small blade concealed in his glove and was working on the ropes binding his hands even as he tried to distract his captor. 'Can't you just use a sword, old man, and kill me like a soldier?'

'You Northerners. Always in a rush.'

'Suit yourself. My people will be along any minute.'

'You're overestimating your popularity, Lord Geta. Yes, I know who you are. The Bombelli brothers were quite explicit that you deserve a traitor's death, should I be lucky enough to find you.'

'I don't suppose you'd consider a bribe?'

'Don't suppose I would.' Ferruccio threw the rope over the branch and dropped the noose around Geta's head just as a horn followed by a volley of gunshot announced the arrival of Leto's rescue party.

'Hark!' exclaimed Geta, 'looks like you have a choice, Doctor. You can stay to see the job done, or you can save your life.'

Ferruccio lassoed the other end of the rope round a handy stump. 'Another overestimation. It don't take that long for a man to strangle.' So saying, he hauled on the rope and Geta was yanked unceremoniously into the air and immediately began to choke. Musketballs sank into the wet mud beside Ferruccio as he coolly looped the slack around the stump, all the while keeping the rope taut.

As Ferruccio rode off, the Concordians arrived. Geta finally got his hands free and dropped his knife in his rush to release the pressure.

Leto studied Geta hanging there, desperately holding on to the noose around his neck and wildly kicking his legs. 'See where your recklessness led you.'

Geta wheezed painfully, 'Cut me down – *acck* – then lecture me, if you would.'

Leto dismissed his guard and then drew his sword. 'Back in Rasenna, you claimed you knew my father.'

'Yes!'

He cut him down. 'Tell me about him.'

Geta lay on his side panting for a minute, then he pulled himself up and rubbed the ripped skin on his neck. 'Your plan worked a treat, by the way. We gave chase, but the bastards had their retreat lined with bolos and tripwire. I had managed to cut Arête free before they came—'

'Geta . . .' Leto still held his sword ready. 'If you are lying, you're going back up.'

'My first posting was on the Francia Major frontier. You weren't born then and he wasn't a general. We weren't friends – he never drank, never gambled – but he taught me what it is to be a soldier.'

'I thought you studied in Rasenna.'

'I only learned to fight there.'

'I'm surprised you know the distinction. He was like me, then?'

'No, he wasn't moderate in all things. In battle he threw himself into the fray – and men loved him for it. I asked him once if he was ever afraid. He asked if I was afraid when I gambled, and then he told me that was how it was for him when the drums pounded, when our banners unfurled from the carroccio, when the Franks sounded their great horns. I'll never forget it. He said, "I set myself on fire, but my enemies burn".' Geta smiled at the memory.

'Times have changed,' Leto said, 'and, if you recall, my father didn't die on the battlefield. His fellow officers – nobles like you – assassinated him.'

'I'd received my first command by then. In the East. I grieved when I heard the news.'

'You'd have been in that circle had you been there . . .'

No point to deny the obvious. 'They wanted him to declare against Filippo Argenti and march on Concord and when he refused to take part, they had no choice but to kill him – he was too close to the Engineers.' He looked up with sudden inspiration. 'That's why you became one, isn't it?' He slapped his thigh and laughed. 'You learned the wrong lesson, son—'

Leto held his sword under Geta's chin; blood started to trickle over the razor-sharp edge. 'Never call me that again.'

'All right, all right. Don't be touchy. So, what now?'

'Now we'll see how good Veii's defences are.'

'Worried?'

'No. Good or bad, it's irrelevant. I just need their attention to be elsewhere when the Moor attacks.'

The Veian captains saw them coming and formed a defensive line across the harbour mouth. The line was impressive, but the variety of craft – from bulky cargo ships to puny fishing vessels, from three-tiered galleys to ungainly catamarans – meant the tactic was doomed. Few of the ships were properly armed – small, antiquated table-cannon with fixed bearing and unimpressive range made up the greater part of the naval artillery – but worse than that, the gun crews were undrilled and undermanned, more used to whipping slaves than fighting free men.

The Ariminumese captains saw the uneven lines and heard the amateur rhythm of their bombard and their high spirits rose higher. At the Moor's signal, the Golden Fleet broke into two columns, presenting the smallest possible target, and sailed along the north and south sides of the harbour – which gave the stationary Veians in the centre nothing to shoot at. They were lame dogs, and the Ariminumese the wolves bearing down on them. The *Bellicose*, the galley the Moor had placed at the forefront of the south column, was aptly named. As her drums urged the rowers on to attack-speed, she sprang forward with bow chasers locked upon the Veian galley ahead.

Her fire was accurate and sustained, while the Veians made plenty of smoke and noise but with little result. Scarcely a shot got off without one of the gun crews getting injured by a recoiling gun, rope burn or powder-flash, and whenever someone fell, the rest made a great hue and cry and were deathly slow replacing them. On the few occasions that their aim might have been true, shaky hands spilling powder and spume-doused wicks ensured that they missed most opportunities to fight back.

The Moor took all this in with glee. The *San Barabaso* was heading the northern column and his crew were artists with a collective consciousness of the ship's pitch and roll. When the moment came to fire, not only had they far more practise, they had the technical edge – their guns were better cast, with clean bores, the powder was better, and dry; the wicks burned slower and more effectively – and there was a new Concordian locking mechanism that minimised misfires.

The Veians prepared to be rammed, but at the last moment, the *Barabaso* turned parallel, its action precisely mirrored by the *Bellicose* on the other side of the harbour, and each sailed majestically towards the centre, steadily peppering the Veian line. Their broadside cannons had no great range, but this close they had wonderfully destructive powers – and whilst they themselves were equally exposed to close-range retaliatory fire, the Veians were in no position to deliver it, for they were being simultaneously raked with fire from swinging siphons fore and aft of the lead galleys. The *Barabaso* and the *Bellicose* were followed by two more galleys performing exactly the same manoeuvre, denying them any respite.

As they passed each other in the middle of the harbour, the Moor called over the thunder, 'Fine hunting, eh?'

Scaevola declined to respond. He was taking his first command very seriously.

It was the sheer volume of shot that broke the Veian line more than accuracy. After each ship had traversed the line, it spat a final shot from the stern, then turned and turned again to meet in the middle. Coming parallel once more and facing the centre of the fractured line, they surged forward at ramming speed, breaking through like a spear-thrust, and the battle, till now a stately pavane, became a free-for-all. Even through the thick smoke that hung over the estuary, the Golden Fleet could see vessels breaking ranks and trying to flee. The worthless fishing boats they chased down and sank; others – those vessels that might have some worth – they took as prizes, including one large cargo ship after the crew mutinied and ran up a flag of surrender.

The wharfs of Veii were chaotic as ships docked wherever they could and the crews fled back to the city. Some of those who had not been part of the defensive line now broke their mooring ropes attempting to flee, and the Moor's captains, loath to let even any reasonable prize escape, followed them out of the harbour.

Scaevola put his ship alongside the *San Barabaso* and ordered the Moor to stop them, but the admiral laughed at the notion. 'These are the fruits of victory!' he shouted back.

Those captains who neither fled nor fought but waited for the battle to decide paid the price for their lethargy when a new order came through from the duke, who commanded they scupper their ships rather than let them fall into Ariminumese hands.

The Moor cursed to see so many prizes burn, and now it was Scaevola's turn to chide him. 'Cheer up, Admiral. Tomorrow, we'll have a whole city to enjoy.'

CHAPTER 42

'I told her—'

. . .

'—the midwife, *cretino*—!'

. . .

'—about the Furies of course. *Madonna*, you don't listen any more. I told her how they rattle my window frame and snap the flags outside so I can't sleep. She just laughed and said it was the Tramontane. She also assures me that nightmares are perfectly *normal* for new mothers. Everything is normal with her. An excess of choler, she said.' Maddalena smiled slyly. 'I didn't tell her what I dream about. She wouldn't say *that's* normal.'

. . .

'Of course I'll tell *you*. There's a wedding feast in the piazza but – oh, it's *so* dull – no one's dancing. And the dancers outside the walls hear the music and want to get in and one of my enemies opens the gates and they burst into the city and the music is everywhere, and they're after me. They scream, "Come and dance, Maddalena, or we'll tell everyone what you did!" and I say "Not so loud!"'

The infant in her arms writhed peevishly – the servants despaired at how roughly she handled the sickly creature. 'Hush! I'm talking to your grandpapa.'

. . .

'His grip? Weak but, between you and me, I suspect the midwife botched it. That hag was always jealous of Mama, wasn't she? All she was interested in was bleeding me. I told her I'd bled quite enough, but still she insisted.'

. . .

'No, you're quite right. Normally I wouldn't take orders from the likes of her, but she did rather have me at a disadvantage. Ha!'

The gleam in Maddalena's eyes and the shine on her skin were not the healthy glow of a new mother. Her child had come early and with a great deal of pain, and she had been bedbound since with a fever – which had apparently finally broken this morning. Her servants, who had been assiduously keeping knives and hairpins away from her, now risked the Midnight Road to cross the Irenicon. They followed her to the Palazzo Bombelli, which they had abandoned so many months before. Now they sat quietly watching their mistress talking to an empty seat behind the banco in the overgrown courtyard and realised that the fever had merely entered a more dangerous phase.

'Oh, don't be squeamish! You saw your fair share of blood when Mama was around. Well, I wrote to my absent husband, telling him that the child looks nothing like him and that people are saying I put horns on him.'

. . .

'Bah, don't be so pious – he'll laugh at that. But I told him another thing he won't like. He wanted me to call the child after one of his illustrious ancestors but I told him – I said no. The very idea! A Concordian name? I said we're going to name him after Papa!' She threw the squealing child into the air again. 'My little Fabbro – shall we weigh you? Yes, let's do that!'

She attempted to put the child onto the scales, but the servant restrained her.

'Get away, you harpies! He's *mine*!'

She clawed them away with one hand and held the child to her bosom with the other, whispering, 'See how they treat me,

Papa? They nag and interfere and whisper. They whisper that—
Oh no, I can't tell you that. You'll never forgive me,' and she
spun and spun through the desolate courtyard until she sprawled
across the floor of the banco. She sat up suddenly, staring at the
servants. 'Why are you just standing there, fools? Let's go, or we'll
be late for the baptism.'

The baptistery's roof had suffered some damage in the fire, but
the formidable bronze doorway had remained intact.

'All right now. Places everyone!' Maddalena said strictly. 'No,
not like that – like this, see? You here, and you here. And when
I come out, you applaud me.'

The women exchanged worried glances, but they made the
guard of honour as their mistress instructed. Once she was inside
the baptistery, she whipped out the letter knife she had taken
from Fabbro's banco. 'Keep back!' she shrieked.

'Please, mistress, don't—'

With a shrill giggle, she rammed her shoulder against the door
and bolted it shut.

The interior was dim and cool, and water puddles fed by the
leaking roof reflected what remained of the ceiling's golden
mosaic. She solemnly approached the font, her steps slowing as
she got nearer. The small painted panels round the base showed
terrible scenes – scenes from the dreams that plagued her:
Herod's soldiers tearing babies from their mothers' arms and
dashing their brains out on pillars. She darted a guilty glance at
the sword hanging over the child shivering in her arms.

She placed the knife on the edge of the font before bending to
put him on the cold stone floor, ignoring his wails of discomfort.
She dipped her hand in the font and made the sign of the Sword
and blessed herself, then dipped and again blessed herself, then
once more. She began washing each finger separately, staring all
the while at the vengeful hanging blade. With a sudden groan

she stumbled back from the font, narrowly avoiding treading on the bawling baby, and fell to her knees before the Madonna of Rasenna.

'Hear my confession, gracious Lady. I have sinned. I've been – oh, the usual: proud, wrathful, envious–'

. . .

'What? No. Who told you that? I *did* nothing of the sort. Oh, we talked about it – I was angry! – but I never thought we'd go through with it. Why does everyone blame me? All I wanted is to be respected and loved, like the Contessa. Is that too much to ask? You're a fine one to judge – you never let a man get away with beating you!'

Locked in her reverie, Maddalena didn't hear the hands pounding on the door. She picked up her child and hugged him so tightly that he screamed. 'Oh, my little Fabbro, Mama was foolish! But it's not too late. We can wash ourselves clean.'

She lifted him to the font and gently dipped the crown of his head into the icy water. As she did so, strong hands came from behind and held her in a tight embrace. Lips at her ear whispered, '*Murderer.*'

Maddalena screamed helplessly as her child slid into the font, its face, body and finally its legs kicking against her. The letter knife was inches away from her fingers – a great gulf. A stream of bubbles troubled the surface.

'You betrayed Rasenna like you betrayed me. Admit it: you killed Fabbro.'

'Uggeri, stop–'

'Confess.'

'You don't understand–'

'Confess!'

'I confess–!'

'*Bene.* This is your penance.' And he pushed her face close to the water. She screamed, writhed, howled until the little legs stopped kicking. A single bubble trembled on the surface and was gone. Uggeri released her and stepped back, breathing hard.

Maddalena picked up the knife. 'Dogs eat cats and cats eat mice and you won't enter paradise.' She pointed it slowly at him, 'Burn the candle. Ring the bell. Uggeri's going straight to hell.'

Something about her crazy certainty made his flesh crawl. 'That's rich coming from a woman who murdered her father.'

'Straight to hell. That wasn't Geta's son.'

'Then you're a bigger whore than I thought. Whose was it?'

'Yours.'

Uggeri threw the blade and her aside. She struck her head as she fell. He ripped the little pink body from the water. 'Oh, oh – Oh *Dio* – I didn't *know*.' He embraced the body and stared up at the Herod's Sword glistening over the font. 'Don't do this to me – *don't!* I've lost too much—'

The knife slipped neatly into his throat, puncturing the artery. Uggeri placed his son's body gently on the edge of the font and turned around. He put one hand to his neck to staunch the flow and the other went instinctively to his assailant's neck.

He found himself looking into Carmella's eyes and the knife's edge prodding his ribs.

'We loved you, and this is how you repay us?' Uggeri's grip, always so strong, was weak as a babe's. She rammed it in to the hilt. 'This is how Herod was repaid.' She pulled the blade out. Blood followed like watered wine.

He fell back against the font, watching Carmella drop the blade and kneel beside Maddalena. He was so thirsty. He turned to scoop a cool handful from the font, but before he could drink, the darkness swallowed him.

Whatever battle Maddalena had been fighting against the Furies was lost the moment she woke to see her child and her lover dead. She scrambled for the knife, but Carmella restrained her in an embrace and crooned the Virgin's Song. Maddalena tried to look away from the Herod's Sword, but it was reflected in the blood seeping from the font towards her and she screamed – for herself, for her baby, for Uggeri, for Rasenna, for the innocent and guilty alike.

She *screamed*.

CHAPTER 43

In the second year of the consulship of Publius Cornelius Dolabella, Veian haruspices persuaded Jupiter to relocate using the *Evocato* ritual. Without its protector, Rome swiftly fell. The kings of Veii swiftly repudiated their promise of eternal fidelity, and the Roman deity, homeless and without worshippers, drowned himself in the Albula . . .

The Etruscan Annals

The shell spun in a lazy arc over the harbour, seemed to pause in mid-air like some low-hanging celestial body, and then plunged screaming towards Veii. First a small dust cloud blossomed on the distant wall, then came the muted crash of shattered masonry.

Leto looked up from the chessboard and shouted up at the lookout, 'Well?'

'Just shy, general.'

'Adjust five points east.'

The bombardier made the corrections with a spring-line attached to a windlass and varied the amount of charge.

The Moor stalked the deck, sighing anew each time he caught a glimpse of the anchors keeping his ship pinned fore and aft. After the excitement of battle, this was crushingly dull. He loved the straightforward destruction rendered by the ships' cannons, the drama of the fire-siphons, but mortars were sneaky, oblique things, Engineers' weapons, not for seamen.

'Sure I can't give you a game, Azizi? We can play for gold.'

'Thank you, no.'

'Then what's bothering you? You've a face like a slapped arse.'

He stamped his foot. 'The deck is obscenely level.'

'So I can shoot straight.'

'Exactly. You're using my flagship as a *platform*. It's like using a sceptre to swat a fly.'

'If you lack the stomach for this—'

The Moor leaned on the railings and watched fires bloom in the distant city. 'I was born at the foot of the Atlas Mountains where the lions roam. From the first I have known the breadth and cruelty of the world, but this ignoble business of calculating arcs and slight adjustments—' He paused and sighed again. 'Without the element of chance, war is so . . . *grey*.'

Leto laughed. 'You're a romantic.'

The Moor made another impatient round, then tried another tack. 'Your wheedling fool of a quartermaster advises that loading the hold with so much powder is unsafe.'

'Since when are *you* worried about regulations? Besides, you've seen the range of the Veian cannons. There's no danger.' Leto covered his ears as the mortar fired again and emerged from a cloud of yellow smoke, coughing. 'Ah, that wonderful smell!' he said. 'It reminds me of my Guild Hall days. That's where I learned that *Labor Vincit Omnia*. Nothing in the world is so strong that it can withstand consistently applied pressure.'

'I thought you just butchered corpses in that place.'

'We dissected earthly bodies as practise. Dissecting the perfect shapes that cannot exist in our sub-lunar world takes great skill – take, for example, the cone. To understand how cannon-shot falls, one must slice it into its constituents – the ellipse, the parabola, and so on. It was Apollonius of—'

The Moor's monstrous yawn interrupted his discourse. 'Very fascinating, General, but I can resist my hammock's siren song no longer. Wake me if anyone needs to be dispatched at closer quarters.'

Though the future hammered on Veii's walls, older rhythms played on inside. The town elders, representing the voices of the Small People, stood silently behind Duke Grimani as always as he opened ceremonies with a prayer to Saint Eligius. The rain of explosive shells made both horses and citizens skittish, and the duke had his personal guard block the exit to the horseshoe piazza to ensure everyone stayed. The Palio di Veii was symbolic of Grimani rule: whatever happened, it *must* be run.

The happy tolling from the bell tower sounded like a grim jest amid the bombardment, but the horses had been trained all year for those notes and they broke into a gallop before their jockeys could apply the whip. Immediately two horses collided on the slippery cobbles, and took down two more with them. One jockey shot from his saddle and flew an impressive distance before landing face-down with a sickening *crunch*. The soldiers moved in to dispatch the fallen: men and beasts lay tangled like the aftermath of a battle of centaurs. The corpses were dragged off together, a droll spectacle that ignited the crowd's laughter. They forgot their hunger, the danger, how much they hated the duke, and cheered as passionately as any other year.

Again the thunder passed by, a lunatic rainbow of green and yellow and chequered purples and gold bands and horses gnashing at each other's necks, removing great chunks of flesh, and the jockeys using their whips on each other, then *this one* leans over to cut the girth and *that one*'s falling onto the cobbles and bones are splintering and now the two front-runners are in scarlet and midnight-blue, surging forward, and scarlet takes the turn badly and stumbles and rolls and crashes into the crowd, who are crawling over each other, trying to escape the carnage, and a cart of roast chestnuts spills out onto the cobbles and brings down the next rider and midnight-blue has a clear run now and Grimani's mouth is foaming as he screams, '*Avanti—!*'

As one, the tightly packed contestants leap their fallen rivals in an infernal steeplechase, and they take the last lap and thirty-something hooves strike the stone and somewhere a snare drum misses the beat and there's a mosquito whine – can you hear it? Only the young do at first, and then it's a whistle everyone can hear but no one can place, and then it's a scream that comes from *everywhere*.

The shell lands in the centre of the pack, sending stone and metal and legs and arms and tack and teeth shooting up into the air and the rainbow is unwoven into a single colour and the colour is red and it spatters the crowd and the few, those ones who have not been deafened, hear Duke Grimani cheering midnight-blue across the finish line.

'I win! I win! I win!'

A horn blew and the gates of Veii creaked open. The town elders wandered out, stunned as newborns. They wore hair shirts and had daubed their foreheads with mud. Signor Marsuppini, the eldest of the four, was the only one with hair, though it was white as cotton. He was a crook-backed old goat with a prominent Adam's apple. Amongst subordinates, he had a bullish manner. Now he held up a severed head and cried in a voice that could be heard over the roar of the Albula, 'On his head our sins.'

After some confusion, a centurion rode up to accept the delegation's surrender. The burghers were dissatisfied; they could not act the penitent long. 'We have exposed our broken bodies to your darts, humbled ourselves, painted our heads with filth and removed that of the devil who led us to this pass.' Marsuppini threw the head of Duke Grimani at the soldier's feet. 'And by this token, we've earned the right to speak to General Spinther.'

Some bunting still lined the horseshoe piazza, but the course had been washed and tidied, leaving the fragmented cobblestones around the crater the only evidence of the recent disaster. Leto's guards were made to wait outside while he was ushered inside Castello Grimani. The hall that had been the ducal court was a windowless chamber deep within. It was lit by stout candles and lined with tall niches decorated with frowning jowled busts of the Family Grimani. Every generation was represented, but for the last scion of that illustrious line; his head now graced a spike on the city gates.

At the top of a small set of steps sat the burghers in four high chairs. The hair shirts had been replaced with sumptuous gowns. At the bottom of the steps was a long table. At one end of it sat a notary, his paper and quills at the ready. In the centre was a wine decanter and five glasses. The single stool provided for Leto was a pointed insult, but he sat without fuss.

'I'm here to accept your surrender,' he said. 'I could remonstrate at how long it was coming, but that would be ungracious. Instead, Signori, I salute your valour and congratulate you on your wisdom. If you had not capitulated—'

The burghers became suddenly agitated. 'We have agreed to *treat*, but we do not *capitulate*,' said Marsuppini pedantically. 'If those terms do not satisfy, let the siege continue.'

Leto sighed. Burghers were all alike: small, pretentious men who believe their small dominion to be the world entire.

'A treaty may suffice if it provides the assurances my master needs. I'm sure you'd be willing to let your people starve a few more weeks, but if I have to break my way in, there will be no mercy.'

Marsuppini glanced wryly at the others as though Leto had said something gauche. but when he turned back, he was not smiling. 'Our walls have withstood your missiles. You think words will scare us? We Veians stand aloof from the follies of Etruria, but that doesn't mean we are uninformed. You dare not tarry for winter will soon be upon you.'

'It is already too late to continue south. One way or another, we will be boarding amongst you for the season. You should be worried about finding good terms on which we can co-habit.'

'We've demonstrated our good faith: the birds are feeding on his eyes. What do you bring to the table, *boy*?'

Leto smiled reflexively at the epitaph. He had heard it often from his adversaries and had never understood exactly why they regarded it as an insult. It crossed his mind that the birds would enjoy a few more heads— But no. A rash soldier like Geta might choose that course, but he was a Spinther; to resort to violence before exploring alternatives was seldom necessary and always vulgar.

He took the decanter, filled and distributed the glasses like a squire. 'I must tell you, Signori, I have seen many civic palazzi, but Castello Grimani is the most splendid by far. I understand,' he continued, 'that Veii was once a republic?'

The gesture disarmed the others, but Marsuppini remained suspicious. 'She still is. The Signoria constitutionally appointed each Grimani as dictator.'

'Indeed? Then let the next Signoria assemble here, in surroundings that reflect its dignity.'

The suggestion pleased the burghers enormously, who were more used to being imperiously summoned to the castello or threatened with a stay in its notorious 'basement'. To be the ones summoning and threatening would be marvellous. They exchanged quick grins before resuming their stony demeanours.

'You presume to give us what we already have,' said Marsuppini, but his manner was noticeably more civil.

'Forgive my presumption. Concord allows its clients to govern themselves as they see fit.'

A wise and prudent policy, the burghers agreed. Leto played

along; for these Small People, these wretches, who had been stooped and bowed their whole lives, the smallest taste of power would prove addictive, and to keep it they would soon agree to any betrayal of their people. They fidgeted and squirmed in their seats like amateur card players who found themselves possessed of a miracle hand.

The walls were breached.

'The First Apprentice will be satisfied if Veii stands aside from this war, provides succour and supplies from time to time, and allows a small garrison be stationed within the city.'

The bald heads drew together around Marsuppini: vulture chicks dissecting a meal. After a minute of whispering, Marsuppini popped his head up. 'Some clarifications, General, if you please: what size garrison? To be built upon which hill? Also, "time to time" isn't very specific; how often is that likely to be, precisely?'

Leto excused himself briefly in order to dispatch a rider to Concord with word of Veii's surrender. He knew he was in for a long night, but that was fine: the walls had fallen.

CHAPTER 44

The waves bisected the light into gleaming knives, but nothing could mitigate its merciless heat. The scuttles and hatches were open on every ship in the vain hope of catching a passing cool breeze. Tar dripped from the rigging and pitch bubbled up from the seams. The tribesmen were familiar with the sun, an old enemy, and they promptly rigged awnings over the decks and sat in the shade telling stories, sharpening their knifes, chewing khat. Only with difficulty did Khoril prevent them from lighting fires at night.

Sofia found their listlessness strange, until Bakhbukh explained, 'They know nothing of the sea except that it is a desert, and knowing deserts are merciless to the ignorant, they have put themselves entirely in Admiral Khoril's hands.'

Their notions of private property were similarly problematic; the deckhands grumbled when treasured scrimshaws and lucky dice, straw hats and sandals went missing with increasing frequency.

'I'm a mariner, not a magus,' Khoril remonstrated, 'and I require a ship to cross the sea – so if they'd be so kind to leave the dowels in my planks—'

Bakhbukh promised to make them behave but did nothing. The challenge of the sea affects each man differently, and he was a man adrift. Sofia had Khoril now, and Fulk, and her own restless destiny pulling her forward. He had memories of plans that had come to nothing in a land far behind and a time far gone. He had been desperate to leave the Sands, but whatever sadness he had hoped to flee had pursued him here.

The fleet had set forth with its newly promoted admiral doggedly insisting that the whole enterprise was flawed. Once they passed Cyprus they were committed, for good or ill, and while Khoril continued to believe they were doomed, at least he ceased predicting it.

As the tribesmen attempted to pass the hours as they would in the desert, so the Lazars attempted to replicate their Akkan life of servility and discipline. They occupied themselves with drills, loading, aiming, firing and cleaning the guns, and then again and again until every man could operate the cannon like an engineer. More usefully, at least at this point, they put their backs to the oars when the winds ebbed.

For the tribesmen, alas, no such use could be found. 'These fellows might be virtuoso throat-cutters, Contessa, but not one can hand, reef or steer a damn – and we're going up against able seamen.'

Khoril did allow that they were wonderful climbers, and as they entered cooler seas, they took to the upper rigging and hung there like bats.

The fleet, being neither Oltremarine nor Ebionite, accepted Sofia's suggestion and called themselves the Sirocco. It pleased them to think of themselves as incontrovertible as the wind, though – not that they would ever admit this to the Contessa – they all shared Khoril's belief, to some degree at least, that the whole scheme was doomed.

The Sirocco had forty ships sailing in chevron formation. Little more than half had been built for combat, and they came in a myriad of designs. The rest were converted merchant cogs. Four of the lantern ships were as grand as the *Tancred*, but they were instead built on the lines of Byzantine dromons, with large squared-off hulls and three rows for oarsmen. The *Tancred* made the point of the arrow, with the *Megiddo* and the *Santa Terra* following half a league away on either side; another half-league behind them were the *Jerusalem* and *Ira Princeps*. Within those floating walls were the transports, great broad-beamed whales carrying mostly infantry and various irregulars, besides the squires and pages of the Lazars. Whilst rigged with large sea-going sails, their navigators were careful to keep first Cyprus and Rhodes and then Crete in view as they sailed up the Middle Sea. The xebecs were interspersed between the flagships, and though they kept perfect formation with the lanterns, their captains complained of the sluggish pace.

Sofia overruled Khoril's initial plan, to assign the Lazars and Ebionites to different ships (lest for want of other occupation they started recalling old feuds) but his caution proved unnecessary: there was a general goodwill amongst the fleet as constant as the wind that now carried it along. The brotherhood between the tribes was remarkable enough, but between men who had been bitter opponents for generations, it was nothing short of miraculous. Sofia remembered tense nights in the Lion's Fountain, back when Rasenna's bridge was being built, calmed by the arrival of Giovanni, who hadn't even needed to speak. His mere presence vanquished rancour. And so it was with Iscanno. The men came frequently aboard the *Tancred* to consult with Bakhbukh and Fulk, and they invariably brought gifts of carved toys and medicines their mothers had given them before they left. Sofia, knowing they really came to see Iscanno, accepted all these gewgaws with gratitude.

Behind the islands they were passing lay the pale coastline of northern Oltremare, to where Prince Jorge was now marching, coming home to raise an army.

'Or just marching home,' said Khoril, who, Sofia was beginnng to think, positively relished predicting the worst. 'Once he passes the Bosporus and hears the cheering crowds in the hippodrome he'll think better, mark my words.'

They passed Crete, but instead of the expected escort of well-armed dromons, the only person watching their approach was a solitary fisherman in a kaika.

'Your prince is as trustworthy as every other Byzantine,' Khoril crowed, not bothering to hide his pleasure at seeing his prediction borne out.

'Surely that fisherman,' Fulk observed, 'does not encounter invasions every day?'

'I wouldn't read too much into it,' Khoril said. 'I doubt he'd bat an eyelid if Neptune came up and shook his hoary locks.'

To prove his point he leaned over and saluted the little vessel. 'Ahoy, old fellow,' he bellowed. 'What news?'

'Oh, nothing of consequence,' the fisherman replied. 'The world is changeless, the land is barren, the sea is cruel. There's a rebellion in Sicily, but what else is new? Veii has fallen and the Concordians march on Salerno. Some people find these events of interest, but I'm old and I lose track of who is who. Oh, there was something else – what was it? Ah yes. Young Prince Jorge says hello. He suggests you might follow me if you want a safe harbour. Good fishing.' And without waiting for a response, he tacked about and sailed due north.

'Some escort,' Khoril muttered in embarrassment.

Sofia asked, 'You're certain about this, Fulk?'

'We need the Byzants, that's certain.'

'I meant about dividing our forces.'

Khoril snorted. 'No loss to shift ballast. Somewhere up ahead, the Moor's waiting for us. To reach Salerno, we have to avoid or outrun him and they're just slowing us down.'

The transports trailed behind the little kaika, their captains wary: Thessalonika's Claw was every bit as treacherous as the Black Hand, and the old fisherman could set the pace. He sailed on, apparently indifferent to the host in his wake.

'Good riddance, says I,' said Khoril. 'Flatfooted land crabs won't be no use where we're going.'

CHAPTER 45

The hall flickered rancid yellow. The fat candles were exhausted, as was the notary. His quill had three times worn down and his last bottle of ink was all but dry. Several bottles of wine had been consumed during the course of the negotiation and the town fathers had grown loquacious as they settled into their new roles. Marsuppini warned that giving power to an inexperienced Signoria would be disastrous in a town trained to obey one voice, and the notary dutifully recorded his suggestion that 'the best interim government would be a tetrarchy, preferably composed of men experienced in the vexatious art of management.'

Although Leto thought he could guess which three heads would shortly be joining the duke's, he made no objection. Internal squabbles in client states were not just to be expected, but encouraged.

The notary had just blotted his final piece of paper when the hall's great door opened suddenly.

Scaevola's face was pale. His surcoat was splattered with blood.

'Treachery!' Leto had been so calm for the last hour that his sudden anger made the burghers jump.

'Yes, General,' Scaevola said, 'but not Veian treachery.'

Leto pulled him closer and demanded, 'What do you mean?'

'An hour after you entered the city, the Moor and his crew landed in force and insisted on their right to prizes. They set about taking them, very roughly, I fear, and some of the hills resisted—'

'And not one Concordian thought to stop them?' His voice

349

might have been quiet, but no one listening could have doubted the force of his anger.

'Well, no— That is, Lord Geta said we should join in.'

From the steps of Castello Grimani they could see each of Veii's hills glowing. One was entirely ablaze; others were dotted with fires that had yet to combine. The town bell chimed away to no particular rhythm – the bellringer was trapped by a fire on a lower storey. From the top floors of the palazzi around the piazza, jewels and cameos and silverware rained down on the marauding soldiers, and carved chests worth small fortunes were smashed for the baubles within.

A horse with a burning tail sprinted round the piazza's curve. The slain Veian soldiers, women and children who lined the piazza were an unappreciative audience. The horse's auburn coat was slimy with sweat and foam gushed from its mouth. Its eyes were huge and rolling wildly as it crashed through the doors of the cathedral. In the apse stood a legionary with a leathern carafe in one hand and a baby, held by the ankles, in the other. His men were busy with the mother. He finished the wine, swung the infant against the cathedral's thick pillars and went to join the sport.

While the Concordians indulged themselves, the Moor's men took a more focused approach – this, after all, was their business. They had already cordoned off one quarter of the piazza into two separate pens for slaves and horses.

'You look ridiculous, Azizi.'

'I bow to you, General, in military matters. Not in fashion.' Around the Moor's neck were rows of pearls and jewels and his shoulders were draped with a fur-lined cape, luxurious as a bishop's. His fingers were laden with as many rings as fit.

Before Leto could say more, the Moor cupped his ear. 'Hark!'

Leto was confused, but then he heard the silence as the fires reached the belfry and the ringer finally let go. Then came the bell's death-cry: a repeated, discordant clanging as it plummeted through floor after floor, sending sparks out of the tower's windows like cannon-shot. The bell struck the earth with a magnificent *duhoonong!!* and every Veian still alive to hear it knew that summer was over, that tomorrow the slaves working the Cagligarian mines would be their own children.

It told Leto something else entirely: it was too late to salvage this mess – but perhaps it might be for the best. The Moor was still grieving the loss of his beautiful ensign and it was better that he vented his spleen on these wretches and satisfied his greed with these scraps.

The real prize won this day was ownership of the Cagligarian Isles. Leto marched away, meditating more happily upon that, until he came upon something sprawled on the steps of the Castello that once again upset his tranquillity.

'Geta–'

'None other!' The swordsman leaped to his feet and clicked his heels. He was drunk, and incredibly pleased with his prize: a ridiculous wide-brimmed hat with an ostrich feather that bounced along to his drunken swaying. He gestured at the Moor's assembly line in disgust and declared, 'That's no way to enjoy a sack! Time enough for that in the morning. Drink?' When Leto demurred, he wagged a finger. 'I'm disappointed, young man. I thought we were making progress after our heart-to-heart.'

'I blame the Moor no more than I would blame a wolf for savaging livestock, but you–' Leto was trying hard to rein in his fury; it would get him nowhere. '*You* are a Concordian officer.'

'You expect me *not* to kick a fellow when he's down? I'm only human, dear boy.'

'Veii *surrendered*. Displaying leniency would have encouraged other towns to quit. We've just given them a reason to fight us to the death–'

'Your trouble, Spinther, is that you want everyone to like you.'

'Not *everyone* . . . I promise you this: when we go south, you'll be the vanguard.'

'Spare me your sanctimony. You meant to do to Veii over years what we did in a night.'

'You're a short-sighted fool, Geta – how are we supposed to winter in a ravaged town?'

'Oh, we'll find enough to get by, don't you worry.'

Leto noticed the town fathers had emerged from the chamber and were now huddled together on the steps. They were staring, speechless, at their ruined city, until at last their putative leader piped up, 'General Spinther, this doesn't change our agreement, does it? We're still in charge . . . aren't we?'

'I take it,' said Geta to Leto, 'that these – hm – *patriots* are the new government? My good fellows, your names will be listed in the Annals and remembered for ever. I congratulate you.' He bowed low, sweeping his hat from his head, and brushing Marsuppini with the ostrich feather. 'May your rule usher in a new era of peace. Mind you, after tonight I daresay anything will be an improvement—'

His voice faded away as an ominous creaking followed by a sharp report like the death-crack of a great tree heralded the final seconds of Veii's great bell tower before it crashed into the piazza, demolishing the pirates' pens and setting people and horses running madly for freedom. The Moor hurled oaths as his men chased after them.

Geta threw his head back and roared with laughter. 'Serves them bloody well right!' he bellowed.

There was nothing else to do, so Leto joined him.

Marsuppini cleared his throat awkwardly.

'Hello,' said Geta, 'looks like the father of his country has something to tell us.'

The prisoner looked up as a key rattled in the lock. He heard Marsuppini speaking rapidly: 'Our first act after overthrowing the tyrant, besides removing his head, was to release the victims of his oppression.'

The prisoner groaned as his cell was flooded with early-morning light.

Marsuppini continued, 'That's when we found the Rasenneisi banker. My colleagues were all for setting him free, but I thought it best to keep him here till—'

'Be quiet,' said Leto as they entered the dark, ill-smelling chamber. He took one look at the man in shackles with frank amazement, then shouted at Marsuppini, 'Remove these shackles at once! Don't you know who this is? Signore Bombelli, forgive me. Had I known Duke Grimani had imprisoned you, I would have doubled my efforts to unseat him. The scoundrel was obviously holding you in reserve as a bargaining chip. I see he treated you ill. If it's any consolation, he will trouble you no longer.'

Salvatore rubbed his wrists. 'It is not, and apologies are unnecessary. War is no respecter of persons. Why should I be singled out?' His tone was nonchalant, but he eyed Geta coldly.

'Because you are singular, sir – I had some dealings with your brother Guido when I was stationed on the northern frontier, but the head of the Tower Bombelli is someone I would like to consider a friend. I speak not merely for myself, you understand, but for Concord.'

'Do you now? Correct me then, but didn't that base-looking fellow standing next to you declare himself head of the Bombelli Family? He bases his claim, if I am not mistaken, on his dishonourable association with my sister.'

Geta bowed in acknowledgement. 'Forgive me, dear brother-in-law, but for once you are misinformed. I wish we had met in happier circumstances, before such jealous whispers reached your ears. I am honoured to call myself a Bombelli – that much is true – but I do not dispute your authority.' He fell solemnly to one knee. 'Pray, not for my sake but for Maddalena's, let us be reconciled.'

Salvatore had been denied water for too long. His spittle didn't reach its target.

Geta looked up, grinning. 'Perhaps other considerations will sway you then. You're known as a man with a talent for keeping track of things, a prudent judge of good and bad investments. I daresay that even buried in this cell you know the way the war's going. Rasenna, Ariminum, now Veii – detect a pattern? The towers of Etruria are tumbling. Isn't yours stronger for an infusion of Concordian blood?'

'I'd sooner see it fall. *Madonna*, you have a nerve to ask that after murdering my father – don't bother to deny it – and making a whore of my sister.'

'Maddalena,' said Geta proudly, 'makes her own decisions.'

'That she does. I judge by your smile that her latest crime has not yet reached *your* ears.'

Leto glanced nervously at Geta.

'I thought all Etruria knew,' said Salvatore with satisfaction. 'She's made a cuckold of you – and her poor bastard child, who-ever sired it, has paid the ultimate price for her sins.'

'Enough of this!' Leto grabbed Geta's sword-hand and made him step back before turning back to the cell door. 'Salvatore, you're a businessman. I'm an Engineer. We both know that allowing emotion to infect calculation is foolish. While other bancos let themselves be tumbled by the winds of speculation, you have increased your family's fortune by discipline and prudent diver-sification. Show that prudence now, and if that quick-boiling Rasenneisi blood impedes you, consider this: were you to sud-denly lose your head, the Bombelli family would get a new one. Perhaps one that—'

'Guido would not prove false – if he did, my brothers would

no longer consider him Bombelli; he would be a stranger to us like Maddalena.'

Geta whistled. 'They are a stubborn breed, these Rasenneisi.'

Leto sighed. 'I'm sorry you take this attitude, truly sorry. Please excuse me. Come, Marsuppini. You don't need to see this.'

After the door closed, Geta wearily pulled out his sword. 'Family get-togethers are such grief.'

CHAPTER 46

The Peoples of the Black Hand: A Bestiary

Salernitan perversity is a product of circumstance. After the fall of the Etruscans, Salerno was ruled by a succession of tyrants,[8] as were so many Etrurian states, but when Crusading fervour swept over Etruria, Salerno took a unique turn. They repudiated all kings and declared they would rule themselves. Many peoples have aspired to be free, but what makes the Salernitans unique is the commitment they have shown to that aspiration.

Understanding that hitherto, every democracy had been rent first by faction and then overturned by oligarchy, they resolved to devise a way of life that would protect them from corruption. According to the histories, this Gordian knot was cut by the philosopher Fra Copho.[9] He recognised the paradox at the heart of civilisation: that the city ennobles and corrupts men. His solution was as elegant as it was severe: every man of Salerno would henceforth spend the greater part of his life in self-imposed exile.

To preserve the city, the menfolk are kept away from it. The Salernitans

---

8 The last of these tyrants now rules Akka. It is a matter of some controversy whether the Guiscards left voluntarily for the Crusade or were expelled. They have never renounced their claim to Salerno, and the Snake of Asclepius still features in the Guiscard coat of arms.

9 Copho was one of the founders of the Schola Salernitana. Although mythmaking has made him into a cross between Moses and Solomon, he was simply the notary at Salerno's constitutional congress.

glory in this self-discipline. They claim the dichotomy between the civilised and the savage is an unhealthy illusion; they argue that just as each year has four seasons, so does a man.[10] And just as each season has its humour, so it has its proper activity.[11]

10 As must be apparent by now, argument by analogy is typical of Salerno's primitive philosophy.
11 According to Fra Copho, 'The cardinal virtue is Harmony.' Besides his *Anatome Porci*, Copho's most influential treatise was the *De Mensurabili Musica*; in this erudite dissection of polyphonic music, he proposed the notation system now used throughout Etruria.

CHAPTER 47

The busts of Grimani's ancestors all wore fool's caps and were painted up as courtesans and carnival clowns, part of Geta's redecoration of the former duke's throne room to turn it into a banquet hall. Leto had promised Castello Grimani to the city fathers, but might have omitted to tell them they would have to share it for the duration of the cold season.

The Moor's men were making extravagant bets on a spinning knife, winning and losing their new fortunes according to who ended up with the sharp end.

Geta, thoroughly enjoying the hospitality of the 'liberated' Veians, concentrated on filling his belly. 'Come on, Spinther. Eat before it gets cold. Don't look so dour – you're putting me off. I plan to fatten myself up this winter, starting tonight.'

'Don't you have a grieving wife somewhere?'

'She'll understand the sacrifices I have to make.' He burped and reached for the nearest flagon of wine.

The party was in mid-swing when a petrified herald announced the First Apprentice was at the gate.

'Let him in, man!' said Leto and, close to panic, tried to dismiss the revellers. He was pacing the hall while Geta and the Moor tried to keep the party going on either side of the table. All of them were trying to ignore the dread sitting in their bellies; the Moor hid it by drinking, while Geta continued wrestling slices off a roast pig sitting in a bed of salt.

'What do you think he wants, Spinther?' Geta asked through a mouthful.

'To admonish me . . .'

'Well, if you're left with a head on your shoulders when he's done, you can't have done anything *that* bad.'

'Disobeying orders now and again is good practise,' said the Moor.

'Then you three must be virtuosi by now.' Torbidda's crisp young voice echoed through the hall. 'Gentlemen, I fear I have interrupted your revels.'

He stood in the doorway as his praetorians filed by, taking up positions against the walls. Geta, fearing the worst, sprang to his feet and cried, 'Welcome First Apprentice!'

'Lord Geta! You left Concord in such a hurry that you forgot to say goodbye.'

When Geta looked about for a window through which to hurl himself, the First Apprentice hastened to put him at ease. 'My dear fellow, *tranquillo*. I look upon those events as in another lifetime. Whatever your sins, your subsequent actions have more than atoned for them. As Podesta and Gonfaloniere of Rasenna you did more damage than we ever could. The general is my dear friend, but he is too careful. He needs men who are not. It's *so* important in life,' Torbidda continued, 'to do as rivers do and find one's true course. Your vocation, Lord Geta, is destruction. Continue to practise it and we'll continue to get along.'

'Yes, First Apprentice,' said Geta, thoroughly confused, sitting back down. This was not the dour, murderous boy he had fled from a year ago. As much as Spinther got on his nerves, he felt almost sorry for him as he watched the two old friends size each other up.

'Leto, you've met Malapert Omodeo. I had to drag him away from his counting table to get him to come along. I always say that it's good to see your money at work.'

Leto nodded perfunctorily at the financier, who was accompanied by a slender young man with hair coiffed in the Byzantine fashion.

'That is why I am here too. After I received your letter, I decided I had to hear you explain yourself in person.' His polite smile vanished. 'Well, get on with it.'

Leto began a long account of what had happened at Ariminum, and why – after the disaster – he thought it vital to use the fleet to bring Veii to heel. The First Apprentice listened with growing irritation and finally silenced him with an imperious wave. 'Let me get this clear: you do not know how Ariminum burned – you *surmise*, but the only certainty is that the Serenissima is ash. Yet you are bold enough to imply that it would not have happened had you known the prisoner's condition. Believe what you like – I *never* confide with subordinates and I do not propose to start. I see it was pure luck that you escaped with part of the fleet – had I been of a conspiratorial bent, I might even think you burned Ariminum on purpose to give you an excuse to bring the fleet here. I see now that you always intended to disobey my orders.'

'Torbidda, when conditions change, it is—'

'I suppose you thought success would mollify me. Despite your mistakes and defiance, your resignation is refused. I need you yet. Our purpose was to terrify Etruria and now that Ariminum is burned, that is achieved.'

He looked around the room, then asked, 'What's this about the Cagligarians being in revolt?'

Leto had no time to wonder where Torbidda got his information. 'As soon as Veii was subdued, I dispatched a new governor to the colony—'

'But?'

'But the islanders were not content to exchange one master for another. It may have been an act of emulation – there have been rumours for months of civic unrest in the Sicilies – or perhaps it was merely simple opportunism. In any case, I was obliged to send reinforcements.'

'That is unfortunate. They'll be missed when you go south.'

'Oh, I think they'll have the situation under control before spring.'

'While we're getting the bad news out of the way,' Geta interrupted, ignoring Leto's glare, 'Salvatore Bombelli revealed before he died – ah, trying to escape – that the Contessa is on her way back to Etruria. She's not alone either. Somehow she's recruited the Oltremarines. She has Akkan ships and Byzantine troops.'

Torbidda turned to Leto with a look of vindication. '*Now* do you see, Leto, what comes of disobeying your Apprentice? The storm is coming here.'

'The Contessa of Rasenna has no authority in the Black Hand,' Leto pointed out. 'How could she get the south to follow her?'

'She'll use the same charm that worked on the Oltremarines. They won't "follow her" any more than the fanciulli "follow" me. We are each of us only the furthermost drop of two great waves rushing towards each other.'

Leto made a face. 'Well, that's all very picturesque but it's hardly reasonable to—'

'—Reason,' Torbidda interrupted. 'You're too old to still worship that idol. My predecessors justified their rule by claiming that they were ruled by Reason, yet they did nothing but squabble. How is it that Reason cannot agree? Is Reason divided? A thing is true or it is false, is it not? Consiglio, Signoria, the committee, bah! The wisdom of the collective is a game for lukewarm times and when war comes, games must end. We must be ready before they arrive. Now that we have Veii, we have central Etruria. When we take Salerno, we will have the Black Hand. They can take to the hills, but we'll have every city of consequence and the Contessa will find a cold welcome.'

'Unfortunately,' said Geta, 'they'll be arriving in a matter of weeks.'

'Which is why it's imperative that you march *now*. The arrow is in deep and pulling it out would only cause more pain. The thing is to push it through—'

'You *can't* be serious,' Leto exclaimed. 'We need to restore our strength, heal our wounds, stock up. If we wait, all the petty potentates south of the Albula will come crawling to us – we may conquer Etruria by force but we cannot long rule it that way. Bernoulli knew this—'

'What Bernoulli knew, I know. You must harry the south. The lessons they must learn must be taught with fire and steel. You will go, now, and meanwhile the fleet will sail south and blockade Salerno.'

The Moor looked up from his cups. 'That would be a mistake.'

'Have I wandered into a Communard council? Shall we put it to a vote? Don't tell me you're afraid of a fight, too, Admiral. Didn't you used to be condottiere?'

Though Azizi's speech was slurred, his earnestness was apparent. 'Yes – and I learnt that nothing but trouble comes from fighting men who don't do it for the money. The Veians are not brave, and see how they resisted. Every Salernitan is a soldier. If we allow reinforcements to come to their doorstep, they'll fight to the last. A better idea would be to meet the Contessa on the way – and I know just the place.'

While the First Apprentice listened to the Moor's plan, Leto noticed Malapert Omodeo filling his glass. His hand was trembling.

'I'm surprised that Torbidda was able to drag you away from the forge,' he said quietly.

'I welcome the chance, General. I have a favour to ask of you.'

The young man with the Byzantine sense of dress must have known he was being spoken of, for he came closer.

'Go on,' said Leto.

'This is my sister's boy, Horatius. Could you give him a commission? He's no head for figures, but he's brave as any.'

'We can always use new talent,' said Leto diplomatically. 'How are things in the capital?'

'Wonderful – production's up – spectacular efficiency—' As they talked, Omodeo manoeuvred him to a corner out of earshot of Torbidda's praetorians. '—every target met. It's wonderful.' Once he was certain no one was paying him any attention, he started, 'When the First Apprentice invited me back, he told me I would have influence. Instead I am being used as a milk-cow – he keeps me close lest I flee.'

'You're in no position to complain. You knew the terms under which you accepted amnesty.'

'My loans were given to fund the war-effort and I accepted no interest on them because I am a patriot, believe it or not. But I'm beginning to understand that I will never be paid back.'

'You'll get your money when the war is won,' said Leto, wondering at Omodeo's unfeigned fear. Was this just about his money?

'How can we win without weapons? Don't expect your annunciators any time soon – the factories are empty. All of the Small People are working on the Sangrail. And even if there were workers, they could produce nothing, for all of the metal from the north has gone into this damn needle.'

'Why are you telling me this? Do not, I pray you, say "patriotism" again; I'm not a complete fool.'

'Nor I, General. When my fortune is exhausted, he'll throw me to my enemies; that I know. Burning me might placate Numitor Fuscus a while and I know you would not mourn me – but what then of Concord? If the Contessa truly has enlisted Prince Jorge, the danger is greater than you know.'

'I've fought Byzantines before.'

'Aye, but you have not seen the Purple City. Its wealth is *vast*.'

'There are other considerations besides money—'

'What are you two whispering about?' Torbidda shouted. 'Hiding away in the corner there? Anyone would think you're plotting. Come, partake of this fine feast, Leto. It'll be your last for a while.'

When the order to decamp came, the men set about loading their loot with alacrity, too busy to realise the full implications. As the Grand Legion slowly poured out of Veii the following morning, Leto wondered if Malapert Omodeo was the only one who had worked out that the aftermath didn't interest Torbidda in the least. There was no one he could tell, no one he could talk to who would even care. They would just shrug and carry on as decades of Guild governance had taught them. Everyone had too much invested in this diabolical deal – wealth for complicity – to risk saying anything awry. There was no sin so base that they could not excuse it: Rasenna had the Wave coming, and as for blameless Gubbio – well, that was an example for all Etruria. The bloody work went on while everybody pretended that there was no choice; they would keep their heads low and wait it out.

But this is a storm no one will survive.

Then he remembered that Numitor Fuscus had warned him of just that. He had dismissed the consul as ambitious, but he was right: Torbidda *had* changed, and it was something to do with Fra Norcino. Some philosophers risked their souls for new knowledge, like Old Democritus, who had put out his own eyes that he might better contemplate. His friend had done himself some mischief . . .

Geta, still half-drunk from last night, trotted alongside with a merry grin. 'Where's Scaevola?'

'I told him I wanted someone I trusted to go with the Moor,

keep an eye on him. Did you know Scaevola was keeping an eye on me? Sending secret reports to the First Apprentice?'

'Can't say I'm surprised. Why so glum, Spinther? Will you miss the sycophantic tight-arse? Or were you expecting the First Apprentice to give you a Triumph?'

'I wasn't expecting this,' Leto admitted.

'I may have been a little merry last night but if the First Apprentice explained his thinking, I missed it. Why are we going again?'

'Orders.'

'Madonna, you're as much in the dark as the rest of us, aren't you? I know it's useful to keep the enemy guessing at your strategy, but to keep it from your general? That's a new one to me. But then, I'm not as learned as you. There must be some use to a Guild Hall education – I'm sure you can cite precedents from the Etruscan Annals. I can't help but feel that we're being punished, though—'

'Trying to set me against Torbidda is a waste of time.'

Geta smiled at that. Discord was a weed that needed little encouragement.

Irritated by Geta's smug silence, Leto said, 'He deserves our—'

'He's deserving of the same treatment as any other lunatic: chains, flogging and a straw bed. If you care for Concord—'

'The Spinthers have nothing to prove on that subject. Our escutcheon is riddled with chevrons of honour.'

'Stop waving your bloody medals at me,' Geta growled. 'You've never fought against the Black Hand, have you?'

'I've studied previous campaigns. Torbidda studied them too, so if he's ordered this, it's because it's vital that the Black Hand is broken before spring.' Geta was taken by surprise when the boy suddenly dropped his assured act, and whispered, 'What should I do? If I refuse, I won't just lose my commission – I'll lose my head.'

'By the holy face of Lucca – don't you realise you have a sword in your hand? The Grand Legion might be riddled with flux and pox, but what does he have to oppose it? A fancy title and a yard of red cloth. Turn around while the legion's still intact and march on Concord.'

Leto stiffened, realising that he should never have let his guard down. 'After everything, you're plotting still. You had your chance to overthrow the Collegio and all you succeeded in doing was destabilising the empire and giving Veii time to mount the defence that has so ruinously delayed us. I should have left you hanging on that tree.'

'I'm beginning to wish you had, lad,' Geta sighed.

CHAPTER 48

The lanterns still retarded the Sirocco's pace but the passage westward was faster now that they were no longer burdened with pack animals and foot soldiers. They looked like what Khoril insisted they were: a raiding party. The tribesmen were comfortable with this style of warfare and remained confident – but they had never seen the productivity of Ariminum's arsenal, or the earth-trembling mass of Concord's legions.

Yellow-spotted dolphins escorted the convoy across the Strait of Otranto, much to the delighted admiration of the Ebionites. It was a restful evening and they were sailing through warm green waters into a blinding setting sun when a Sicarii lazing in the rigging drawled, 'Scout ship ahoy!'

Moments later, the lead crow's nest confirmed it by raising a red flag.

The xebecs either side of the *Tancred* took off like loosed arrows. Sofia was in the first xebec, the *Solomon*, which was beating at attack-speed, while the other xebec, following at battle-speed, began firing its forward chasers.

The scout ship had spotted them now and briefly presented its beam as it tacked to bring itself about; the xebecs' light guns fired and it completed the turn with only a shattered bowsprit. Every hand not at the oars lined the weather rail to stiffen the xebec and increase its speed. The cutwater struck the cresting waves like a hammer, shattering them to foamy spindrift, till an apparent snowstorm enveloped them. Captured wind moulded the sail to stiffness and the yards were braced taut.

The scout's stern chasers were aimed squarely at them and a ball went hissing over Sofia's head and punctured the mainsail. The gap increased. The Lazars were strong, but the scout's crew were more practised.

Then they struck a lucky stroke: the sniping xebec missed, but the shot skidded along the scout's portside and tore through the oarsmen. The havoc it wreaked below deck was apparent from its sudden stop. The uninjured rowers on the other side succeeded only in exposing their beam again and this time two volleys struck home.

A thin plume of white smoke rose up from the becalmed scout.

A cheer went up from the rest of the Sirocco, who had been watching the chase, but it died when the scout fired a shot into the westward sky which exploded into green sparks. Sofia's worst fears were realised when she heard the cry from above, but she ascended the rigging herself to confirm it. There, a league to the west, was a second scout ship silhouetted against the dying sun, going about.

'Shall we give chase?' the tillerman panted. 'We've reserve rowers – we could pump out our water and throw the guns overboard to give us more speed—'

'Save your energy,' she said. Even if they did manage to run the second ship down, there was likely another further west still.

Instead, she had the stranded ship's slaves unchained and let loose on their former masters.

As the rest of the xebecs returned to formation, Sofia came aboard the *Tancred*.

'They know we're coming.' She spoke casually, but they all knew that their odds, never good to begin with, had just got even longer. The moon rose and the stars became visible, merging with the running lights and glowing battle-lanterns. The ships spread out to avoid collision, and each sailed alone with its fears on the dark sea.

*

Next morning's blue-green sea was beautiful, but Khoril was wary of the slow, pregnant swells beating against the starboard bow. 'Augurs storms in the west. Madonna help us if a nasty Gregale comes upon us.'

There was nowhere to seek cover, though Taranto – the thumb of Etruria – was due north. It was Sofia's first sight of her motherland in a year. She held up her child and said softly, 'Look, Iscanno! That's *home*.'

He solemnly chewed on a lock of her hair and looked. Taranto was the Black Hand's best port, so the Moor would have it well-blockaded, Khoril assured them. Besides, it was capacious enough for the better-armed Ariminumese galleys to keep their distance – just the type of fight he wanted to avoid. They needed somehow to fight a land battle at sea. Besides, their destination was on the far side of Etruria. If they rescued Salerno, the war was not won, but if Salerno fell it was most certainly lost.

Even so, once they passed Taranto all of them felt another fatal irrevocable step had been taken. That feeling was confirmed when a dozen Ariminumese galleys emerged from the port in hot pursuit.

While each ship was being stripped for battle – the yards padded and slung with chains, splinter-netting rigged, powder prepared and shot stacked – the leadership held a midnight council on the *Tancred*'s foredeck. The Messina Strait was leagues away yet, but they could just make it out, stretching before them in the moonlight.

The creased corners of Khoril's old map, pinned down with a sextant and a spyglass, trembled in the wind. The lines might be faded, but it clearly showed the dread gauntlet between the Black Hand and the Three Sicilies. Besides what lay ahead, they could see the distant lights of the chasing galleys behind them.

'They've not increased their pace since Taranto,' Khoril said.

'They're content to keep us in sight. They're herding us towards the strait, knowing we'll never cross it.' He drew a half-circle around the Sicilies. 'We have to go round to get to Salerno.'

Sofia stared at the map. 'Let's cross the strait then – they won't be expecting that, and if we go now, by the time they see us, we'll be through.'

'Navigate the strait by moonlight?' Khoril was aghast. 'I'd not do it for all the silver in Ariminum.'

Bakhbukh was with her, but his voice lacked his usual authority. In this liquid desert, he was an alien. Sofia couldn't explain her urgency, but now that Etruria was in her sight, the Darkness could see her: she could feel it reaching out for her and for Iscanno. 'To get this far and have our nerves fail—'

'If you had ever seen Charybdis, believe me, you'd not be so casual,' Khoril said. 'Think of your child.'

'I am!' she insisted, but saner heads agreed with Khoril.

'West it is.'

After the council broke up, Fulk climbed down to the *Tancred*'s rowing deck. Whatever happened in the next few hours, there would be no further time for talk. Over the last weeks, the Lazars had sought to lose themselves in servitude, but this voyage into the unknown had been an ordeal for their faith.

They knew the hour was imminent and they were all leaning at their stations, praying. Here in the ship's bowels, the air was thick, the walls caulked with the congealed fog of sweat.

'Brothers,' he said softly.

They made the sign of the Sword and warily, grudgingly, gave their Grand Master their attention.

'This day you are Crusaders.'

'We are orphans, Grand Master,' said Gustav dryly. Such back-talk would have been unthinkable a year ago.

'Yes – just as the first Crusaders were orphans. They had no fortune at home, so they sought it doing God's work. For them, Crusade meant protecting the Holy Land from the devil. Things were more complicated than they could have imagined. The Ebionites aren't the infidel – their fidelity to God is equal to ours.'

'But they are not so handsome,' said the old knight.

Fulk chuckled with the rest. 'I'll give you that, Gustav.' He looked over the rows, *seeing* each man despite the masks. Even those the disease had ravaged still wanted to hold onto their self-respect. 'I won't lie: most of us will never see Akka again, and I know some of you begin to fear that we have given our lives for a dead cause. Brothers, Crusade *never* ends. This night has brought us to the very shores of the land our fathers left. We made the devil so unwelcome at home that he has retreated here – and we will not let that worm rest. All lands are holy lands, even Etruria. We are as fortunate as our fathers, for like them, we are doing God's work. Like them, we fight wherever we can make our sacrifice count most. Tonight that's here. Be brave: fight for Akka, fight for your brothers – fight because *God wills it!*'

The chant of *Deus lo Volt!* made the deck vibrate beneath the Ebionites' feet, and though they rolled their eyes at the gauche manners of the Marians, it cheered them to know such madmen were at their side this night.

The Sicilian coast was dark except for the light of burning Syracuse. The Sicilies' division into a trinity was a convenient fiction of the geographers – the same queer breed that fancied the archipelago formed a stiletto for which Etruria was eternally reaching. Beside the three principal islands – Palermo, Messina and Syracuse – there were any number of islets, not to mention hidden mile-wide reefs waiting to tear into the hulls of careless ships like a fishmonger's gutting knife.

In an instant the night was impaled by a trail of fire that streaked across the starry sky and hung for a moment before melting into flaming drops that hissed where they landed on the water – hissed, and kept burning like lime-coloured lights of a ghostly puppetshow. The glare pulled back the curtain of darkness to reveal some forty ships directly ahead, lined up beam to beam. At the far end of the line was the source of the fiery rainbow, and several smaller ships were extending the barricade of fire in case they should try to circumnavigate.

Khoril ordered a full stop before they came within range of the fire-siphons. The gun crews were ready: slow-matches smoking in little tubs along the deck, the men at their stations. 'We could go south,' his navigator suggested hopefully. 'Creep along the Barbary coast for a few days then turn north?'

'And if they intercept us? We run away again? If we take that craven course then Salerno is done for.' He shouted across to the *Solomon*, 'Looks like you got your wish, Contessa. The strait it is, Madonna help us. The strait it is.'

The Moor's men cheered as the *Tancred* changed course. He only nodded and scanned his formation again, not to ensure the line was straight – he trusted his captains' seamanship. Their greed, that was another matter. Pirates practically considered it a sacred duty to pursue a feeing enemy but – *mirabile dictu!* – they restrained themselves. He was strangely disappointed. How soft the Serenissima had made them.

Khoril too was bothered by the restraint. 'Not that I'm complaining, but usually they'd fall on us like wolves.'

Sofia, on board the *Solomon*, was looking back at the wall of ships just waiting. Yes, it was ominous. She was almost relieved to see the wall slowly beginning to turn. The most southerly ship travelled a wide arc while the ship nearest to the coast merely turned about forty degrees. It looked like a great door shutting behind them, an image compounded as the fifteen galleys from Taranto arrived to complete the encirclement.

Khoril could not bury his misgivings. He hovered near the tiller. Their pursuers' pace had not increased; it was just a slowly tightening noose. 'What's he waiting for?' he grumbled.

'They don't think we have the salt,' the tillerman said. 'Well, he's in for a—'

'Full stop!' Khoril shouted.

The *Tancred*'s oars lifted – the action was simultaneously replicated by the thirty ships behind it – and the Moor grinned. He could just imagine Khoril's crestfallen face.

Beyond the strait, beyond Scylla's rocky teeth and swirling Charybdis, fifteen ships were waiting, five of them copper-plated lanterns armed with the heaviest of Concordian guns.

CHAPTER 49

Salerno is one hundred and fifty miles south of Veii as the crow flies – but in Etruria, the eel was a more reliable pacemaker. The route was complicated by endless lakes and circuitous rivers which were especially high at this time of year, and the Minturnae Marsh was treacherous at all times, so they had to go some distance east to where the Albula narrowed. The pontonniers assembling the bridges were constantly harassed by a small band of butteri – but such a host could only be delayed, not defeated.

Leto sent hundreds of skirmishers across in small rafts to protect the bridge, and supported them with a flock of annunciators. Stocks were perilously low but Leto was in no mood for half-measures. Soon enough the Grand Legion was assembled on the far side, complete with the carroccio displaying their banners.

They had to cross the Allia before the day ended. Frustrated at their pace, retarded by wagons in need of repair, Leto declared that all unnecessary baggage was to be burnt, and to show a good example to his men, he set fire to his own books. But few were inspired, and the order had to be carried out forcibly. The men grumbled as they watched all their Veian loot go up in smoke. The next day's march brought no rivers worth recording, but no reprieve either: the land got progressively more wet, and the men more despondent.

Exhausted and hungry, they stopped early and while the surveyors marked out the camp, Leto made a short address. 'I daresay this is familiar to a few of you. For the rest of you, the name of this place is Tagliacozzo. Three years ago, John Acuto fought and lost here. Three years ago, your countrymen smashed an army of the south. We can do it again.'

The men listened patiently, desperate for encouragement, but who could be impressed by a *field*? A skin of bright yellow lichen and dark green covered the ruined engines, softening their edges so they resembled disembodied limbs, as though titans did battle here. Weeds grew thickly through collapsed earthworks. The trenches had turned into connected canals of stagnant water, hazed over with the last of the year's mosquitoes – the hardy *zanzara*, big as wrens, that delighted to feast on the eyeballs of buffalo or, even more succulent, those of their shepherds. As for the thousands who had died here, they had left no mark. More impressive were the ash-blue mountains to the east: massive, impassive and changeless. In this land, time alone was victorious. The officers were glum for other reasons: they knew their general proposed to take the highlands route to the south. The Great Pebble, as it was called, had three summits: Big Horn, Middle Horn and Small Horn, which together resembled the profile of a sleeping giant.

'Look around and be assured,' Leto shouted, 'that whatever force we come up against shall meet with the same fate. We shall finish the work begun in Forty-Seven – and be assured that the eyes of the noble dead are upon you today. Those cowards who were routed that day, they too have their jealous eyes upon you. So cry out, and let these hidden watchers, from the mountains to the marshes, know that we are here to stay!'

Malapert Omodeo's nephew Horatius erupted in loud hurrahs, but he was alone; they rest received the speech with a perfunctory cheer that quickly vanished into the darkness of the evening. The feeling that retreat was no longer an option was too strong – and the reference to 'hidden watchers' had confirmed all their paranoid suspicions.

Aware that his oration had failed, Leto peevishly dismissed the assembly.

If the site of the battle was disappointing, the town itself was worse. Tagliacozzo possessed one shabby piazza, and it was burning. The scorched circle had but one shack left standing – and that would not last long if someone did not put out the fire.

'Bastards,' Horatius exclaimed indignantly. 'They mean to deny us bread and dry beds.'

Geta said, 'We must become accustomed to these warm welcomes. Is everything burned?' He was here for supplies. Since leaving Veii, General Spinther had taken a petty satisfaction in assigning him menial tasks.

'Everything worth a soldi. We managed to pull this rogue out of the church cellar before it collapsed.' Horatius pointed to a scruffy prisoner whose hands were still bound and whose boots were still smouldering. His long moustache was a little singed too – as were the bushy eyebrows. 'The other prisoners were—'

'—cooked,' the man drawled.

'Well, that can't be helped. Now, my dear fellow,' Geta said solicitously, 'I assume by your delightfully rustic costume that you're not from these parts.'

'Ain't you the smart one.'

'I don't suppose you have any information that might save your life?'

The buttero's coal-black eyes glowered under his brows. 'I know a thing or two about a thing or two.'

'An educated buttero. This *is* a surprise. For example?'

He nodded at the shack that was beginning to smoulder. 'That there's a tavern.'

Geta smacked the nearest officer's helmet off and cried, 'Look lively, man!'

After the fire had been subdued and a firebreak made, the

soldiers went in to sample the wares. Geta insisted the prisoner join them. He expected the fellow would try to cut some sort of a deal, but Sergio – that was apparently his name – was interested only in cards.

Geta was intrigued, and after an hour's play, enquired, 'Don't you want to know our plans?'

Sergio sucked at his moustache. 'Figure you'll play that three you've been nursing.'

'I mean the Grand Legion's – there's plenty would pay plenty to know them.'

'Never saw much point in thinking on tomorrow till I wake up in it.'

'We're going south.'

'Hell, I knowed that. How you fixing to go?'

'The highlands,' said Geta.

The buttero supped his grappa. '*Bona fortuna.*'

'You don't think that wise?'

'Look at me. I lost my hat, my bolos and my buffalo and my boots got holes in them.'

'*Salute*,' said Geta. 'To misfortune. What's your point?'

'Point is, I ain't no authority on what's wise and what ain't. But since yer asking, that's got to be the most fool *transumanza* I've ever heard.'

'I assume that's some delightfully obscure Black Hand custom,' said Geta, growing vexed. 'What does it involve, sleeping with your sister's sheep?'

'Come fall, we bring our herds on down from the hills so they have a chance of surviving. Spring comes, we take 'em back up. You aim to cross the land, but you're going about it ass-backwards. I wouldn't lead men, *any* amount, let alone that horde you got, up yonder mountain. Them highlanders ain't got no buffalo, no grass, no grappa. All they got is the Big Pebble.'

'So?'

'The thing a man holds, that thing he prizes – if you go aloft, you better be in the Madonna's good graces, because you will *not* be welcomed.'

'We didn't come to make friends.'

'Huh, I knowed that too. What I'm telling you if you got ears is you'll suffer snowfalls and landslides. You'll go to sleep cold and when you wake up, your engines'll be gone or busted and your beasts'll get their necks cut or legs broked up. That's *if* you wake and your head ain't cracked by an unlucky midnight rockfall. There'll be lots of them. See, it ain't just Highlanders that don't take to strangers. The mountain ain't fond of them neither.'

'You mean to scare us,' said Geta with a smile. 'No Southerner loves Northerners.'

'Well, you're not wrong: I got no affection to spare you. It's a quirk of ours, I suppose, that we don't like being invaded, and I suppose I wouldn't warn you if I expected you to believe me. Your boys pulled me out of the fire and I'm returning the favour is all. You want to jump back in, that's your business. If you do, take a few jugs of grappa and concerto. Cold nights up there. I'll see you when you get back, and if I don't, I'll guess you're dead. *Salute.*'

Geta returned to camp next morning, drunk again. Leto was poring over maps surrounded by officers in the command tent, still angry at the men's stubborn refusal to be moved by his address.

'We don't all have your Guild Hall grooming,' Geta protested. 'But you must really disdain our intelligence – we can hardly forget the legion that won here was the same legion that was destroyed in Rasenna.'

'You find this funny. Can't you even act like you care?'

Geta uncorked his wineskin. 'Do you care for dog-fighting, Spinther? It's wonderful sport. The best dog I ever saw – it was in Ariminum, I think – he'd lost an eye, had his paw gnawed off, ribs broke and still he kept coming. *Madonna*, that dog was game! I swore I'd buy him if he won.'

Leto continued to study his map. 'What happened?'

'He practically beheaded the other mutt before they dragged him off. I won a packet.'

'Was he expensive?'

Geta chuckled. 'Lord, I didn't buy him! He'd ruined himself in the process. They threw him in the lagoon that very night. My point, dear Spinther, is that these Southerners are like that: no matter how severely we beat them, they'll keep coming.'

'Keep your penny philosophising to yourself,' Leto snapped. 'And for Reason's sake, keep your drinking to respectable hours.'

'Why stop here if not to pour libations to the glorious dead?'

'We've stopped because something's *off* and you'd have realised that if you weren't half-drunk all day. The butteri are proud people and the Allia River has always been a frontier against invaders. I expected more resistance – but there's been *nothing*. Now here we are, camped without a fight at Tagliacozzo. They're letting us get deep.'

'You give those cowards too much credit.'

'They want us to proceed confidently and leave our flanks exposed. Here's us,' said Leto, tapping the map, 'between Pescara and Caieta.'

'If we stop to subdue every hovel, we'll never get to Salerno.'

'Unless we proceed methodically, we'll end up surrounded.'

'You take counsel from your fears.'

Feeling the officers' eyes on him, Leto spoke loudly and slowly. 'Patience, Lord Geta. When we get to Salerno, you'll have ample opportunity to charge about waving your sword like the ridiculous anachronism you are.'

Unabashed, Geta insisted, 'We should press on.'

Leto hammered a fist on the table. 'This is *not* a joint command!

You are my subordinate and your mercenaries' lives are mine to spend. Take them west to Caieta. Secure it. I'll investigate Pescara. We rendezvous back here at noon on Giovedi, and only *then* will we proceed south. Dismissed.'

As Geta rode for Caieta, his anger at Spinther's imperiousness faded in the face of his anticipation of the fun of falling on the fishing town unawares. His indignation returned when dense obelisks of smoke segmenting the sky told him that someone already had the same idea. Caieta was ablaze and most of the berths in the small harbour were empty – the fishermen had either fled south with their boats or sunk them at their moorings. There was no one to kill or rape, nothing to eat or loot.

Pointless.

Back in Tagliacozzo, Leto admitted he had fared little better in Pescara.

'Burnt to the ground too?' said Geta.

'No, but it was similarly denuded. The town fathers were obviously terrified of the butteri. From what I could understand of their barbarous dialect, they claim not to support either side in the war.'

'How nice of them.'

'I politely informed them that neutrality was not an option. The translators had trouble conveying this point, so I had their families brought out.'

Geta chuckled. 'And what was lost in translation was suddenly found?'

'After the town fathers had made their proper obeisance, I set out for our rendezvous – but I'd only gone a few miles when I glanced behind and saw Pescara burning. There was nothing to do but ride on. I wonder was it self-sacrifice, or punishment by the butteri?'

'At least we don't have to wonder about their loyalty. What a bloody waste of time.'

'For the last time, it is simple prudence to protect our flanks,' Leto insisted. 'Moving an army is no different from building a bridge: if you calculate stress and load conservatively and use good materials, success is assured.'

'You've spent too much time in Scaevola's company,' Geta grumbled. 'Our lives are in Fortune's hands. The prudent do not win her favour.'

Geta might be infuriating, but Leto knew he was right: war was *not* that arid subject he had mastered in the Guild Hall; it was a savage dream, primitive as the swamps ahead of them, where inspiration and phantasms had form, where an artistic temperament like Geta's could bring ruin or wrest victory from impossible odds while pedants like himself could only plod behind, making sure the horses were fed and the machinery kept dry. He was not a general, but a quartermaster.

But admitting that was another matter entirely. 'Tomorrow, we take the Big Pebble. Dress warmly.'

CHAPTER 50

Scaevola was enthusiastic about the Moor's plan in part because it resembled a land battle, with static lines and neat encirclements, but mainly because he alone had command north of the strait. He took this as a mark of respect from the Moor, although in truth it was the only station where the quartermaster's naval inexperience would not matter. His wing merely had to float there and attack whatever emerged from the strait.

Despite a growing swell, Scaevola insisted on binding the ships together. He had employed the same tactic in Gaul once to prevent an allied tribe from retreating. An hour before dawn, he summoned his captains to the *Bernoulli*, the splendid lantern he commanded. They had already rehearsed several times, but once more wouldn't hurt. Scaevola began lecturing to the increasingly surly captains at once: 'It's crucial that you maintain the intervals. Who's captaining the two ships nearest the vortex?' He consulted his list. 'The *Ariminus* and the *Bellicose*. You two? Look, I know you're dealing with the shifting currents but you're both sagging to leeward.'

The captain of the *Bellicose* wasn't about to listen to an amateur. 'Your bloody line's too long, Concordian. Each end's experiencing different conditions.' The others agreed, and began to clamour about becoming entangled in the chain.

Scaevola was unmoved. 'I know very well why you want to be unchained, but we're not here for prize-hunting.'

'What if they break for the Sybaritic coast?' demanded the

captain of the *Serenissima*, at the most westerly end of the line. 'We'll have to pursue.'

'No, our role is to keep them bottled up in the strait and we'll only achieve that by concentrating our forces, not dispersing them. The few that do escape – if there are any – can be easily hunted down later. Until the day's issue is settled, you will conduct yourselves like soldiers.'

The meeting broke up with angry muttering, and as the morning went on, the folly of such a long line became clear even to Scaevola. The exasperated captains tried to maintain their stations by heaving to with sails so that the winds cancelled each other – but the winds of the strait were almost as contrary as its waters. Though Scaevola suspected deception at play, he dreaded being out of position when the battle began and reluctantly he ordered the line divided.

This manoeuvre wasted another few hours, and when it was done, three untethered ships hung back between two groups of six chained. The untethered ships' role was to lend support wherever and whenever necessary. One of these was the *Bernoulli*; from here Scaevola planned to control each wing like a conductor.

'Ships ahead!'

The cry from the crow's nest of one of the advance line was audible back in the *Bernoulli*.

'Daft bugger,' the man at the tiller said. 'It's only the *Fata Morgana*!'

Scaevola said nothing as he looked steadily past the bowsprit. His heart began pounding. This was no castle in the air. Between the *niponti* appeared the thin foresails of several ships.

'I thought there'd be more,' he said, a little disappointed.

'Commander?' said an eager ship's boy. 'Shall I signal the others to engage?'

'For the fifth time, *no!* We keep our positions and let them come to us.'

The dimensions of the trap were clear before them but neither Khoril nor Sofia nor Bakhbukh despaired. Once the scout had escaped, an ambush was practically assured. They had plans of their own. Nine xebecs sped forward for the strait while the remainder turned about and rallied on the lanterns, making a crescent to face the crescent now encircling them.

'They mean to push us onto the *niponti*,' cried Khoril, and changed the glass in the lantern to yellow. At his signal yet more xebecs broke rank and went for the enemy in four groups of two, each pair aimed at a lantern.

Between each of the Moor's five lanterns sheltered ten 'regulars' of the Golden Fleet, and with the wind now in their favour, they came forth to meet the approaching xebecs, targeting them with cannon.

The heavy swell would inevitably impede accuracy. 'Wait for the upward roll,' the Moor cautioned, though the *San Barabaso*'s gun crews knew their work as well as any.

Then he roared, 'Fire!'

One of the xebecs was immediately dealt a crippling blow; its shattered mainmast toppled sideways and smashed through the starboard oars before plunging down to the abyssal depths. The other lanterns, drawn by the scent of weakness, turned about to target it.

All of the heavy cannon were on the lanterns, and most of their fire flew harmlessly over the low-lying xebecs, which began weaving, as if to confound the unfixed guns.

The Moor was puzzled. Such little ships couldn't possibly hope to board them, or sink them by ramming . . .

He signalled to the four siphon-ships to prepare. Their fuel would be quickly exhausted and he had planned to save them for

AIDAN HARTE

later in the engagement – but it could not be helped. He delayed
until the xebecs were in range, then shouted: 'Fire!'

Eight burning swords illuminated the morning gloom, forming
great arcs until they intersected. When each pair met, the flames
strove to consume each other like fugitive stars brought to earth.
The weaving xebec pairs could not dodge them – and they did not
try. They passed through with their momentum unchecked, transformed from menacing black darts to fiery arrows. Below deck, the
drummers beat them to ramming-speed, the Lazars chanted, 'Deus
lo Volt!' and they rowed for the Contessa's son. They had lived with
pain all their lives; it was easy enough to ignore the smoke and
falling embers, the dripping pitch and melting tar. The glowing
ships pushed forward, faster and faster, throwing a sizzling bow-
wave in front and trailing a cloud of steam.

When the Moor finally realised what they meant to do, the
first sincere prayer he had ever made escaped his lips – but no
one was listening. The xebec-arrows were aimed at their hearts:
the magazines on board, which were all dangerously overstocked
since Veii. The great wooden world rocked as the first xebec
struck, splintering timbers with her small but deathly-sharp ram.
Men fell screaming from the rigging, the lucky ones hitting the
water. Those few who had managed to hang on were dislodged
when the second arrow stuck home.

The Moor was one of the few on deck to keep his feet. He leaped
out of the way of a falling block and looked down the line. The
two most easterly lanterns were hit too; the closest to the *San
Barabaso* had managed to avoid one of the suicide-boats, which
had instead collided with the galley next to the siphon-ship,
impaling itself in its magazine with horribly predictable results.

The blast of scalding air and licking flames enveloped its neighbours and the siphon-ship expired like a sea-serpent flailing its
tentacles in general outrage at the world. A cracking explosion
made the Moor turn to port just in time to see the lantern closest

385

to the Syracusan coast erupt in white light, raining incendiary drops and flaming spars upon its neighbours.

As a hot wind brushed by, he watched incredulously as some Ariminumese officers rushed down into the *San Barabaso's* hold carrying sloshing water-buckets. Such fools gave heroism a bad name. He cast away his great cloak, cried, 'Swim for your lives!' and bolted, not waiting to see who followed.

The deck beneath his feet buckled as if suppressed by some great weight and he waited no longer: he leaped the rails and dived in a great arc as behind him, the night detonated.

The main mast shot skywards like a great javelin, trailing all manner of things caught up in the rigging: men cooked like spitted pigs, smoking cannon, charred blocks and twisted hot metal that hummed as it flew through the air and sighed sadly when it hit the water. And everything was shrouded in the deadly shredding cloud of a great forest reduced to splinters.

Under the waves, the Moor opened his eyes and saw the surface of the water above him was *glowing* like midsummer noon. Its beauty was so distracting that it was a moment before he noticed the water itself was beginning to boil. He swam deeper, and let the strange currents carry him away from his ruined ship before pulling himself free. He resurfaced next to one of the inner galleys and took a breath of scalding – *delicious* – air before surveying the destruction.

A less jaded mariner might have quailed at the apocalyptic vista. Though the neat order of his line had vanished together with the other three lanterns, he still had the numbers – and his quarry still had nowhere to flee. Scorning to be hauled aboard on a bosun's chair, he scrambled up the ratlines and threw himself on deck. The traumatised crew of the *Mars* stood gawping at him.

'Not a bad overture, gentlemen,' he said cheerily. 'Let's show them our appreciation, shall we? Step lively now!'

*

Leagues to the north, a dozen galleys fired steadily into the strait, but it was hard enough to keep both wings in line while remaining stationary, so they drew no closer. Had Scaevola been less cautious, the trap would have been perfect; as it was, at least the xebecs did not have to navigate the *niponti* under very close fire.

Even so, the crossing proved immediately fatal as a chasm suddenly opened in front of the first xebec, and the other nine watched in horror as the whirlpool dashed the ship against one of the *niponti*. With no way to help and no time to grieve, they immediately turned to the next channel, which luckily proved to be vortex-free – but still the ceaseless battery contrived to complicate their progress.

Scaevola was not surprised when the first five through turned for the mainland – west was certain death at the hands of the endlessly wheeling maelstrom. He had the eastern wing hold fire till the xebecs made their run, and when he finally gave the signal, the din was stunning. Soon a dirty cloud drifted over the strait, blinding friend and foe alike.

By the time the sixth xebec zipped through the strait, the gunnery of the western wing had found their range and an excellent shot broke through the xebec's mast. The next found its target too, less spectacularly but no less destructively, breaking through below the waterline, and the stricken vessel stopped midway in the channel. With that way blocked, the final three xebecs were forced to divide and risk the next two channels. The *Solomon* was lucky, as was the ship following, but the third was not. The Ariminumese took potshots as it spun in its death-spiral.

The sound of the shallow reef scraping the *Solomon*'s hull was awful, but once they had cleared it, their ears were assaulted by something worse: Charybdis' endless roar. Her sons might roam, but she was chained eternally to the seabed. The luck of the ship behind ran out as it impaled itself on a rocky outcrop; it was an easy target stranded there, and there was nothing the *Solomon* could do.

Even if they could have got close enough to rescue anyone, they had their own dilemma: an unenviable choice between likely or certain death, whether to risk the long passage east, exposing her beams to the both wings' fire, or—

'Are you certain you can do this, Mistress?'

'This is no time to start doubting me, Bakhbukh. Straight ahead!'

Scaevola signalled the most westerly galley, the *Bellicose*, to tackle the *Solomon* and then watched nonplussed as the xebec sailed directly into the maws of Charybdis.

The *Bernoulli*'s tillerman was equally bemused. 'They're either fools or suicides.'

'Then let us not detain them,' said Scaevola, who was more concerned at the queer behaviour of the xebecs which had crossed first. The Contessa must surely be on one of these five vessels, now aligned in a row and racing towards the distant craggy cliffs of the Sybaritic coast. It was sensible to use each other's slipstreams like that – but why were they were running so close to the eastern wing, allowing their guns to pound them so remorselessly?

In order to keep their cannon fixed on the fast-moving targets, the eastern wing had gradually tilted away, out of line. All at once the xebecs turned, each aiming for a different ship. Scaevola, watching from afar, was dumbfounded, but the intention was immediately clear to his far more experienced captains on board – bound as they were, no evasion would be possible. All they could do was to pour fire at the incoming xebecs and brace themselves.

One of the xebecs was quickly crippled, but the other four found their targets simultaneously.

*

The tension on the *Solomon* was palpable. Bakhbukh was standing at the bow, watching Sofia. Her cool exterior was no front; it was clear her only concern now was Iscanno, safe in his cot in her cabin. Whatever happened to her, he *must* survive this day. He doubted the child would be sleeping. He responded to people's mood as a sail to the wind.

Sofia gave the nod and Bakhbukh roared, 'Now!'

Up went the oars – just in time, for Charybdis grabbed them in the next moment. Bakhbukh tried to ignore the feeling of mounting pressure under his feet, and the foreboding that this day would end tragically. 'How's this supposed to work, exactly?'

'I'm exactly damned if I know,' Sofia said, her grin slightly manic. 'But if it does, I'll be useless for a spell. It'll be up to the Sicarii.'

'We shall not fail you.'

Sofia tutted. 'You didn't say God willing.'

'God has willed *you*, Mistress. There is no *if* any more.'

The *Solomon* was dragged in a great circle with less volition than a leaf carried away on a mountain torrent. They passed by the innermost line of chained galleys – who totally ignored them, now that they were in the monster's grip – then bore west, and then back till the southern coasts of the Sicilies faced them. Below deck, the Lazars sat at their posts, conserving their energy and waiting for the Grand Master to beat the drum.

The timing must be precise.

She didn't know if it could be done – or if it could, for how long. She had seen Giovanni stop a Wave, though the effort had ripped him apart. She'd never moved much more than a glassful. Was this folly? Had she condemned them all? What if—?

No: the Darkness was trying to intimidate her with these doubts; they were shadows that had been burned away in the Sands. There was no essential difference between a glass and a maelstrom; water was water. A drop contained a sea.

She raised her hands from her sides and a wind, unfelt by any other on deck, assailed her. She leaned back into it, tipping over impossibly. Tonnes of water hammered against her back and the beams of the fragile vessel creaked as a splintering crack came from the mast and the planks she stood on buckled, but still she did not cry out. She did not move.

Then – a thing that had not been seen since the Great Flood: the maelstrom stopped. In the suddenly stilled water, a thousand doomed sea creatures scuttled and swam for freedom. Charybdis roared in outraged majesty.

The helmsman gave Bakhbukh the nod and he turned and roared, 'Now!' down the hatchway.

Fulk pounded the drum and twenty oars hit the water as one. Sofia had begun when they were bearing east, away from the Sicilies, and carried along by momentum in addition to the heaving oar-power they were now approaching the innermost chain again.

At last, with everyone below straining together, with Bakhbukh and the helmsman wrestling the tiller and Sofia feeling that her body must surely crack in two just as the mast had done, they broke free.

The crew's cheer was drowned by a hideous sucking noise as the unleashed monster stirred the seas behind them. They were a missile now, aimed straight at the Ariminumese galley.

Bakhbukh caught Sofia as she fell. 'Mistress, you did it!'

'Iscanno,' she whispered. Her eyes were open, but she was spent. He carried her to the cabin and laid her down beside her son – then he paused awkwardly.

'Go where you're needed, you chivalrous fool,' she rasped.

He didn't need to be told twice. He rushed out of the cabin, glancing above as he loaded his sling. The Sicarii in the rigging were weaving between the hail of arrows from the *Bellicose* so they must be close now. He shot out the eye of a crossbow sniper then took to the beams where the reserve Lazars were lined up, grappling hooks at the ready.

'For the Contessa!' he shouted.

Across the diminishing gap, they heard the captain of the *Bellicose* cry, 'Brace yourselves, lads. Have courage!' – though this last looked to be in scarce supply, for the *Solomon*'s miraculous escape from Charybdis had obviously awed his superstitious mariners.

The impact threw the Sicarii forward and like the seedpods of those thorny succulents that explode across the Sands only once a century they flew across the void and caught in the *Bellicose*'s rigging, even as the arsenalotti were shaken loose, falling to the deck or into the water. Those who did manage to hold on were faced with another terrifying shock: an invasion of savage fighters as adept at climbing as they.

Once secured to the *Bellicose*, the Lazar oarsmen abandoned their oars to join their brothers. Fulk fought his way, his axe swinging, to Bakhbukh's side.

The gaps between the chained ships had lessened with the westerly-tending wind. The next ship over, the *Ariminus,* was in range, but reluctant to fire on one of their own; they had not yet recognised that the *Bellicose* was already lost.

The invaders had varied tactics – the Sicarii worked in pairs while the Lazars preferred one-on-one duels – but all were unknown to the Moor's men, who were accustomed to fighting terrified seamen. As the battle drew to a close, the Sicarii made death-defying leaps to invade the rigging of the *Ariminus*, while the Lazars took control of the *Bellicose*'s cannons and raked the lantern's deck. They were not practised enough to be precise, but at this range precision was irrelevant: any shots that missed the *Ariminus* struck the enchained ships behind her.

South of the strait, the situation was quite different. Though Khoril's initial blow had been magnificent, the Moor had recovered to wreak a grievous revenge. He was still stationed on the *Mars*, now his last surviving lantern, and his captains were at home in mêlée. Khoril's inner crescent, now reduced to ten, had become ever more circular as they were pushed back towards the strait. Burning and sinking ships presented another obstacle to both sides, and between the smoke and rain and increasingly turbulent west wind, all was confusion.

The *Mars* was an embarrassment to its name, the Moor had decided, equipped as it was with only one large cannon. His sunk lanterns had all the long-range guns, so the remainder were obliged to fight at intimate distance. The first galley that closely engaged a Sirocco ship had been overrun by swarms of Sicarii, leaving the Moor no choice but to sink them both.

Since he couldn't board them, he had the Golden Fleet – or what was left of it – attack Khoril's ships in pairs, hammering at them from both sides until their decks were reduced to charred splinters. They were left drifting aimless, unable to do further harm , while the Moor's men moved on to the next enemy vessel. At the start he had superior numbers in the region of two to one and now, despite his initial losses, it was more like three to one.

It wouldn't be long now . . . His relish was interrupted by an unexpected cry from the crow's nest: 'Admiral, vessels portside!'

'Portside?' He scrambled aloft, ready to throw down the blind fool, but the boy spoke true: a fleet of galleys was coming from the Port of Syracuse. Their formation was tight; their speed, with sail and oar pulling together, good – their intention as obvious as it was incredible: to break through his now-dispersed line with a concentrated punch and to relieve his beset quarry. But why would *Sicilians* wish to antagonise distant Concord? It made no sense – but he had been too long amongst the heathens to be much surprised at anything they might do.

His orders were precise and not up for interpretation. There was time for only half the line to turn about, no more than that, and though they still had the numerical advantage, fighting with another enemy at your back was rarely pleasant.

On the far northern rim of this intense struggle, the *Bernoulli* and the two reserve galleys sat untouched and uninvolved. Instinct said flee, but Scaevola knew it was his duty to lend help where needed. The question was: which side's need was greater?

To the west they were contending with Charybdis' crazed currents and even more crazed Sicarii invading from all directions, and the fight had descended into a mêlée. He watched with terrible fascination as a ship drifting on its beam ends was swallowed by the whirlpool and vanished in seconds.

To the east, the xebecs had struck the chain at several points at once and completely destroyed his neat formation. In the confusion two galleys had collided, and although neither was going fast enough to do real damage to their hulls, they still became entangled. More troublesome yet, the collision had broken loose an improperly secured cannon, and after crushing the deck-crew, it had acquired a taste for murder and finished the job by plunging down the forehatch and straight through the galley's bottom. As the first ship sank, it dragged the other galley with it.

Faced with the awful reality that this battle had no centre, Scaevola decided there was no deciding and sent one reserve galley east and one west. The *Bernoulli* remained uncommitted: a monument to caution.

A tin cup slid off the edge of the shelf and Sofia opened her eyes. Everything in the cabin was at a weird angle: were they sinking? It wasn't the creaking or the muffled explosions that pierced her grogginess but the fact that Iscanno was not smiling. She rolled over to see a grim arsenalotti standing over her wielding a rigging-pin.

'Forgive the intrusion, Signorina, but there's a pretty reward for you.'

He took a step towards her and then stopped, sighed wistfully and fell to the ground.

Bakhbukh wiped his blade clean. 'Time to go, Mistress.'

He helped her to her feet and over the body. The scene on deck was hellish. A pall of black smoke hung over everything like a sickness, and parts of men were littered everywhere, caught in the rigging, piled on the deck, floating in the waves. Ahead of them was a forest of swaying masts and from the crow's nests to the rowing decks she could see men locked in earnest conflict. The general drift towards Charybdis was tangible now; that monster would not be twice denied.

The eastern wing was entangled with the xebecs and had by now turned so it was perpendicular with the strait. The conflagration drifted west like a great trawler net, trapping everything it touched, and explosions started fires on those few ships not already burning and infused the cloud of gun smoke drifting before it with foggy blackness. Storms of men draw storms in nature: the sulphur merged with the gathering storm clouds and the cannons' report was now echoed by real thunder.

The ships of the western wing were thoroughly entwined: one great rootless island drifting west. The arsenalotti had regrouped sufficiently to stop the Sicarii advance, yet it was too late to do more. The Lazars took control of the guns of each ship as she was claimed and spread confusion with random fire; those not yet taken did the enemy's work by firing pre-emptively on each other.

The galleys Scaevola had sent ahead had already become hopelessly entangled in the fray. The *Bernoulli* itself was in a corridor of sorts between the two merging wings, and burning debris surrounded them. If they tarried much longer they would be trapped – so surely now the imperative must be survival. He desperately wanted to turn north and sail back to Veii, but his navigator insisted the corridor behind them was closing too fast.

'We can't take the *niponti!*' Scaevola screamed.

'Well, if you have any better—?' The navigator's head was whisked off by a piece of spinning spar as a portside explosion buffeted the *Bernoulli*. She listed precariously. Grappling hooks flew from the clouded island to starboard and when the *Bernoulli* righted herself, she pulled dozens of Sicarii up into her yards. More hooks portside came flying from the smoke as arsenalotti, Sicarii, Lazar and pirate alike sought to escape the general doom.

'Cut the ropes!' Scaevola screamed at the deck-crew, but they were too few and the enemy too many.

CHAPTER 51

'How can I serve?' she asked again, but taunting silence was the only answer Carmella got from the stained-glass Madonna. She'd called Isabella a child, but here she was, dumbly replicating her actions. Why was she praying in the chapel? Because Isabella had done so – but it hadn't worked. The Madonna in the window looked reproachful, certainly, but there was no forgiveness.

As was just. Carmella believed in old Rasenna's law: blood for blood. She'd blamed Isabella for not letting her shine, but there was no one to blame now. This wreckage was her doing. She alone had elected to stay, and she alone had stained the baptismal font with blood. Uggeri's blood.

'What do I do? Speak!'

This time she heard something.

'Unhand me, you dirty peasant!'

'Shut up. It's time you made your confession.'

Carmella went out into the garden to investigate the raised voices. Bocca came striding into the baptistery, pulling a young woman along. 'Hello, Sister. Still take orphans here?' He did not wait for an answer before throwing the woman at Carmella's feet.

Maddalena's head had been roughly sheared and her lip and cheek were bleeding and swollen. She stared at the font. Her lips moved, but she was dumb with terror.

Carmella said, 'Who did this?'

'Me,' Bocca said resolutely, 'and I'll happily do worse if you don't keep her from mischief. Them dancers outside is nearly all dead now, so the last thing we need is for some lunatic to open the gates and start it all over again. If she wants to kill herself, I'll provide the rope, but I won't let her endanger Rasenna.'

'Papa will have you whipped!' Maddalena screamed.

'I told you already, slut: your papa's dead and even that criminal Geta's abandoned you. The Signoria is back in charge.'

'Signor, there's no cause to abuse her,' Carmella said calmly.

'Perhaps not, but it feels great to give a Bombelli a good hiding. You should try it – you look like you need a laugh. Or treat her like a principessa if you prefer, she's now your responsibility. But if you don't keep her here, out of trouble' – he leaned close – 'I'll chain her up like the bitch she – *ahhh—!*'

Maddalena's claws drew blood and Bocca raised his fist, but Carmella deflected the blow with one hand and with the other spun him around and off his feet.

He got to his feet with an offended dignity and said, 'You've been warned.'

When he was gone, Carmella led Maddalena into the garden. Away from the font, she calmed down and began to speak. 'There's no justice. Our podesta has fled. The Furies have come for the rent and my purse is empty. I've seen them knocking on our gates and they won't let me sleep and if we cannot give them justice, we must show them hospitality '

'How long since your last confession?'

Somehow Carmella's question cut through her mania. 'I've never made one,' Maddalena answered. 'Not truthfully, anyway.'

Carmella took her hand. 'Then do so now. It'll ease your mind, I swear.'

Maddalena pulled her hand away, rigid and proud, and Carmella braced herself for a tirade. Instead, she collapsed and buried her face in Carmella's habit. 'Sister, I killed my papa – what penance answers that?'

Carmella glanced towards the font inside the baptistery. 'You've already been punished for that.'

'I want to be whole again,' she wept. 'I want to be . . . like you.'

Carmella grabbed her by the shoulders. 'You shall be!'

Geta and Leto entered the tavern together. The old buttero was surrounded by stacks of empty bottles and strumming a mandolin.

'You've been busy.'

'I have not been inactive, signori. Will you assist me with the last jug that Tagliacozzo has to offer?'

'Certainly. You didn't lie about the Big Pebble, Sergio, or the Highlanders.'

'They know how to make a fella feel welcome, don't they?'

'We return poorer in men and equipment,' said Geta, mournfully concluding, 'I lost a toe.'

'You'll recover,' Sergio said, waving his four-fingered hand. 'I was always afeared of losing a finger and then it happened. Weren't all that bad after all – nothing's bad as all that.'

'The mind conjures monsters,' Leto remarked, sceptically studying the buttero.

'Well put, young fella. This your boy, Geta?' Sergio pinched his cheek before Geta could stop him.

Leto kicked his chair back and drew his dagger. 'Back off, you drunken oaf.'

Geta faked a coughing fit to stifle his amusement. 'Sergio, this is General Spinther.'

'This is the mighty warrior? I ain't going to lie, I expected taller. I heard they started young in Concord, but I never rightly believed it. Hell of a thing, to see a calf leading bulls.'

'Don't be so touchy, Spinther,' said Geta patting the empty chair. When Leto sat down, Geta refilled Sergio's glass. 'The general has a proposition.'

'That so?'

'As the mountains are closed to us, we need a guide, Signore.

The Minturnae has a fearsome reputation but you butteri pass over it as easy as the birds of the air.'

'That's a flat-out exaggeration but I *can* find my way across, just about. Don't rightly know whether to be flattered at the offer or offended by the implication. What makes you think I'd betray my folk?'

Leto stared at him coldly. 'We've been making our way south these last months. Some towns we have to burn, most are handed to us. There's always someone willing to strike a deal. I was given to understand that you were left to burn in this town's dungeon – that or be executed – which would surely have been your fate had anyone but Geta here found you. Your folk, as you call them, consider you an enemy.'

'I ain't from round here, for your information.'

'No, you're a Salernitan. And butteri don't let their brothers get locked up. I see you're missing more than one digit.'

Sergio self-consciously pulled his other hand into his poncho. 'Ain't you sharp. What of it?'

'The transgression that led your folk to permanently ostracise you was not your first, which makes you a recidivist. And it gives you two choices: you can try to drown your criminal nature in this hovel' – he leaned forward – 'or you can accept what you are and strike a blow to make your countrymen rue the day they shunned you.'

The buttero had begun by staring defiantly at Leto. He ended with his head bowed. When Leto had finished speaking he turned to Geta. 'He don't talk like no calf.'

Geta tilted his head. 'Maybe not – but he does talk sense. What do you say? We'll pay.'

'*Corpo di Bacco!* Why'd you leave that till last?' He grabbed his hat. 'I'll show you the way, but let me warn you this before you all start grumbling that I sold you something you didn't want: the Big Pebble offers frostbite and pneumonia; the marsh offers footrot, flux and fever. She's a treacherous bitch, even for those who know her intimately. My former partners won't make it easy on us neither—'

'Men we can afford to lose,' said Leto. 'It's the attacks on the wagon-trains that are causing the longest delays. Even when the engines survive, the wagons are often beyond repair. I'm damned if I know how they know which to attack – it's not like we announce which are carrying our engines and which carry supplies . . .'

Sergio laughed. '*You* don't need to say a damned thing,' he said. 'The tracks announce it loud and clear. And even if they didn't, it don't take much smarts to know folks'll take the best roads when they're hauling something worth something. Once you cross the Liri, it's all marsh till you get to the Garigliano. They'll expect you to avoid the lowlands with your heaviest loads but I know some lowland ways what're dry. That won't fool 'em fer long, but if we keep up a pace it won't take long. So what now, young fella? You want another finger to make sure I'm bonifide, or do we just shake on it?'

'Let's drink,' said Geta, 'to revenge.'

'To justice,' Leto corrected.

'Long as I get to settle the score,' said Sergio, 'I don't give a cuss what it's called. *Salute!*'

The three men drained their glasses, and Geta and Sergio threw them over their shoulders. Much to their amusement, Leto keeled over, coughing and spluttering.

'He don't talk like a calf but he sure drinks like one,' Sergio observed.

Maddalena cast off her clothes onto the cold stone. Despite the night's chill, she smiled rapturously and repeated, 'Sisters!'

Carmella lit a circle of candles around the font and in front of the pedestal of the Madonna of Rasenna. Without turning, she began, 'Madonna, I present a poor candidate in a state of darkness.' She waited till Maddalena had stood up next to her, then took her hand. 'The first rule is obedience.'

Maddalena didn't even flinch when Carmella took the Herod's Sword from around her neck and pricked her small finger. She placed the bloodied icon around Maddalena's neck, then stepped up to the font. Looking into its dark water, she whispered, 'Come into the light, Sister.'

'Sisters,' Maddalena echoed softly as she approached the font.

Carmella took her hand and squeezed out a red drop. 'Let your blood be mingled with those innocents.'

'Sisters!' she wept as Carmella slowly pushed her head into the water.

'Become innocent once more.'

Carmella numbly repeated the questions she had once herself been asked: 'Do you solemnly swear to obey the Madonna, without secret evasion of mind; binding yourself under no less a penalty than that of having your body severed in twain, your bowels taken thence, burned to ashes, and the ashes thereof scattered to the four winds . . .'

As the seconds passed, the trail of bubbles coming steadily to the water's surface slowed. Carmella tightened her grip on the back of Maddalena's neck. It would be *so* easy . . .

'—of so vile and perjured a wretch as you should be, should you ever violate this solemn obligation?'

She yanked her up and Maddalena spluttered and gasped for air and sobbed, 'I swear! I swear! *I swear!*'

While Maddalena spun rapturously around the moonlit garden, Carmella kneeled before the Madonna of Rasenna and gave thanks herself. She had held her enemy's life in her hands and spared her. If *that* wasn't Grace, Grace was a myth.

CHAPTER 52

The Peoples of the Black Hand: A Bestiary

A Salernitan's first decade is considered spring; it is spent in training body and mind. When he attains manhood he is 'exiled' from the city, to spend his summer and autumn years in the contato as a buttero. The butteri herd water buffalo over the river-scarred Campania plains and learn to accommodate themselves to the rigours of the Minturnae marshes or perish. Though the life is hard, the butteri learn to treat nature gently. They hate only the flies that plague their flocks in summer; their buffalo do not know the yoke. When two-score years have passed, the buttero's banishment is lifted, for he is deemed to have attained wisdom. He returns to the city, less vigorous but wiser, to live out the winter of his life training the next generation. These elders are called Doctors.

In the last century, Salerno's Doctors began to explore Natural philosophy just as their Concordian contemporaries were doing. Though hypothetical questions are ordinarily worthless[12] the conscientious scholar inevitably asks why it is that Concord dominates Etruria, not Salerno? Many explanations have been proposed[13] but the reason Salerno did not conquer the South as

---

12 There are two errors which the historian must avoid as mariners avoid Scylla and Charybdis. The first is to ascribe contemporary values to our ancestors; the second more grievous error is to speculate on the sundry ways events might have been different. To consider untaken pathways can be a diverting game, but ultimately it is an idle one. History, like a river, chooses the path of least resistance: what is so is so because it must be so.

13 Some have suggested that Bernoulli dissected in order to build better machines, while the Doctors studied man's humours to become better healers. Some have argued that they failed because they failed to abandon the Curia's stifling dogmas. Some have contrasted their indolence with our vigour.

Concord conquered the North is simple. The Black Hand has suffered under a succession of yokes; having shirked them off themselves, they do not seek to subdue others. No doubt this is very worthy, but it is also a failure of ambition that has left Salerno no part in Etruria's glorious future.

CHAPTER 53

The Concordians were a river of green and black banners winding their way along the narrow *tratturi*. Attacks occurred, but Sergio's juggling managed to keep the engine-carriage safe. Leto was not pleased that the old paths Sergio chose often meant dividing the legion into smaller cohorts, but he could not complain, for they were finally making progress.

The general was so intent on moving his pawns over the maps that he could not see what Geta saw very plainly: every day they were regressing. The south was more than another country; it was another age. The green of the Concordian banners was a cold teal, but the green of the Minturnae was the remorseless colour of moss burying a grave. Nature grew strange and engorged down here. The men's chief terror was the *grosso*, a massive leech that left limbs withered to dry bone. It could not be burned off and the only treatment – digging it out, together with the surrounding flesh – was usually fatal to the patient. Every mile they waded deeper into this primitive land they backslid further into that long night when Man did not hold the whip and when the darkness belonged to the wild things . . .

The horsemen of the south rode out to harass, delay and complicate the Concordians' progress. The butteri were less an army than a collection of autonomous bands who kept their raiding parties small by necessity and preference. They were capable of hitting hard and swift, and then vanishing into the marshlands where none but the foolhardy could – or would – follow. They rode to battle well warmed by their moonshine grappa while the

Concordians slurped down slimy grass soup and weevilly oat-cakes.

Hungry and maddened by an enemy that did not fight fair, according to their rules, the legionaries developed a particular loathing for Spinther's pontonniers, who needed all available wood for trestles, beams and planks. They had declared camp fires a luxury that all must forgo and immediately confiscated the rare tree the butteri had left standing and the few logs the legionaries managed to drag intact from burning cabins.

They didn't try hard to hide their glee when the butteri methodically targeted each battalion's pontonniers, leaving the rest alone – only later did they realise that without pontonniers, the legion was like a great Man o' War without oars: it was moribund and vulnerable.

Sergio called the marsh *Campania Felix* as a grim joke. One liquid continuity, moisture permeated every inch: it swam in front of their eyes as they slouched through frozen bindweed and brackish puddles. The foul-smelling quagmire clung to their boots until the leather was sodden, then lapped at their exposed feet till they too reeked of decay. At night, they pulled off their soaking clothes and burned off and ate the silver worms that have been feeding on them all day. Any man venturing forth in the darkness to defecate took his life in his hands; all too often he failed to return.

With every mile, memories of Concord's dread walls, pristine aqueducts and night-defying globes became more threadbare; and the feeling deepened that this chaos was the natural state of things and that fighting it was as great a folly as trying to fight a river – and when their hardy chauvinism reminded them that they *had* mastered the rivers once, a louder whisper insisted that Bernoulli was long-dead.

Palisades, embankments, sharpened poles and a full watch kept throughout the night: the camp was as thorough as any Geta had seen on the Europa front. He sat outside the shelter of its wooden walls, whittling a piece of wood and staring up at the mountain as though daring the tormentors who'd made their march so hellish to come and attack him and be done with all subterfuge.

Sergio called the highland *Ursonia*, the Kingdom of Bears, but if so it was a kingdom contested by wolves and foxes and wild cats and boars, and their wars were overshadowed by the quarrels of eagles and peregrines against the sparrows and pipits. Their shrieks and barks and grunts and howls filled the darkness between vespers and matins. And amidst this incessant bestial chorus was an interloper: the owl-whoop of bolos, somewhere not too distant, and answered by another set, some miles away.

He was listening so keenly that he jumped when someone nearby whispered his name. He saw who it was, sheathed his sword and continued whittling. 'Isn't it past your bedtime, Spinther?'

The slot shut and the gate was hauled open. 'The Night Watch told me you were keeping solitary vigil.'

'So you came to keep me company? Shall we tell each other stories? No? I must say I don't know how you can sleep so easily, Spinther, with all our forces packed together like buffalo. We've surrendered the initiative.'

'Every day we're pushing forward.'

'But into what? Every day we lose more men, we have less dry food and less clean water, and all the while we're dragging those useless baubles along. A sword's dead weight when there's no one to use it on.'

'Only children and fools live for the moment. The engines may be heavy but I promise you won't think them useless when we reach Salerno. If we're suffering, they're suffering too.'

'*They*'ve been raised here! *They* call this hell home.'

Leto had heard enough. 'For God's sake, don't let me hear you talking like this to the other officers.'

'Hush!' Geta hissed.

'What is it?' he whispered. 'Is someone out there?' He hated to admit it but the swordsman's instincts were keen.

'*Listen.*'

Leto could hear only the usual barbarous wail. 'What?'

'They're sending messages to each other, you complacent ass. They're using bolos the way the Rasenneisi use flags, the way we use annunciators.'

'You're giving them too much—' Leto's condescending smile vanished as he heard a rider approaching. 'Who goes there?'

'Me,' drawled a familiar voice.

'I didn't give you permission to leave camp,' Leto snapped, fear turning swiftly to irritation.

'Don't recall asking,' said Sergio, leaping down from his horse. Another person was slung over the saddle.

'Where were you?' Geta asked.

'Hunting. I didn't catch nothing 'cept this fellow.' He pulled him roughly to the ground roughly. 'Whoever he is, he ain't no *cavalcante*. He managed to drown his horse and was fixing to drown himself when I happened along. All the griping and hollering he was doing, I figured he must be one of yours.'

Leto walked over to the prisoner. 'He's not.'

'That so? Well, have him all the same. I'm plumb tired of him. Hoy! Open the gate there!'

Geta saluted Sergio as he went into the camp and was looking after him when Leto asked, 'You know who this is, Geta?'

'Should I?'

'I should say so. It's another of your brothers-in-law. It has been too long, Signor Bombelli.'

'That it has, General. Would that it was under other circumstances.' After shaking Leto's hand, Guido looked Geta over coldly.

'So, you are the one who made a wife of Maddalena? A bad investment, Signore. She is quite mad.'

Before Geta could respond, Leto said, 'Apologies are in order
for Salvatore: had we broken though earlier, I could have saved
him. Out of sheer pique, the Veians executed him before they
capitulated.'

Geta, watching, saw that Guido knew the story was a lie and,
more importantly, did not care.

'I'm sure you did everything practicable,' Guido said amicably.
'What's done is done. You know our network can be useful to you.
The League is a going concern as long as the free cities think it
has a hope. Cut off its silver and you cut its hamstrings.'

'Can you do that?'

'My other brothers are scattered across Europa. I am the senior
Bombelli now in the Etrurian market. They must trust my judgement.'

'And Costanzo? Does he trust your judgement?'

He pursed his lips. 'My little brother cannot see that continuing resistance is throwing good money after bad. Passion is an
excellent quality in a poet, but a banker must see things object-
ively. The League fought the best fight they could, hurt you by
delaying your march, but at last you are here. Reality is not subject to argument. Two is greater than one. You are the greater
force. You must win out.'

'And so you are here,' said Leto, considering.

'It goes without saying – but I'll say it anyway – that I will look
favourably on whoever represents my offer to the First Apprentice
in a fair light.'

'What do you think, Geta?'

'I think he mistakes us for one of his couriers. Give the word
and I'll put up a scaffold so the bears can watch him dangle and
tell the butteri about it. That'll concentrate minds in Salerno
wonderfully.'

Leto had already considered that, but Omodeo had said weeks ago that the Concordian treasury was perilously low. It must now be empty. To be forced to retreat when they were so close to victory, and by insolvency of all things? That would be ignominious indeed. Guido Bombelli represented salvation. Leto doubted that Guido's brothers would fall in line as easily as he intimated, but his defection would set the Bombelli firm at war with itself.

Leto's long silence unnerved Guido. 'I implore you, General Spinther, don't listen to this animal.'

'*Tranquillo*, Signor. No need to beg – not while we need each other anyway.'

Next day, Leto sent to Concord an optimistic report of progress, and along with it, Guido Bombelli: a prize to keep Torbidda happy, and hopefully a spur to send more annunciators.

That morning, Sergio as usual outlined separate routes for men and machines. Leto took the infantry by a lowland route and left Geta the thankless task of leading the engine-train. Geta declared that if he saw another leech that day he would defect and Sergio grudgingly admitted they *could* avoid some wetlands if they took a tapering path that circumnavigated a stretch of coastal cliff – but he could not advise such a precarious route.

'We'll risk it,' said Geta.

Spinther's precious carriage was an inconspicuous unit in the vanguard. Geta would have very much enjoyed pushing it off the side, but he could not think of a way to make it look like a plausible accident – and anyway, there was no time. The narrow path hugged an undulating cliff and required careful negotiation. They were to rendezvous with the main army during the next day and the thought of spending more than one night on this desolate and vulnerable spot held little appeal.

The height made the horses skittish. The road was poor, and the looming ravine promised death for any false step. The stops were so frequent and exhausting that he decided that Sergio had the right idea: the buttero was as usual sleeping contentedly in the back of the wagon in front of him. Geta dismounted and led Arête along. A little ahead the path turned into a steep slope. As he could not see beyond it he could entertain the pleasant thought that it would be downhill and easy going hereafter. Feeling suddenly optimistic, he looked towards the sea. Perhaps the Moor had already finished with the Oltremarines and was even now blockading Salerno – how pleasant it would be, when they finally escaped this mire, to arrive and find the city already broken and begging to surrender.

An odd rumble startled Geta out of his reverie.

Quakes were common enough in the south, but this wasn't that. He spun around in time to see a boulder tumbling down and into the rear of the train. A carriage shattered and as splinters of wood and flesh fell into the ravine, the horses bolted, pulling their wagons along at breakneck pace. A terrible moment passed as Geta watched this stampede approaching. He took a step back, but Arête was frozen – this was almost as shocking as the stampede, for Arête did not quail easily.

'Move, you brute!' he cried and tugged the bridle, but the war-horse just as viciously wrested it away. Geta looked down: the ground wasn't just shaking, it was giving away. Arête scrambled backwards as Geta leaped forward for Sergio's wagon. He caught the edge of the feed trough just as a chasm opened behind him.

Sergio woke up, cursing. 'Can't a fella get some sleep—?'

Geta hung on tightly as the cart was dragged along, craning his neck to try to see what was happening with the stampede. Arête's fearsome whinnying had alerted the panicked beasts, but they dragged the lead carriage to the edge of the chasm and then stopped so abruptly that the driver went flying headlong into the gulf, closely followed by the cargo of iron pipes. Geta twisted his body to avoid being impaled. Sergio was not so lucky.

Men shouted. Horses bawled. Wood cracked. Pipes clanged and tolled – and amidst all this cacophony was one errant sound he could not mistake: the whoop of an owl.

Geta let go of the cart and scrambled to his feet, his sword drawn. Up ahead, a butteri posse was descending the slope. They rode by the first and second carriage and stopped at the third – the one in front of Sergio's cart. Geta darted behind the cart again, breathing fast.

'Geta,' said Sergio, 'get on out of here.' He was trying to drag the pipe out of his thigh. The one through his chest was immobile.

'That's Spinther's carriage—'

'You want to die for it?'

'Got to die for something,' he muttered. The wail of horses made him stick his head out and he saw the first wagon being pushed over the edge. The second swiftly followed. Now its path was cleared, the general's carriage started forward again. Butteri were hanging from its canvas flanks.

With no better idea, Geta stood up and shouted, 'That's it, flee, you heartless cowards—' He stopped short. 'Doctor Ferruccio – we meet again!'

The old buttero turned and in one graceful movement whirled and released his bolos. Geta dived behind the cart again and a burst of fire pushed him over the chasm. He managed to catch hold of a pipe caught between the ledges, but it began bending under his weight. There was no way it was going to hold long enough for him to climb to the other side.

'Geta!'

He turned to trace the voice and saw Sergio's hand. When he hesitated, the buttero grated, 'Hurry, you ass. They got what they came for.'

Sergio lay there panting in the ferocious heat of his burning wagon. 'Make yourself useful and fetch that jug there afore the flames get it.'

'Medicine, I suppose?' Geta hunkered down beside him and uncorked the jug.

'Manner of speaking,' said Sergio. While he drank savagely, Geta lifted his poncho. It was sticky with blood. He whistled and replaced it gently.

Sergio took a gasping breath. 'Can't help noticing you ain't telling how bad it don't look.'

Tears were stinging Geta's eyes. 'Take another drink.'

'Ain't thirsty no more.'

'*Dio*, it's a miracle,' Geta said, then, 'where were you last night?'

'Told you where. Off hunting.'

'And you didn't catch a single cotton-tail?'

'Shoulda known then that my luck'd turned.'

'Funny they knew Spinther's carriage.'

The buttero's eyes were closed. 'Got something to say, say it. Case you missed it, I'm fixing to quit this here mortal coil.'

'Hell, you don't need to confirm it. Just tell me why.'

No answer came for a long time. Geta was about to check if he was gone when Sergio's eyes opened wide. He felt pinned by the strength of the buttero's stare. 'I feel sorry for you, Geta. You got salt, but you don't know what to do with it. You got to live for something. Your folk is your folk – no matter if they hate you and you hate them, they're all you got.'

Geta listened to Sergio's breathing getting more ragged until it finally stopped. He took the jug from the corpse's grip and poured the scalding liquid down his own throat.

'*Salute*, partner.'

CHAPTER 54

Dawn found Pedro shivering uncontrollably and his nurse much wearied; Trotula forced herself out into the wind to collect fresh herbs. As she carried her baskets through the wings of the Asclepeion, she found the tension in the air was making the novices' singing strained. Salerno's citizens were a hardy lot and Trotula had never known them so nervous. She did not tarry to enquire into it; right now her prime responsibility was her patient.

She found Ferruccio waiting in the apothecary with a leather satchel over his shoulder. His eyes were heavy with weariness. 'How is he?'

'Worse,' said Trotula briefly. 'One can fight only one monster at a time.'

'You don't look so wonderful yourself.'

A strained smile. 'It's my own fault. I prayed for patience, but the Madonna sent me patients.'

'Get some rest. I need to show him something.'

Her anger was sudden. 'Do your ears need sluicing again, Doctor? He needs to concentrate on fighting or he's dead.'

'We're all dead, unless he can help,' said Ferruccio and pushed by her. He knelt beside Pedro. '*Madonna*, what a healthy shade of green you are. The salubrious south agrees with you, lad.'

'Hey, Doc! You been lighting candles for me?'

'A bushel's-worth. Catch.'

Pedro caught the slender leather satchel and noted the Concordian squared circle impressed upon it. 'What's this?' he asked, fiddling with the strap.

'Rather hoping you'd tell me. I'll leave you before your nurse decides to test her poisons on me.'

After chasing Ferruccio out, Trotula retired to her bench. Once Pedro thought she was otherwise occupied, he spread out the sheaves of schematics. Trotula of course only affected not to notice. She knew that work for young men of Pedro's stamp was medicine. Even as feverish as he was, he saw immediately the great potential of the design – and just as quickly, that there was some deep flaw in it.

The captured documents were the work of two hands. The first hand was clearly the one who had conceived the idea of the 'bouncing bridge'. Whoever this was, he had described it theoretically in an elegant but infuriatingly terse abstract. Pedro followed the steps: a cannon mounted on a river bank fired a projectile to the far bank. The projectile was fired at an acute angle, so it skipped along the river's surface. The ingenious part – and the most brazenly impractical – was that the arcs of its bounce would trace the arches of a bridge, and wherever the projectile briefly connected with the water it would emit a pulse downwards to the riverbed, and somehow, this pulse would generate pillars of ice which would form the weight-bearing columns of the bridge. Pedro knew enough Wave Theory now to recognise that the equations describing the induced phase-shifts were superficial, incomplete. The idea's originator had either thought them sufficient – or had lost interest.

The rest of the documents were the work of a second hand – General Spinther's. Half-done diagrams, repetitive iterations of the same unsatisfactory equations, scribbled notes and sketches – these were the work of a lesser mind floundering in the depths and reminded him painfully of his attempts to understand Giovanni's journal. The first hand was showing off a clever idea; the second was trying to realise it and repeatedly coming up against the limits of his wits and Nature's bounds.

Trotula returned to his side and handed him a goblet of the steaming pink brew she'd given him before.'Enough,' she said sternly. 'You must rest.'

He drank quickly, showing more appetite than he had in days. 'Do you know what this is?' he asked between sips.

'I'm sure it's very important. So's staying alive.'

'Sorry, I can't . . . sleep . . .' He dropped the empty goblet, which clattered to the floor. '*Strega!* What've you— Did you—? Give me what did . . .'

'I gave you what you need,' she said unrepentantly. 'The war will be waiting when you get back.'

He did not sink into the darkness; he fell.

He struck the water. It was hard as granite. He wasn't dreaming – there was no pain in dreams. This was another place, as real as the world he had left. The past. He could smell the earthy iron tang of the sottosuolo and hear the dissonant roar of the shadow Irenicon. Trotula was right: he had never really left Rasenna.

He tried to pull himself up, but the water was viscous and held his hands and legs fast. It took a real effort to pull his head free but now he saw the buio all around. They filed by him as if on pilgrimage and amongst these wraiths he saw the Vaccarelli and the Borselinno brothers, and Frog and Sister Lucia, Doc Bardini and the Reverend Mother, Fabbro Bombelli and his wife, the two giants Jacques and Yuri; he saw Valerius Luparelli and Marcus Marius Messallinus and Isabella Vaccarelli and her father Guercho, and he saw a sullen Uggeri, holding Hog Galati's hand. Trailing behind all of them was the frail, hunched form of Vettori Vanzetti.

'Papa, wait for me!'

His father turned slowly and said something, but he could not hear over the water's roar. The current carried him into the darkness. Pedro tried to wade after him, but only succeeded in getting stuck deeper. The river and all the souls that were part of it were fleeing the deathly halitus

emitting from Concord and he would be left alone, in the sterile place
between death and life. He was sinking. The ice-cold water reached his
neck, and now his chin.

'Pedro, look up.'

He knew the voice – his teacher, his friend; the only man who had ever
believed he was worth something, even though he was too weak to hold
a flag. But he could not turn his head to see him.

'Look up!'

'Giovanni, I can't see you—!'

The water's roar melted imperceptibly into a melody ascending
on a single voice. It attained a summit and hung there, pure as
the North Star. Then a cascade of other voices joined it in different registers, one after another, deepening and broadening
the harmony.

A rough hand touched his cheek gently. 'Pedro. It's passed.'

He breathed deeply – and yes, he could feel it; he could taste
the fresh air.

'Matron. I'm very sorry I called you a—'

'I've been called worse.'

Pedro tried to get up but Trotula held him down firmly. 'You
need sleep to recover your strength. I'll go and tell the girls to
keep it down.'

'No – no, don't. It's very pleasant.'

It was more than pleasant. *It was the answer*. The notion had ger-
minated while he had been sleeping, and it had broken through
when he'd opened his eyes. He knew what was missing from the
Bouncing Bridge: *harmony*.

The Concordians regrouped, bridged the chasm and arrived very
late at the rendezvous point. Leto had clearly had an eventful few
days too – his head was freshly bandaged and his temper short.

After Geta reported their losses, Leto shook his head. 'Our pet buttero got it too? Ah well, perhaps that's for the best. We would have had to dispose of him shortly anyway.'

Leto's callousness didn't surprise Geta, but he hadn't expected him to take the loss of his wagon so lightly.

'What use are my papers to a pack of illiterates? If they're wasting their time on vain hopes, I'm glad. We're through the worst now.'

'Are we, though?' Geta asked earnestly. 'Even if we beat them here, what do we win but stewardship of a people who hate us?'

'*Madonna!* I've had enough surprises today without you trying to convince me of your patriotism. You're worrying about your pelt? Don't. Victory's imminent. Salerno is but days away – one more push and the war's won.'

CHAPTER 55

Trotula found Pedro next morning bent over a sheet, scribbling and humming.

'I've been meaning to ask you, Matron' – he pointed his stylus to the vault – 'what's that?'

'An old symbol. Generals carry a baton to war, do they not? Well, that is the baton of the god of medicine.'

Before she could say more, a booming voice bellowed, 'Madonna! I was ready to take you out in a box, Pedro!'

'Just the man I wanted to see. Here's a list of materials . . .'

Doctor Ferruccio looked it over sceptically. 'This fellow still feverish, Matron? You don't ask much, lad, do you? How, dare I ask, did you get it working when the best minds of Concord failed?'

'It remains to be seen if it will actually work, but I think I'm on the right track. The Concordians' problem is they're too used to thinking in straight lines. They were trying to apply the same principle behind their measuring instruments.'

'The Whistlers?'

'Yes, a signal bounced off the river bed. We used something similar to render the Irenicon safe while we were building the bridge. The buio find dense water unpleasant, and the Concordians aimed to take that a step further – not just to make the water denser, but to induce a phase-shift.'

Doctor Ferruccio was looking at the dense notations on the sheet.

'When a liquid turns to steam or ice, that's a phase-shift.'

'I know that, you pup.'

'Sorry. From what I gather, Spinther and whoever came up with the idea got stuck here. They couldn't make a signal strong enough to form a column that would last more than a few seconds.'

'And for the bridge to work, they need it to be weight-bearing. You can make it work?'

'Nothing's certain, Doctor – but I do know something about sound. Three years ago we held the Wave back by disrupting the Molè's signal. A sound's power can be measured in decibels, but its *quality* is more elusive. One of the first things my maestro taught me about architecture is that scale is trivial compared to proportion. In acoustical terms, proportion is *harmony*.'

Ferruccio smiled at last. 'Music I understand.'

Pedro turned the paper over and sketched three concentric circles with a sequence of notes on each level. 'This is a geometrical representation of a chromatic scale, their corresponding key signatures and their flats and sharps.'

'My word, a drawing of music,' Ferruccio said brightly. 'Fresco painters have a similar device to discover colours that sit well together.'

'Yes, the colour-wheel is analogous,' said Pedro. 'Look here,' he tapped the top of outer circle, 'at the apex, the key of C Major –'

'—with no sharps or flats—'

'Right. Now proceeding clockwise, the key of G has one sharp. Next is D.'

'With two sharps,' said Ferruccio, following closely.

'Exactly and the next key, A, has three sharps; the next after that, four. And if you go counter-clockwise, you get the corresponding flats. Starting at any pitch, you can create a twelve-tone scale with just pure perfect fifths and octaves.'

'Very clever – but what's the point of it? Does it make you a better singer?'

'It shows the distance between the chords at which they are

harmonious. That distance is governed by proportion. This is only a simple model. You can make a far more sophisticated model of pitch relations with other forms – a helix, for example.'

'This is sufficiently complex already, thank you,' he said drily.

'The point, Doctor, is that a musician doesn't light upon a pleasing chord progression by accident. Those harmonies existed before the world existed. Whoever conceived this bridge was very brilliant, but he couldn't make it work because he wasn't a mathematician like Bernoulli. Few of us are. I only got it because it was right in front of me.'

'Well, don't keep me in suspense . . .'

'Euclid said that the shortest path between two points is a straight line. And that's true of a plane, but not necessarily a curved surface. Sound doesn't travel in straight lines. It's a wave that describes a sphere as it travels out from the source. You keep the land around Salerno drained, right? If you tried to use suction instead of an Archimedean screw—'

'—I'd be a bloody fool.'

'Exactly. It'd be a waste of energy.' He rolled up the drawing and pointed over Ferruccio's shoulder to the central column. 'Spinther kept trying to make the signal stronger by making it *louder*. It's easier to find an efficient proportion – and there is no better proportion than the one which Bernoulli used to model the Molè. Just like harmony can be represented with a circle of fifths, the Golden Ratio can be represented as a spiral that gets wider by a factor of *phi* every quarter-turn. Now imagine that spiral travelling in space' – he pointed to the central column – 'just like the snake, winding up and down eternally.'

'I have to admit it's beyond me,' said Ferruccio finally, 'but if it does what I think it does—'

'—it does—'

'—then that's good enough for me.'

*

Refugees from the north were allowed to attend the assembly, but not to speak or vote. Salerno's population had tripled in the last month, not counting the exiles – the butteri who had returned to the city in its time of need were a ragged mob, but they listened attentively to the speaker. The congestion of so many pointed-ear caps made the amphitheatre resemble nothing so much as a parliament of wolves.

'In the north, the disease of *campanilismo* – that imbecilic loyalty to a certain bell – is rife. There *are* some things that the north can learn from the south – we certainly have a nobler conception of the city than they. Salerno is nothing more or less than its people. You—' Ferruccio slowly traced his pointed finger across over his listeners and then jabbed it to north. 'Concord is coming, my friends. What shall we do – build walls to crouch behind? Veii's walls still stand, but the Veians are slaves within them: a pitiful fate, but well deserved. Men who refuse to reason are dogs and a city defined by her walls is no true city but a prison. The Ariminumese too, they burned with their city and her hoarded vanities. Shall we emulate them? We have never fought as the Northerners do. Why should we lie supine and wait as they have?'

He paused as a resounding rejection circled the amphitheatre.

'Remember, not *every* northern city has fallen to these locusts. There are those who say that Rasenna too is dead. Believe it not. Her towers have fallen, but Rasenna is *not* her towers. As long as there are Rasenneisi willing to fight, Rasenna lives on.'

He turned to where Pedro and Costanzo were sitting with their countrymen.

'If you see *exiles*, you need to look better: here is *Rasenna* before you. And it is the same for us, my countrymen: where we are, *there* is Salerno.

'I say again: Concord is coming. I ask again, what ought we do? What is *reasonable*? They are many, but slow. We are few, but swift. Should we fight on their terms, at the place and time of their choosing? I for one don't plan to make it so convenient.'

The Asclepeion's garden was filled with sweet-smelling flowers to perfume the air and the paths were planted with herbs like burret and wild thyme and watermint that released their odours when trod upon. The blissful scent was complemented by the view of the old aqueduct; the stone creation seemed almost to fuse into the mountain.

When Pedro looked upon the old stone he fancied he heard the horns of Montaperti. Then the sun painted them orange and his eye was dazzled and his doubting heart armoured anew.

'You like it here, Maestro?' Trotula asked.

'I like the people. They don't fear adversity.'

'We take pains to instil our children with courage.'

'You exile them.'

'Yes, so that they learn the folly of opposing nature. It's not a lesson men learn easily, and without courage it would never take. Men are like those spices that reveal their goodness only when they are crushed. You are too. I think illness agrees with you – you are looking positively handsome.'

Pedro blushed. 'Hardly, Matron.'

'You don't believe me,' Trotula teased, 'but I've had to remind several of my girls of their vows.'

'I'm no bandieratoro—'

'Perhaps carrying a flag was the acme of manhood in Rasenna, but this is another country. You may become someone else here if you choose.'

After the assembly, Ferruccio found a small Tolfetano horse for Pedro and together they rode the length of Silarus, the river dividing the contato south of the Salerno. Like almost every southern river the headwaters rose in Etruria's central mountains and flowed down almost perpendicularly to the coast. The Silarus and the Calore, her main tributary, were known as Mother and Daughter. They converged gradually, travelled parallel for fifteen miles or so before finally intersecting to deluge the rocky shore with silt.

'This large triangular plain is where we'll fight, Maestro.'

'We? Who else is coming?'

'Bari, Brundisium, Taranto – they have some admirable horsemen.'

'How many do you expect?'

'Not enough to win, I fear, but perhaps we'll bloody their nose before we depart.'

After the ordeal of the Minturnae, the last substantial river to cross was the Volturno. Salerno was only fifty miles away and Leto was certain the butteri would make their stand there. Geta suggested giving each man an inflated animal hide and crossing *en masse* at night, but Leto would not hear of such a risky manoeuvre.

Pontonniers were now in short supply and they had no annunciators, so Leto sent Geta with a cavalry troop to cross the ice-cold river and secure the far bank, to protect them while they worked, while he reordered what remained of the Grand Legion. Thirty thousand men had set out from Concord, but disease, desertion and attrition had taken some five thousand men. That was still more than equal to the job, but Concordian warfare was a geometrical affair and asymmetries in the cohorts reduced their efficiency – besides being distasteful. Leto moved men about until each century was restored to strength – or rather, they were all made equally weak. He was determined to leave nothing to chance; that was after all why he had built not one wide, solid pontoon but three. The reorganised army would cross in strength and surprise and overwhelm whatever force the Salernitans had managed to muster to meet them.

After all this preparation, their crossing was as uncontested as the crossing of the Allia had been. Geta had recovered from his melancholy at Sergio's betrayal and the unnecessary delay made him frantically impatient. 'More womanly caution,' he ranted to Leto. 'Our food stores are gone and we're running through our powder reserves just trying to flavour the horse-meat.'

'It's common sense,' said Leto patiently. 'They want to lure us forward without securing our lines of supply and retreat.'

'That's exactly your problem right there: you're thinking of running away when you should be attacking. All the supplies we need are waiting in Salerno's granaries.'

Leto was unmoved, and as if to make the point that he would not be bullied into a rash charge, he left an entire cohort behind to guard the pontoons.

'After all, who knows what's ahead of us,' he said to Horatius.

Ferruccio climbed the aqueduct for his evening passeggiata to find Costanzo waiting for him. He noticed that the younger Bombelli no longer dressed like a rake but instead wore sober clothes more suited to his new position as head of the family.

'That was a nice speech, Doctor.'

'The truth's a bell that always rings sweet. Any more news from Oltremare?'

'Some say the queen's won; others say the Byzantines overthrew her and cut a deal with the Ebionites.'

'You believe that?' the Doctor asked.

'Tales warp as they pass from ship to ship and harbour to harbour. The Byzantines are capable of it, certainly. They've had nothing but disdain from Akka for decades,' Costanzo said bitterly, 'and no one really believes in Crusade any more.'

'Your *paesano* still has faith.'

'Pedro *needs* to believe. If he can't win here, he'll have to admit he abandoned Rasenna for nothing. Even if his bridge works, it changes nothing.'

'It gives us a chance, Costanzo.'

'A chance for what? To outrun the hounds for a while – but the day will come there'll be nowhere left for us in Etruria.'

'Did you come up here to throw yourself off?' Ferruccio took Costanzo's wrist to measure his pulse, 'Dear me, this *is* a serious case of melancholy. I prescribe acorns. I don't want to wake one morning and find you have vanished like' – he checked himself – 'that foolish alchemist.'

Costanzo snapped his hand away. 'Like Guido, you mean. You know very well I'm with you to the end, whatever that is – but that's no reason to stop being realistic of our chances.'

'But I *am*. That's what you're failing to see. The Concordians have all the clocks, but we have all the time. The trick to beating most infections isn't bleeding or purges or colics. It's simply to keep the patient alive. No matter how many of our cities they burn, as long as the League lives, the odds are in our favour. They are far from home and every day that passes they have less food, less money, and most of all, less will.'

CHAPTER 56

The Peoples of the Black Hand: A Bestiary

At its decadent height, Sybaris, the City of Welcomes, cast a shadow over all Etruria. It ruled or received tribute from every city in the Black Hand and its very name was a byword for luxury – but luxury robbed its people of vigour and strength.

When an empire withers, new empires spring to life from its ruins. Far to the north, the Etruscan League crushed the Latins, the Samnites, the Picenes and the Apuli. Knowing that they could not match Etruscan arms, the Sybarites sought to overawe the upstart. They invited the League's ambassadors to Sybaris and plied them with cuisine and courtesans. The condescending exhibition[14] instead showed the Etruscans what wealth they could win and so they declared war and sacked the cities of the Sybaritic League one by one.[15]

Finally, Sybaris alone was left. The Etruscans' cunning philosophers diverted the River Crathis so that it flooded the ancient city and the peninsula which had hitherto as many names as it had peoples became known exclusively as Etrusca.[16]

The unhappy survivors of the deluge meanwhile relocated further south.

---

14 The failure of this ploy may be why the Sybarites' descendants are so notoriously inhospitable.

15 This is a simplified retelling of what was the penultimate chapter of a wider conflict between Magna Grecia and the alliance of Etrusca and Carthage. Etrusca sought to dominate the peninsula; Carthage wanted Sicily. After Sybaris fell, the allies promptly went to war.

16 Whence our modern Etruria. It is a diverting game to imagine how Etruria might differ were it known by one of the sonorous old names: Víteliú or Oenotria or Latium or Hesperia or Ausonia or Saturnia Terra or Italia.

On a map, the *digitus auricularis* of Etruria's Black Hand looks almost dainty. The reality disappoints. On the Isolated extremity, the harsh winds of intervening centuries have hewn the Sybarites into creatures as rugged as the shores upon which they eke out their bestial existence.

CHAPTER 57

For lack of iron to cap his spear, the savage had hardened the wood with fire. Despite this, and though he had but one eye to aim at the fish in the tidal pool, his aim was unerring, and what he caught he skewered on another stick. It was barely half full – a poor day's work, but he must be content. The tide was coming in with the evening. With one stick over his shoulder and using the other as a staff, he climbed until the wind's howl was louder than the sea's roar.

The black idol stood on the promontory overlooking the bay. Its great age was evident in the way the elements had polished the volcanic rock till it resembled black metal. The carving was superficial, but despite this and other crudities – its outsized head and hands – it bore a simple dignity. The tenderness with which the Madonna held the Babe to her breast was moving, even to a savage.

In front of it, he placed two fish, one large, one small – one for mother; one for baby – and muttered a prayer in mongrel Etruscan. It did not matter that he did not understand the magic words; they were not for him. The Madonna was the Sea's mistress; only She could make it behave.

He climbed down, whistling to himself, not watching his step though the rocks were jagged and uneven. He had prayed – as always – for luck, something with which he had never been blessed. Usually the Sybil passed on to sons their fathers' names, but he had never known a father; he'd been slain years ago by a cruel man named Hellebore. So when the savage had come of age, he'd been given a name without honour. Old Befana had dubbed him No Man.

He reached the shore and was about to turn for home when he saw a large skiff in the uncharitable shoaling waters of the bay. Whoever was at the tiller was no fool, for he was neatly navigating the sharp rocks, both seen and unseen. No Man darted behind some rocks, trembling and panting, and remembered the promise he had made when he had plucked out his eye: Sybaris would never again suffer invasion. That he was the only one around was irrelevant. An oath was an oath.

He pulled the day's catch off his other spear, praying that the Madonna would grant him time for a second throw, and leaped up with a great war cry. The first dart was loose before he realised his target was a woman carrying a child. This surprise was swiftly followed by another: moving with the reflexes of a mountain-cat, she simply *stood aside*. His spear splashed harmlessly in a rockpool and before No Man could cast his second spear, another of the invaders snapped his sling. No Man spun his spear to deflect the stone, but as he did so a second, much larger, rock came hurling towards him. It snapped his stick and slammed into his chest.

A moment passed before he realised he was on his back.

One of the invaders picked up the rock again and was about to brain the groaning savage when the woman said, 'Zayid, enough.'

No Man had never heard of a female Top Man before, but clearly she was in charge.

Footsteps approached. His death was certain, but he resolved to take the invader's Top Man with him to the Underworld. He leaped up—

—and found the point of his spear an inch away from his remaining eye.

She spun the stick with a warrior's deftness and said in a Salernitan dialect, 'I return what's yours. We mean you no harm.'

No Man gawped. Was he dreaming, even slain, perhaps? The

woman who stood before him, tanned skin grimy with the soot of battle and dressed in Ebionite fashion and with babe on arm, was his idol made flesh.

'I am Contessa Scaligeri.'

The Contessa, she who had burned Bernoulli's Molè, she whom the Concordians feared above all, was famous throughout Etruria – the Small People, who always suffered most in times of war, included her in their prayers to the Madonna, asking her to deliver them from evil as she had delivered the Rasenneisi – but on this rock her name was unknown.

'Contessa,' he repeated reverently.

'My friend is wounded. Can you help us?'

South of the Messina Strait, a dense web of grappling hooks bound each ship to each other. They slowly turned about, listlessly slapping at each other like lovers in the last dregs of an orgy. The ferocity of the Sicilians had breathed new life into Khoril's men, and at these close quarters their stilettos were lethal as Sicarii steel. In the teeth of the attack, the Moor's men shook off the sluggish enchantment of the Serenissima and fought like the savages they were. The Moor was too experienced to imagine he could play the admiral at this hour of the dance and fought alongside his men.

Holes gaped in the bulwark of the *Mars* and its deck was strewn with bodies half-buried in knee-deep splinters. As a dozen more Sicilians swung aboard, the Moor and his men grudgingly gave ground. Amongst them was a tall scarecrow of a man with a floral-patterned green kerchief wrapped about his long neck.

'I declare! It's the condottiere who thinks he's a Crusader,' the Moor bellowed. 'Podesta Levi, wherever least wanted, you invariably appear. I don't know if I'd call it a talent, but it certainly is remarkable. General Spinther said the League was broke – what did you pay the Sicilians to join you? I'm almost offended that you didn't bribe me.'

'So imagine how offended you'll feel when I kill you.'

'I'm glad you're game, but we both know that's unlikely. Have at it!'

Levi's broadsword clashed against the Moor's scimitar. Levi had always been a better talker than a fighter, but his spell manning the oars had given him an iron strength that took his foe aback. But the dance of the Moor's curved steel was too subtle and Levi had to duck and roll under a cannon to escape what would have been a beheading stroke. The swaying deck forced him into the railings. The Moor leaped on top of the cannon, laughing, and in desperation Levi slashed one of the binding ropes. Almost at once the cannon began to roll like a thing alive. The Moor fell and twisted out of its passage, but Levi hacked the second rope. It was loose, a thing of terrible volition, heading straight for its master. The Moor swung himself behind the mainmast. The great cedar trunk took the full force of the blow and blocks and ropes were shaken loose to fall about him harmlessly and drape the cannon in netting. As the swell tilted the deck up, the cannon began to roll back towards Levi, who dived headfirst down the hatch towards the rowers' benches. The cannon rolled down the deck, catching three unlucky ship's hands in its nets. It crashed through the railing and plunged into the turbulent waves of the strait, dragging the hapless sailors to their doom.

The Moor peeked down the hatch and saw Levi groaning and rubbing his back. He had landed awkwardly in the aisle between the rowers. As the admiral climbed down the ladder, he remarked, 'You've worked enough mischief for one day, Levi – we really must use that energy more productively. I'm sure we can find an empty seat down here.'

'Thank you, no,' said Levi. 'I tried my hand at being a slave. It didn't agree.' He scrambled onto the timber storage grid over the rowers' heads.

The Moor followed, and as the low roof forced them to fight each other crouching low they were soon panting and dripping sweat on the slaves chained below.

'Whoever takes this bastard down is a free man,' cried the Moor, and turned and kicked Levi in the chest.

Levi fell back onto the backs and shoulders and grasping hands of the rowers. His ripped shirt was pulled from his torso, but he fought like a lunatic to regain his feet.

He finally succeeded when a voice behind him called out, 'Look! He's one of us!' The Moor's opponent was branded, like them: his back was a web of whip-scars. And now those clutching fingers constrained the Moor's movements, pulling on his boots and breeches, then entwining around his belt, until he sank into a morass of slaves, cursing them roundly. 'Release me – I am your master,' he croaked even as a forearm tightened around his neck.

'And I am their brother,' said Levi, pointing his sword down at him. 'I didn't *pay* the Sicilians to join me: those ships are sailed by the men who were formerly slaves upon them.'

'Levi the revolutionary,' the Moor sneered. 'When did you become so *principled*?'

Levi heard rapid steps climbing down into the rowing deck, and then Khoril's voice, asking, 'What are you waiting for?'

The Moor could not move so much as a finger. 'Speaking of masters,' he said, 'I once made a bet with yours.'

'John Acuto is dead.'

'Aye, and we are yet alive! The day can be yours without one more drop of blood. The Concordians have used me ill, and I would have done altogether with the vexatious races of Etruria. Spin your dagger. If I win, I'll strike my colours and set sail for Barbary with every ship I have this side of the strait.'

'And if you get the sharp end?'

'I get the sharp end, and my captains will fight to their deaths, or yours.'

'You can't trust him, Levi,' Khoril said furiously. 'Cut his throat now. Better yet let me.'

'No.' Levi placed his dagger in the aisle between the decks. 'When it comes to gambling, Admiral Azizi is as honest as a mendicant.' He spun.

No Man said his mother was a healer. Crooning delightedly, he led them back to Neo-Sybaris, taking a treacherous path along the coast. Making contact with strangers was bad enough; leading them to the village was the ultimate taboo – but he wasn't worried because the others would see what he had seen: Befana's prophecies made flesh. He had to admit that the Madonna's companions were certainly odd: strange knights who hid their faces, Ebionites with slings and daggers, some of them dark as Moors. But that too was part of the prophecy – She came for all men, the shadowed and sunlit, the named and the nameless.

Zayid and Fulk carried Bakhbukh on a stretcher. Sofia thought he was concussed, but what else was wrong, she couldn't be sure. He'd been injured when they'd boarded the *Bernoulli* and found complete chaos, guns blown to pieces, shattered spars everywhere, water gushing from her scuppers, tangled ropes, the mainmast barely standing . . . but it was only when they saw the lantern's commander boarding a skiff and fleeing that they realised the *Bernoulli* was actually sinking. Sofia had had no idea who'd won on the other side of the strait; the smoke obscured everything. With the maelstrom gobbling down the wreckage of the battle, there'd been no sense in waiting to find out, so they'd set off in another skiff, initially in pursuit of the fleeing captain, but they'd soon lost him – and themselves – in the haze of gunsmoke that turned gradually to coastal mist. That's when they'd come to shore, only to be attacked by a one-eyed native.

Now they followed the muddy track to a storm-tossed bay shaped like a twisted horseshoe. There was no harbour as such, just some rotted piles and a few warped planks, but that was all that was needed: the Sybarites took to their crude canoes for a few summer weeks only, and even then they never ventured out of the bay.

No Man expressed surprise when he saw a strange boat tied up at the moorings, but Sofia recognised it as the skiff in which the *Bernoulli's* captain had escaped. Their fears took shape as they walked up the path to Neo-Sybaris. It was lined by rows of flaming beacons and the sour yellow light and the smell of burning pitch drew them on. As they drew closer, they saw what was burning: Concordian heads, freshly harvested.

'You sure about this, Contessa?' said Fulk. This welcome to the land of his forefathers left much to be desired.

'Don't see that we have much choice,' she murmured.

The Sybaris of legend was a place of vaunting fountains, lofty marble temples, of spacious agoras. Neo-Sybaris was a dismal, sparsely populated hamlet. Its grey stone huts formed a circle, and in the centre of this rude piazza was a perpetually burning fire. Beside it, Sofia could see a squinting old man perched upon a broken column. He gripped a corroded trident coated by browning flakes. His protruding navel was circled with red paint so that his belly was one great unblinking eye. Tufts of grey hair, an ancient loincloth and a ratty blanket covered his pink nakedness. His pale arms were wound tightly with strings lined with white seashells. This, patently, was the all-powerful Hellebore.

As the people made a circle round the strangers, No Man's mother came to his side. After a quick exchange she indicated that the stretcher-bearers should put Bakhbukh down.

'I think,' Fulk whispered to Sofia, 'that their wounds are self-inflicted.'

434

'I was just thinking it was some coincidence . . .'

Hellebore heard the commotion of his people, and asked, 'What do you see, my Son?' He was old, and increasingly relied on his son's strength and the Whisperer's wit to rule the Sybarites.

Femus glowered. He was a brute swaddled in muscle – as the Top Man's son he'd always had the pick of the catch from childhood and now towered over the rest of the tribe. 'A parade of foreign mongrels,' he rumbled, 'and led here by the nameless one.'

'What? Saw their heads off!'

'Peace, my lord,' said the tall man at his left ear. 'There's some strangeness here. Let us first see what's what.'

'No Man, you clot!' The Top Man tapped his trident against his column throne. 'Have you forgotten the Law, or do you intentionally flout it by bringing an invader to the Umbikee Urbee of our empire?'

'This is no invader, Far Seeing One. This is She.'

'It is She. It is She,' the villagers repeated in tones of hushed awe.

'We must show her to Befana,' said No Man.

'*Must* is not a word you use to Top Man,' said the Whisperer.

'But Befana will tell us if she is She—'

'Who doubts my vision?' the old man croaked.

Hellebore took the tribe's silence for affirmation, but they were silent for another reason: this exotic maiden held a child whose smile was like spring dawn in the heart of these half-blind barbarians. They looked from one to another, marvelling, waiting for Hellebore's judgement.

Sofia could barely follow the discussion, but it was clear that her life was in the balance. The boy was good-hearted, she could see that, but hardly an advocate for them. She wished Bakhbukh was fit to move. Fulk was getting ready to fight, not a good sign.

435

No Man too was nervous. Hellebore had plucked out his remaining eye when he became Top Man, as custom demanded. He was blessed with absolute blindness so that the snares of the material world could not beguile him. But it meant that he could not see what was so obvious to his subjects. He tugged on the roots of his beard as the Whisperer described the scene. The Whisperer was no friend to No Man, but he was attendant to the Law – surely *he* must recognise the truth? Hellebore's son stood behind them, still glowering at the excited crowd, who were being untypically vocal.

Hellebore threw the blanket from his knees and, with Femus' aid, stood up. He thudded his trident against the pillar and called for silence.

'Children, the Sea has cast up this siren to tempt us. The Great Eye wants to see if you are steadfast or not. Redemption *is* at hand, but today is not the day. We must cleave to our traditions like limpets to rocks.'

The crowd murmured. He might be blind, but Hellebore could see this was unpopular. 'Who are you going to believe,' he bellowed, 'your eyes, or me?'

Femus stared down the crowd on his father's behalf while the Whisperer whispered some more.

No Man's mother was shaking stones over Bakhbukh. He was awake, though his breathing was shallow. Sofia knelt beside. 'I'm glad,' he whispered in Ebionite, 'that I got to touch Etrurian soil, Mistress, but I do not think it agrees with me.'

'Don't be melodramatic. You're coming with me, all the way to Rasenna. I'm going to show you Tower Scaligeri and that's all there is to it. Stay awake,' she said as she gave him a parting kiss.

'Yes, my Nasi.'

Fulk looked at her. 'Say the word.'

'No – I didn't cross the sea to slaughter Etrurians,' she said crossly. 'You're going to stay here and make sure everyone behaves.'

'And you?'

'The Old Man told me that one of his kindred would seek me out. He said her name was Befana.'

No Man turned to her, eagerly nodding. 'Yes, Befana!' he repeated.

Hellebore slapped his belly for attention and said, 'Very well. Hellebore is fair and far-seeing. Let her go to Befana's cave, if she can find it, but let no man help her. If she is She, the Great Eye will guide and protect her. If she is a siren, the rocks will break her.'

'That is just,' the Whisperer bellowed, and the villagers, who had forgotten how to argue, said nothing and looked at the stranger.

'I accept,' Sofia said.

No Man walked over to Sofia. 'Come, I will show you the way. My mother will mind your boy.'

'What's this?' cried Femus indignantly.

'Where are you going?' shouted the Whisperer.

'Top man said no man may help her. I am No Man.'

The people murmured happily at this unexpected turn of events.

'Indeed you are,' said Hellebore, trapped by his own words. 'You are that, and your father's son. Go then and be careful, lest like your father you stumble.'

CHAPTER 58

The Peoples of the Black Hand: A Bestiary

The pirates of Barbary had raided the Black Hand since antiquity, but one dreadful day they decided to stay. The memory of the occupation, which lasted several centuries,[17] remains traumatic for the primitive coastal peoples: the devil is represented in Sybarite village totems as a Moor and their greatest fear is that of polluted blood.[18]

The Sybaritic religion is a strange hybrid too.[19] Much as the Marianism of Oltremare was infected by its proximity to the Ebionite heresy, so the Marianism of Sybaris bears few similarities to that creed practised in the North.[20] Perversely, the Sybarites worship a Black Madonna.[21] They hold, like the Ebionites, that the Virgin was occluded and await Her return, confident that She and Her luminous child will restore Sybaris' fortune.

Sybaritic self-segregation may suit their neighbours, but it has left the colony deformed by interbreeding. The men mutilate themselves further with a ritual cruel even by Black Hand standards. When a warrior comes of age, he

---

17 Self-invited guests invariably stay too long. The Eighth Century was the Radinate's zenith, a period of expansion in which Byzant was won.

18 Owing to their Grecian heritage all Southerners are dark, but the Sybarites are decidedly so.

19 Even before the occupation, the Etruscan Mysteries cast a taint on Southern Marian practices. Readers are directed to the *Mongrel Madonna: Religious Miscegenation of the Sub-Peninsula,* by this author.

20 Which tradition is faithful to the original faith is a question that once animated Curial scholars – who naturally decided it was theirs. Why fidelity should matter is a mystery to the current author; surely traditions should be judged not by how static they remain but how useful they are?

21 Even today, they carry charred totems of their goddess into battle.

brings a lamb or a goat to the cave of the Sybil. The animal buys an audience with the crone, but to win a new name he must make a more lasting sacrifice: an eye. In return, she reveals his name. If the initiate lives, he returns to the tribe a man.[22]

22 This bizarre rite, apparently, recalls a Sybarite revolt when an exasperated governor had all the men blinded.

439

CHAPTER 59

The peaks afforded views of the wide sea. To the south, the storm over the strait was dispersing, though Sofia could still see nothing of the two fleets. She turned back to the flat stones interspersed with aromatic juniper and cistus scrub, which were giving way to a steep, sparse scape of jagged rocks. She quickly understood that by sending her to seek Befana alone, Hellebore had intended to kill her.

No Man crouched on a rock, staring vacantly, his nose occasionally twitching. 'We're being followed,' he announced.

She turned and looked the way they had come, but she could see nothing but cloud shadow rippling over boulders.

'Come on,' he said, and scurried up a crag, as surefooted as the ibex of the Sands.

Sofia had expected to find the cave at the peak, but instead No Man brought her to the edge of the great pit.

He pointed and said, 'Her grotto is within.'

All she could see at the bottom of the pit was a small green lake. Just as she noticed how sluggishly the gulls were circling the pit, a deftly cast stone struck one's breast and it dropped without a squawk into the water.

No Man told Sofia to stay close as he climbed down. The scree made it hard at first, but the ivy thickened the further down they got. When she reached the bottom, she saw the bones of birds and other small creatures scattered all around the edge of the lake. It was much warmer here, and smelled of sulphur. Scarcely a chink of water showed through the tiny round lotus leaves which covered the lake; it shuddered like the skin of some great sleeping lizard when a noxious bubble rose from its depths or when winds whistled through the porous rock. No Man spotted the slain bird and manoeuvred it with his spear until it was close enough to grab it. He lifted it out and gave it to Sofia, then walked up to the ivy wall, stuck his hand in up to his shoulder and then pulled it back out. Sofia stood blinking in amazement until she saw the hanging ivy subtly swaying with the wind's respiration.

'Go inside. Lay your gift in front of the crater, then step back and close your eyes. If you are lucky she will accept your gift. If you are very lucky, she will speak to you. You may want to listen for days, but do not tarry. The inside air is fatal to men.'

'And you?'

'When you emerge, I will be waiting – or the men who have killed me.'

She pushed the ivy aside, found an arch cut into the stone and crawled inside, grimacing as bird bones crunched under her hands and knees. It wasn't long before it opened into a circular space. The only light inside came from the tunnel, but the green glow illuminated the domed cavern surprisingly well, for its curved walls twinkled more like glass than rock. There was a crater in the centre of the floor, however, and that seemed hungry for light. The wafting blue fumes, a revolting blend of rotting eggs and putrid meat, made her gag. She laid the bird in front of the crater and then scampered back to the side and covered her face as she'd been instructed.

A wheezing cough echoed from the crater as a set of ancient fingers emerged, looking like the tendrils of a vast, bloated spider. As they explored the crater's edge, the rest of an ancient old woman gradually emerged. Her claws found the carcase and she eyed it warily as she took an exploratory bite. She ate it up, feathers and flesh, then burped and wiped the blood from her face.

'*Sallalation de ta leanamh.*'

The words were Etruscan. When Sofia didn't respond, she broke a small bone and picked her teeth with it. Then in Ebionite, 'A fine boy, your son. Congratulations.'

'Thank you,' said Sofia.

The crone tilted her head, rook-like, and switched to a northern Etrurian dialect. 'Stop pretending not to look, Child. I'm the last of my kind. The Winds consumed the star-gazers and I shall give myself to the Waters presently, so time is short. Thirty years ago a girl who spoke this tongue sat where you now sit. She and her brother fled from a drowned world. They came south to start anew. He stopped in Salerno to study with the Doctors. She came here. I told her of great changes afoot.' She pointed to the crater with her bone. 'In the earth's bowels, a war blazes. I helped her to perfect her art so that she would be ready when it erupted.'

'The Reverend Mother died for me.'

'I told her she would have to if she returned to the north. A brave one, she was. Are you that brave?'

'I'll do what I must to save my boy.'

She scampered over to Sofia like a spider. Her grizzled face came close. Her breath was earthy and ripe. 'What would you do? Would you tear your breast like the pelican? The star-gazer told you that your boy was born to die. Even if you save Him from the worm, the debt must be discharged.' She sniffed at her. 'Ah, you don't like that. I have long pondered it and in truth, it little pleases me either. Follow me and I will tell you the Earth's secrets.' She crawled back towards the crater.

'No Man said that air is fatal to men.'

'So it is. But we are not men, are we? Besides, you must die a little if you wish to be wise.' And, like a flower drawing in its petals at night, she sank into the crater.

*

Even the seriousness of his wound could not dim Bakhbukh's curiosity. 'What's happening?'

Warily Fulk watched Hellebore and the Whisperer conferring. There was some controversy upsetting the assembly, but there at Bakhbukh's side he could not tell what. 'Don't concern yourself.'

'Easy for you to say, Grand Master. Minding other people's business has been my occupation.' Bakhbukh attempted to smile but the pain made him grimace.

'Chew this,' said Fulk, offering some khat. No Man's mother snapped it from his hand, sniffed it suspiciously and tasted a sprig. She made a face, but evidently satisfied that it was not poisonous, handed it to Bakhbukh.

'Thank you, Madame.' He chewed meditatively for a while as Fulk watched the argument growing more and more animated. ''Tis right that I depart now, Grand Master. I have overstayed my welcome, and the scenery has changed about me. This is a stage I hardly know. My nasi is dead, and I helped to finish his bloodline.'

'You were not responsible for Arik's fate,' said Fulk, still watching the Sybarite chief.

'Being advisor means everything is your responsibility, and by taking Yūsuf's part, I drove Arik into the embrace of the *franj*. Tell the Contessa, I could not wait. But you must promise me something, Fulk Guiscard.'

He turned and looked at Bakhbukh. 'Tell it.'

'Go and see the Contessa's tower on my behalf, and then take my bones back to the Sands. I will not rest until my dust is mingled with the Sands.'

Then, satisfied with Fulk's word, he drifted in sleep, until coming suddenly back to lucidity, he added, 'And since I cannot leave you without a word of advice: Melisende Ibelin is a good woman, but you are the rightful king of Akka. Your tribe needs its nasi no less than any other. Go home and take your throne.'

There was more than that to his words, Fulk knew. Without the axe to keep the tribes honest, they might easily fall back on their own turbulent ways.

The old Ebionite fell into a deep slumber from which Fulk knew there was no return. He contemplated the chair he had left empty in Akka when a sudden squall of raised voices brought him back to his present predicament.

He looked over to his knights. 'Perhaps our Crusade shall end here too, brothers,' he murmured.

It was hours before Sofia returned to the surface. Just before she crawled out, she stopped and – not looking back as instructed – said, 'Back in the village, my friend is—'

Two ancient coins shot out of the hole and the crone's voice came from far away. 'Gone. Your spoiled knight saw him out and his soul has already merged with the Winds. And you shall find another friend waiting. You shall never lack for friends, until the very end. Then, when most you need one, you shall be friendless . . .'

Sofia peeked out of the ivy warily and found No Man calmly sitting by the pool. The body of Hellebore's son was floating in the reflection of the moon. They didn't speak until they were close again to the village.

'Will you get in trouble?'

'I'll be killed,' he said without regret. 'What did she tell you?'

Sofia glanced back before answering, 'Everything, except what I wanted to hear.'

When the villagers saw No Man return with the Contessa, they fell down and wept at their deliverance.

No Man's mother returned Iscanno to Sofia.

'Fulk,' Sofia cried, 'what have you done?'

'Not a thing,' he said. 'We merely looked on as justice was

444

done. There was uproar when the Sybarites discovered Femus was missing. Knowing Hellebore, they knew exactly what he'd sent his over-muscled son do. The other one – they call him the Whisperer – he tried to stop them, but I think they'd had enough. They'd kept the Law – they'd been faithful for centuries, waiting for this day – and I guess they weren't going to let it pass because one old blind fool wished to hold on to power. The Whisperer got off lightly – they only took his tongue. The Top Man's head is over there, next to the Concordian captain.'

'Where's Bakhbukh?'

'Paradise,' Fulk said simply, and showed her the body. The old man looked restful.

Sofia laid the ancient Etruscan pennies on his eyes and whispered, 'Godspeed, my friend.' That hour when she would be friendless was one hour closer.

The day's miracles were not over. For the first time in centuries, strange ships came to the sharp-toothed mouth of Neo-Sybaris' harbour. The Sybarites gathered at the moorings, spears and rocks in hand, ready to attack if the Contessa commanded it, but tears sprang to her eyes as she recognised the tall scarecrow of a man in the foremost boat.

'These are my friends.' she said.

Even with a paranoid, hesitant commander, the Concordians accomplished the final push in two days and made camp near the slopes of unsleeping Vesuvius before entering the pass between the Lattari and the Picentini Mountains. Much to Geta's annoyance, Leto again slowed the pace, fearing ambush at every step.

Finally, they saw Salerno. Far from the fierce fight they were expecting, the city was not just abandoned; it was burning. To discover all the agony of dragging the siege-engines south had been for naught? That was the final insult.

Some four thousand horsemen formed up beside the River Silarus. The muster of the men of the south was a grand sight, and not just for Pedro. The butteri themselves lived such solitary lives that they had not properly realised their collective strength; it awed them. Even so, Pedro could not forget that the Legion that had besieged Rasenna was a thousand men more, and that Spinther's Grand Legion was the sum of six such hosts. Doubtless the campaign had reduced that number, but it would still be a disproportionate match.

Ferruccio did not like to look at the smoke covering Salerno. He turned and found Pedro watching the yellowish haze approaching from the south. 'How many did the Tarentines promise?' Pedro said, taking out his eyepiece.

'Two thousand – but it looks like they brought considerably more.'

'It's not them.'

It was a strange host indeed, coming down from the Pollino Mountains. Sofia had set out from Neo-Sybaris with a few hundred men. Along the way, the other villages of the Sybari Plain – each of whom thought of themselves the sole descendants of Sybaris – had been drawn to their banner, a crudely drawn eye.

It was unusual enough to see Sybarites venturing out of their caves, but what alarmed the butteri even more was the sight of their companions; such knights had left this land a century ago – and marching beside them in loose-fitting robes were the Ebionite foe they had gone to fight!

Pedro suddenly snapped his eyepiece shut and urged his mount to a gallop.

'Maestro, wait!' cried Ferruccio, but Pedro Vanzetti couldn't stop for another moment. Three years ago he had found hope in the midst of utter despair when he had spied the Scaligeri flag in the front ranks of John Acuto's Hawk's Company.

He had just found it again.

CHAPTER 60

As they headed south of Salerno, General Spinther reviewed the old Bernoullian maps of the unfamiliar territory and pointed out interesting features of the terrain to Horatius, who had become something of an acolyte. The general was missing Scaevola more than he realised.

The Grand Legion found their foe at last, arrayed on the far bank of the Silarus. The rather ragged-looking pikemen jeered at them to cross the antique stone bridge.

As Geta surveyed the situation, Spinther asked, 'What do you make of it, Horatius?'

'They picked a good spot for it, General. The steep-banked rivers surrounding the plain make it a natural fortress, the thick forest provides cover – and probably conceals butteri reserves. The marshy patches will retard the ability of large numbers to manoeuvre. The scouts report that the bridge where the Silarus meets the sea has recently been demolished.' After this grim catalogue, he paused for effect, then added, 'There is another bridge further inland which has been left undefended. I wish to volunteer—'

'Undefended indeed,' said Geta irritably. 'It's a ruse, boy. They want us to waste time looking for a chink in their defence.'

Horatius ignored the interruption and said earnestly, 'If we fight them here, General, I strongly recommend luring them to this side before we engage. They could have easily destroyed this bridge before our approach. It's obvious they wish to make it the focus of the contest. And it's obvious why: only small numbers

447

can cross at once so a few sturdy pikemen could hold us back almost indefinitely.'

'Everything you say is true – but what are we to eat while we are waiting – grass?' Leto was by now as impatient for blood-letting as Geta. 'We're out of time, so damn the difficulty. I'm through playing according to their rules. Bring up the catapults. Might as well get some use of them.'

Horatius saw the general was decided. 'In that case,' he said with studied élan, 'might I lead the cavalry charge?'

'You would volunteer in spite of your reservations? I must say I'm impressed. But no, you shall stay by my side. That baton is an honour that must go to another.'

'Too kind, Spinther,' said Geta wearily. 'Just make sure you soften them up first.'

The bombardiers assumed that this would be their last chance this campaign to practise their art, and they were liberal with the powder. The intensity of the bombardment quickly forced the pikemen back, then the artillery slowly increased their range. Geta's cavalrymen were first across the bridge. They formed up quickly on the far bank, all the while waiting in vain for any counter-attack.

Behind them, a cursing centurion herded eighty infantrymen across. The century formed an intimidating semi-circular wall of steel in front of the mouth of the bridge, and it expanded as more infantry poured across.

After five more centuries had crossed, Geta ordered them to form a cohort. He was disgusted that the butteri had not even attempted to contest the crossing. 'If they won't come and get it, we'll bring the fight to them.'

Leto had altered his plans. After seeing how easily they had crossed over, he decided to push the advantage. He left a cohort protecting the artillery on the first bridge and led a march for the second – if he could get across that one before the Salernitans found the nerve to attack, they could attack at two points.

The pikemen were repugnant one-eyed creatures, and almost as gruesome were the Moorish-looking fellows beside them hurling stones from leather slings with deadly accuracy. They stood together so firmly, and Geta belatedly realised they had *intended* to draw the Concordian forces as far forward as they could. Behind the first rows was the League's carroccio, and amongst the coalition flags he could see the same red banner that the Tartaruchi of Rasenna had flown: the Scaligeri lion.

Dio, how he'd love to capture that one.

Fond hope. The mounted butteri never charged the centre, but instead pressed either flank, one darting forward and flinging his bolos before turning away and immediately being replaced by another. Geta did not like to imagine the results if one wing collapsed under the pressure.

'What do we do, Lord Geta?' cried the centurion.

'For God's sake, give me a moment.' It was hard to fight and even harder to think while keeping one eye over his shoulder, where the situation across the river was looking distinctly troubled.

The cohort that was supposed to be protecting his own rear was pulling back, and to the east he could see Spinther too was giving ground – but what on earth to?

He saw it.

A purple river had poured down the slopes of the Picantini Mountains and flooded the plain, and there in the front rank was the master of the purple river, riding in a quadriga. The two-headed eagle emblems, the massive square banners – they were horribly familiar.

The Byzantine Army – Geta didn't care to think about how it had got there – might not be as large as the Grand Legion, but it was almost certainly fresher. And he knew from painful experience the skill of their cavalry. It was only a matter of time before the bridge behind him was cut off; if he ordered a general retreat, the butteri would turn it into a rout in moments.

Only one thing for it.

Geta dug his heels hard into Arête's flanks and galloped into the thickest fighting, slashing left and right, before turning to face his beleaguered men. He held his baton aloft and flung it into the enemy ranks. 'A thousand soldi for the hero who retrieves it!'

After a stampede of inspired soldiers passed by, he turned about and galloped headlong for the bridge – but before he reached it, he found his way blocked by an ancient buttero with a thick white beard and a long starry cloak.

'No further, Lord Geta.'

'Dear me, Doctor, this is too exciting a place for an elder statesman.'

'I'll make it fair,' said Ferruccio as he dismounted. 'My mazza. Your steel.'

Geta remained in his saddle. 'Very good of you – I'm ordinarily game for daft romantic gestures, but the thing of it is, I *am* in rather a hurry.'

'Oh, it won't take long. You're overestimating again.'

'And you've already had your chance to kill me. YAAH!'

Arête went straight for him. Ferruccio would have done better to strike at the horse instead of its rider, but that a true buttero could never do.

Leto could hardly believe it. The Byzantines were pressing his line back, pushing them away from the Silarus and cutting them off from the men he had already sent across. He was not so much concerned for them but worried that the Byzantines would envelop his forces; it would be inevitable if they continued to grapple.

Horatius was still at his side, injured in the leg but fighting on gamely. 'Look who it is, General,' he said with a curled lip.

Leto turned to see a dreadful figure approach. The legs and belly of Geta's horse were spattered in gore, and Geta himself was breathless. 'You saved my life once, Spinther. Permit me to repay the favour. Our position is untenable. Order a retreat while you can.'

Leto's face fell. He knew it was true, but he hadn't dared admit it to himself. 'But the artillery—'

'Already lost. The only question is whether you give them your life today, or preserve it. I've harried enough disorderly retreats to know how they end.'

The centuries fighting on the far side of the Silarus were almost entirely encircled and – once it got round that Lord Geta, whose survival instincts were the stuff of barracks legend, had abandoned them – utterly hopeless. A few months ago they might have fought to the last man, but the Minturnae had leached that spirit. Instead, they struck their colours and prayed their foes were men who treated prisoners better than they did.

CHAPTER 61

The Concordians passed once more into the funnel of the Lattari and the Picentini Mountains, constantly looking over their shoulders, checking out any number of concealed passes from which butteri could burst to harass their straggling columns and tumble their exhausted horses with bolos before dispatching their riders with mazzas.

After reaching the Vesuvius camp, the Concordians threw down their arms in exhaustion. Geta, forgetting the men he'd abandoned behind the Silarus, fulminated through the long night at the ignominy, 'They left us this one escape route so they could herd us like buffalo – you know this means the Moor failed.'

'That's not certain.' Leto did believe the Moor had failed, but he considered Geta's wallowing unprofessional and refused to indulge it. 'Once we cross the Volturno, we can regroup and fight on more agreeable terms. The rivers are as much an impediment to them as us.' He took a breath. 'Under the circumstances, we did well to conduct an orderly retreat.'

'*Dio*, I pray I never see what you'd consider a rout.'

After a night of sleepless watches, they embarked early and marched on at the same unforgiving pace. The infantry lines became stretched out, and it was the cavalry – looking to their own safety – who reached the Volturno first.

It was not to be the promised deliverance.

All that remained of the cohort the general had left to guard the three pontoons was a field of broken men and spears. Only the middle pontoon was still standing, and that, he knew, was quite intentional. If he attempted to get everyone across none of them would see the morrow; the crush would collapse the pontoon long before the butteri arrived to finish off the rest.

As he considered his options, Geta said quietly, 'Pick someone else.'

Leto marvelled at Geta's instincts, but he pretended to be disappointed. 'I thought you many things, but never a coward.'

'Does that kind of thing often work? I fight when there's a fighting chance, otherwise I run.'

'Horatius,' Leto shouted, 'how's the leg?'

He trotted up to the general eagerly. 'I fear my galliard days might be over, but I'll live.'

'I want you to lead the rearguard and protect the crossing.'

'Yes, Sir!' cried the young officer.

Geta wondered when Horatius would work out that he had just been handed a death sentence. He didn't wait for Leto's order before crossing, and a stampede of cavalry soon emulated him. The pontoon was not designed to bear such weight all at once and the rearguard would not hold out long against the Byzants and butteri. Leto's choice was simple: stand on protocol – or follow Geta and live.

As soon as he rode onto the pontoon a hundred hands of entreaty raised up, begging for succour even as they dragged at him. It was impossible to reason with that blind hydra. He let himself be pulled down from his saddle and carried along on the pressing, pulling river of flesh, enduring the pinches and biting, stabbing with his dagger when necessary, all the while hearing the fearful creaking of the timber slowly growing louder than the screams.

When he was finally vomited out of the crush onto the muddied bank he found Geta looking down on him with a grin. 'Orders, General?'

'Burn it and fall back'

It was just one more sacrifice, after days of little else. The more he could leave behind to delay the enemy, the better it would be. The very worst outcome would be to let the dogs have any means of reaching them. His bedraggled men could not long hold the pass – his abandoned artillery would surely be brought up and used against them. And he was wary of the butteri taking some unknown ford in the highlands and flanking them.

When the legionaries who had safely crossed saw the pontonniers packing the foundation with powder, their despair turned to rage: they had comrades still crossing. Geta had to beat back the rioting legionaries while Leto ordered his cannoneers to fire *into* the bridge to stem the flood. As the survivors backed away, their frantic comrades began shouting that they were being abandoned.

A frantic few risked it, but the charges exploded with a strangely displaced *bang!* and the ripple threw most of them off. Those who remained began crawling forward with pathetic optimism – but all at once the pontoon collapsed, a dead thing, all rigour gone, and fell away into the cold rushing river.

By the time Leto and Geta had restored order, the battle on the other side of the Volturno was over. After Horatius fell, the abandoned Concordians threw down their swords, hoping for better treatment from their foes than from their masters.

While the rest began marching back towards the Minturnae, Leto hung back in the rearguard, looking at the host on the far bank though his spy-glass. He would not give that rabble credit for the victory; it was this cursed land that had beguiled him with its wearing rhythm of river after river after river till he had lost his wits. Surely the ultimate fault lay in a misconceived strategy: they had ventured too far, and fought the enemy in a hellish arena where his small strength was maximised and their myriad advantages completely negated. This defeat was not *his* fault; it was Torbidda's.

As Leto portioned out the blame, he watched with growing curiosity as a gun crew wheeled a pair of queer-looking mortars to the edge of the bank under the direction of a young man wearing a sleeveless leather jacket. When the fellow removed the long hood wrapped around his face Leto recognised the young engineer who had accompanied the Rasenneisi delegation in Ariminum. The engineer knelt between the cannons and fitted a peculiar device to them, then spent a while getting each operator to minutely adjust their angles.

Despite the disastrous day, Leto was amused to see such amateurism. Such puny cannon could not do much damage, and they were aimed too low, besides. They fired simultaneously, and Leto laughed at the tiny report, and laughed harder when he saw a disc come from the mouth of each mortar at too low a trajectory to even clear the river; the idiot had badly underestimated the range.

Leto stopped laughing.

Now he could see each disc was spinning as it skipped over the water, and trailed a thin wire that traced its flight arc and held its shape. Each brief landing emitted an exquisitely harmonious sequence of notes, accompanied by a cracking, splintering sound. At every point the disc touched the river, the water swiftly turned pale as the ice columns formed to support the frozen wire. One, two, three, four . . . the discs skipped on, the arc of each bounce slightly shorter, slightly lower than the last – but the final one landed both discs on the far bank.

Leto, more than anyone else watching, recognised this for the prodigy it was – and nearly as miraculous was its significance: the problem that had defeated Concord's First Apprentice – and *him* – had been solved by some rustic mechanic.

'We are lost,' the general remarked to no one in particular. 'Lost entirely.'

CHAPTER 62

> The Masons knew not the Tower's purpose, only
> that King Nimrod paid gold. And when Nimrod
> heard them bark and hiss and gibber and com-
> port themselves as Beasts, he took it as a sign that
> he was close; for his Tower was a dagger aimed at
> the Almighty; and the injuries it did to God would
> be visited on Men also. He sent more Masons to
> the cloud-wreathed summit, urging them to
> toil faster. Likewise were they afflicted: their
> right hands forgot their cunning; their tongues
> cleaved to the roof of their mouths. Too late did
> they realise the Tower was an abomination in the
> eyes of the Lord.
>
> *Nimrod 15:2*

The windowless carriage was little better than a cage, but
nothing of import escaped the prisoner. Though he had wealth
enough to bribe his captors to free him, he paid instead for gossip
– Guido Bombelli had made his fortune by knowing things, and
by quickly deducing the implications. So when he heard that
the Grand Legion was retreating following the Battle of the Volturno, he realised not only what was obvious – that he'd picked
the wrong side – but also that by the time he arrived in Concord
he would be worse than an embarrassment.

His second deduction was not altogether correct.

*

The Etruscan cloacae under the city of Concord still functioned, but it was not uncommon for the sewers to overrun and flood the lowest quarters of the Depths. This year's *aqua alto* had risen to an unprecedented level, causing whole boroughs to empty. The refugees fled to more elevated neighbourhoods, which did not make them welcome. Tensions rose alongside the water.

Few but lunatics and animals connected the flood to the erection of the Sangrail, which was now complete, with a cold-gleaming spine and a great needle that pointed skywards like a threat. For the fanciulli, the needle was the realisation of a promise. For their parents, who had grown up with the Molè's domes eclipsing the sun, it was a restoration. And when the days became darker and small children grew weak and the weak fell ill, that was attributed to the exceptionally harsh winter. Summer's enchantment would surely put things to rights.

The Collegio were waiting to hear the news from the front – always a more pressing matter than the Small People's comfort – when a panicked orderly burst in to say that a crowd was gathering outside. From the balcony of the Collegio, Malapert Omodeo and Numitor Fuscus stood side by side, their differences momentarily forgotten, looking on with disbelief as the piazza filled with fanciulli. Torbidda stood at the podium below and while the praetorians formed a wall in front of the crowd, their prefect led a prisoner with a sack over his head to the podium.

'Children,' the First Apprentice solemnly began, his voice ringing out over the crowd, 'we have made ourselves perfect by stripping away our fetters – the chains of Curia, of Guild, of false religion and false reason. We have rejected them all, that we might carry a greater burden, one which purifies our souls even as it annihilates our weak flesh. Our freedom is terrifying to our enemies. Some of you will have heard that our Crusaders have suffered a terrible reverse, and it is true. More: an ungodly coalition of southern apostates and foreign infidels now marches on

Concord. They send their agents ahead to work mischief within our walls. They are too subtle to poison our wells and aqueducts. Instead they have sent to confuse us a false prophet of false profit.'

Torbidda ripped off the prisoner's hood and quickly stood back. The crowd pelted Guido Bombelli with stones and pieces of glass. They didn't know who he was, only that he was an enemy.

'The boy's insane,' said Fuscus.

'No,' Omodeo said bitterly. 'He knows exactly what he's doing.'

Torbidda smiled up at them before turning back to the crowd. 'These are godly stones – but hold back a moment.' He leaped in front of the prisoner and the rain of missiles instantly ceased. 'Innocents that you are, you recognise the devil. Innocence is the only *true* armour against evil; wisdom has its use, but it has many chinks. O Children, it pains me to tell you, but some of your wise men have been tempted by this prophet's wicked doctrines.'

A wail of terror and revulsion and rage spread over the piazza. Now the consuls were pelted, though they were out of range. The hail battered the massive green banner that hung beneath the balcony.

'And what is the blasphemous doctrine that misled those philosophers? I must not tell you, lest you too are misled.'

'Tell us!' they cried, squeezing their stones so hard their fists bled.

'I must not. You are mere children – you are not strong enough.'

'We are strong!'

'Are you not afraid?'

'We fear nothing!' they cried, brandishing their bloody fists as proof.

'Children, I believe you. This devil tempted the consuls with the pestiferous worm of *usury*. He told them he would teach them that unholy art – unnatural as sodomy – which would make fertile unions where nature has decreed there can be no issue.

'Ah – I see you do not believe me. O simple children, you know not the wiles of calculating men: you say coins are barren, so how could coins beget coins? Or Time beget Time? But I have seen it myself, even in the Collegio – yes, even there.

'They have made my temple into a gambling house. This consul has sixty silver pieces and so he rents out thirty pieces to a consul in need, for a small fee. What has changed hands here if not Time? If it is not given to any but God to know the Time, how much worse to sell it? Will Our Father allow it? Will He sit idle while vice flourishes?'

'No!'

'What was the Serpent's reward for seducing Eve with unfit knowledge?'

'Death!'

'It was Ariminum that schooled Etruria's merchants in the degenerate art of lending with interest and now that city of pimps is one with Tyre and Sodom. But their wicked doctrine escaped the fire that purified them. Our enemy, this League of Sin, is sustained by usury – and here is a high priest of that dark art: Guido Bombelli.'

The piazza became a sustained roar, a trembling of hands outstretched to strangle and rip and rend.

'You are zealous – we cannot suffer a false prophet to live, that is sure. What to do with the Collegio is the harder question.'

The crowd didn't find it complicated: 'Death!'

'Peace, Children. The Lord respects the righteous, but the merciful He loves. The consuls have been led astray. Before they ruin themselves with too much cleverness, we must lead them back to rectitude. How shall we instruct them? Shall we burn the sinner?'

Once more a thousand hands reached for Guido Bombelli, an inchoate screaming leviathan bellow that echoed into the Depths.

Torbidda looked around slowly. 'I hear you. You are wiser

together than any single judge. The sentence is most just: schismatics should be themselves parted.'

He nodded to the praetorians who lifted the prisoner high up and cast him far into the sea of hands.

Everyone got a share.

CHAPTER 63

Death marked, winter owned; they belonged to those shrill sisters. The carts wheeled over bodies frozen in the mud and the legionaries, recognising beneath their boots the faces of old comrades left behind, mourned afresh. The League might have turned the retreat into a rout by pursuing them; instead, for the most part, it let them flee unmolested. Some called it charity, but General Spinther knew better. Once the marsh had them, the screws would tighten.

Even though an elongated line was vulnerable to attack, it proved impossible to keep the men tighter together. The whip's snap no longer made the legionaries flinch, but if they did not cross the Albula soon they would perish to a man. Leto, anxious to get on, rode to the rearguard to investigate the delay and discovered Geta patiently whipping a pair of horses bound to a mud-mired wagon.

He left off his toil to salute. 'Hail Imperator!'

'There's only wounded in this wagon,' Leto observed.

'So?'

'We don't haul machinery when it's broken. These horses are useful, but soldiers unable to march are no longer soldiers. Our engines may yet save us; misplaced charity will condemn us all.'

Geta lowered his voice. 'We can't just abandon them.'

'Since when are you so tender-hearted?'

'Call it self-preservation. The men are on the point of mutiny as it is – they simply won't countenance more abandonment.'

461

'You'll be surprised how soon their tears will dry. It's hard, but we are on a hard road. Get it done.'

Sure enough, the marsh was an ordeal that made their first crossing seem easy. Leto soon realised that the meticulous destruction of the pontoons behind them was a waste of time: with the Bouncing Bridge and their knowledge of the marshes, the butteri advance riders could easily flank them. The devils did not use this greater mobility to launch substantial attacks, but preferred rather an exhausting schedule of skirmishes – ceaselessly pestering them like a swarm of zanzara. The daily mounting anxiety was worse than trenchfoot, worse than fever, worse than the cold. They trekked across the field of Tagliacozzo and did not pause for libations. The Albula, when they came to it at last, was partially frozen, but the pontonniers judged the ice too weak to bear so many. They lacked material to make a pontoon, but managed a raft, large enough to ferry whole battalions. It was tied off at either end and hauling it through the broken ice was slow work.

The butteri finally swooped in after the main corps had passed over. Leto did not hesitate to cut the rope and the unlucky battalion halfway across could only curse him as they were released to the mercy of the river. The despairing hundreds who remained tried to cross the half-frozen river, with ghastly results.

The Concordians had their fill of horror. They turned their backs and hastened away from the unlucky site, only to be intercepted by a small party of horsemen. Leto recognised the slain she-wolf adorning their yellow banners, but the man at the head of the Veian embassy he barely recognised at all. Power gnaws some men like consumption; others it emboldens like mother's love; Marsuppini was one of the happy few. For his part, he smiled fondly to see Leto Spinther as bedraggled as his army.

'You come alone, I see,' said Leto, offering his hand. When Marsuppini did not kiss it, he said, 'Your fellow patricians are well I hope.'

'Alas, there was a constitutional crisis and they quite lost their heads.' He handed Leto a scroll. 'Fresh from Concord. The First Apprentice orders us, his vassels, and you, his general, not to surrender an inch beyond the Albula. Thus far and no further, he says.'

'And is this your idea of a martial array?'

'This is merely a courtesy. I must look to Veii's interests, not Concord's. Our walls are restored and manned by a strong militia. I've come to warn you to pass by. I will not make you welcome.'

'I won't waste my time reminding you of your oath of fealty. I'll remind you instead that we broke our way into Veii once—'

'The point is,' Marsuppini cut him off, 'can you do it again with the League at your heels? I think not.'

'A point you may have neglected in your calculations: how do you think Costanzo Bombelli will look upon the man who gave his brother to us?'

'I doubt I'll have much luck getting any loans from him, but perhaps that's a blessing in disguise. My predecessor bequeathed Veii enough debts to service as it is. Costanzo's a man of the world. He'll understand that I was constrained by circumstances. Denying succour to you – Salvatore's *actual* murderers – will repair some of the damage. Besides, there are other sources of credit in Etruria – Malapert Omodeo for one. Speaking of which—' Marsuppini produced another scroll. 'The same herald who delivered the First Apprentice's diktat brought this private communication for your eyes only.'

Leto noted the broken seal. 'You've learned the game quickly.'

Marsuppini bowed at the compliment. 'That's the only way this unforgiving sport can be played. Godspeed you home, General. From what I gather, Concord needs a strong hand now more than ever.'

As the Veians rode away, Geta sidled up to the nonplussed boy. 'Let me guess: we're not invited to supper?'

By way of answer, Leto silently handed him the second scroll.

'This is co-signed by—'

'Keep reading,' Leto said.

Geta wondered what prodigy could bring Omodeo and Numitor together. When he finished he knew the answer, and could hardly credit it. Neither, he saw, could Leto.

'The Bombelli are the keystone of the League. After all we've suffered, I can't understand why Torbidda would be so rash. Whenever he made a sacrifice, there was always a good reason.'

'I despair of you, Spinther. I doubt he's thinking further than tomorrow. The boy knows he has a mad dog on the leash with the fanciulli; he's sacrificing us to save himself and the capital.'

'But it won't even do that.'

'In my experience, the deepest thinkers make the worst blunders,' Geta said with an odd satisfaction. 'They're so fond of complications that finally they deceive themselves. The unlettered at least know when they are lying. Very well. We'll make our stand at Rasenna and I shall see my dear wife again. I'll wager she looks elegant in mourning clothes.'

The League moved up the west coast and the Byzantines the east like two parallel rivers. To avoid overburdening the exhausted land, each army kept itself supplied by sea. Khoril's wounded fleet was fit for little else, but the boundlessness of Byzant's power was becoming increasingly apparent to the Etrurians. The Adriatic was carpeted with dromons, more each day. The Byzantines had old trade contacts in towns like Pescara and Ancona and Jorge was made welcome by a people still delighted at shaking off the Ariminumese yoke.

As Sofia rode with the butteri, she noticed the rhythm that followed them: the whoop of the bolas, the patter of the hooves in the day and the crackle of campfires and the husky breath of the buffalo at night. Like the Ebionites, they loved poetry, favouring ballads and laments which they rendered so sweetly that the prosaic lyrics were transfigured.

She noticed too how comfortable Pedro was amongst them. He had been quieter than usual since the battle, and she knew well the warring states of mind he was likely feeling.

'I was scared, elated – I don't know what,' he confessed. 'The remarkable thing is that I fought at all.'

'It's not that remarkable – Vettori Vanzetti had plenty of salt, and the Doc always said no one fights like a man with something to lose or something to prove.'

'I am the latter, I fear. The City of Towers lost its towers on my watch.'

'You cannot carry that burden: we all lost Rasenna.'

They were both silent, thinking of the things lost in the fire: Isabella and Uggeri, casualties of the war, no less than her father, Doc Bardini, John Acuto, Arik ben Uriah, Jabari, Bakhbukh or—

'Doctor Ferruccio would have liked your savage, Contessa. The butteri have really taken to him.'

'They have that.' It gladdened her to see them showing No Man how to ride and throw the bolas. The boy proved to be skilful at whatever he tried, and hardy enough to keep pace with them. The humidity that so bothered the *Stranieri* – as the Byzants and Sicarii were being collectively called – did not fatigue him. He became adept at hunting the wild long-eared Minturnae hare, which the butteri considered a great delicacy. The Sybarites had naïvely believed that only the Madonna could restore them to past glory; No Man was only the first of his people to realise that all that was holding them back was themselves. Rejoining the life of the Black Hand was the first step to the restoration.

As the Sirocco's forces drew further north, strains between the Byzantines and the League began to manifest. Costanzo spoke for many when he said, 'I don't want to clear the way for one set of weeds by burning another.'

Fulk was riding alongside, sniffling with a cold. He reminded Costanzo that Jorge had agreed to join them only reluctantly.

'Aye – because he thought Concord stronger than it has proved. Once a man takes a bite out of an apple, he usually finishes it. We've let his troops rove over Etruria. What if he does not leave?'

Fulk turned to Sofia. In Ebionite, he said, 'Your country is a little damper than Oltremare, but truly, nesi'im are the same everywhere.'

'Identical, and I weary of it,' she said, before answering Costanzo, 'Let's take it one war at a time.'

CHAPTER 64

A thousand empty stomachs lumbering through a sodden desert. It was the Grand Legion's passage months ago that had denuded the contato – though they had not wreaked the damage through greed or sadism; it was simply a function of moving such numbers across the land. This fact did not console them now that they had to retrace their steps.

In the absence of better nourishment, they subsisted on desperation. Concordians had long mocked their enemies' atavistic suspicion of technology but the League's 'wonder bridge' was like a judgement in their hunger-crazed minds. Every man knew it would be death to fall behind, so they trekked exhaustedly on through the bad lands of Gubbio, where the carrion and wolves were equally fat, to the Rasenneisi contato, which was littered with the skeletal remains of the dancers for whom the music had finally ceased.

The Rasenneisi did not cheer the Concordians; neither did they resist. Many said a restoration of order was welcome, whatever flag it came under. Bocca the brewer had not excelled at keeping the peace. The persecution of collaborators he had permitted was initially popular, but rapidly became an excuse for opportunistic score-settling between rival families. Once they lost any reputation for impartiality, the Signoria lost all authority and Bocca could do nothing but watch as Rasenna descended into factionalism worse than the worst of the old days.

Geta was looking forward to playing the magnanimous lord welcoming his harassed countrymen to the warmth of his hearth, but all such illusions were quickly dispelled: General Spinther took over the Gonfaloniere's Palazzo and left him to bunk with the infantry in the Fortezza del Falco.

Carmella did not like to admit it but the Baptismal Font had become something awful for her. The scenes on its base – of murder and mourning – were an accusation. Yet she kept picking the scab – the water drew her to it. Sometimes she fancied she heard voices – Uggeri's, Isabella's – and she strained to hear what they were saying for hours.

She was startled by the booming knock at the baptistery door and she ran to pull it open. When she saw who it was, she pushed it closed.

The toe of Geta's boot prevented her. 'I'm her husband, Sister. She'll want to see me.'

'So sure? They spat at her in the piazza because of you. She's lucky it went no further.'

'Now you're being silly. No one's going to hang the sister of the Bombelli Brothers.' He put his full weight behind the door and pushed, crying, '*Amore*! I'm home!'

Carmella followed him out into the garden as he called Maddalena's name again. 'Where is she, Sister? I'm asking nicely.'

'I've no idea.' Carmella was not a practised liar.

'Thank you, Sister,' Geta said, striding in the direction she'd glanced. '*Amore*?'

The door of the little chapel was open and Geta stopped abruptly. There inside sat his wife, staring with a manic intensity at a single glass of water on a little table in front of her. That was bad enough, but it was her unkempt appearance that told him something was seriously wrong. She'd never been full-figured but she had always dressed well. The woman before him was a skeleton lost in the folds of her coarse habit. Her hair was growing back in sporadic clumps that made her resemble some emaciated Frankish Amazon. 'Maddalena. It's me. Didn't you hear me calling?'

Like a sleepwalker, she turned towards him. 'I thought I imagined it.' She spoke slowly, as though drunk. 'Kneel beside me, *amore*. We'll confess together.'

Geta grabbed Carmella's arm roughly. 'What have you done to my wife? '

She pulled her arm away. 'I gave her something to live for.'

'You made her a bloody nun! *Dio*, she even talks like one—'

'You can't imagine what a relief it is – I don't know why I avoided it so long. It wasn't Uggeri's fault – he was just God's arm. I hadn't confessed what we did and so my baby had to die, you see, because I hadn't paid my debt and the interest was growing. It's like Papa used to say: that's where you make your percentage. Now I confess every day so it doesn't get a chance to build up. I tell the Madonna all the bad things I think and do and no one else needs to die. Come, tell her what we did to Papa. That's a good one. She'll like that.'

'. . . It sounds great fun,' said Geta in a strangled voice. 'Truly it does.' He backed away from the door with a terrified rictus grin. 'I do however have some pressing Signoria business to attend to first. Tell you what – you start without me and I'll be along shortly with my list of misdeeds.' He backed up a few more steps, then turned and ran.

Alone in the dining room of the Gonfaloniere's residence, Leto stared at the exquisitely carved chessboard. As usual, he reset the pieces to an interesting midgame, this one from a match he had played in the autumn of Sixty-Eight against Torbidda. Torbidda's preference was to play black. To begin with, he feigned indifference, but this apathy was a ruse. He studiously avoided exchanges until a hideously complex mid-game had developed, at which point, with the multifarious combinations and possibilities stacked large, he would shift in his seat and become engaged.

Leto interrogated the silent pieces, searching for some explanation for Torbidda's actions.

With a hopeless sigh, he played out the game as it had transpired four years ago. Torbidda's audacious queen sacrifice. Check. Leto takes queen. Torbidda's rook smashes down to his second rank. Check. Leto takes rook. And now the unseen knight protecting that humble pawn rears up like Nemesis. Check. Leto must retreat and see the pawn reborn into something new and deadly.

Mate.

He felt the surprise of it afresh and wistfully smiled. Geta, for all this pride and recklessness, was correct: one could not be an Engineer *and* a soldier. Only confusion arose from lukewarm commitment. In memory of his father, he had devoted himself to Apollo – but blood, like water, finds its natural level. It had brought him back here to the altar of Mars.

Bocca looked sullenly at the only customer in the piazzetta. 'If you still think you can have credit, you're sadly mistaken.'

'Bocca, after all I did for you—'

'I should pour you arsenic.'

'Oh, come on. I've had a simply awful day. My wife's gone mad, and everyone thinks it's fine to make horns at me in the streets. *Me!* Their rightfully elected gonfaloniere! I must kill someone or have a drink. What's it going to be?'

'I'm not scared of you any more either. If you want a drink, I want silver.'

Geta took his hat off and put his hand through his hair. 'My horse. I'll give you my horse.'

Bocca knew Arête's temper, but if he could not sell him, he could always make mince of the brute. 'Go on then.' He took down a bottle. 'So, reckon you'll be staying?'

'All depends on the little general. I've never known his arrogance to falter but if I didn't know better, I'd say he's having a crisis of confidence.'

'I heard you got your arses handed to you at Salerno.'

'It's not that. The Volturno *was* a blow, but after the initial shock, Spinther convinced himself that was just a setback. What's made him despondent was a letter from Concord.'

'Ah,' said Bocca. 'The lad's homesick.'

'No, *idiota*. Spinther's always revered the First Apprentice – but his faith's been shaken. It transpires his hero has taken to senselessly murdering valuable prisoners-of-war.'

'What's he fixing to do?'

'That, Bocca, is the question. Put it this way – I won't be turning my back on him any time soon.'

An hour later, Geta was delivering an impromptu diatribe against Rasenna. 'You wretches haven't thought how bereft you'd be if you defeated us,' he shouted defiantly. 'Without hatred of Concord to hold you together, what would you have? Who will you blame when you inherit Etruria in all its absurdity?'

Bocca, who knew better than to interrupt an angry drunk, looked past him – and dropped the glass he was polishing. 'General Spinther!'

Geta's reaction was similar. He took a deep breath and was suddenly sober, before turning around. 'Care for a drink, Spinther? My credit's excellent here. Can't say the same for the wine, haw haw.'

'I'm buying,' said Leto, and signalled for a bottle.

Geta pretended not to notice the guards he'd brought along. 'Well, whatever else I achieved on this campaign, I taught you to drink. What's the occasion? Let me guess, you're giving me a citation for bravery—'

'I wanted you to hear it from me. We're leaving.'

'Oh. I see.'

Geta's muted response was not what Leto had expected, and he went on as if he'd been challenged, 'It's senseless taking positions that can't be defended. The Byzants have retaken Ariminum, what's left of it. With them coming from the east and the League coming from the south, Rasenna's too exposed.'

Geta's leg began nervously tapping under the table. He drank the glass in one mouthful. 'Where then, Montaperti?' he said, naming the field where disagreements between north and south were traditionally settled.

'One for the road?' said Leto. He poured without waiting for Geta's answer. 'As I said, it's futile to hold indefensible positions. Fight at Montaperti and what's the outcome? If we lose, Concord's lost. If we win, that lunatic's rule will continue to its inevitable end. The only way Concord survives is if I make peace.'

Geta stilled his tapping leg with his hand and discreetly unsheathed his boot dagger. He cleared his throat. 'Overthrow the Apprentice by all means, Spinther. Take the Red, or any colour that takes your fancy, and I'll carry your banner. But this duel's too far gone for to end with an exchange of handshakes and hostages.'

Without responding, Leto filled his own glass. He finished by tapping the rim with the decanter. 'The war's unwinnable.'

'You don't know that.' Geta began arguing that a change in fortune was imminent.

Leto let him ramble, amused by his volte-face, before interrupting, 'Let's be candid, Geta. You care about preserving your neck, not Concord. You know that any peace negotiation must include the Rasenneisi, and that any settlement that the Rasenneisi negotiate will require you to be hanged.'

'I'll drink to that,' Bocca mumbled behind his counter.

Geta picked up his glass again and laughed.

'What's so amusing?'

'I thought I'd taught you well over the course of this campaign.

I clearly failed – if this is your idea of springing a trap!' He flung the wine at Leto and the empty glass at a praetorian. He plunged his dagger into the other one and bolted from the piazzetta into the night.

The guards gave pursuit, but Geta knew every bolthole the Tartaruchi had ever used. As he crawled on his belly through the damps of the *sottosuolo* he considered his abruptly reduced options. Leto was serious about taking over, so he must therefore cleave to the First Apprentice – but that malignant imp would hang him just for spite if he returned to Concord bearing only bad news.

CHAPTER 65

Lucius Priscus, fifth king of Etrusca, made a
pilgrimage to Cumae, to ask the three wise
women how he might expand his League into an
Empire. The sisters duly consulted the *Disciplina
Etrusca*, and revealed Etrusca's future to the king
– its glorious rise, and its inevitable fall, naming
the very hour of nemesis centuries hence. The
appalled king pledged to renounce ambition if
only the doom could be revoked. But it was not
in the sisters' gift to divert Fortune's river. They
could only foretell its course. 'Then ye art doomed
also,' said he. One only, the youngest, escaped the
king's wrath, by finding refuge in the Kingdom
of Sybaris.

The Etruscan Annals

The unburied dancers should have confirmed Pedro's warning,
but it was only when she saw what was left of Rasenna that Sofia
realised there was to be no homecoming. Home was gone, lost
somewhere in the years gone by, and what was left was as pointless as a eunuch.

'I don't suppose Akka will be the same when I return to it,'
said Fulk.

Sofia wiped away her tears and turned to him. 'You've kept
your promise, every promise. You need not go further.'

At last he said, 'Whatever comes, Akka stands with the League. I must see this Crusade through to the end.'

While they gazed upon that towerless skyline, Levi, Pedro and Costanzo watched the chariot approaching from the east.

Anticipating that Rasenna would be strongly defended, both armies had converged in the field where John Acuto had met his end. Costanzo's paranoid intimations about the Byzantines had not abated, so Sofia decided to simply ask Jorge his intentions. She'd begun to have misgivings of her own. All she had to rely upon was Fulk's estimation of the prince's quality.

Jorge was straightforward. 'We're not fighting for land,' he said, 'we're fighting for water.'

Costanzo was quick to comprehend. 'The Adriatic.'

'It's our sea. The only foothold on the Etrurian peninsula we seek is Ariminum.'

Sofia was confused. 'There is no Ariminum.'

'Its harbour remains,' said Costanzo.

'We understand each other, Signore Bombelli. I will rebuild the City of Bridges – *Cam'era, dov'era* as the natives used to say – and run it as a client state.'

'What of the Rhineland?'

Jorge's manner became colder. 'We ought to finish *this* war before worrying about prizes – but let me say that those won by Byzantine arms alone concern Byzantines alone. Just as the peace Etruria devises is none of our concern.'

Sofia noted how Jorge included Fulk in that 'our', and that Fulk did not object. Both apparently considered Akka a Byzantine dominion.

'Whatever arrangement you make, ' the prince continued, 'I'm sure that some other state, a year or a few decades hence, will take Concord's place. You're fighting for liberty, a splendid cause. Ours is more prosaic but no less vital: security.'

After that frank exchange, the captains waited in a tense

silence as a single rider emerged from the wounded city. Pedro saw he was carrying the red flag that Rasenna had once united behind. Before the rider got close, it became clear he was having difficulty controlling his horse. It danced around in a circle, before bucking him off. The unseated rider had to scramble to avoid its hoofs. The captains exchanged a wry glance and trotted forward together.

'Hail Liberators!' cried Bocca as he slapped the dust from his arse.

'I recognise that beast,' said Pedro.

'That truculent nag,' said Bocca, picking up the flag, 'belonged to the tyrant who usurped the rightful powers of the Signoria. Where you now sit, he and the boy general begged for succour but a few days ago. We gave them passage but made it clear they were not welcome.'

'If another lie escapes that tongue of yours,' said Pedro solemnly, 'it'll get the same treatment as Jacques the Hammer's got. What really happened?'

Bocca wiped his lips, his mouth suddenly dry. 'The part about it being Geta's horse is true. He sold it to me just before he and the general had an altercation at my tavern.'

'Why were they fighting?' said Levi.

'The general wishes to make peace. Geta – well, he knew what *that* meant.' Bocca was not sure that his implication was understood and so illustrated with an elaborate mime of a man being hanged.

'Go on, man,' said Levi impatiently.

'After he fled, the Concordians up and left too. The general told me to inform you that he was surrendering Rasenna as a mark of his good intentions. Which is what I am doing. Here. Now.'

There was a long silence as they looked down on him. He lowered the flag. 'On behalf of the Signoria, Contessa Scaligeri, I humbly beg amnesty.'

Prince Jorge lacked a dog in this fight, but he waited to hear the Contessa's response with curiosity.

'You, who sat silently as Rasenna's towers were burned,' she said, 'ask for lenience?'

'What could we do, Contessa! We were prisoners of the Concordians, isn't that so, Maestro Vanzetti?'

Before Pedro could respond, Sofia said, 'We're not here to settle scores, Bocca. You're pardoned.'

'All but one,' corrected Costanzo. 'Maddalena Bombelli must answer for her crimes.'

Bocca was drunk with relief. 'Do what you like to her. It was only out of respect to your family, Signore Bombelli, that she wasn't hanged with the rest of the whores.'

'Watch your mouth,' said Levi.

'No, he's quite right,' said Costanzo. 'The Signoria's enormities were forced upon it by my sister and her Concordian lover.'

'God's beard, Costanzo, you forgave the Veians!' said Pedro.

'Marsuppini will be paying for his treachery for the rest of his life. He has no credit with Tower Bombelli.'

'But you'll still do business with him—'

'Veii's our chief source of alum.'

'And Maddalena is your sister!'

'That makes it worse!'

Bocca stood before the liberators uncomfortably as they began to shout at each other. Sofia noticed the Byzantine's embarrassment. 'I'm sorry, Prince Jorge.'

'Unnecessary, Contessa. This is a family matter,' he said, taking up his reins.

'I mean, sorry for not trusting you.'

'Scepticism's healthy. There are no lifelong friendships in diplomacy. Today the Byzantines, the Akkans, the Salernitans and the Rasenneisi are pulling the same chariot. Tomorrow we may be pitted against each other.' He tipped his head to Bocca.

'This dog may be lying about General Spinther's change of heart, but until we know for certain, we should press our advantage. I shall return to Ariminum and send my dromons into the Venetian gulf. I'll take my men by the coast until we're north of Concord, at which point we'll double back.'

'And we'll be the other claw of that pincer. Until then, Prince, Godspeed.'

He gave Fulk an expectant look before turning.

Fulk touched Sofia's shoulder, 'Contessa, my place—'

'—is at his side, yes. These fools will ever be suspicious of each other, but that is enough to give me assurance. At Concord then.'

'At Concord.'

Carmella leaned over the font. The whispers had stopped, and left behind a question: what would it feel like to *kiss* water? She leaned closer, closer and—

'Ahem.'

She leaped back and bowed to hide her blushes. 'Contessa Scaligeri, Maestro Vanzetti. Our prayers are answered. You have delivered Rasenna.'

'We all played a part,' Pedro said. It had been the right decision, but guilt at leaving Uggeri behind lingered. 'We're here to ask what we can do for you.'

Carmella nervously confessed that she was afraid for the safety of the women who'd taken up with Concordians during the occupation.

Sofia said that Levi had resumed the office of podesta. 'Justice will be done by him, or not at all,' she promised. 'There'll be no score settling, no purges.'

'I see.' Carmella was taken aback. She had pictured the Contessa as an angel of vengeance. 'In that case, I'd like to introduce you to our newest novice.'

Sofia followed her into the garden and to the chapel.

Carmella cleared her throat nervously, 'This is—'

'The Contessa knows me well,' said Maddalena without looking away from the Madonna in the stained-glass window.

Sofia stared in amazement at the girl sitting in front of the table in the same cramped position she had spent so many hours.

'I was haughty when she most needed sisterhood. I slandered her while playing the whore.'

'The Contessa will surely forgive you,' Carmella said, looking at Sofia with pleading eyes.

Maddalena wept, 'I do not deserve forgiveness!'

After fighting so long to keep Iscanno alive, Sofia could take no satisfaction in a widow's grief. She didn't believe the self-serving account of the occupation that Bocca and his cronies had painted, nor did she imagine there was justice to be extracted from Uggeri's sordid end – *vendetta*, that old ghost that haunted Rasenna's towers could never be fully exorcised, but she would not feed it either.

She came out of her reverie to see Pedro had joined them. He was staring at her expectantly.

'We fought our battles, but what sisters do not quarrel now and then?'

'Sisters!' cried Maddalena in ecstasy.

'Sisters,' Sofia repeated, and bounced Iscanno in her arms so that he giggled. 'Would you like to hold him?'

'Oh no.' Maddalena drew back in alarm. 'You don't understand, Contessa. I'm not *safe*.'

Sofia had to force Iscanno into her trembling arms. She started weeping and laughing at once.

'Now I require something from each of you. Carmella, will you baptise Iscanno?'

Carmella concealed her anxiety well. 'I would be honoured, Contessa.'

Sofia thanked her and took a deep breath. 'Maddalena, if your mother were alive I would have asked her to be Iscanno's god-mother. Will you to do me the honour in her stead?'

Maddalena scarcely appeared to have heard; she was twirling Iscanno round the chapel, sweetly laughing together. 'Yes! Yes! Yes!'

Pedro was proud of Sofia – and of Maddalena too, for all her sins. Knowing how deep the two young women's enmity had run, he could not help being moved. He was caught unawares when Sofia asked, 'Will you be godfather, Maestro?'

'Of course he will!' cried Maddalena with something of her old spirit, rushing over with the baby. 'We shall outdo each other in showering Iscanno with gifts, won't we? What saint-name are you giving him, Contessa?'

Sofia didn't have to think. 'Giovanni.'

After the baptism of Iscanno Giovanni Scaligeri, Maddalena took her godson into the garden. Sofia and Carmella watched them from the baptistery.

'We should go to the Signoria, Contessa,' said Pedro.

'Yes,' said Sofia, with a sigh. 'There's much to discuss.'

Neither said it outright, but they were both resolved to rec-oncile Costanzo with his sister. If he saw her pitiful condition, surely he would bend? The Bombelli family had been a rock for Rasenna first, then for the League. To heal that schism would complete their victory.

'We'll be back in an hour or two' said Sofia glancing out into the enclosed garden where Maddalena was rolling in the grass with Iscanno in the dying evening's light. 'Could you—'

'Go,' said Carmella. 'I'll watch over them. Don't worry. Here at least they're safe.'

Costanzo had convened the new Signoria in Palazzo Bombelli, in the same capacious courtyard where Fabbro used to hold court, but now weeds pressed up between the tiles. The olive trees had overgrown their pots and the fountain in the centre was long-dry. There was no notary and no handing round of the mace; instead, Costanzo sat at his father's banco behind the scales and fired questions as though they were employees and not parliamentary colleagues: 'If General Spinther's offer is genuine, why did he run off at our approach?'

Pedro noticed that Fabbro's old cronies had come out of the shadows to pay obeisance to the new head of the family.

'He can't very well make peace without possession of the capital,' said Levi. 'He's probably afraid we'd hang him.'

'I just want the First Apprentice hanged,' said Sofia.

'Nothing would give me greater pleasure,' said Costanzo airily, 'but remember, Contessa, he's just one boy. Someone would take his place in a moment. And we can't very well let the Byzantines march to Concord's gates and sit here waiting for an annunciator to tell us how they get on. We need to be part of it. We need to make sure Concord never threatens us again. We need to grind its walls to dust, burn the Guild Halls down and sow the foundations with salt.'

Iscanno sat in Maddalena's lap, exhausted from their play. He was staring up at the window and its kaleidoscope of colours. His godmother was tired too. Her joy had become something else – she didn't quite know what. All that she knew was that the surface tension of the water was captivating. So thin, that boundary between air and water, and yet what a difference. That's how it was with boundaries. One step too far and the world dropped from under you. The Contessa's baby was alive; hers was dead. Such trivial differences.

The water coiled up the surface of the glass and then poured in a balloon-like form over the lip and onto the table. Iscanno's eyes went wide with fear, but before he could cry out, her hand covered his mouth. The water left an oily trail across the table as it flowed gloopously into the garden.

In the baptistery's perennial twilight, Carmella grasped the rim of the font and glanced into the garden to confirm no one was watching. She slowly put her hand out and rested it on the surface, so gently that she barely caused a ripple. She pulled her hand back. Something – *someone* – had touched her hand. The gold ceiling and the sword were reflected on the water's surface, but that was an illusion. The water was not water; it was a window into another space. There was a boy at the other side. A fighter even in death, Uggeri was fighting to return to her – to tell her that he was not angry about what she had done. That he was grateful – she had set him free.

She leaned in and as soon as her lips touched the water, she tasted it.

It was *foul*, but before she could pull away, Maddalena's hands were pushing her head under.

As Carmella fought back, her eyes opened under water. She saw the boy looking up at her: not Uggeri but someone else, a pale boy with an ox-like brow, a frowning jaw and eyes with no pity.

Maddalena held her until the thrashing had stopped, then pulled her out. Her body flopped listlessly to the ground beside the bawling baby. Maddalena picked him up and held him to her breast as she examined the font suspiciously. She warily scooped a handful of water and sprinkled it over the baby. 'Now, Fabbro, let's find Father.'

Geta was curled up in an earthen tunnel scarcely a brachia wide and holding his breath. The horrors of the *sottosuolo* were beyond comprehension: rats big as cats, and – *Dio!* – the stink . . . How the Tartaruchi had managed it for so long was beyond him. He'd chosen this tunnel expressly for his last stand and it was not likely to be glorious. It was a dead end that could only be reached by wading through a deep pool, and right now *something* was wading towards him. He watched the lumbering shadow approaching and at the last moment, he thrust with his knife – then pulled back in surprise. 'Maddalena?'

She was shivering uncontrollably, and her lips were blue. 'Oh, my love. It's so cold. Take him from me.'

He took the baby – it was close to frozen too. 'But whose is it?'

Maddalena's stubborn anger had not left her. 'He's *not* the Contessa's! She has too much. He's my Little Fabbro returned. We're going to be a family again.'

'I see.' He rocked the baby thoughtfully. 'How did you find me down in this maze?'

'The water showed me the way. It wants us to be together.' She stumbled, and her head went under momentarily. She reached out a hand, but Geta did not take it.

She rested it against his leg. 'Can you keep a secret?'

'I'm famous for my discretion, *amore*.'

'There's something *hungry* in the baptistery. That's why I fled. It wants to harm my little Fabbro!'

'Well, we can't have that, can we?'

CHAPTER 66

It was Pedro who found Maddalena and dragged her from the underworld. Costanzo embraced her lifeless body, crying, 'Oh my sweet sister, forgive me!'

Sofia backed away in horror and ran to the only place that offered any refuge. Maddalena was just one more casualty of her own ineptitude. She been warned, after all –Befana had told her what was waiting:

'*Once before, the Darkness had a tool as terrible as Bernoulli – a wicked king who tried to quench the light. The Lord sent a flood to destroy the wicked race who had crowned such a king. The deep rivers of the world would have drowned the world, had not a few worthy men begged for mercy. The Lord relented and He swore never to loose again the Waters, and the men swore to choose better kings. Man has broken the covenant, but the light will not suffer itself to be quenched. If Iscanno dies before the appointed hour, if his blood is wasted and it's a choice between giving the world to Darkness and starting anew – then every hidden river and sea will overspill. Nor will the flood stop at Concord: the world will be washed clean.*'

She stood by the Irenicon, looking at the ruins of Giovanni's bridge. The rubble sat in piles, making islands in the river. The Irenicon was unseasonably high and fast. In the absence of a body to mourn, the bridge had been the closest thing she had to a memorial. This was desecration: just one more thing taken from her.

She walked into the water. The cold made her gasp. A few braccia from where she stood, a mound of water swelled up on the river's surface, indifferent to the current. As she continued to wade in until she was waist-deep, the water approached her.

The bridge had been a place where deals were made: that was why she was here. The buio stood looking at her. Before she could ask *Is that you?* she heard the answer unreeling in her head:

He is here amongst us, but not . . . as you knew him.

'I want you to pass on a message. Can you do that?'

Speak.

'You made me Handmaid to protect Iscanno, and I've failed. I know now I should have leaped from some high place in the desert with my boy in my arms. I know now that Bernoulli has been running to *lose*. He led us on – he left his armies overexposed, he gave us our victories to draw us – to draw *me* – close to him. He threw the fight and vain fool that I am, I fell for it. I brought Iscanno to Etruria – I practically laid him on the altar. I can't be your Handmaid any more . . .'

Every inch of Monte Nero's summit was thronged with the fanciulli except for the shallow lake of liquid black from which the needle projected. The tripod overshadowed all. Its legs met two-thirds of the way up the needle, and were so darned with glow-globes that it looked a structure of permeable light rather than of stone, a momentary thing that did not pretend to permanence. Since the needle's erection, the turbulence around the mount had spread until it overhung all Concord, and wherever its bloated shadow fell, it dulled men and made them brutish.

For want of a pulpit, the First Apprentice stood on the shattered base of the Angel of Reason, one foot on each fragment. 'We shall show these pretended Crusaders the extent of our devotion,' he cried, 'for no Crusader could be more worthy than we, God's own children. But look into your heart before ye drink, for only the righteous may consume of His blood and live.'

He pointed to a golden-haired girl who was grinding her teeth.

'You, Sister! You must not drink if in your heart there is any doubt.'

'I have no doubt!' she cried and ran to the edge of the pool. She squatted like a dog and began lapping up the filthy stuff. The fanciulli waited in silence until she sat bolt-upright. She turned around with her face covered in the noxious black juice. Her eyes were wide, her pupils dilated. 'O, it is delicious!' she cried.

At that, the mob pushed forward like thirsty cattle in summer, clamouring and tearing at each other, pushing, even drowning each other, to get a pint, a mouthful, a drop . . .

The children of Concord might be united, but their elders were irrevocably divided. The inner rotunda of the Collegio was empty, but the vestibule outside was full of nervous consuls waiting for the First Apprentice's address. Numitor Fuscus and Malapert Omodeo had brought their factions together, but there was small comfort in numbers. The Grand Legion billeted outside the city, the legionaries General Spinther had brought – unconstitutionally – inside the walls, the approaching armies, the rising waters, the ceaseless rain and the fanciulli's predictions of imminent destruction – these things had made them timorous. They could not decide with whom they were more outraged: the First Apprentice, who ignored them, or General Spinther, who sought their support in deposing said Apprentice in such a vulgar fashion. Whispered conspiracy might be integral to Concordian politics, but the art was best practised in shady taverns; it was not done to debate such matters in the vestibule of the Collegio itself.

Consul Fuscus was not scared, but he too was divided: he was elated that his revolution was at hand, but was anxious to keep the general in a subordinate position, lest they be 'accidentally' dispatched along with the Apprentice. 'You had no authority to offer terms to the League,' he said pompously.

Leto had no time for stately intrigues. Girolamo Bernoulli had unleashed two Waves upon his enemies, and now like Nemeses, two vast armies were descending upon the city he had made glorious. He exposed the blade of his sword. 'What is this if not authority? You charged me to use it in the defence of Concord. Do not blame me if you did not realise what you were doing.'

'We gave you that sword to tame Etruria, something you have signally failed to do.'

'I was forced to march into the worst territory at the worst time, while desperately-needed iron went into that architectural atrocity that defaces fair Monte Nero. Tell him, Omodeo: your gallant nephew is dead because the Grand Legion was stabbed in the back.'

'It's true.' The financier was still in shock after learning that young Horatius had fallen at the Volturno.

'Have you forgotten,' one consul groaned, his head in his hand, 'what happened to Corvis?'

'Hardly: I was the one who flayed him,' Leto said. 'Has the First Apprentice addled your brains along with the fanciulli? Courage, Consuls! You sound like a school of cardinals. I'm here because your leaders asked for my help. If we do this, there can be no half-measures. He is mortal. Everyone here was trained by Grand Selector Flaccus too. We can take him.'

'That's hardly a mathematical certainty,' said Omodeo gloomily.

'Yes, you're right. There is another possibility: that he survives. What of it? We'll be dead if we do nothing.' Leto saw they all needed stiffening, 'Nothing is certain when you pick up a sword: I learned that on the northern front in my father's camp. My father told me, "You cannot succeed without knowing your enemy," so I asked him who were our enemies, that I might learn. "Barbarians," said he. I knew he used certain Frankish tribes – who wore rank furs and spoke poor Etrurian – as auxiliaries, but to me they seemed no more barbaric than our own legionaries.

My father brought me to a funeral of the chief of a tribe allied to us. They lived up to expectations, getting blind drunk at the feast before lighting the chief's pyre. They threw his weapons into the flames, then his cattle, then his slaves and finally his wives. My father held me close enough that I could smell the cooking flesh. "This is barbarism," he said. I never forgot it. When he was killed – by his own officers – I learned that even he did not know his true enemy. I learned that your enemy may speak your own dialect, salute the same flag. And such enemies are deadliest of all.' Leto looked around. 'The First Apprentice must die. The question is: must we throw ourselves on the fire with him? A wise man once told me never to take counsel from fear, for it chases away opportunity and leads nowhere. There is no certainty but that, Consuls. The rules are the same as they were in the Guild Hall. Strike first or die first.'

The oppressive atmosphere of impending storm encased the Sangrail. Enervated air built up on the needle's skin until it was repelled in thunderous charges that created turbulence even as the lower pressure sucked in more air. A vortex as vast and terrible as Charybdis was churning the sky.

'O faithless generation, not one of you was worthy.' The First Apprentice leaped down from his pulpit and walked over the bodies of his congregation. Most of the fanciulli were lying still, but some were twitching like legless insects or vomiting endless bile into the pool they had so recently supped from.

The girl who'd drunk first was stronger than most. She grabbed his ankles as he passed and spat out, 'Poison!'

He knelt beside her and rubbed her golden hair tenderly. 'Oh no, Child. It was Judgement. And you must not say that you were harshly judged – you must not say anything again. Your tongues will cleave to the roof of your mouths to ensure that. You will have to find other ways to express your love.'

CHAPTER 67

The tavern was a braccia deep in foul water, and it was rising. Bottles floated between the legs of the customers, along with an occasional cloaca rat. Madame Filangeiri hadn't planned to spend her final years with those whose ruin she had facilitated, but life is full of surprises, few of them pleasant. Since the Dolore Ostello had burned down, she had become a great customer of the Rule and Compass, along with many of her former clientele.

Empty bottles formed a little wall between her and her neighbour.

'You're something resembling a woman, Madame,' said a disembodied voice behind the glass wall. 'Why, pray tell, would a loving mother want to scare her child? Mine used to tell awful stories about wolves and buio and the barbarians of the north.'

She sipped her pint of gin thoughtfully. 'It's no puzzle, Lord Geta. Youngsters love a scare, simple as that.'

'Some perhaps' – he reached for her hand so suddenly that his barricade of bottles collapsed and revealed a basket on his table – 'but I always liked the parts where the beast gets to do his worst.'

Madame Filangeiri might not be a procuress any more, but she still knew a guilty conscience when she heard one. 'What's troubling you, ducky?'

'I have been' – he flicked a finger at his glass to make it ring – 'debating my course since my return. I am fixing to attain a new low.'

She pulled her hand free. 'Well, practise makes perfect.'

'I'm selling,' he confessed, tilting the basket towards her.

'Oh, isn't he a lovely little fella. With a smile like that, he'll fetch a good price.'

'I have not shocked you?'

Madame Filangeiri had trafficked in depravity and was skilled in the sophistry of tolerance. 'People do anything when they're starving.'

'I am not starving, Madame,' he said sharply. 'I don't *want* to do it, but I can't seem to stop myself.

'Doing the low thing gets to be a habit. You could always quit.' She burped and tottered off to the bar. When she returned with a new bottle, Geta's shoulders were shaking. She couldn't tell if he was laughing or weeping until he looked up and she realised it was both.

'Progress would cease if Man stopped doing things that sicken us. *Semper Eadem,* that's my motto. Same, same, always the bloody same . . .' He straightened up and raised a glass to constancy. 'A valiant fellow told me you've got to live for something. I've been heading for the hot place for years; to veer now would be disgraceful.'

He set down his drink unfinished and waded out into the streets with his basket, careful to avoid the floaters.

The Angel of Death hovered over the mount but did not alight on the bodies of the children, for they had been marked by another power, and now it called them to service. Their stiff limbs snapped to life and pulled them helplessly to their feet like a marionette army. Their black eyes looked up and saw at last the needle for the fell idol it was. They could not decry it; they could only bark and gibber – and so they were silent. They had imbibed the truth and that was that there was only one commandment, and that commandment was to dance. They twirled and swayed and pirouetted to the stairway to spread the news to the city below.

The general's troops billeted in the Piazza dei Collegio did not salute the First Apprentice when he alighted from his gondola. The intimidating silence was interrupted only by the billowing of the great banner that hung from the Collegio's empty balcony. Its rumblings augured a coming storm. He entered the vestibule to discover his general, together with Consuls Fuscus and Omodeo and their respective supporters, all with scrolls in hand.

'What a reception – and to think that I was beginning to fear I'd become unpopular.' He glanced from Fuscus to Omodeo and finally to Leto. 'Your Triumph isn't ready, Imperator, if that's why you're back in Concord.'

Leto ignored the derision. 'I'm here as a disinterested patriot. The consuls are here to petition you. They want peace. So do I.'

Torbidda backed into the rotunda. 'War is your profession, General. Pacifism will not win you laurels.'

'I care not,' said Leto as he led the consuls into the speaking chamber.

'Good for you. It's so rare to hear a rapist voluntarily take a vow of chastity,' said Torbidda as he retreated to his place at the stone table. He turned to address the consuls, none of whom had yet taken a seat. 'Be careful of soldiers who would befriend you. I speak from experience. Remember, the League was able to dissect our retreating army because of the good general's incompetence – it was he, remember, who allowed the Bouncing Bridge to fall into enemy hands and now he is panicking, flailing about looking for someone to blame. That's very natural – but panicking men make poor judges. Our position is not so dire. Be steadfast a little longer, friends, and you shall have your peace. General Spinther has also, in his wisdom, abandoned the territory north of the Irenicon without lifting his sword, but his cowardice has at least preserved the core of the Grand Legion. I've summoned the three legions guarding the northern border and they will arrive before the League reaches Montaperti where our bolstered forces can meet them in strength. This campaign has been wearying for our enemies too: if we are close to exhaustion, so are they. If we prove that our will is unbroken, they will sue for peace, on terms more honourable than any you'll get lying supine.'

The vestibule had finally emptied of consuls and now the praetorians followed and hauled the two large doors shut. He ignored this, and continued, 'And then we'll do as we've always done: we'll make promises – different promises to every party. The Contessa's coalition will dissolve in acrimony and all will be as it was. Any questions?'

There was a long, tense pause before Leto said mildly, 'One springs to mind: *are you insane?* Those legions were *guarding* our northern border. What remains to prevent the Franks from crossing into Etruria?'

'Not a thing, but that's a fire we can quench later.'

'You speak as if we have unlimited resources and time. We're out of both. The Byzantines have made an art of manipulating barbarians. They'll goad the Franks into revolt and follow in their wake as they spill over the Alps. You haven't *saved* Concord. You've guaranteed its destruction.'

The circle tightened, with Omodeo coming towards Torbidda from the left and Fuscus from the right.

He did not appear to notice. 'You exaggerate: there will be incursions, of course, and I don't doubt they'll take resolve to repel, but repel them we will. It's a necessary risk. If the Contessa's army is not stopped, there is no empire.'

'Torbidda, I beg you one last time,' Leto pleaded. 'Step from the brink. See Reason! We've lost the south – make peace before we lose the north too.'

Omodeo leaned from behind and whispered into his ear, 'Spinther's right, First Apprentice. The iron mines are better security than any walls.'

Fuscus' lips were at his other ear, 'While we hold them, we can rebuild our empty coffers and broken army—'

'There can be no peace!' Torbidda roared. 'Not while the Contessa or I both live. One of us must perish.'

'So be it,' said Leto.

The consuls grabbed Torbidda from behind. Their followers dropped their petitions to reveal the daggers within.

'Praetorians!' Torbidda cried, but the black-robed soldiers at the door did not budge.

'These men are mine, First Apprentice. You have no friends here.'

'No, I see that.'

The consuls nervously drew round with their daggers up, as though Torbidda was a lion at bay.

Leto pushed them back impatiently. 'No. A knife's too clean for this traitor.' He picked up the mace. 'Omodeo, Fuscus, hold him down.'

Torbidda struggled to keep his head up. *'Traitor?'* The fear vanished from his face, leaving a sneer. 'That would make you – what, *loyal*? Isn't this how they came for your father?'

Leto smashed down the mace and hit—

Nothing but stone. A consul's dagger stuck into the chair where Torbidda had been a moment ago; he landed behind Fuscus and Omodeo and slammed their heads together. There was a hollow crumbling sound. He pulled back the chair and removed the blade as the consuls crowded around him, keeping the chair between as they circled at a safe distance. Leto was at the outer rim of the circle. When they finally attacked, he could see an occasional flash of steel, and jets of arterial blood – then, one by one, the consuls dropped, leaving the two boys facing each other.

Leto backed away and risked a glance over his shoulder. 'Praetorians,' he started, but Torbidda laughed.

'Really?' he said as he advanced on Leto. 'You think they'll be able to stop me?'

Leto took out his dagger. 'They may delay you a little.'

'To what end? You're supposed to be the best and brightest, and yet you've never understood: all this ritual' – he gestured at the bodies, the endless rows – 'this building's finely tuned proportions, the title I hold, the red I once wore and the rags I now wear: these are merely tools to concentrate my will, so that I could influence not only humanity's muck, but people like you. Leto, you too are my tool, and harnessing your will, I have magnified my own till God himself cannot ignore me.'

As the praetorians assembled behind the general, he said, 'You're mad.'

'No – but I *am* a little disappointed. All I asked for was the Contessa and her son, and you failed me. No matter: another of my tools is bringing the child to me as we speak. O, and then shall the world see such a winter—'

'Who do you think you are?' Leto demanded.

'So blind. I am what remains of Girolamo Bernoulli. Torbidda's in here too, and others – legions. We are made one in the Darkness. Would you like to join us?'

'Go to hell!' Leto cried, and flung the mace. It stuck Torbidda hard in the chest and took him off his feet and the praetorians rushed him.

Leto ran for the balcony. He knew he had only seconds. He leaped over the balustrade, crouched down and plunged his dagger into the Concordian banner – then let himself fall. The dagger ripped through the thick green fabric, and for as long as it did, it slowed his descent – but before he was halfway down, it came free and he hit the ground hard, landing badly. There was no time to moan about it. The legionaries surrounding the Collegio were panicking, for a queer mob of fanciulli was invading the Piazza dei Collegio, apparently with every intent of transforming it into a bacchanal.

The sentries on the walls looked down at their brothers billeted in the Wastes and wondered if they knew their role was to break the wave descending on Concord. And after they'd fought and died, it would be the sentries' turn to fight, and Concord's turn – at long last – to suffer the torture with which it had broken so many other cities. They wondered how long the gate would hold.

Bells and alarums from the city behind them spun them round in time to see General Spinther riding from the Piazza dei Collegio directly across the Ponte Bernoulliana. 'If you love Concord,' he cried, 'open this gate.'

CHAPTER 68

The dead eyes of the Wastes had witnessed countless prodigies but none as odd as this: Concord's general had ridden out, over his officers' protests, to the unclaimed dirt in front of the uncountable ranks of the League. The captains of the armies that had scorched Etruria stared at each other. Their horses sensed their masters' animosity; they gnashed their teeth and pawed the dirt.

'Why should I believe you, Spinther?'

'You want the First Apprentice dead, Contessa. I'm saying I will help you kill him if you will help me.'

'We have to get to the summit,' said Pedro urgently.

'Why?'

'Because we do,' Sofia snapped. 'You want our help or not? But I *will* get an answer first, General. In Ariminum, you told me that if we trusted each other, the day would come when our grandchildren would look on each other as friends. You said that peace is worth the risk – but that was a trick.'

'Look in my eyes, Contessa Scaligeri, and tell me if I'm lying. I would have lined the rivers of Etruria from here and back to the Black Hand with the crucified bodies of you and every soldier of your cursed League if I had not been sabotaged and undercut by the First Apprentice. Old Town has flooded and he has done nothing, and now he's loosed a plague – the plague I watched consume Ariminum – on New City. He's *mad* – he believes himself to be Girolamo Bernoulli. He told me so. I saw the Serenissima burn, and I shall not stand by as Concord drowns.'

*

Water boiled up from deep beneath Monte Nero as if the earth had determined to rid itself of the pestilent lice poisoning its skin. The cloacae belched an unending flow of filth into the Depths, burying the poorest shacks first, and then the factories on the foothills of Monte Nero. The two-way current of the New City canals ceased to function and they overspilled their bounds and rained down still more water into the Depths. Enclosed by the city walls, there was nowhere for the water to go but up and up.

Geta used his sword until the crush became so great that even that had no effect. He found himself pushed into a corner of a narrow stairway, protecting the child from the blows of the passing throng as best he could. He tried to avoid the baby's eyes, but whenever he caught them, he felt his own eyes water and a burning desire to apologise. He turned his face away and was met with that familiar scrawled graffito of a rising sun and a Herod's Sword. He read aloud the motto underneath: 'Her Kingdom Come.'

'I'm afraid it won't,' said a voice that was smooth as beetle shells. 'Lord Geta, I believe you have something for me?'

He scrambled to his feet. 'First Apprentice! I— No, this isn't the one – I stole this from a whore in the Depths.'

The dark-browed boy took a slow step closer – and somehow the panicked citizens running past knew to avoid him. 'You cannot lie to me. I am the father of them.'

Geta flushed hot and his heart pounded. He thrust his sword at the boy. 'I won't give him to you.'

'My dear Geta, I fear you don't quite understand the situation. I know you don't *want* to, but you've belonged to me for a long time. You cannot refuse me.'

'Back away. I'm no one's man.'

'And therein lies the problem: Men who belong to no one belong to me. How can you doubt it? You killed the only woman you ever loved – of course you're mine! Drop the sword.'

He watched his hand let go, watched it fall, heard it clang against the steps.

'No, please,' he attempted one last bargain. 'Leave me this—'

'Alas, I cannot.' He pulled Iscanno from Geta's grasp and the baby immediately began to weep miserably. 'But I have a reward for you, my good and faithful servant. It's waiting for you down below. Go back and finish your drink.'

Geta was powerless to resist. He turned and fought his way against the flow of the terrified crowds until he came to the water. He waded through the debris, and kept walking down the steps, even when his head went under, and when he could no longer walk, he swam. Before he got to the Rule and Compass his lungs were bursting. *Up*, his mind pleaded, but another more compelling voice said, *Down*. He opened the tavern's door, pulled himself in, closed it – and then floated to the ceiling with the other empty vessels.

And still the waters rose. A lone gondola with three passengers – two boys and a young woman – pulled through the sea of bodies – dogs and cats and rats, and people young and old; a vision of the Apocalypse to Pedro but oddly familiar to Sofia. Somehow she'd sailed this awful sea before.

The League's armies had flooded into the city to join with the Concordians in fighting the dancers. Right now the hordes of manic children had been contained, but it would be impossible to reach the mount through those who remained. It was Leto who had suggested this alternate route via the Guild Hall.

The fight continued above their heads, and bodies dropped periodically from the sky. Most lay still where they fell, but some paddled towards them. Pedro watched their approach, resting his hand on his basket of annunciators, but whenever they got close enough to touch the gondola, Leto would neatly and dispassionately dispatch them with his oar. After the fifth of these, he turned back to his passengers and said, 'Tell me why you need to get to the summit or no further.'

Sofia jumped up. 'I knew we shouldn't trust you.'

Pedro reached up and pulled her back, 'Contessa – we need him.'

Two more dancers were paddling towards them, but Leto did not budge. 'I let you in to save Concord from the First Apprentice, but how do I know your intentions aren't worse?'

Pedro sighed. 'The First Apprentice wasn't lying when he said he was Bernoulli,' he said.

Leto stared hard at the Rasenneisi. 'Maestro Vanzetti, I take you for a reasonable fellow. I have myself seen what engineering feats you're capable of, but—'

'—such a proposition requires more than assertion, I agree. Did the Guild ever guess how Captain Giovanni stopped the Wave?'

'There was speculation,' said Leto warily. 'Obviously he somehow disrupted the signal from the Molè.'

'The needle on Monte Nero is a transmitter too. It was designed to act on a substance which exists between lunar and sublunar space—'

'Called aether. This is Bernoullian eyewash.'

' Just what do you think is causing the cloacae to erupt? Is the water buoying us up empirical enough for you? The aether's level rises and falls in a cycle lasting thousands of years. It's the medium by which God communicates with His creation.'

'I'm no theologian, Maestro Vanzetti, but even I know that the deity isn't some fellow living in the clouds.'

'God isn't as close to humanity as we could wish. His influence depends on the aether level, and that's been low since the last Messiah was killed. The needle doesn't just confuse the signal; it destroys the medium in which it travels. Just as the Molè collected pain, so the Sangrail collects sin, concentrates it and sends it back heavenwards.'

'If it's truly a cycle, what does it matter how low it gets? It'll rise when the tide turns, won't it?'

'Your Bernoulli proved the moon makes the tide turn, did he not? Well, what if you could stop the moon?'

Leto began to see. 'The tide would cease.'

'Exactly, General: the act that prompts the tide to turn is the Son of God's self-sacrifice.'

The dancers were almost at their gondola now; Sofia grabbed the oar from Leto and did what was necessary.

Leto stared at her, then Pedro. 'The Contessa's son—'

'That's why your friend wants him: his blood is imbued with divinity. Killing him will be the ultimate sin, and amplified by the tripod and fired into Heaven, it will sever the connection for ever. No aether, no light, just us, alone on a spinning rock, exposed to the evils of unbounded hell.'

'This is arrant nonsense,' said Leto, desperately clinging to the crumbling foundations of sanity. 'You're asking me to believe the First Apprentice sacrificed the Concordian Empire in order to get her child.'

Sofia handed him back the oar. 'It's hard to credit, but you'll get used to it.'

'Can you explain the First Apprentice's actions otherwise?' Pedro asked. 'This is a chain of reason, and the final link is that he means to degrade all men, Concordians first, to the level of beasts. The question now is: will you let him?'

The Cadets' quarters were partially submerged, so they moored at a second-storey window and crawled inside.

'A thousand secret tunnels riddle the Guild Halls. Some lead to the mount. Torbidda – the First Apprentice – showed me one once.'

The Rasenneisi knew no better but the derelict smell of the Guild Halls reminded Leto of how far his city had fallen. Webs covered the nooks where he used to hide from the Fuscus twins, and dirt marked the doorknob of the Drawing Room. 'This is where we perfected our art, Maestro Vanzetti.'

A few dancers who had found their way down the mountain by alternate routes were roaming the halls, so Sofia stood watch at the doorway as the two engineers searched through the schematics. 'We don't have time for sweet reminiscence, Spinther,' she remarked acidly.

'Patience, Contessa. If you want to bring down the needle, a little homework's going to be necessary.' He pulled out a drawing of the tripod and the needle and the engineers studied them together in silence for a moment.

'Looks like your basketful of annunciators won't suffice, Maestro.'

'There's no powder in these annunciators,' said Pedro. 'They're beacons. We just have to land them on the weight-bearing parts of the tripod.'

'Ah, very clever. Even so, look at this cross-section of the needle. There's even a mass dampener to counteract the natural sway. We'll need to weaken it first.'

'True. Any ideas?'

Leto rummaged through one of the drawers, then threw Pedro a Whistler. 'I know you're familiar with these. Think you could tune it to emit a harmony that resonates exactly with the needle's oscillation?'

'I could try.'

CHAPTER 69

Those tardy dancers still descending the mountain recognised their master as he ascended and made way by throwing themselves off the steps. Iscanno cried and struggled vainly against the First Apprentice's embrace. The child knew that the thing carrying him was just a shell, an avatar of an old power that hated him. The disguise was worn threadbare now; the worm's hold on this body was weakening and all the froth of mortal memory was spilling over. As the First Apprentice climbed the steps, assailed by the cold wind's fury, he fancied he heard whispering in his ear: *Take nothing that will slow you down.* It was a girl's voice, and a figment. No matter; this shell would not be needed for much longer.

As he came to the top another memory rose, of the first time the boy Torbidda had reached this, the summit of his ambitions. Waiting there had been praetorians, consuls, Apprentices – and, of course, the Molè itself, its doorway a vision of heaven, and hell.

They were all gone now, all swept away by Time's attrition. The men, the Molè and even that scared boy. Today's reception was certainly sparser: two young Engineers crouched beside the melan pool, so absorbed in their work that they did not notice his arrival.

'Dear Leto. You don't know when to quit.' He had to shout over the wind's howl. 'I suppose that after all I've made you suffer you do deserve to witness my apotheosis.'

Leto stood up. 'Your apotheosis. What of Concord?'

'My word, you really *are* a patriot, aren't you? If you saw this city as I see it you'd know the lives you wish to save are already dust.'

'*Torbidda* – you can fight him!'

The First Apprentice's cloying smile faded at being so addressed; he gathered himself. 'Ah. So, General, you've realised that I'm not mad – but do you realise that Torbidda always planned to kill you? He knew it was inevitable from the moment you introduced yourself. He used you, but you were always expendable, in the same way Agrippina was expendable.'

'You don't know him: Torbidda killed Agrippina because he *had* to.'

'Ah yes: *necessity*, a most malleable tool which can justify any crime. In my first life I made use of such arguments, but I no longer have any need of hypocrisy.' He looked at the other engineer, who had not ceased his toil. 'Who's your guest?'

'The Chief Engineer of Rasenna.'

'Ah, the one who's given us so much trouble? You too are welcome, Maestro Vanzetti. Alas, all three of us had poor timing: I was born too early, and you, dear children, were born too late. The reign of Engineers is over and another age is at hand: an age of blissful darkness with neither philosophy nor prayer, nor reason nor faith to complicate it.'

'I can't let you go through with this,' said Leto.

'You *can't*? I'm afraid you have no authority here, little general '

Bolos wound round Torbidda's feet and he tumbled and dropped the baby, who rolled ahead of him, howling over the wind. He lay there staring at him in a kind of daze – had he not dreamt this? He looked at his hands doubtfully, almost expecting claws.

A young woman walked by and picked up the child. She looked back at him.

This was no dream. It was *her*.

'Behold,' he said, sitting up to pull the bolos apart, 'the Handmaid of the Lord.'

Sofia backed away and handed Iscanno to Pedro. 'Get him out of here. I'll deal with this devil.'

'No, Contessa,' said Leto, drawing his sword. 'That is my honour'

The First Apprentice got to his feet. 'You don't have the salt, Cadet.'

Leto circled carefully, his wounded leg making him awkward. He made a few tentative thrusts, but Torbidda did not even raise his hands to defend himself. 'You must have forgotten that I saw you weep at your first blooding.'

'I won't cry for you,' Leto promised, and he ran him through.

'Uck! Well done, Cadet!' With inhuman strength, he grasped Leto's sword with one hand and his shoulder in the other. 'The most important lesson of the Guild, the one you never learned, was to leave behind everything that might detain you.' He stepped forward, pushing the blade deeper into his own chest, until he could hold Leto's head in a vice-like grip. 'Pain's a luxury a philosopher can ill afford.' He battered his forehead into Leto's face, once, twice, three times, and when he released him, Leto simply crumpled.

Torbidda picked a tooth from his forehead and cast a glance at the others. The Contessa stood between him and the other engineer, who was busy affixing annunciators to the handles of the basket.

'With you momentarily, Handmaid.' He knelt and gently put his hand over Leto's face. When he felt his breath, he rubbed until the boy's face was covered in gore. 'I have no laurels to give you, General, but here's your mask of Triumph.' Then he lifted Leto's head and smashed it down. He lifted it again, but stopped as Leto's eyes rolled back in his head.

The hum of annunciator wings made him look around: the Rasenneisi engineer was standing on the shattered base of the statue, holding the basket aloft.

'Do it, Pedro!' Sofia cried, and he released the basket. It lifted from the mount, slowly at first – then it was caught by the powerful wind and borne away.

Before the First Apprentice could react, Sofia threw herself at him, riding a wind gust, twisting in its whirling embrace and hitting him like a cannonball. She knocked him off his feet and they landed and rolled together until Sofia came out on top, sitting astride his chest. His head whipped left and right with her blows until she paused for a moment to see where the basket was – giving the boy a chance to wriggle his arms free. He smashed his fists against the ground and the impact threw her off.

She let herself be carried on the wind so that she touched down gently, poised like a dancer on the balls of her feet. His fire had neither light nor grace in it, only power, only rage: he threw himself at her with no feinting, simply direct. She crossed both of her arms against his downward fists, tilting left so that he came off-balance. Her leg whipped out and slapped against his chest, rested momentarily and neatly kicked his howling jaw shut with an audible bite.

It worried her that he was not fighting more warily. Was he so strong? She felt her tension and made herself relax. Whatever she was in for, that wouldn't help. She let her breath be guided by the rhythm of the dust-laden wind, so that when he leaped at her, she was ready.

He spun like a crazed Jinni, kicking on each turn, touching down momentarily, then springing at her, pounding at her. And she was water, so fluid that his fury was something she could slap down without getting burned. He stopped mid-turn and thrust his torso close. She crunched his nose but still he kept coming until she was forced to lock arms to keep him back. His grip was iron and she could not pull away without letting him closer.

Against her heel she felt a piece of masonry some deluded child had hauled up to the mount. She scooped it up with her foot, kneed it into the air while she pulled one arm free, caught it in her hand and slammed it into his jaw.

The blow snapped his head back, way too far, and she paused, a little shocked at what she had done.

An error. He suddenly grabbed her hair in both hands and whipping his head round like a mazza, slammed his forehead into hers.

Before she could rise, he kicked her in the ribs and something broke. 'You seek to deny me my Lamb but the Wind too is my servant,' he shouted, and ran – fast as thought – in the direction the basket had flown.

When she finally got her breath back, Sofia rolled over and saw Pedro crouch behind the shattered base, then take off running for the stairway. She turned back in time to see the First Apprentice leap and soar into the air. His body tumbled aimlessly like a leaf, but always upwards, and always towards the basket until at last he caught hold of it, smacked the annunciators to pieces and drifted back to the mount.

He landed beside her with an impact that shattered rock, held out the basket so she could see too – and then threw it aside with an oath. 'Where is he?'

He grabbed her leg and turned with the wind that had whipped itself into hysteria. He turned her once and released, and she went with it, letting herself roll with the wind's torque so that she landed on her feet. It was simple dizziness that made her tumble.

He advanced on her again and now there was no deflecting, Water or Wind. If she sidestepped one blow, there was another fist waiting, another rib-shattering kick. His knuckles tore her lip and something gave in her jaw. She landed on her back, a sharp stone piercing her side. She rolled off with an anguished groan.

He stared down at her pitilessly. 'I can tear it out of you—'

She coughed up a mouthful of blood. 'Get on with it then.'

'Oh, I'm not going to rush this meal.' He placed his heel on her cheek. 'I've waited for you for so long, I shall savour it.'

CHAPTER 70

An echoing sound slowly became a voice that dripped into her ear like curdled milk. 'Are you awake, Handmaid?'

Sofia tried to feign unconsciousness, but a sharp slap to her face made her eyes fly open.

'There you are!' The First Apprentice was leaning over her, reaching up to her wrists. 'We've danced this dance for so long and yet only now, at one minute to midnight, do we find an opportunity to talk.'

He turned and waded away from her, through the melan pool. Behind him, General Spinther lay still beside the steps. Pedro was nowhere to be seen. She looked up at her wrists and saw they were bound to the needle. She looked down at her feet and screamed: the melan was clinging to the needle's base, and it was slowly rising.

'You understand that this is no idle construction – you know my methods, having seen the Molè from inside – its best vantage, I always thought.'

'I didn't appreciate the view. That's why I burnt it,' Sofia said, trying to keep the terror from her voice though the melan was flowing inexorably up the curved surface. It was rising at a steady rate, with occasional lurches when dark slivers like elongated maggots burst from its smooth surface and found a new purchase. It was just a braccia from her feet now, and it was getting closer.

'You saved me a lot of work that night,' the First Apprentice admitted. 'The Molè's work was done; fire was necessary to make way for the new crop. I have been ruminating upon this tower for millennia – once or twice in other lives I have even begun it, but it has always been torn down before it could do its work. I do not regret it; all those iterations have perfected it.'

The melan touched her toes and Sofia gasped. It was like wet ice enveloping her feet, so cold it burned.

'Yes, it is breathtaking.' The Apprentice was looking skywards. 'The graceless age it ushers in will extinguish Man – oh, not at first. He will pine and gratefully fade away. This needle reaches as high into the air as it reaches down into the pit below, which even now is filling with pure water from the subterranean rivers. The great animal I am hunting knows my intent; it can smell how close I am. Truly, He is a jealous God. Man has chosen me, by a thousand admissions and compromises, and He would rather drown the world than lose His pet. I ask you, Handmaid: is that *love*?'

She remembered Ezra telling her why Abraham had been willing to sacrifice Isaac. The melan was clinging to her thighs now, making her shiver uncontrollably. 'Better drowned by our Father than enslaved by you.'

'You don't know how right you are. That pain you're feeling now? It is a mere *fraction* of my range. Tell me where Maestro Vanzetti has taken the child and I'll end your suffering. You're only brave because you don't know how much I can make you suffer – but let me be plain, child: there is *no* limit. If it makes it easier, you should know that your boy was foreordained to die here. You tried to break free of the chains of necessity, but there never was any possibility of escape. Like all your species, you imagine you have free will – but if you are free, it is the freedom of the most infinitesimal drop of water in a torrent. Ah, but what misery you create for yourselves with that modicum of power.'

'You're no better—' she started, but he cut her off contemptuously.

'Ah, there you are wrong: I only *wear* this incompetent form. You shouldn't have too much trouble with the concept; after all, you loved a creature pretending to be a man, didn't you? And your boy – well, he's something else entirely.'

'You'll never find him.'

'Now you're just being silly. Where can they hide him?' he cackled. 'Somewhere men are incorruptible? God made you imperfect in His image – poor thinkers, selfish lovers. Even now – admit it – your clenched fists still hold onto the memory of my grandson, or rather the buio that took Giovanni's form. What do the minstrels say? True love is about letting go. But you take after your grasping, selfish Father. He seeks to drown me, but I will blind and poison Him. One eye of the needle scratches away the aether, the other has gone deep already. The melan is diffusing into the earth's veins and arteries. The world is dying.'

'And you will grow fat on its corpse like a worm.'

'You think to insult me? If you could see my true form, you would fall down and worship.'

The melan had reached her neck. Its tendrils coiled over her skin like sentient ivy.

'Not long now,' he crowed. 'Die and keep your secret. I've waited patiently through a thousand turns of the wheel – I can wait another day. As for you, this is your last turn. You finally get to lay down your burden, Handmaid. You should thank me.'

'I do,' Sofia cried with joy.

He stared at her, bemused – and suddenly doubt struck like a gut-punch. He wailed, 'Why do you exalt so?'

'Because I made a new Covenant. I am the Lamb, and I have lain freely upon your altar. Worm, thou art undone!'

Comprehension came at last. 'No. No. *No!*'

'Yes.' Sofia closed her eyes tight as the melan bled into her. The pain was horrific, but she could bear it: she was going home.

Giovanni, wait for me. I'm coming.

The melan discovered – too late – that it had crawled into a holy furnace, and it was consumed. And so was Sofia. Her shoulders sagged, her body gave up the ghost.

Deep beneath the mountain, chambers collapsed and stones began grinding together. The heavy stormclouds over the city were illuminated by sheets of lightning within.

The dancers in the Piazza dei Collegio ceased to hear any music and fell down, incapacitated by exhaustion. All those who loved the Contessa looked to Mount Nero and the divine storm that flashed about the mount.

In astonishment Bernoulli's ghost relaxed his grip on his earthly vessel and Torbidda, waiting and watching, shattered the coffin binding him. If it had been an equal contest between the will of Bernoulli and Torbidda, then the latter *might* have triumphed, for he knew that he fought for more than flesh and that the chance would not come again – but Bernoulli was a vessel himself of the Darkness, that will that eternally contested with God, and so the outcome was preordained. Yet while the two spirits wrestled for the boy, his uncaptained body did a queer circular jig that left him standing on the edge of the steps.

His eyes sparked open to see Leto, conscious again and looking at him fearfully. 'Leto, it's *me*!' Torbidda cried. 'I can't do it, his grip's too strong. If you love me, Leto, *kill* me – do it *now*!'

Leto didn't hesitate. He threw himself into his truest friend, striking him with his shoulder and taking him from his feet. He kept going, and pushed them both into empty space until they were falling together down the stairway they had both struggled so long and so hard to climb.

After a minute of shambling, cracking, rolling, falling, they came to rest: two broken dolls.

Thunder clapped and dropped earthbound in heavy sheets. One of the dolls shifted. It was not the wind's doing. It shifted again, and then, like a tumbled house of cards rearranging itself, it stood and once more ascended the steps. Those bones that were not shattered obeyed the commands that came from the commanding spirit, but the abused tendons and ligaments gave way before it reached the summit.

And above the foul crawling groaning thing came a flock of little shadows that leaped and danced over the stones of Monte Nero. The host of annunciators loosed by Pedro Vanzetti were drawn by the homing beacons atop the tripod. There were hundreds of them. Some failed before they reached the top, some collided and exploded into little metallic fires, some were plucked away by the winds, but most converged on their destination and there erupted. The upper ring of the tripod was silhouetted against the blast – and then the shredded halo caught fire.

As lumps of masonry crashed down onto the mount, what remained of the First Apprentice oozed over the final steps and pulled itself to the edge of the pool. Its head was facing behind, away from its chest, and it had to roll over like some alluvial fish. It regarded itself in the shiny glutinous tar and with a voice belched from inside, said, 'I must be born and born again, and again—'

The body shuddered with a prolonged death-rattle and then sagged and was still – for a moment.

A bulge distended the throat. The cheek bulged. The jaw dropped open, as though the dead boy had remembered something of import. A long, wet and shiny thing emerged, too thick to be a tongue. Its brilliant white flesh was covered in a bloody mucus, like a newborn. It wriggled from the corpse's mouth into the melan. As the storm gathered strength, it sank under the surface. Raindrops landing on the black liquid vanished in a hiss of vapour. After a few moments, the worm burst through the melan, shivering and throwing its coils around aimlessly. It resembled a flayed, limbless cat that did not know how to decently die. Even as it writhed there, it grew at a fantastic rate. Great bulges engorged one segment, and others followed in spasmodic rhythm. The sheets of rain formed a barrage of caustic darts that punctured the pale membrane and it coiled itself against the base of the needle in agony. Even as it did so, its tail – or head, perhaps – slapped blindly against one of the tripod legs.

The abused leg went first, crumbling like lice-riddled wood, and with that crutch gone, the other two tumbled towards the centre, dropping all their weight on the weakened needle, which groaned like a wounded beast. The upper third cracked and bent, slowly at first.

The bloated white worm below was battered by that masonic rain until it was impaled by the falling spear. Its taut skin gave way and the bile that filled it spilled over the mountain. It died screaming from both ends – a strange reverberating sound that was heard miles away.

Indeed, it was heard in heaven.

In every nook of the dark white city men slowly uncovered their ears and eyes. They walked out into the pelting rain and let it wash them. Concord, for all its error, crimes and weakness, was reprieved. So was the race of men.

In the ruin that was left of the Piazza dei Collegio, Pedro Vanzetti felt the cold rain and knew that Sofia and Giovanni were one. It was not logical, but he had seen the limits of logic.

He held Iscanno aloft so that he could see Levi flaunt the Lion of Rasenna, along with all the other banners – Sybaritic, Salernitan, Akkan and Byzantine. He thought of the man who had woven it and of how parents bequeath more than life to their children. By their characters, good and ill, parents delineated the bounds of their lives as sharply as rivers shaped fallen rain. He prayed that Iscanno's life would be ordinary, and that he would be loved: not because his nature commanded it, but because that was the birthright of the children of this new world.

He had enough experience of miracles to know they were shy things, that change would overtake them so slowly that people would take the remade world – a world where love came easy – for granted. One day he would tell Iscanno how his mother had made it so.

'Where are you going, Maestro Vanzetti?' asked a bandieratoro who saw him briskly walking towards the Ponte Bernoulliana.

'Rasenna. I have a bridge to rebuild.'

THE END

ACKNOWLEDGEMENTS

Thanks to my brother Michael Harte for subjecting himself to an early draft. Thanks to Fergal Haran, and Michael again, for advice on matters technical and for finding a vaguely believable basis in science for Aether, ice bridges and other mediaeval esoterica. If errors or improbabilities remain, that's when I foolishly chose to ignore your council.

To all hands on the HMS Fletcher, to Nicola Budd who unravel all knots however complicated, answers all questions however inane and sees that I'm pointed in the right direction at conventions, to the new kid in the splendid jumper Andrew Turner, and to all the Quercus sales team who holler about The Wave Trilogy in a market where one needs to SHOUT, thanks.

Thanks to my agent Ian Drury for swooping *Irenicon* – back when it was still called *Drytown* – off the pile that is slushy. Thanks to my editor Jo Fletcher who's had a rough year but never lets it show. Lazy readers make for lazy writers, but Jo is the type of attentive reader – severe and sympathetic as required – that brings out the best in me, and all the writers that come her way.

Aidan Harte 2013

THE WAVE TRILOGY TIMELINE

400–510	Etruscan League conquers Rome; then Sybaris
500 to 01	Expansion of Etruscan Empire
01 *Anno Domina*	Christ killed in the Massacre of the Innocents
01–30	Jewish Revolt; Etruscans expelled from Holy Land
33	Madonna dies; Schism of Judaism between Marian and Ebionite
30–150	Decline and Fall of the Etruscan Empire; Rise of the Radinate
600–1100	Rise of Ariminumese commercial empire
850–950	Radinate occupation of Southern Etruria ends, Radinate declining
1098	First Crusade; Etrurian knights capture Jerusalem
1180–1225	Ariminumese establish trade links with Ebionite Byzant; St Francis of Gubbio active
1260	Battle of Ain Jalut won by Crusader-Ebionite coalition led by Old Man
1260 to 80	Old Man disappears; King Tancred takes Byzant from weakened Radinate
1309	Girolamo Bernoulli born; Duke Scaligeri born
1321	Twelve-year-old Bernoulli wows Curia
1325	Bernoulli writes *Dialogue with Myself*
1327 to 1347	Second Concord Rasenna conflict
1327	Jacopo, Bernoulli's son (Giovanni's father) born
1328	Engineers' Guild founded with Bernoulli Chief Engineer; Construction on Molè begins
1329–	Doc Bardini and Sofia's father born

1340	Rasenna defeats Concord at Montaperti
1347	Wave hits Rasenna, Engineer Revolution in Concord
1347–53	Expanding Concordian Empire; Experimentation on buio begins
1349	Giovanni Bernoulli born
1352	Counter-coup fails; Jacopo, Giovanni's father executed; Purge begins
1353	Sofia Scaligeri born; Girolamo Bernoulli dies, Luca Pacioli becomes First Apprentice
1356	Sofia's father assassinated
1357	Giovanni Bernoulli enters Guild Hall
1359	Hawk's Company conducts Gubbio massacre; Giovanni Bernoulli killed by buio
1360	Levi joins Hawk's Company
1364	Hawk's Company declares war on Concord
1367	Torbidda enters Guild Hall
1368	Torbidda becomes Apprentice candidate in his second year
1369	Giovanni builds Rasenna bridge; Hawk's Company defeated at Tagliacozzo; Molè burned
1370	12th Legion lays siege to Rasenna and is routed
1371	Spinther invades Dalmatia; Sofia conceives and flees Etruria; Moor's coup in Ariminum
1372	Sofia gives birth in Akka